Settled on a Mountain

Love is a Cabin Series
Book 3

Jacque Jacobs

Drawings by Ken Czarnomski
Cover Photography by Bill Johnston

An Imprint of
Drellag Press, LLC

Other Works by
JACQUE JACOBS

Love is a Cabin Series

High on a Mountain – Book 1 (*August, 2021*)
Life on a Mountain – Book 2 (*November, 2021*)

Coming Soon:

New Beginnings on a Mountain – Book 4
The Community Unites on a Mountain – Book 5
Holidays on a Mountain – Book 6

Drawings by
Ken Czarnomski

Cover Photo by
Bill Johnston

An Imprint of
Drellag Press, LLC
Vero Beach FL

Acknowledgements

Many have provided ongoing support and encouragement in the writing and publishing of this series, and I am deeply appreciative. With love, as always, to my family members who read, comment, and cheer me on: Amy, Bonnie, Cheri, David, Nancy, Chuck and Tom. With special thanks to Ruth Jackson Johnston, Dondra T. Maney, Ph.D., Donna Duffy, Nancy Gorneau, Sandra Council, Ph.D., Marilyn Burton, Paula VanHooser, Peggy Jones, Ed.D. and Ann Alexander, Ph.D. An overdue thanks to Marlowe Mager, Ed.D. whose expertise and real-life experiences at his store, the Blue Ridge Beer Hub. in Waynesville, N.C., provided context for the characters in their beer choices. Drop in to see him sometime—friendly folks abound.

I offer special thanks to Jennifer Horne, Poet Laureate of Alabama, with gratitude for her workshops through the Laura (Riding) Jackson Foundation in Vero Beach and with respect and admiration for her talent and expertise. You are an inspiration.

Writing is a solitary process, but publishing a book takes a team.

With thanks to my very talented friends for their contributions:

Ken Czarnomski for your drawings
Bill Johnston for your photograph on the cover

Thanks to the team who put it all together for the continued interest and support of my readers:

Elaine Massung, editor extraordinaire at
https://academic-smartcuts.com
Arkonna, format professional at http://fiverr.com
Pixelstudio, book cover designer professional at http://fiverr.com

Dedication

This book is dedicated to the many fine educational professionals with whom I have worked around the world. Unsung heroes that you are, your dedication every day educates the minds of children, young people, and adults. Thank you.

Keep close to Nature's heart. . . and break clear away, once in a while,
and climb a mountain or spend a week in the woods.
Wash your spirit clean...

John Muir, 1838 1914

Drawing by Ken Czarnomski

Chapter 1

Blue Lights and Anxious Moments

Bella's heart was pounding. She sat up in bed, looked around—and slowly, the blue flashing lights of her dream faded. She needed to figure out where she was. The room was unfamiliar and the feelings swirling through her mind more so. It was clear she was not in Drellag Caban: her cabin. She swung her feet out of the bed and onto the floor, enjoying the warmth of a braided wool rug. She admired the muted burgundies and blues under her feet. The light creeping in around the edges of the window gave the space an ethereal feel.

Slowly, Bella moved the curtains aside and lifted the shade. The sun was nearing the top of the jagged ridgeline of the mountains. The brilliant yellows, reds, and oranges of the autumn leaves, some already fallen to the ground, hovered like a warm blanket over the earth, preparing it for the coming cold of winter. She already knew by the look of the room that she also was not in Joshua's guest room; it could only be Chad's—she just didn't remember coming here.

Deep breaths, exhaled slowly, calmed her racing pulse as the events of the last several days started to settle in her mind. She gently moved her hand across the sheets on the bed as she recalled the speed at which Chad had driven down the mountain from Drellag Caban. Her shoulders slumped as she remembered the reason they rushed to the hospital: *Joe. I can't believe Joe is gone. Why? No one deserves to lose his life that way.*

Bella ran her fingers through her long brown hair, pulled on her robe, and stepped into her slippers. She quietly opened the bedroom door and glanced down the hall. She had not bothered to look at her watch on the nightstand and did not know what time it was. She saw a soft light coming from the far end of the hall, what she presumed was the living room. Her feet carried her towards the light, even though she was not fully conscious of deciding to do so.

"Good morning, Bella," Chad's voice carried a touch of tenderness. "Were you able to rest at all?"

She smiled at him. She was glad to see him, but she knew that being at Chad's had nothing to do with her and Chad's... *Relationship? Flirtation? I'm not really sure what we have going on, but I know this isn't part of it.*

"Good morning, Chad. I slept. I don't know if I rested. How about you?"

"Managed a few hours before the phone rang—" He saw fear creep into her face.

She interrupted him; her voice panicky. "What's up? I must have heard the phone because I woke up with my heart racing and feeling disoriented."

Bella sat down on the sofa, slid her feet out of her slippers, and automatically pulled her legs up under her. *Did something else happen?*

Watching her with gentle eyes, Chad waited. *I could get used to that scene in front of me to start each day.*

Suddenly, Bella put her feet on the floor and looked towards Chad but not at him. "I'm so sorry. Whatever possessed me to put my feet on your sofa?" She brushed at some imaginary dirt then found herself caressing the smoothness of the fine leather. "This is a beautiful sofa."

"Bella, please look at me." He waited. She turned her gaze to him, but he had the feeling she wasn't actually seeing him. His voice carried the quiet assurance of the sheriff he was. "The last thirty hours have been pretty surreal for all of us, Joshua especially."

"Was the call about Joshua? Should we go to him?" There was a quiver in her voice.

Chad stood from his recliner and walked to the sofa. He sat beside her but not so close as to startle her by his proximity. He was not displeased when she slid next to him and put her head on his shoulder. He slipped his arm around her. *I could get used to this, too.*

He could feel the slight tremor of her head on his shoulder. "I'm sorry the phone woke you; it was work related. Carla's with Joshua and she'll let us know if there is anything he needs. Right now, there are two things that will help him. The obvious one is time, though there is no way to tell how much time anyone needs to process loss. The second is for my team to figure out who is responsible for robbing and assaulting Joe at the Valley Store."

Bella sat up and looked at him. "What time is it? What day is it?"

"It's Sunday morning, about ten o'clock. And, before you ask, you're in my home after sitting up very late with Joshua at his house. I finally dragged you away..." She looked at him askance. "Okay, I didn't literally drag you away. You didn't, however, argue when I insisted you get some sleep. You brought things down from the mountain with you when we left Drellag Caban late yesterday."

She put her hand out in front of her and saw it shake. It wasn't like her to be so shaken by death. She had experienced too much loss in her own life.

"Oh, Chad. I honestly don't have a clear memory of what's happened. It has to be from the shock."

"No doubt. We went from a lovely afternoon hike and starting supper to rushing to the hospital to check on Joe..."

She nodded. Chad's words helped her piece together the events from yesterday. She had known Joe Johnson and his son, Joshua, her entire life. Joe was the last link to her own father; the two had grown up in the valley and had hiked the mountains together as boys. *This is not about me. Joshua lost his father last night. How will Joshua ever run the Valley Store without his dad?*

Chad looked at her bewildered face. "I have a suggestion." He knew she needed to get into a routine. "You took a shower late last night, well, early this morning. . ."

She sat up and stared wide-eyed at him.

"By yourself." He tried to suppress a laugh at the look of surprise on her face. "Let me start again. You were, as I said, exhausted. Here's what I'm going to suggest. Go take a hot shower and get dressed. It'll relax you. I'll make breakfast, and then we'll talk about what you want to do today."

"I want to see Joshua." She could not understand the complete disorientation that had come over her. It felt more extreme than other struggles she had experienced since her husband, Matt, had died nearly five years ago.

Gently taking her elbow, Chad stood up, helping her up at the same time. He pointed her towards the guest bedroom. "Go shower and dress. It'll help. I promise."

She looked at him, smiled wanly, and headed towards the bedroom.

"I can't promise my cooking will help, though."

Bella looked back over her shoulder and smiled more softly. "I'll take my chances. All of a sudden I'm ravenous."

Ahhh, there's Dr. Anderson; the retired English professor speaks. Ravenous. Chad walked into the kitchen with a smile of his own and started breakfast.

Settling Her Nerves

Chad was right. The shower helped. I'm starting to feel human. Dressed, Bella stood looking at the bed trying to decide whether she should take off the sheets. She rolled her shoulders, a movement which generally helped her relax. There was a soft knock on the door.

"Breakfast is ready when you are."

She opened the door as Chad walked back towards the kitchen. Bella absolutely could not remember the last time anyone had made breakfast for her. She and Matt had a ritual of making breakfast for each other on weekends. *It's been more than four years, that's for sure.* She pulled the memory of Matt in close as she reached the kitchen door.

Chad watched her carefully. "All the same to you if we eat out on the porch? Nice morning coming over the mountains, and some fresh air will do us both good. What do you say?"

"Let's do it."

She entered the kitchen ready to help out. She saw he had an unopened box of Earl Grey tea with a mug sitting next to it on the counter. Then she heard the kettle start to whistle. Without asking, she opened the box of tea, put a tea bag in the cup, and turned to him with the mug in her hand. "Water, kind sir?"

"My pleasure. Any problem with me serving up the food on our plates?"

"Not a problem for me."

"Good, then mosey on out to the porch, and I'll be there momentarily."

Bella headed towards the open French doors. The slight chill in the autumn air caused her to shiver a bit, but once she sat down and sipped her tea, she decided it was perfect: enough clear, crisp mountain air to shake out the cobwebs but not enough to give her goosebumps. She was totally absorbed in the kaleidoscope of colors presented by the leaves draping across the ridgeline of the mountains, the colors at the peak of their brilliance. She knew the East Tennessee mountains like the palm of her hand. The blood of its European settlers flowed in her veins, and a lifetime of summers in Drellag Caban shaped her memories.

Chad set the plate of scrambled eggs, ham, and toast on the place setting in front of her. Bella looked down at the plate and noticed he had a small bowl with blackberry jam on the table next to the milk and sugar. He flourished a hand at the milk pitcher and sugar bowl. "Help yourself."

"I take it straight, but thanks for the effort."

Relieved she was sounding more like herself, Chad sat down next to her, and they both looked out at the mountains. Before he knew it, Bella was all but shoveling the eggs into her mouth. He watched her reach for the blackberry jam.

"How did you know blackberry preserves are my favorite? Did I tell you that?"

Chad turned to her. "Maybe you would consider you don't have exclusivity on that preference?"

For the first time since they were at her home on Saturday, he heard her chuckle, almost laugh. It helped him settle, and he suspected it meant she was settling too.

"Fair enough, Sheriff Oliver. Fair enough." She leaned back in her chair and looked at him. "I don't know why I'm having so much trouble processing Joe's death and how it happened. But, before we talk about it, what time did I go to bed last night?"

"About two forty-five this morning."

She turned her head sharply and looked at him. "Two forty-five! What time is it now?"

"Twenty minutes later than I told you before."

"Oh, you want to play those kinds of games, do you?" The smirk on her face was one he liked.

"Okay, okay. I surrender. It's about ten twenty. We arrived at the hospital a little after six last night. After Fred told us Joe didn't survive the assault, we went to Joshua's home. Mostly we listened to Joshua talk about his dad, and occasionally one of us would share something special about him. I think it was good for Joshua. But by two a.m. it was clear we were all exhausted, physically and emotionally. I convinced you to get some sleep. Carla was trying to convince

Joshua to shower and get some sleep, too. I assume she stayed the rest of the night."

Bella nodded as things started to fall into place. Carla was the head server to locals at The Corral Restaurant and Bar, and, although Bella hadn't known her very long, she had taken a liking to Carla and her quick wit. Bella had only recently learned that Carla's parents were killed in a car wreck when she was in her twenties, leaving the restaurant to her and her brother, James. They, too, were deeply rooted in the community

Chad watched her. *I might start to recognize the signs of that deep thinking of hers if I pay attention.* He waited until she turned her head towards him. "You didn't eat any supper, so I convinced you to eat something. You said you would eat half a peanut butter sandwich." He saw the look of shock on her face.

"I did?" A gentle chuckle gave way to uncontrollable laughter. Her shoulders heaved as she sputtered, "I... never... I think, never... asked anyone... for a peanut butter... sandwich!" The gasping for air between words gave way to absolute silence. She looked at him in disbelief.

Chad knew it was the release she needed, but he had not expected it to happen over a peanut butter sandwich. He gently placed his hand on top of hers.

"Pretty big fan of peanut butter sandwiches myself. In fact, I cut the sandwich in half, and we stood at the kitchen counter and ate it."

"You ate one too?" Her eyes widened.

"You betcha! Protein, starch, and a vegetable all in one fell swoop."

"Not according to *my* mother! She was *quite* insistent that peanut butter was not a vegetable; it didn't matter how much I argued it was." *Did I tell him that last night?*

Now Chad was laughing. "Okay, we've already figured out we're likely related, distantly, on the Oliver side. But maybe our mothers were related, or at least educated at the same school of 'what's proper.'" He could tell she was regaining her equilibrium.

"Entirely possible. My guess is they were educated in the same school of East Tennessee propriety."

Now he knew she was back. *Propriety? Have I ever used that word? I'm endlessly intrigued how this woman bounces from her own very well-educated self to her mountain talk roots even in the midst of traumatic events.*

Bella flipped her hand over and held Chad's for a moment. She looked at him, her eyes holding back tears. "Let's finish eating, and then I seriously need to get myself organized and let you get on with your day."

They chatted about the call they could hear of the eastern towhee: "drink-your-tea," "drink-your-tea."

"Is that why you don't drink coffee?" Chad tapped his finger on her mug of tea.

"It's entirely possible. Grandmother Hazel wanted me rooted to these mountains, and she wanted me to know as much as I could about them. We both loved the call of the eastern towhee."

Finishing her last bite of toast with blackberry preserves, she turned and looked at him. "Chad, I don't know how to thank you for this. *All* of this: getting me down the mountain to be with Joshua and Joe, taking care of the pup on Friday night... taking care of me. Someday I'll tell you about my 'bear bite' moments, how strong emotional events take me to dark memories I don't want to recall." Her somberness shifted as she smiled. "In the meantime, I don't know how to thank you."

"I do." He leaned towards her and kissed her.

She returned the kiss and looked at him, her eyes smiling. "Hmm... a kiss from such a lovely lady with blackberry preserves on her lips."

She gave him a playful tap on the hand. She dropped into her very southern mountain drawl. "A gentleman does not disgrace a lady by telling her she's made such a serious social faux-pas. Imagine my mother's shock if she knew I did not pat my mouth with a napkin after taking a bite of toast with preserves."

"Well, this gentleman enjoyed both, so no disgrace intended." He leaned in and kissed her again. "Now, let's think about what you want to do today, and we'll go from there."

They sat silently for several minutes, drinking their tea and coffee, looking out at the mountains.

"Bella, I didn't mention contacting the funeral home last night because we have to let the medical examiner do an autopsy. But we'll need to have Joshua start the process of making arrangements today." He watched her for any reaction before he continued. "Just so you know, I have things covered, especially on finding out who robbed the Valley Store and assaulted Joe." He knew his matter-of-fact words hit her hard, but she did not show it.

"I knew you would have things covered, Chad. I'll try to find the right time to help Joshua contact the funeral home." She continued to look out at the mountains. She knew he wouldn't tell her anymore until he could, but she wondered how he dealt with the impact of so many crimes. She couldn't imagine how he kept all of them straight: sex trafficking of minors, illegal immigrants, robbery, assault.

"Penny for your thoughts."

"Chad, right now there are too many. But my biggest concern is being supportive to Joshua. I think the first thing I will do is call Carla. At the jamboree, Joshua had invited us to eat a late lunch at his house today, remember?" Chad nodded. "I was thinking we could take food over." She sat back and sighed. "Death is a horrible life event to navigate. It's so hard to know if you're doing the right thing."

"I think the right thing is doing what you can for a friend, while trying to help that friend determine what he needs."

"You're right, Chad. It's about being there for your friend. It truly is."

"Once you talk to Carla, we can finalize a plan. Joshua may want to open the store tomorrow. His loyalty to his dad has been unwavering in all things, and that includes the Valley Store. I asked Carla to call me if Joshua says he plans to open the store today."

Bella nodded.

"My team finished up at the store late last night. There was no break-in, so it was a matter of cleaning up around the cash register from Joe's fall and the fingerprint dust. I sent a couple of people to clean the store this morning. Arthur was there to repair the stairs, so they worked together to get it cleaned up and ready for Joshua to open tomorrow, if he chooses. Of course, the old timers around here will fully understand if he closes for a few days. Knowing Joshua, he will struggle with what to do."

"I think it might be important for Joshua to go back in the store tomorrow, but not alone. Sometimes it's easier to face the pain while you're still numb." She stood. "Let's clean up these dishes, and I'll call Carla. Then we can decide what to do, fair enough?"

"Fair enough." Chad picked up the dishes, and she took their mugs. Chad put the food away, and Bella put the dishes in the dishwasher. He stood in front of her when they finished. His voice was serious, "I could get accustomed to this, Bella, very easily."

"Could be nice." She kissed him lightly on the lips. She turned to walk out of the kitchen but stopped when he spoke.

"Sorry, something else?" She looked back at him.

"I need to check in at the station, and before you apologize for not thinking about my work, it's covered. I have multiple people who can handle things, and I meant what I told you yesterday afternoon. I'm going to learn to back off." He looked at her earnestly.

She could see in the tenderness of his deep gray eyes that he was intent on keeping that promise.

"I believe you, and that makes me happy for you... and for me." She smiled and he could hear a lessening of her grief. "I have two more questions. First, did I take you from your room? Second, normally I would strip the bed and fold the sheets . . . "

He looked at her—his eyes wide and his brow furrowed.

She recognized the look. "Blame my mother and that 'school of what's proper!' She taught me to take the sheets off the bed, pull the cover up, fold the sheets, and put them at the foot of the bed. I know, I know. Just humor me, old habits die hard." She took a deep breath. "Anyway, I was going to ask if I could impose another night if Joshua needs me down here?"

They had been standing in the kitchen. He stepped over and pulled her into him. "Bella, Bella, Bella. Stop worrying about being polite. I don't need an explanation, although I'm sure I have much to learn from you. My home is yours, and no, you did not take me from my room, although I would have been happy to give it to you. I built this cabin after my divorce and purposely put bathrooms in each bedroom because I wanted my guests to be comfortable. As for the day, let's just take it easy and see what it brings." He kept his arms around her but, at the same time, leaned back to look her in the eye. "Let's see what Joshua needs, and then there'll be plenty of time for decisions. Fair enough?"

"More than." She kissed him deeply then stepped back. "Now, I'm going to call Carla, and you do whatever you need to do at this moment to protect us in these hills." With that, she turned and walked to the bedroom to get her phone.

Chad watched her walk away. He'd received the "I'm interested" message in her kiss.

Chapter 2

Joshua

Joshua was groggy when he got out of bed. He left his bed unmade and headed to the kitchen to get coffee. He was thankful the cool morning had prompted him to put on his robe when he saw Carla sitting at his kitchen counter. *How could I not remember she was here?*

She looked up from reading his trade magazine. "Good morning, Joshua. Get some sleep?"

The smell of the freshly brewed coffee was drawing him towards it. "I must have. I don't remember much about last night." He reached for the coffee pot. *I wonder if the smell of coffee is what woke me?*

He set his full mug on the counter. His eyes were still heavy with sleep, but they suddenly shot open. "Carla, did *you* get any sleep?"

"Yep. That's a pretty comfortable couch you have. I slept almost six hours. Might be a record for me." She chuckled, hoping it would make him smile.

Now he remembered Carla had come to the hospital. He had no sense of time, though.

"Carla…"

"Joshua…"

They spoke at the same time, sputtered, choked, and stopped.

Joshua looked at Carla, "Thank you for coming to the hospital last night. How did you know to come?"

"Small community." She used her usual restaurant server banter, then her voice softened. "Chad had his dispatcher call me."

He nodded his head. "I've given you so much grief over the years at The Corral and the bluegrass jamborees. I hope you always knew it was in good fun."

"Joshua Johnson!" She wagged her finger as if scolding a child. "Do you have any doubt I can take teasing as well as I dish it out?"

At this, his lips moved into a slight smile. "No, ma'am. No doubt. No doubt at all."

She smiled at his use of the mountain double speak. She knew they were just filling time and understood Joshua would need to fill lots of time over the next weeks.

He saw the clock on the stove showed ten thirty. "Carla, don't you need to be at The Corral?" His voice was quick, almost panicked.

"Only if it means we're going to go have breakfast while you sort out what you want to do today, and how I can help you. My brother knows I'll be out for the duration. No problem. I work to keep busy, not 'cause it makes any real difference in my paycheck; it's a major benefit of owning half the business."

His shoulders sagged in both relief and dread. "Mighty fine of you, Carla. Appreciate it. Pretty sure neither of us is up to cooking, so what do you say I buy you breakfast?"

Twenty minutes later they walked into The Corral. Carla's brother happened to be on the floor helping out when they entered; she whispered to him to keep well-meaning folks away. It was unlikely many folks knew about Joe yet, but, either way, she didn't want the wrong question coming at Joshua. She maneuvered Joshua to the back corner table so that he sat with his back to the rest of the restaurant.

The young server was at the table as fast as Carla would have been with water and the coffee pot. She knew Carla was the owner and she didn't say a word but just looked at Carla— who ordered for both of them. It wasn't like Carla didn't know what Joshua would eat: eggs over easy on toast. Even though breakfast was not his usual meal to eat at the restaurant, no matter what meal he ordered, it was always the same thing depending on the time of day.

"Thanks, Natalia. Your mom was okay with you coming in today?" Carla knew Natalia's mother only allowed her to work on Saturdays and the occasional Friday night, if a regular server was out.

"Yes, ma'am. We don't have school tomorrow. It's a teacher workday, so my mom was fine with me coming in today. Glad I could help out." She quickly glanced at Joshua but didn't say anything.

Joshua suddenly spoke up. "What year are you in school, Natalia? Junior?"

"Yes, sir, Mr. Joshua."

Carla grinned. "She's the top student in her class, right, Natalia?"

Natalia avoided looking at either of them. "Yes, ma'am."

"That's great news. You know the top *senior* at the high school works in our store . . ." Joshua stumbled a bit.

Carla felt a mix of sadness and relief that Natalia's presence was giving Joshua a distraction from the horror of losing his father. She was concerned about the difficulties of the week ahead.

"Yes, sir. It's Melody. She's my neighbor, and we help each other study."

Joshua steadied himself. "Good. Then you already know the high bar you have to keep the tradition going."

"Sorry, Mr. Joshua, what tradition?"

"A young woman as valedictorian!" He looked up and smiled at her. "I have no doubt you'll come through just like Melody will. She'll be valedictorian at graduation."

"Yessir, I'll try." She smiled, nodded at Carla, and headed towards the kitchen.

Carla hoped to keep him distracted. "Real fine family. I just found out a while back that her dad teaches at the university in Knoxville. Not sure why I didn't already know that. A jazz musician, I hear. Apparently, Natalia's parents are from a mountainous region in Europe. Seems they wanted to be a little higher up than they could be in Knoxville, so they bought a house here and he commutes. Lucky for us." *Does it matter what I say? I just want to distract him.*

Joshua just nodded his head. He was already slipping back into the reality of losing his dad, finding the monster who attacked him, and wondering how he could ever run the store by himself.

"Carla, you know I'm not a big talker, but I need help to think this through. Do you mind being my sounding board?"

How can I tell you I would be thrilled to be your sounding board? I know you loved Jan, and rightly so, but I have been in love with you forever. You've just never known it.

"Joshua, I will help you in any way you need. We've never had much time to just sit and talk, but for all the mouthing off I do working here, I'm a pretty good listener. So, have at it."

Joshua laid out what he thought were all the considerations he had at the moment: planning a funeral for his dad, running the store and the propane business, finding out what progress Chad was making on the robbery and assault, and just getting through the day.

He looked closely at Carla. "So, any perspective you have will be greatly appreciated."

She was about to speak when her mobile phone rang. She glanced down at the screen to see who was calling. "It's Bella. I'll take it if you don't mind?"

"Oh my gosh! Bella. I totally forgot. Bella and Chad were at the hospital. Yes, yes, take it. Please."

"Hey, Bella, what's up?" Carla listened intently and decided Bella presented a good solution to offer Joshua. "Okay. Well, Joshua and I are eating breakfast at The Corral. Maybe you and Chad could join us?" She listened carefully to what Bella had to say. "Right. See you soon."

Joshua had a look in his eyes that Carla wasn't sure she wanted to see. At almost forty-nine and with the instincts of someone who had been single all her life, she was aware that Joshua was taken with Bella. She felt a pang of jealousy over a woman she was growing to like immensely, but who she could easily hate for having two men vying for her attention. Although Carla was pretty sure that Chad Oliver, the esteemed sheriff, was intrigued with Bella, the one thing that kept her from becoming a total green-eyed monster was that Carla was equally sure Bella was interested in Chad.

"Sorry, Joshua, what did you say?"

"I gather Bella is on her way here. Right?"

"Right." She didn't want to show the jealousy she was trying to tamp down.

"Okay, so any thoughts on what I laid out for you?"

Carla had her own thoughts and wasn't afraid to share them. "Let's start with..." She reached over and put her hand on top of his and let it rest there. "Joe is at peace. Doc Fred has seen to it that he's being taken care of now. Okay?" Joshua nodded. "Now, Chad's folks will be all over the robbery, and they will check with you if they need something. You know that, right?"

"Yes."

"Now, for the store and propane business," Carla said with assurance, "can you give me the names of the folks who help you out when you get busy?" She grabbed a napkin and took a pen out of her purse. "Who are your most reliable helpers?"

Carla wrote them down as Joshua named them. "Okay, I think I know or can get phone numbers for those three. Melody is off school tomorrow too, so I can call her. I think we can get folks to the store tomorrow, and as soon as Bella and Chad get here, we'll map out the rest. Deal?"

"Yeah. Thanks, Carla." Joshua pulled his hand out from under Carla's and patted the top of her hand, like a brother thanking his sister. Carla knew she would take whatever attention he was willing to give. After all, she had been a patient woman her entire life. Her musings were soon interrupted when she saw the side door open and Bella walk in with Chad.

Friends Helping Friends

When they reached the table, Joshua stood up slowly and shook hands with Chad and accepted Bella's kiss on the cheek. Carla was surprised when Bella hugged her. Bella stepped back.

"Oh, Carla, I'm sorry. I should have asked if I could give you a hug." She smiled and continued, "I need to wear a button that gives full disclosure, something like, 'Fair warning: I'm a hugger.' I forget that not everyone's a hugger."

"No problem. No problem at all. Be a better world if everyone hugged and meant it." Carla smiled and nodded her head. "Sit, you two."

Chad and Bella took the seats opposite each other, and Natalia was there the moment they sat down.

"Sheriff. Ma'am. Good morning. Coffee?"

"The lady will have?" Chad looked at Bella.

"Ice tea, unsweet, please. And thank you."

"And black coffee for me. Thanks, Natalia. Hope your family is well."

"Yes, sir. We're all fine. Thank you."

Natalia was back before they could start talking. Her hand slipped on the glass of ice tea, and she almost dropped it on Bella. "So sorry, ma'am. Did it splash on you?"

"No, no. We're good. Hi, Natalia, I'm—"

Joshua interrupted. "Natalia, this is Dr. Bella Anderson. Her family has lived in these mountains for over a hundred years. Bella, this is Natalia. She's the top student in the junior class at the high school." Everyone at the table knew Joshua's rapid-fire speech was the talk of grief.

"Natalia, I'm so happy to meet you. What a lovely name, the pronunciation must be from central Europe, is that right?"

Natalia was surprised. "Yes, ma'am. My parents are from the Czech Republic. I was born here though. Nice to meet you, Dr. Anderson." She backed up and turned to walk away.

"Very nice to meet you too, Natalia. I hope to chat with you some other time. Thanks for such prompt service." Natalia nodded and walked towards the kitchen.

"So, Carla, you have the younger version of Joshua's Melody. I'd say it makes you both pretty lucky to have such bright young women working for you." Bella smiled at the other woman.

Carla nodded.

Joshua sat staring at the wall.

"How're you holding up, Joshua?" Chad hoped to get a sense of how Joshua was coping with things. It was bad enough his wife died last month, and now this—even mountain men with a strong backbone sagged sometimes. He was pretty sure Joshua might be at "sometime."

Joshua shrugged his shoulders in a non-committal expression of "I'm here." He didn't speak.

Chad had his answer.

After several seconds of quiet, all eyes turned to Bella as she spoke. "Joshua, what I mentioned to Carla on the phone had to do with this afternoon." She knew in these circumstances you just had to move ahead and hope you could keep the one with the greatest loss from drowning under the weight of it.

"We were already planning to come to your house for a late lunch."

Joshua interrupted her. "Oh no, I completely forgot." Now there was panic in his eyes.

"Joshua," Bella continued quietly, "Chad and I will take care of what I think now might need to be an early supper. Would you prefer to do it at your house or Chad's?"

She looked at Chad.

Chad nodded.

The panicked note in Joshua's voice subsided. "We can go to Chad's. Carla, is that okay?"

"Absolutely, my brother has the restaurant covered." With the habit of so many years of bantering in The Corral, she couldn't stop herself from continuing, "Do him some good to remember what it's like to take care of customers face-to-face, not just to shake their hands when he decides to step away from the accounting in his office."

It turned out to be a good thing; they all laughed.

Carla thought the levity was good for Joshua, so she continued, "Granted you probably do *not* want to be under a coffee pot my brother's trying to pour, but, short of that, he can manage. So, will you trust us, Joshua? We're here for you—for whatever you need."

Joshua hesitated. "Thanks. Thanks to all of you. Friends matter to me. I'm feeling pretty guilty right now that I may not have shown the best friendship to you folks over the years. Makes it hard to accept." He stopped and they all remained quiet. Each knew Joshua well enough to know he was contemplative on a normal day; this was anything but a normal day.

Chad spoke first. "Joshua, is there anything you need covered that you don't have someone to do? Stocking shelves, anything?"

Joshua let out a deep sigh. "The store can pretty much run itself. Doug and Melody can handle the cash registers, although I have to say until you catch who did this, it makes me nervous to be responsible for anyone being in the store."

"We're on the hunt for whoever did this. You know Billy Williams is a fine detective, and he will not sleep 'til he finds those responsible.

You'll be the first to know when we succeed. Now, what else? The propane side of the business?"

Joshua looked at him. *Are you a mind reader, Chad? That's my biggest worry.* He cleared his throat and said what he was thinking out loud. "The propane has me most worried. Folks are starting to use more and more gas with the colder weather. I don't think I can handle deliveries right now, especially since some of them are pretty far up in the mountains."

Chad thought for a moment. "I have several deputies and my work crew who are used to handling the gas pumps at the station. I know it's a different kind of gas, but safety is safety. They all have hazmat training so if you give them a quick training on propane, I'd trust them to handle it for you. I can put the word out, and when they're off-duty, they're free to help out however you need them. I'm pretty sure you'll have to turn some away. What do you say?"

Bella was relieved to see the breakfast crowd had thinned out to a few tables at the front of the restaurant as Joshua put his hands to his face and wept softly. All three of his friends reached over to touch him on the arm or shoulder but did not speak. Not one of them could imagine the depth of his suffering. Even when you're sixty-three, you still aren't ready for the loss of your father or your spouse and especially within a month of each other.

Standing up, Joshua excused himself and headed to the men's room. The other three sat quietly. All were old enough to have figured out they just had to jump in and do what needed to be done. Chad pulled out his phone and called his desk sergeant.

"Yes, that's right. Have me a list of who's willing and when they're available. I'll be in within half an hour." He listened to the desk sergeant. "Glad Williams is there, please ask him to text me with a time he can meet. Thanks." He knew the deputies would be aware of the robbery itself, but he was hoping that Billy and Sergeant White-horse were the only ones who knew the robbery had resulted in Joe's death.

Carla whispered to Bella. "I'd like to run home and shower, but I don't want to leave Joshua alone."

"You go do that. Sounds like Chad needs to go to the station. I can stay with Joshua. Once we know what he wants to do, you can meet up with us."

"Great. Thanks, Bella."

Chad nodded at Bella and Carla as he saw Joshua head back to the table. Chad had his wallet out and put money on the table to cover the food and drinks for all of them.

Carla handed it back. "No need, Chad. Thanks all the same. If you want to leave something for Natalia, that'd be great."

Chad nodded and left a generous tip for Natalia. He and Bella stood. He slapped Joshua on the back. "I'll have a list of folks for propane delivery in about thirty minutes."

Once they were out the door, Bella touched Joshua's arm. "What would you like to do?"

Joshua shrugged.

"Would you feel better if you checked on the store? We could do that." Bella hoped seeing the store would help Joshua move beyond thinking about it as a crime scene and make it easier for him to get into a routine.

Joshua nodded. "Sure, let's go by the store."

Carla spoke up. "I'm going to run home and change. I'll meet you there."

"I'll drop Joshua and Bella off then run by the station. I'll swing by the Valley Store as soon as I'm done." Chad knew that Bella and Joshua both had the experience of loss, and he thought it would be best for them to go by themselves.

Carla kissed Joshua on the cheek, gave Bella a hug, and nodded to Chad. No one saw the sadness on Carla's face as she walked towards her Jeep Cherokee. *Joshua Johnson, how do I get you to see that I'd go to the moon and back for you, and always would have?*

Bella would have been stunned if she had known what Carla was thinking. She, Joshua and Chad go in his Ford Interceptor and headed to the Valley Store.

Chapter 3

On the Trail

After dropping off Bella and Joshua, Chad headed to the station and made a beeline for the desk sergeant. He was handed a list of deputies and maintenance workers available to help Joshua with propane deliveries. He planned to give it to Carla when they met up again. *I'm pretty sure Carla will run things for Joshua for a few days.* He looked at the list. He had been right that there would be plenty of people willing to help out; it made him proud of his employees.

There were other things he had to sort out, but he didn't want to be gone too long. He knew his detectives would be turning over every rock to find whoever committed the crimes at the Valley Store. But new crime didn't wipe out the need to follow up on the immigrants they found on the plateau, the prostitution and likely trafficking of young girls they uncovered on Friday night, and how or if Commissioner Zimmerman was involved in any of it. There were a lot of balls in the air already, but none of that hinted at what the day might bring.

Detective Billy Williams was waiting at the sheriff's door when Chad walked down the hall.

"Morning, boss. Need a bit more time?"

"No, Detective, I'm good. Come in and have a seat."

Billy headed to the round table, which he now understood Chad had in his office to encourage his folks to problem solve and talk out a crime investigation. Billy was glad Sergeant Sylvia Whitehorse had explained the Native American custom of the "talking circle" to him. He sat and waited.

Chad shut the door, picked up his coffee mug, and walked to the table. "We have a number of cases right now, and I need to be available to Joshua. So, updates, please."

"Yes, sir. I assume the most immediate is Mr. Joe. We found some good prints, and we're still trying to eliminate those that might be Mr. Joe or Joshua, or anyone else who ran a cash register for them. But we got a hit on one of them."

Chad had been staring at his empty coffee mug, wondering why he had brought it to the table. He looked up immediately. Before he could comment, Billy continued, "Another kid, Jason Kirk, who's been in juvie. Lives across the street from that Nick Brown kid—the one who overdosed."

"Yes. I know who Nick Brown was. I didn't think Brown had been in juvenile detention."

"No, sir, he never was. But Jason was in juvie for breaking and entering. He got off pretty light, really. I think the judge was trying to put the fear of God in him at the time by sending him up for three months. Seems it was a relative's house, and he stole some Budweiser. Judge might have been trying to send the dad a message. I suspect the Bud was for him. The dad was in the front yard guzzling down pretty good when we were investigating the Brown death. In fact, when we finished interviewing Nick's dad, he went over and drank with him. Some role models."

Chad did not speak, and Billy knew it meant to keep quiet. Billy made a note on his pad of paper to tell Chad about the call from the DA regarding Steve Phillips.

"Go on."

"Deputies picked up Jason. I'll interrogate him as soon as he's processed in holding, which should be anytime now. I saw Jason looking out the front door the night Nick died, but he wasn't around later that evening when we interviewed his dad. When we asked where Jason was, Mr. Kirk claimed he had gone to visit an uncle. As that case evolved, we didn't have any reason to suspect Jason was involved with Nick's death, so we didn't do a follow-up to talk to him. We'll see how he reacts when he sees me." *I may have really messed up not interviewing him then. I bet the boss is thinking that too.*

"How old is this boy?" Chad always hated it when teenagers were involved in a crime.

"Eighteen. I would have thought younger the night I saw him behind the screen door, but he disappeared, and the dad insisted he had left. Anyway, he's still in school. I'll talk with Dr. Bennett, the high school principal."

Chad let it go that Billy felt the need to tell him who Dr. Bennett was. He could tell Billy was nervous. *Hope it doesn't turn out we should have interviewed Jason Kirk before.*

He looked at Billy. "Okay. Let me know after your interrogation. Meantime, I need to know the current status on getting Gertrude to talk. Have you been able to find out who she's working for? Who might be running the prostitution ring? She has to know several of those girls in that house were underage. No way she's paying the rent."

"I let her sit Saturday morning and then dropped in during the evening. She doesn't want a lawyer, but she was quite adamant one of the commissioners would make sure we knew 'what was what' and she'd be out of there. Then she clammed up again."

"Really now? A commissioner? Say which one?"

"No, sir. I'll have another talk with her this afternoon. She knows she's here at least until she asks for a lawyer or tells me what I need to know."

"Good work, Billy."

"One more thing. I heard from the district attorney yesterday afternoon. She's taking the case on Steve Phillips to the grand jury in the overdose death of Nick Brown. She expects to get a charge of homicide added to the trespassing and property damage. They convene Tuesday morning."

Chad nodded his head. *Another young life gone astray. We have to do better.*

"Boss, lots of folks are asking about Mr. Joe. Anything we can tell them?"

Chad stared at Billy, his expression a mix of "Are you kidding me?" and "I get it."

"Sheriff, I know it's not our job to inform folks, but they're asking after a long-standing member of our community."

"Sorry. I hate the conflict between knowing our staff and neighbors truly care about Joe, and making sure we protect his, and Joshua's, right to privacy. We have to follow Joshua's lead on this one. He'll let folks know when he's ready." Chad stood and Billy knew the meeting was over.

"Sure thing, boss. Sure thing." Billy stood. He hoped his mountain double speak reassured the sheriff he would do the right thing. "Hope Joshua's going to be all right." He walked out.

Chad returned to his desk; reasonably confident he would soon be able to tell Joshua they had a suspect from the robbery in custody. He was counting on it. At the same time, he was concerned about the increase in the number of crimes involving young people in the valley. He needed to have a meeting with his sergeants to try and get a handle on any root causes. He sent a calendar request for Wednesday morning, then he did a quick scan of emails and messages. Although he half hoped to see something from Detective Lewis with any update about the motel ownership in Round City, he realistically didn't expect anything until Monday as the detective had previously reported. He walked to the front to speak to the deputy and sergeant on the desk before he headed to the Valley Store.

At the Valley Store

Bella and Joshua walked towards the front door of the Valley Store. Joshua stopped on the front steps and turned to look at Bella. "I'm sorry, Bella, you can wait out here. I shouldn't have agreed to you coming to the store with me. I came so I could clean up. I don't want you to see the place, and I sure don't want you to have to help me. I didn't even think to ask Chad if I could clean up."

"It's okay, Joshua, it's all been taken care of. Let's go in." The bell above the door jingled as Joshua unlocked the door and they stepped inside.

Joshua stopped and looked around.

"Bella?" He looked at her. "Who cleaned up?" He leaned against the wall. "I thought I'd have to do that."

Bella hoped he didn't faint. She knew she couldn't stop him from falling to the floor. "Chad arranged it. They were able to get the evidence they needed pretty quickly, and Arthur came in earlier this morning and fixed the steps."

Joshua looked confused.

"Carla said you told her he was supposed to come fix them today, so she sent him a text and he ran by your house to get the keys. He dropped them back off before you got up." Bella kept talking, hoping to distract him. "The steps look pretty good, don't you think? Chad had some folks come in to clean the store, and Arthur helped them."

Joshua stared at her. "Bella, how can I thank all of you? I don't know what to say."

She smiled and nodded. "It's all good." She grabbed Joshua's elbow, thinking this time he *was* about to faint. "Let's go sit in the back, and I can make you a cup of coffee. Then, when Chad gets here, we can take you home."

Once they were in the back, Joshua sat down at the table where he and his dad always had their lunch. He stared into space. Bella remained quiet as she began to make him coffee.

Out of the blue, Joshua started talking. "Deliveries come in tomorrow. It's usually around eleven this time of year. I hope the driver is Skip. He knows what to do. Not sure I can sort it out for a new driver."

"Let's see how you feel tomorrow morning, okay? I'm sure Carla and I can help." Bella felt like she was flying blind trying to navigate Joshua through this.

They chatted about their time as kids when Bella came up in the summer. She looked at Joshua's haggard face. "I've always been grateful for the connection our families have. Joe always helped me imagine what my daddy would have been like." She touched the back of his hand and smiled.

The jingling of the bell over the front door got their attention.

"Hey?" Chad called out.

Bella stepped to the double doors that separated the storeroom from the front of the store.

"Back here, Chad."

Chad walked straight to the table and sat down by Joshua. He had to figure out how much Joshua could handle right now, and how much he should tell him without getting Joshua's hopes up.

"Any news, Chad?" Joshua didn't look at him.

Bella poured Joshua's coffee, but she stayed by the counter.

Chad was caring but spoke with the authority he had as sheriff. "Joshua, we're making progress and we were able to get some good fingerprints. Billy is on it. I promise you we're going to track this down."

Joshua nodded his head but didn't say anything.

Bella took the coffee to Joshua.

"Thanks, Bella." Joshua stared at the mug. He lifted it to his mouth to drink, paused for a moment, and then flung it across the room. The mug hit the concrete of the loading dock and shattered. He put his head down on the table and sobbed silently, his shoulders shaking.

Chad nodded to Bella to come to the table. She walked up behind Joshua and put her hand on his shoulder, not knowing whether she should say something as she felt the tremors course through his body. After a rapid debate with herself, she decided her presence would be enough. *After all, there is nothing I can say that will make any of this better.*

Chad picked up the broken mug and put it in the trash can with a clatter. There was another jingle from the silver bell over the front door. He stuck his head out of the double doors and saw it was Carla; he waved her back. Chad walked to the table and sat down with Joshua. The tears that wracked him had stopped, and Bella moved to meet Carla at the entrance to the storeroom. Bella turned Carla around and they headed back into the store.

Bella quietly told Carla what had just happened.

Carla's face was stricken. "Do you think I should come back later and clean up?"

"Chad cleaned up the mug. I think the coffee is only on the loading dock; it can wait. Whatever staining is done... is done."

The women turned and looked towards the back as Chad and Joshua walked towards them.

Chad's voice was soft but direct. "I think it's time to head out, and maybe get some Sunday afternoon football and eat. Good with that, Joshua?

"Okay." Joshua kept walking towards the front door.

Bella was about to ask Joshua for the key to lock up when Chad held the key up in his hand. She realized Joshua must have left the key in the front door.

"Joshua, you ride with Carla and keep her company. We'll head out and see you when you get to my place." Chad nodded his head towards his SUV.

Joshua let Carla take his hand and walked to her Jeep.

Bella looked at Chad when he closed his door. "Do you have anything we can fix for an early supper?"

"Sadly, no. Not used to keeping groceries in the house. Carla or I can call James at The Corral and he'll send over something. Let's just keep this easy. That work?"

"Works fine. Just fine."

They rode the rest of the way to Chad's home in silence, each lost in their own thoughts.

Interrogation Begins

Detective Billy Williams walked into the holding cell area and spoke to the matron. "Kirk processed?"

A deputy had picked up Jason walking down the road from his house, and it was likely his parents had no idea he was in jail. Jason had not asked to speak to anyone.

"Yes, Detective. He's ready when you are. We moved Steve Phillips to another area since we weren't sure if they knew each other."

"Good thinking! Which room's open?" He turned his head as Deputy Susan Thomas came around the corner. He nodded at her. "Thanks for coming in. Glad you could make it." He told her briefly what was going on with the boy they were about to interrogate. She nodded with understanding as he spoke.

"Okay, Matron, if you'll bring Kirk to Room 2, we'll get started."

A few minutes later, Jason Kirk shuffled his shackled feet into Room 2. His eyes were glazed, and his scrawny frame drooped. He glanced at the deputy and detective, and slowly moved to the empty chair next to the wall. Deputy Thomas sat in the chair by the table, and Billy was stationed near the door. He straddled his chair, with the back of it facing Kirk. Once they were in position, Billy nodded to Susan to start the tape recorder. Both of them knew the camera in the wall was already recording.

"Mornin', Jason. I'm Detective Williams and this is—"

"Deputy Thomas," Susan's cadence was quiet but professional. She gave the date and time.

Jason just sat there.

"Please state your name and date of birth." They waited.

He sat for a second and finally sighed, "Jason Kirk." He gave his date of birth.

"I'm going to read you your Miranda rights." While she did so, Jason tapped his heels against the floor causing the chain to jangle. Susan ignored it, and instead tried to look Jason in the eye. "Do you understand these rights?"

Jason nodded.

"I need you to answer for the recording." A mother trying to coax her child to eat could not have been more caring.

"Yes, I understan'."

She continued in the same placating voice. "Do you wish to have an attorney?"

He shook his head no and moved his eyes up a bit but didn't look at her from his slouched position. He could see her finger point at the recorder. "Don't want no attorney." It was barely loud enough to be recorded.

Billy waited a few beats. "Need something to drink? Some water? Tea?"

Jason shook his head no.

Billy had already told the deputy they were going to leave the cuffs and ankle bracelets on for the time being.

"Think I saw you last week, didn't I?" Billy looked at him but didn't stare.

Jason glanced sideways to look at Billy and continued to tap his feet.

"Saw you standing at the screen door the night things happened across the street at the Brown's. That *was* you, right?"

Susan and Billy could see he was trembling, but they couldn't tell if he was scared or coming down off a high. His glazed eyes were obvious, but he didn't look up long enough for them to see if his pupils were dilated.

"Yessir, it was me."

"Good, Jason. Glad you remember. Real sad what happened to Nick. What do you know about Nick's death?"

Jason shook his head. "Nothin, really. He'd been acting all weird after he started hanging around with that guy from them villages over the mountain. He didn't talk to me much anymore. His mama told my ma that he died from some kind of poison."

Billy and Susan looked at each other. He nodded to her to continue the questioning.

"Where were you yesterday? Saturday afternoon."

"Home."

"All afternoon, Jason?"

"No, ma'am."

"Let's start with Saturday when you got up and tell me what you did the rest of the day. Just take your time and try to remember."

When he looked up at her, she could see his eyes were dilated. *Oh boy, this might not be good. He's on something.* "What did you eat for breakfast?"

"Toast."

"Anything else?"

"Nope, don't like eatin'."

Susan glanced at Billy.

"Tell me what you did after you ate your toast."

Jason spoke directly to her. He didn't look at Billy. "I watched TV most of the day. Then my cousin come over in the afternoon and we went riding on his ATV. We just rode around the hills behind my house." He took a breath. "Then my cousin wanted to go get some cigarettes, so we done went to the Valley Store."

Billy and Susan just sat, barely moving, hoping not to distract the boy from his story. Billy was trying to figure out what was wrong with the kid. *He can't be too bright telling us he went to the store. Word spreads fast in these hills. Likely lots of folks already know something happened to Joe.*

A moan emerged from Jason that was so feral Billy pulled out his secure phone, expecting to call for an ambulance. The words gushed out of Jason. "I didn't hurt, Mr. Joe. Honest. I didn't. I took the money, gave it to my pappy, but I didn't hurt Mr. Joe."

That may explain his prints on the cash register. Billy looked at Susan and waited. They didn't want the boy to clam up.

Susan spoke very softly. "Thanks, Jason. Thanks for telling me that. Did you think it was okay to take the money?"

Jason shook his head. "No, ma'am, I know it's wrong. My momma always says you can't hurt nobody either. I never did."

"Who did, Jason?" Susan hoped she was using her *best* mother's voice. There was something about this boy that was not quite typical of an eighteen-year-old. She had the feeling he could be easily led.

"My cousin, Bobby. Bobby Kirk." He waited a second. "Ma'am, please don't say I told. I'm scared. Bobby'll hurt me. My pappy'll hurt me, too." The whimper in his voice now was sadder than a crying baby. They both knew there was going to be more to learn about this boy than what they could see at the moment.

"Let me get you something to drink, Jason," Deputy Thomas started to stand.

Billy stood. "I'll get it." He recorded that he was exiting the room and quickly got a bottle of water from the matron. He recorded his return as he handed the water to Susan to give to Jason. He saw Susan shake her head to indicate the boy had said nothing while he was out of the room.

Jason gulped the water, almost choking on it. He lowered his head. "Thanks."

"Jason, it would be really helpful if you could tell me everything that happened yesterday." Susan smiled at him.

Jason took another gulp from the bottle. In a rush of words, they often saw in young suspects who were both guilty and afraid, he told them they were just going to get some juice and cigarettes. "When Bobby saw Mr. Joe by himself, he pushed him to the side and jumped behind the counter and grabbed a couple of cartons of cigarettes." He raced on. "Mr. Joe tried to stop Bobby. Then Bobby hit him really hard, and Mr. Joe fell and hit his head on the corner of the counter." The look of fear on his face was palpable.

"My pappy always fusses at me and my momma 'cause he needs money. Sometimes he hits us, so I just grabbed some money to take home." He started crying. They let him.

Deputy Thomas leaned towards him but didn't touch him. "One more question, Jason. Did you call 9-1-1 to help Mr. Joe?"

The boy shook his head.

"I need you to answer me, please."

"No, ma'am."

"You've been really helpful. I think we can stop for now. I'm going to ask the matron to put you someplace you can sleep for a while." Given how much he had been in motion the whole time he spoke, she doubted he would sleep, but she also didn't want him scared someone else would hurt him.

Billy's tone was somber. "Jason, you did a good job here. Thanks for your cooperation." He stood. "Detective Williams and . . . "

"Deputy Thomas exiting interview Room 2 and returning... Please state your name."

"Jason Kirk."

"Returning Jason Kirk to holding." She turned off the recorder, slipped it in her pocket, and followed Jason out.

As soon as he was in the custody of the matron, the two officers stepped into a room. "You okay, Deputy?"

"Good as can be given the circumstances."

"Shouldn't be hard to find his cousin Bobby. Let's see what we can do."

"Yes, sir."

As much as Billy liked the sound of being addressed as a senior officer of the sheriff's department, he was equally uncomfortable with it. "Detective is fine, Deputy. No need for the 'sir.' Save that for the sheriff."

Chapter 4

There need be no lasting sorrow for the death of any of Nature's creations, because for every death there is always born a corresponding life.

John Muir, 1838-1914

The Value of Friendship

Joshua shuffled into Chad's living room and dropped onto the sofa. He sat with his back straight and his eyes vacant. Carla sat down next to him, and Bella left the front door open, hoping the cool fresh air of the fall afternoon would provide some comfort. As she went to the kitchen to let Chad know they had arrived, she gently touched Joshua's shoulder as she walked past.

Chad handed her a glass of water. "Thanks, Chad, I'll take this to Joshua." She turned and, to her surprise, Joshua was standing in the dining room, looking out the French doors to the porch.

"Here, Joshua, let's go sit on the porch." She opened the door and Joshua pulled out a chair for her.

Carla walked into the kitchen and accepted a glass of tea. "Thanks, Chad." She stood quietly and then said, "I'm so worried about Joshua."

"It's good of you to be here for him, Carla." Chad smiled at her.

Out on the porch, Joshua looked at Bella.

"It's true, isn't it, Bella? Dad's gone." The last part was more statement than question.

"Yes, Joshua. It's true. It's a great loss for you. . . for all of us."

He did not look at her. He stared off across the mountains.

"Why? He never hurt anyone. Never." Joshua's words were raw and carried so much love for his dad.

Bella let the question hang in the air. She did not have an answer and knew anything she said would sound trite. They both knew there was no answer to the question of why.

"Joshua, as we both know from experience, this is a time when reason, pain, and the mundane collide. Carla, Chad, and I are here for you—whatever you need. Would you like me to call Pastor Fisk?" She waited.

He continued to look at the mountains.

Bella knew they had to get through some of the difficult issues of planning a funeral. "Doc Fred is going to need to know what arrangements to make. Will you use the funeral home in Round City?"

He nodded but still didn't look at her.

"Do you think you can make the call, or would you like me to do it? I think if I call for you and explain the situation, we can get Joe taken care of. Then we can talk about what you want to do."

"Bella, please call the funeral home. I worked with Director Davis for Jan's funeral. . ." he choked. "Just ask for him. He knows my dad. We can call Pastor Fisk later."

Bella looked at him, trying to read the anguish on the face of a man she considered a friend. She had no experience with a loss in such a tragic way. Joshua had not been told about the autopsy, so Bella knew she would have to make the call to the funeral director from another room.

"I'm going to step into the kitchen. Carla will be out here in a minute. Can I get you anything?" He shook his head. "Okay then, I'll make that call."

She walked into the kitchen. "Joshua has asked me to call the funeral home. Carla, I told him you'd come out and join him, okay?"

"Sure. Should I take him anything?"

"He has some water. He said he didn't want anything. We have food coming, right?" Chad nodded. "Yes, James will send food soon. I'll find out what time the football starts and who's playing, and then we can see if Joshua really wants to watch it."

He and Carla walked out of the kitchen and closed the door. None of them wanted Joshua to hear the details she had to give the funeral director. She found the phone number and was immediately put through to Director Davis. She explained that Joe had passed away and told him the current situation.

"Ms. Anderson, I will just need a brief word with Mr. Johnson, then I can take care of things. May I ask if he knows it may be a day or two before we can get Mr. Joe's remains?"

"He does not. . . at this time. Sheriff Oliver said Dr. Smith and the medical examiner would take care of things over here. I just need to verify that you will be handling things for Joshua."

"If I may speak with Joshua for a moment, I'll take care of everything."

Bella walked out to the porch, grateful there was mobile service at this elevation.

Carla and Joshua were sitting side-by-side—looking out to the mountains.

"Joshua," He looked up at her. "Mr. Davis needs to speak to you for just a moment." She handed him the phone.

Joshua took the phone. "Joshua here." She saw his eyes darting across the mountains. "Yes, yes. Whatever Dr. Anderson told you is fine. Thanks, Dan." His voice was as flat as a river in the heat of summer. He handed the phone to Bella with his left hand. Carla reached over and held Joshua's right hand.

Bella walked back into the kitchen. "Thank you, Mr. Davis, I appreciate—" she stopped when he interrupted her. "No apology needed, Mr. Davis. Dr. Anderson isn't necessary. Please call me Bella. Thanks for your time and help. We'll bring Joshua over in the next day or two to make final arrangements. In the meantime, I'll call if we have any questions."

Bella was startled by the whistle of the tea kettle as she ended the call. She smiled. Chad knew she would want hot tea. She made herself a cup and then walked into the living room to check with Chad about the rest of the day.

"Are you surprised Joshua was okay having a late lunch here?"

Chad was flipping through the channel guide on the TV. "No. I'm not surprised. I suspect he doesn't want to be at home where there are reminders of Joe." He stopped the channel search when he reached ESPN. He looked at Bella.

"You're right, Chad. I saw a framed picture of Joe, Joshua, and Jan on the kitchen window ledge." She stopped. "I don't know when reminders of Matt went from being too hard to look at to becoming a memory I wanted to recall."

Chad stepped over and put his arms around her. He pulled her into a close embrace. "Bella, part of you not remembering where you were this morning is the shock of losing Joe and how he died, but it's also dredging up lots of difficult memories. So, please, tell me when you know a way I can help."

She hugged him; her voice was a whisper. "This helps more than I can tell you." They stood in the embrace for a moment, then she stepped back. "See what you can figure out about football. I need to see if Joshua has any questions about my phone call to Mr. Davis."

Chad wasn't sure what to make of her abrupt move and change in tone. He decided she didn't even realize it.

Bella walked out to the porch with her mug of tea in hand. She sat down and looked out to the mountains just as Joshua and Carla were. *I wonder where your mind goes when the loss of a loved one is not from natural causes? I hope the quiet doesn't swallow us up.*

"Bella, I think I need to call Pastor Fisk. What do you think?"

Bella saw the look of hurt on Carla's face. She was beginning to understand that Carla's interest in Joshua was likely not new. *I need to figure out how to back off, and let Carla have a role here. It's important for her and for Joshua.*

"I think that's a fine idea, Joshua. Let me get the number." She did a search on her phone. "Do you want to talk with him, or do you want me to talk to him?"

"I'll try." Joshua held out his hand.

She dialed the number of the office at the Presbyterian church, hoping it would be answered by Pastor Fisk and not by an answering machine on a Sunday afternoon. As she handed the phone to Joshua, Chad joined them on the porch.

"Afternoon, Pastor, this is Joshua Johnson." His hands started to shake. There was a nip in the air, but it wasn't cold out. Bella wasn't sure he could continue to hold the phone to his ear. She pointed to his glass of water, hoping Joshua might take a sip to steady himself. He picked it up, his hand shaking, but he managed to take a drink. The tremors seemed less as he put the glass back down.

Joshua started again. "Pastor Fisk." Bella thought he sounded a bit more like himself. "Dad didn't make it." He nodded his head while listening. "I'm at Chad's place, can you come here?"

Bella watched him then looked out at the mountains. It sounded like the pastor already knew Joe had been taken to the hospital—she was relieved. She knew there was just no easy way to get through this loss; she wished it could be different.

"Sure, Pastor, come over when you have time. No rush. I'm not going anywhere. Fine, fine. See you then."

Joshua set the phone on the table and seemed to have no awareness of the need to touch the "end" button. Bella reached for the phone but saw the pastor had ended the call.

"Pastor Fisk—" Joshua turned his head when he heard the doorbell.

Bella and Carla both stood and headed to the door. Bella stopped and let Carla go first. It was something Carla could do for Joshua.

Joshua turned to Chad and, with a rush of urgency in his voice, whispered. "Promise you'll get whoever did this to my dad. Promise!"

Chad looked at Joshua's pleading face. "Joshua, your dad is my number one priority. I have folks on it. I think I'll have some answers for you soon. We're doing everything we can."

From where he was sitting, Chad could see Bella and Carla were escorting two people from The Corral into the kitchen with multiple containers. He could imagine that James would have sent enough food for an army. He looked back to Joshua.

"Hang in there, Joshua. I've got the investigation covered. Want something to drink?"

"A beer, if you've got it."

"Should I get one out for Pastor Fisk?" Chad tried to lighten the mood.

"Nah, I think he drinks scotch. Wait 'til he gets here."

Chad grabbed Joshua's shoulder as a friendly gesture. "I've gotcha." He stood and walked into the house.

Attending to Joshua

Chad entered the kitchen where Bella and Carla were talking quietly as they organized the food. Carla was putting aluminum containers in the oven to stay warm. He could see the labels were written in broad black marker showing the contents: barbeque pork, fried chicken, green beans, corn bread, and corn on the cob. He saw Bella putting utensils and plates on the counter buffet style, with empty dishes for what he presumed was the cold food she had put in the refrigerator.

"Finding everything you need?" Chad looked from Bella to Carla.

"Oh, Chad, I hope it's okay that we just searched for what we needed."

He thought Bella sounded like a child who was caught with her hand in the cookie jar.

"Relax. Of course, it's okay. Just tell me what you need if you can't find it. I might not have it, but I may have a substitute."

Carla grinned at him. "Pretty well-equipped kitchen for a bachelor . . . who I suspect we feed more from The Corral than he cooks."

"Credit my daughter for that. Nora equipped the kitchen so that when they're over here she has all the conveniences of home. Of course, by that she means her home!" Chad chuckled.

Bella looked at him and smiled. "I'm sure you enjoy having time with Nora and her family here. I hope to see them again soon."

Chad warmed to the comment; he allowed himself to take her interest in seeing them again as a sign she was comfortable with his family—he sure hoped so.

"I hope it's soon myself. Now, I came to get Joshua a beer. Can I help in any way? Or get either of you anything?"

"Not for me." Carla shook her head and looked at Bella.

Bella shook her head. "Chad, I think it would do Joshua good to have you out on the porch with him. For all my pushing for gender equity, I'm not unaware that sometimes a man just needs to talk to a man—"

"And a woman just needs to talk to a woman." Carla grinned, with a clear bit of mischief in her delivery.

Bella looked at her, nodded, and smiled.

Chad shook his head and rolled his eyes as he walked to the fridge. He saw he had two four packs of Fat Tire Ale; he hoped Joshua liked it. He took two of them, then turned and held one up as a question for the women. Both shook their heads.

"Good. More for Joshua." Chad winked and headed out to the porch.

After she surveyed the kitchen, Bella looked over at Carla. "Looks like we're as organized as we can be for whoever may show up this evening."

"I suspect the pastor will have no small number of people here once he has talked to Joshua." Carla paused. "Or maybe not. Joshua may tell him he doesn't want anyone just yet."

Bella nodded. "Well, either way, we're ready. Nice of your brother to get everything here on such short notice."

"We're used to it. Although… he would have had to do some work himself for a change, given I wasn't there." Carla's laugh carried deep affection for James.

"Well, Carla, for now all we can do is try to anticipate what Joshua might need and take it as it comes. I'm sure Joshua will really need your expert business help tomorrow if he decides to open the store."

Carla nodded her head. "James knows I'm not going to be back to The Corral as long as Joshua needs me."

Bella had already figured out that Carla would be by Joshua's side, and she also thought it might turn out to be much longer than just tomorrow. She refilled her mug of tea and pulled out a stool at the kitchen counter across from Carla. They continued to chat, leaving the two men to themselves on the porch to talk.

"Carla, how are *you* holding up?"

"Bella, it's been a lot of years since my parents died, but it was in a car wreck. Some flatlander was driving too fast for our switchbacks and ran head-on into them. Took both of them. So, though it isn't the same as what happened to Joe, I can't stop thinking that someone was responsible for taking my parents, same as Joshua's. I just wish I could help him."

"Carla, you *are* helping. Just being here helps him. You'll find the right time and the right words to share with him. I know you will."

"You think so?"

"I do." Bella reached across the counter and squeezed Carla's hand.

Anger and Grief

Chad set the Fat Tire ale in front of Joshua.

Joshua peered at the label. "Looks like one of those craft beers that Harold likes."

"That right? Didn't figure Harold for a craft beer kind of guy."

"I think it's just because he has to hobnob with the Mountain Villages folks from time to time."

Chad knew Joshua and Harold were good friends, but he wondered if Harold knew about Joe yet.

Joshua picked up his beer and turned to Chad, automatically lifting the bottle to make a toast. He faltered. Chad picked up on Joshua's dilemma and raised his own bottle: "To a great man, who loved his family, served his community, and is singing with the angels."

Joshua blinked with surprise then started laughing almost maniacally, the recognizable laughter of loss. "Oh no! The angels will not want him singing." He gulped in air. "There were so many good things about my dad, but singing was not one of them." His laugh dwindled to a sputter.

"Then here's to Joe enjoying the serenade!" Chad lifted his bottle again. The two clinked their bottles and fell silent. Chad was actually glad that Joshua was expressing some emotion. He had been concerned he might tamp it down and it would fester inside him.

"Chad?"

"Yes?"

"Do you think they meant to do this to my dad? To hurt him so badly he would die? Do you?" Joshua struggled to say each word.

"Hard to know what's in someone's head or heart, Joshua. I don't know enough yet, but when I do, I'll let you know. I promise." He hoped he was right. He knew this was leaning towards an accidental robbery gone bad, but he was never one to speculate.

"Dad loved a view of the mountains. He didn't really have a mountain view. It was always important to him to live close to the store. The only land close enough all those years ago backed him up against a hill. He loved to joke that he kept an eye on the valley 'cause no one else was paying attention—too busy looking out to the mountains."

Chad nodded and smiled. He knew Joshua needed him to listen. He wasn't surprised that Joshua really had no interest in football today. He just needed to have his friends close. The doorbell rang and, to Chad's surprise, Joshua stood up.

"I suspect it's the pastor. I should go to the door." Joshua walked in and bumped into Carla, who was also heading to answer the door. He smiled at her. "I'll get it. Thanks though." They could see through the front screen door that it was Pastor Fisk. Joshua opened the door and greeted him.

Bella walked out on the porch and stood behind Chad's chair, looking out at the autumn colors spread across the mountains; although beautiful, it was a different perspective compared to her familiar view above the valley. *I miss Drellag Caban.* She realized she had put her hand on Chad's shoulder only when he reached up and squeezed it. He didn't linger. She turned at the sound of the two men talking as they walked onto the porch with Carla. Chad stood up.

"Pastor Fisk, it's nice to see you again, I'm Bella Anderson." She wasn't sure he would remember her. She hadn't been to his church since she and Matt last attended five years ago.

"Dr. Anderson, so nice to see you. I heard you were back in the mountains. Good to have you here."

Bella smiled at him. She didn't hear rebuke in his voice, but she had her own guilt for not coming off the mountain on Sunday mornings. She felt the warmth in his voice as a reminder that she had a church home here.

"Chad, nice to see you. Sorry it's under these circumstances."

"Nice to see you, Albert." Chad extended his hand and nodded in agreement with the pastor's acknowledgement of Joe's passing. "Can I get you something to drink? Joshua and I are having this Fat Tire ale." He pointed to the bottle.

"Pretty much a scotch man myself. But it's a bit early for me. I could use a glass of tea, if that's an option."

"Happy to get it. Sweet or unsweet?" Carla waited.

"There's a choice?" The pastor gave a little chuckle. She nodded. "I'll have unsweet, then."

Chad pulled out a chair for Bella and left the one next to Joshua empty for Carla. Chad and the pastor sat. Chad planned to finish his beer and then step away to check in with the station. He was officially off today, so he had not hesitated to have the one beer he normally allowed himself in a day. He knew Sergeant Whitehorse could handle things and would call him if there was an urgent matter. The urgency for him was finding out if his lead detective had located and been able to interrogate the second suspect in the crime that had resulted in all of them being here on this autumn afternoon.

"Yes, Pastor," Chad heard Joshua say. "It's a beautiful fall day. It's the kind of day my dad," he visibly choked, but continued, "my dad would have said, 'God painted these leaves to remind us He's in control.'"

"Amen to that, Joshua." Pastor Fisk patted Joshua's arm.

Carla handed the glass of tea to the pastor and moved to sit in the chair next to Joshua, as all three men half stood from their chairs. "Thank you, gentlemen, but please, sit."

Bella watched. She imagined southern formalities were going to be on full display over the next few days. They all sat. There was absolute silence.

"Since we're all gathered here, would you like me to say a prayer, Joshua?"

"That would be nice, Pastor, thanks."

Pastor Fisk began: "Father in heaven, thank you for the life of Joe, his good deeds, and his many kindnesses. Bless those mourning him today. Amen." The friends stayed quiet at the end of the prayer, each lost in his or her thoughts.

"Unless you feel an urgent need, Joshua, I think we can talk about final arrangements tomorrow."

"That'll be fine, Pastor, thanks."

Joshua was staring at his bottle of beer. "Chad, could you do something for me?"

"Of course. What do you need?"

"I'd like you to go tell Harold. He's the closest thing I have to a brother, and I don't want him to find out about this from someone else, or on the phone."

"Said and done." Chad stood and Bella followed suit. She saw that Joshua had his hand resting on Carla's.

Bella looked at Pastor Fisk. "If you don't mind, I'll leave you to talk, and I'll get Chad to take me on an errand I need to do. We'll be back shortly."

The pastor nodded. "By all means. I'm here for whatever Joshua needs. It'll give us a chance to chat." That is exactly what Bella had hoped. She noticed Joshua was nodding his approval. Carla remained seated and quiet.

Bella looked from one to the other. "Can I get any of you anything before I leave? There's plenty of food in the kitchen from The Corral."

Carla started to get up. "I can help with that. What would you like?"

Joshua looked up at Carla; his eyes brightened and there was a small smile on his lips. "Carla, you brought food?"

"Not me, Joshua. Chad ordered it, and James brought it over. But you know we're all here for you. Everything is set up in the kitchen so you, and anyone else, can help themselves. Warm food is in the oven and cold in the fridge. So, what shall I get you?"

"That's real nice." Joshua smiled. "Real nice, but just sit, Carla. Let's talk to Pastor Fisk." They all picked up on the reassurance they knew he cherished in the repetitive statements.

Bella bent and kissed Joshua on the cheek, nodded to the pastor and Carla, and headed out to meet Chad at the front door.

Chapter 5

In every walk with Nature, one receives far more than he seeks.

John Muir, 1838-1914

Always More to Learn

Detective Billy Williams had called Dr. Amanda Bennett, the principal of the combined middle and high school, at home on Sunday afternoon. She met him at the front door of the school, and they headed across the entry hall and into her office.

"I have some cold water, but that's about it on Sunday afternoon. Get you one?"

Billy shook his head as he stared at the round table. *Well, apparently, she knows the talking circle tradition too. How come I never learned about it?*

"How are you doing, Amanda? Sorry to get you out on a Sunday afternoon. I saw Ken went off shift this morning for a two-day break. He said things are going pretty well for you two."

"Did he now? He would say that if we were flat broke with a mountain of bills to pay." She looked at Billy. "But he's right. We both have jobs we love, even though sometimes we're like two ships passing in the night. But I'm pretty sure you didn't ask to meet up to check on the state of our marriage."

"No, afraid that's a bit out of my job description and my expertise."

"Well, before we get serious, maybe we need to work on changing your expertise. I might know a nice young woman or two you could meet."

Billy stared at her. It had never occurred to him to have Amanda introduce him to a young, single teacher. Given that he didn't hang out in bars and didn't have the time to be more active in church, he was always trying to figure how to meet a nice woman. "Well, that would be a mighty nice gesture. Yes, ma'am, a nice gesture."

She just nodded. She knew Billy well enough to get down to business. "So, how can I help you, Detective?"

"We arrested Jason Kirk." The look on her face softened and turned to sadness. She didn't speak. They had a long understanding about how she could help law enforcement without violating the privacy of a student. She was quite adept at providing information without stepping over the line, something he had always appreciated.

"Detective, I do know that Jason Kirk is eighteen, but he's protected by law to be in school until he graduates or reaches the age of twenty-one."

Billy turned and looked out the window. He had reviewed his notes from the training Amanda had provided for members of the sheriff's office on the restrictions she had under state and federal law. He had also reviewed the legal training notes he had. He knew she was limited in what she could discuss about a student. She had always cooperated and steered him in the right direction when she could. He nodded and remembered she had explained the conditions for students who have a disability; he realized that was what she was telling him now, without actually saying it. It was the only way Jason could possibly stay until age twenty-one. It probably explained some of the things he and Deputy Thomas had observed.

"Is there any reason to suspect that the boy doesn't know right from wrong?"

"None that I know of or have ever heard about."

"Has he ever been in trouble at school?"

"No. He's in a program with a teacher and a teacher assistant, so he gets the support he needs to be successful. That generally helps keep other behaviors from surfacing at school."

Nodding his head as he thought, Billy was about to thank her when he thought of something else. Although he was pretty sure she wouldn't answer him, he asked anyway. "Can you tell me if he takes any kind of medication?"

She shook her head and all but *tsked* at him. "Now, Detective, we're both well-informed, and you know I couldn't tell you even if I knew. Have to find another way to go after that one. Did you think to ask *him*?"

With any other official, Billy would have ignored the question. He liked Amanda and knew she was pulling his chain. He returned the volley. "Why, Dr. Bennett, ma'am, I may look like I just fell off the turnip truck, but as you so rightly put it, 'we're both well-informed' when it comes to our responsibilities, and I'm not likely to be answering that question."

They both laughed as he stood to leave.

"Thanks, Amanda. I appreciate your help. Unless you need to stay here, I can walk you out."

"Since I'm here, I'll take care of a couple of things that will give me a leg up tomorrow morning. Ken's home with the kids. Good luck, Billy. I just hope this boy wasn't responsible for hurting anyone." She shook his hand then walked to her desk as he walked to the door.

"Tell Ken I'm sorry to drag you out today." Billy hoped he conveyed his understanding of the limited time the two had together given their respective jobs.

As soon as he arrived at the station, he headed to the lab to see if there was anything Elizabeth Alexander, the forensic tech, had on a couple of his cases.

"Morning, Alexander."

"Morning, Detective. Deputy Thomas asked me to tell you she's got news on a suspect, when you have time."

He turned around from his desk and stared at her. "What was that last part?"

"When you have time." Alexander knew full well that wasn't what he wanted to hear.

"Best back up a few more steps and show some respect to your elders." He dished out the teasing pretty easily himself, and he knew she could give it back, though he had to admit she was always respectful.

"By all means." There was great deference in her voice. She acted like he couldn't understand and dragged out each word, "Deputy Thomas... asked..." then she quickly told him the rest, knowing she better not take it too far.

"Thanks, Alexander. Now get back to work before I have to dock your pay for malingering."

Then he gave her a high-five and they both laughed.

He picked up the phone and called Deputy Thomas to hear her update. "Good work, Susan. No telling when he'll show back up at home. Glad the sergeant put a detail watching his house. They'll let us know when they pick him up. I have some things I need to check out on Jason. Want to take a ride with me to his folks?"

"Sure thing. I'll meet you out back."

Billy hung up the phone and turned to Elizabeth. "Anything I need to know before I head out, Alexander?"

She brought him up to date on progress on the other cases they were working, but she had nothing definitive at the moment. "Maybe later today, or it *could* be tomorrow. I'm working as fast as I can and still do it right."

"No doubt, Alexander. No doubt. Catch you later."

He and Deputy Thomas reached the back door at the same time.

"Do you think Jason was hoping he would be out before it got too late so he wouldn't have to tell his parents?"

"Good question, Thomas. Could be. Too bad, 'cause I suspect he's not going home anytime soon." He told her what he had learned from Dr. Bennett and emphasized he didn't know how having an identified disability might play into the direction the DA might decide to go.

"Did she *tell* you he has a disability? Not that I don't believe it, given what we saw with him."

"No, she can't. But in some training for us a couple of years back, she explained that the only students guaranteed a..." his voice trailed off as he tried to think of the words she had used. "Oh, yeah, guaranteed a free appropriate public education, were kids with a disability. She also told us they were the only ones who could stay until age twenty-one. If they don't have that federal protection, they age out if they're not making satisfactory progress towards graduation."

"Wow, I wish she would offer that training again. It sure would help the deputies on the beat."

"Ask the sheriff. He'll be pleased you asked for training."

"I will, thanks."

"Anytime! Just remember free advice is worth what you pay for it."

She laughed, long accustomed to his joking around. "So, what's our plan?"

"Hoping to find the mother home alone. If not, we'll separate them, and you take her. We need to find out if Jason's taking some sort of prescription medication that might cause him to have the jitters and dilated pupils. It sure would help if one of them would own up to it."

Just as they turned onto the street where the Kirks lived, Deputy Thomas finished telling Billy that Bobby Kirk worked at the gas station changing oil and tires, but he was off today. "Deputies are out looking for him. I think it's safe to assume the boys are cousins on the father's side."

"Not necessarily. Things aren't always what they may first appear to be."

She looked at him, puzzled, but decided not to pursue it.

"Still can't get used to the gas station being open on Sunday since that big company bought it from Walter. He was never open on Sunday."

"Ah, modern times are creeping into our little corner of the world." Susan gave a wan smile.

"Yeah. And bringing lots of things to keep our little sheriff's office busier than we've ever been."

They saw there was no vehicle outside the house. Billy remembered seeing a truck when he interviewed Jason's dad last week about Nick Brown's overdose. Both exited the SUV and headed for the front door. Billy knocked on the door, and Susan saw a gaunt woman with furtive eyes peep out behind the thin curtain on the picture window at the front of the little bungalow. Billy knocked again. Slowly, the door opened.

"Mornin', sheriff, my hubby ain't home. He and Mr. Brown done gone fishin'. Don't know when he'll be back."

Billy had long ago quit correcting people when they called him or a deputy by the title sheriff. It wouldn't change a thing—they would still call them sheriff.

"Didn't come to see him this time, Mrs. Kirk. Just have a couple of questions for you. I'm Detective Williams and this is Deputy Thomas. Mind if we come in for a minute?"

"I can come out on the porch, but I ain't allowed to have no one inside the house. Kirk don't like it." She used the hill people's custom of referring to a man by his last name, even when that man was your spouse.

"That'll be fine." Susan stepped back so the woman could come out on the porch. Susan watched Billy push the door open wider, as if giving Mrs. Kirk space to come out. She knew he was trying to see inside the house; a look at how people kept their homes could tell you quite a bit about them.

"Now, Mrs. Kirk, we just need to ask you a few questions about Jason." Susan watched her carefully.

The panic on her face was swift, and her motherly instincts as sharp as any bear protecting her cub. "Whatcha mean? Where's my boy?"

Susan and Billy could see the anxiety rising in her eyes. Billy thought she might reach out and scratch at him like he had seen a mother bear do when someone got too close to her cub.

"Mrs. Kirk, Jason is fine. He's safe and we're just trying to clear up a few questions that have come up. The detective was talking to Dr. Bennett, the principal, and she told him she was sure you would be helpful." She waited a beat. "You can do that for us, can't you, Mrs. Kirk? You will try to help us?"

"Call me Lottie. That's my name, Lottie."

"Okay, Lottie. Do you want a chair? We can get one of those out there under the tree."

"No! He'll beat me silly if he sees I moved a chair."

Now torn between telling this woman how she could get help and finding out what they needed to know, Susan took a quiet breath. "Lottie, does Jason take medicine to help him in school?"

Lottie nodded.

"Did he take his pills this morning?"

"Yeah, he done takes it every day. He don't like it, though. It makes him kind of jumpy, and his eyes always done look like he saw a ghost. Know what I mean?"

"Does it affect his eating?"

"Yeah, he don't eat much. He's skinny as a scarecrow." The sadness in her voice as it trailed off tugged at Susan's heart.

"Do you know the name of the pills?"

Lottie shook her head. "I kin show you. I have to put 'em right back in the same place or Kirk'll hit me."

"Thanks, Lottie. You go get the pills. We may have one or two more questions. Then we'll go."

"Good." Lottie's eyes darted across the street. "Mrs. Brown won't tell Kirk, but if Mr. Brown and Kirk comes home. . . " She trailed off.

Billy and Susan both nodded understanding.

Lottie came back out, and Billy saw the label on the pills: Adderall.

"One more question, Lottie. Where was Jason yesterday?"

Lottie suddenly looked at her with fear in her eyes. "Why?"

"Just need to make sure we cover all our bases."

Billy did not interfere with Susan's questioning.

"He went riding on one of those ATVs with his cousin, Bobby. Did they do somethin' wrong?" It was clear that her worry for Jason had turned to outright fear.

"Just needed to verify his whereabouts yesterday. Thanks, Lottie. You go put those pills back, okay? And, Lottie, you call me if you're ever afraid or if Mr. Kirk hits you." Susan handed her card to Lottie, who slipped it in her pocket.

Lottie nodded. "Okay. Bye." She turned, walked in her house, and shut the door.

Billy and Susan exchanged a glance then headed for the SUV. Billy could see the frustration on Susan's face. "What's up?"

"Oh, nothing." She paused. "Okay, something. That woman's son is in jail, but I can't tell her. She's going to be hysterical when he doesn't come home this afternoon, and there's no telling what the husband might do to her." She leaned back on the headrest and Billy just let her have some time. Neither spoke as they pulled into the back of the sheriff's station and headed for the door.

Nothing To Do but Wait

Chad and Bella drove to Harold's home. "Want to come?" Chad smiled at her.

"I think it's best if you go. I'll wait here."

Chad went to the front door, but no one answered. He turned to walk back to his SUV when Harold's neighbor walked over to the bushes that divided their front lawns.

"Hey, boss, need Harold?" Deputy Ken Bennett asked. Chad could see he was playing catch with his daughter and son.

Chad was so focused on telling Harold himself that he forgot about Ken being Harold's neighbor. He walked over to him. "Know if he's around?" Chad extended his hand. The two men shook.

"They went to Nashville for the weekend. Harold said he didn't think they'd be back until pretty late tonight. Something I can help with?"

"Not on this one, Ken, but thanks. I'll catch him first thing in the morning at his office."

"Any word on Joe?"

"We're making progress on the case." He hated that he couldn't tell the truth even to his deputy. People in these hills cared about Joe. He also knew the deputy wouldn't push him. Chad knew all his deputies would be aware of the robbery by now, but if the laws about privacy held at the hospital and morgue, no one knew Joe had died.

"Good to hear. Enjoy the rest of your day. Tell Dr. Anderson I said 'hey.'"

Chad was surprised at first, then he remembered Bennett had been on the investigation at Bella's property last month. "Sure will, Bennett, sure will. Give my regards to Amanda and the kids."

"Will do when she gets home, boss. She's up at the school meeting with Billy."

Chad looked at him. Maybe Billy had found the cousin. "Sorry to take her away on a Sunday afternoon. Just so you know, it's *really* important or he wouldn't have bothered her today."

"Never a doubt. If I see Harold, should I let him know you stopped by?"

"Only if he asks. If he asks, call me; doesn't matter what time it is. Otherwise, I plan to be at the county offices when he arrives in the morning."

Ken was still standing in his yard as Chad backed down Harold's driveway. They all waved.

"That's Deputy Bennett, isn't it?"

"Yes, he said to tell you 'Hey.' I felt a bit guilty not telling him about Joe, but my being at Harold's wasn't official business, and it's not my place to preempt Joshua letting the community know." He paused. "I hate this stuff."

Bella reached over and put her hand on his and gave it a squeeze. He took his hand off the steering wheel and held hers tightly.

"I know how hard all this is for *me*. I can't imagine what it is for you having to juggle being sheriff and being a friend. But, if it's any consolation, I think you did the right thing in not telling the deputy."

"Thanks. I needed that." He squeezed her hand. He put his hand back on the steering wheel as he approached a sharp switchback on the mountain road.

"The reassurance, or the hand holding?" Bella had a slight lilt in her voice.

"Both." He glanced over at her. Then he purposely took the switchback a little too fast, causing Bella to lean his way before her seat belt locked in.

"Oh, now you're going to play driving games, too? Better be careful, two can play games, you know."

"Counting on it." His grin was from ear to ear. "Now, what was it you needed to do on this difficult Sunday afternoon?"

"I'm fine. I just felt we needed to give the pastor and Joshua, and Carla for that matter, a bit of space."

"Couldn't agree more. There's one more place I'd like to stop, if it's all the same to you."

"I'm along for the ride." Bella leaned back in the seat to enjoy the view; a feeling of contentment settled on her.

Chapter 6

Talking with the Pastor

Pastor Fisk convinced Joshua to eat. Carla offered to serve them. The men insisted they could serve themselves and she should go first. They filled their plates from the abundance of food in the oven and fridge before returning to the porch. As he sat down, Joshua looked at the corn, fried chicken, green beans, and coleslaw on his plate and wondered how he ever thought he could eat it all.

Once settled, the pastor asked for a blessing on Joe, Joshua, Carla, and the food.

"Not sure why I took green beans." Joshua made it as an offhand comment.

"I don't know who came up with the idea of cooking green beans to smithereens, but I just can't eat them." As soon as the words were out of his mouth, Pastor Fisk looked at Carla with regret on his face. "My sincere apologies, Carla. I meant no disrespect."

"I'm right there with you, Pastor. I've told the cook I'm going to fire her if she doesn't stop taking the vitamins out by cooking the beans 'til they're mush."

Joshua chimed-in, "Dad was so happy the first time he ate steamed green beans. He never touched overcooked green beans again."

Carla nodded. "Smart man."

They ate in silence. Joshua took a few bites of food then pushed his plate aside. He continued to look out to the mountains.

"Albert, I don't know if I can hold up through another funeral like Jan's. It was right for her to have everyone in the community. She taught so many of the people here, but I don't think my dad would want what he would consider to be all the folderal. He was a pretty quiet man who lived his life in a simple way."

"Joshua, your parents had a plan for the end of their lives. Did you know that?"

Joshua seemed taken aback. "What?"

"Yes. Before your mother passed away, they each put in writing what they wanted at the time of their death and left it with the pastor. Your dad updated it and made sure I knew about it when I came to the parish. I reviewed it before I came over here today. I suspect Joe didn't think he would be needing it quite so soon, and he surely wouldn't have burdened you by mentioning it when you were dealing with Jan's illness."

Joshua nodded. "Thanks, Albert. I was starting to feel guilty for not knowing what my dad wanted, or expected of me, at the end of his life." He fell silent, his gaze returned to the mountains.

"It's pretty simple, really. He wanted you to tell me who you wanted with you for a small service at the church. Then he said it would be fine if the community wanted to come together at The Corral and remember him during a jamboree." The Pastor watched for Joshua's reaction.

Joshua nodded. "For sure. Sounds like my dad: keep it simple but celebrate the joy of life. He always used to say that."

"How do you feel about that? Do you know who you would want with you for a service?"

"I want to respect my dad's wishes. For sure I want Carla, Bella, Chad, Harold, and Julie." He looked at Carla and smiled. "Pastor, can I let you know tomorrow if I think of anyone else?"

"No problem at all, Joshua. Take your time."

Pastor Fisk stood when he heard a knock on the door and the screen door open. He knew it meant a friend of Chad's or Joshua's had arrived since that is how friends entered a home when visiting. "Just sit, I'll get the door." It was Carla's brother, James.

"Evening, Pastor." James had a metal pan in his hands.

"Evening, James. We just finished eating some of the fine food you sent over. Thanks for that. Joshua didn't eat much. I see that pan is marked blackberry cobbler. Might be just the ticket." He took the pan from James and headed to the kitchen as Carla walked inside from the porch.

"Thanks, big brother, you're the best." Carla and James had always been close.

"Back atcha, Sis. Just wish there was more I could do. Think it's okay if I go out and speak to Joshua?"

Pastor Fisk nodded. "I think that would be great."

Carla took James by the arm, and they walked out to the porch.

Joshua stood when he saw James. "Thanks for coming, James. And thanks for all the food."

James pulled Joshua into a bear hug. "Sorry, man. Don't know what else to say. Let me know what I can do." James backed off, cleared his throat, and glanced at his sister. "Hate to run, but I need to get back."

"Thanks for coming, James. Thanks for everything." Joshua's eyes bore the sadness he felt.

Pastor Fisk reached to clear the plates.

"I can get that, Pastor."

"You do it all the time, Carla. I'm pretty good at it myself. Just relax. I'll clean this up, then I'm going to leave you for this evening." He took the plates and headed for the kitchen.

Joshua and Carla stood at the same time. He almost knocked her over and reached for her arm to steady her. "I'm so sorry, Carla. I wasn't paying a bit of attention."

"Didn't mind a bit." Carla gave him a wink. She could see the flirtation did not register with him.

They walked into the dining room just as Pastor Fisk was exiting the kitchen. "Dishes are in the dishwasher, and the blackberry cobbler is keeping warm in the oven. Joshua, I'll check in with you tomorrow morning. We can make some decisions then." Albert had surmised that Joshua didn't know, or hadn't processed, they would have to wait on the autopsy. He felt sure the medical examiner would make Joe a priority.

"Thanks, Pastor, thanks for everything." Joshua walked towards the front door.

"Call anytime, Joshua. Anytime." The pastor walked down the hill to his car.

Joshua stood in the door watching him leave.

Carla stood watching Joshua.

Check-In

Chad turned onto the main road into the valley and then off onto a street that Bella recognized from Friday night.

She smiled. "We're going to check on the pup, aren't we?"

"Didn't think I'd be able to pull one over on you. I sent a text to Doc Jim. He said it would be fine to stop by this afternoon. I thought it might do us both good to see that one victim of the weekend is going to be fine." He bit his tongue as soon as the words left his mouth. *I've spent too much time around folks in the department who have long since been desensitized to the realities of life and death.* "I'm sorry, Bella. I wasn't thinking."

"Chad, I don't want you to think you have to monitor everything you say. I know you have seen way more of the seamier side of life than I have. If it's too raw for me, I'll tell you. Okay?"

"Sure." He wondered if he could adjust to having someone in his life that he could talk to honestly. He had gotten used to keeping everything to himself when he was married to Mary. They pulled up in front of the veterinarian's home and got out.

Doc Jim was sitting on his porch. "Afternoon, folks." He touched the pipe he had taken out of his mouth to his forehead. The pup stood up from beside Doc Jim's rocker and looked out. His tail started wagging.

"Oh, look, Chad, I think he's glad to see us." Bella hurried towards the porch.

Doc Jim stood and shook hands with Bella and Chad. "It's generally a pretty good sign when a dog wags his tail like that. I think he's a pretty clever dog. Seems he knows you're his friends."

"Looking good there, Doc—you and the dog."

They all laughed.

"Pull up a rocker. Nice evening to sit a spell on my porch."

Chad pulled two of the rockers over. As soon as Bella sat down, the pup was beside her.

"Hey, fella, you're not limping too badly. I'd say you've had pretty good care here with Doc Jim." She reached her hand out to the dog, allowing him to sniff it. Once he seemed comfortable, she petted him on his side; the pup leaned into her and closed his eyes.

"Any luck on finding an owner?" Chad asked.

"None so far. The word has usually spread through the hills at this point if someone is looking for a missing dog. As scrawny as this boy is, I suspect whoever had him isn't apt to come looking for him. Hard to know how far he might have traveled."

"Doc Jim, you've taken such good care of him. In forty-eight hours, he already looks healthier."

"Amazing what a bath and some food will do for animals and people."

"That's the truth!" Chad reached over and petted the pup. "That's the truth, eh, big boy?"

The pup was between Chad and Bella with his head resting on his front paws, the bandaged paw on top of the other one. They all rocked quietly for several minutes.

"Chad, I'll understand if you can't tell me, but I heard some talk that there was a robbery at the Valley Store last night."

Chad looked at Doc Jim and simply nodded his head. Doc Jim knew enough not to push him on it.

"Hard to know what any day is going to bring, Doc." Chad felt he had to say something.

"That's for sure. Well, where's my manners? Can I get you good folks something to drink?"

Chad looked at Bella, who shook her head slightly. "Thanks, no. We just stopped for a minute to check on this fella here and tell you thanks for fixing him up."

Bella stood and the pup rose with her. "Yes, thanks so much, Doc Jim. I'm so relieved to see how well he's doing, but we should leave you to your evening."

"Come here, boy." The pup moved over to Doc Jim but looked at Bella.

Bella scratched his ears. "I'll stop and see you in a day or two if that's okay?"

"You betcha. Miss Bella, you probably ought to be deciding on a name for this fine boy. I'm thinking he's going to be a good companion for you."

Bella smiled. "We'll see." She did not want to get her hopes up.

Chad reached out to shake hands with the vet. "Don't get up, Doc. We'll see you soon. Thanks for everything."

Doc Jim saw that Chad took Bella's hand as they walked off the porch. They both had a bit of skip in their walk on the path down to the truck. He smiled to himself. *You're a good man, Chad Oliver. About time you had a good woman in your life.*

Joshua Needs Rest

Chad pulled into his driveway and saw that the pastor's car was gone. "Looks like it's just Carla and Joshua."

"Sorry, Chad. What did you say? I was lost in thought about the pup . . . and Joe."

"Not important. Want to share your thoughts?"

"Just trying to sort out how two tragedies could end so differently. A pup who no one apparently wants, injured and in need of help, is on his way to recovery. A man, who everyone loved, was brutally injured and dies. I'm glad the dog is going to be okay, but I'm deeply saddened at the loss of Joe's life, especially in such a tragic way."

She fell silent as Chad pulled to the top of the drive. He decided to leave his SUV in the driveway, walked around, and opened her door. He could sense the sorrow Bella was struggling not to show. He took her hand as she stepped out of the SUV. He pulled her into a hug and kissed her—a long kiss. She leaned into the kiss and the embrace. They stood there for several seconds. She kissed him again, and then she took his hand and started walking towards the front steps. "Let's go see what we can do for Joshua."

They walked in the front door and saw Joshua and Carla on the porch.

Bella whispered to Chad. "It doesn't look like they've moved since we left."

Chad called to them, not wanting to startle either one. "Hey! We're back."

Carla stood up and headed towards the door. "Oh, hey, Chad. Bella. Come on back. Well, it's your home, Chad, guess you can go wherever you want." It was clear she was trying to make a joke of it.

Bella looked at the table. "Have you two eaten?"

"Joshua didn't each much. Maybe he'll have some more now that you're back." The look on Carla's face showed her concern.

Bella walked onto the porch and kissed Joshua on the cheek. "Hey, Joshua. What do you say we eat something?" Chad and Carla had already walked into the kitchen. The rustling sound of the food being taken out of the oven and the fridge door closing carried out to the porch.

"Hey, Joshua, join me in a beer?" Chad called out. He knew he would drink another if Joshua did. *But, off duty, or not. Only two.*

"Not deaf, Chad. I'm right here." Joshua stood in the doorway to the kitchen.

"Sorry. I'm used to calling out to my son-in-law when he's sitting on the porch." He raised a beer bottle with a questioning look on his face.

"Sure. I imagine these two fine ladies are going to insist I eat something, so might as well have a good beer to go with it."

They all fixed plates of food then took them and their drinks out to the porch to sit down. Bella didn't know whether to be surprised or not when Joshua started praying, "God is great, God is good, and we thank you for this food. By His hand we all are fed, thank You for our daily bread."

In unison, they all said, "Amen."

Bella smiled as the aroma of the food wafted above the table. "This all smells great, Carla. I'm always amazed that a restaurant can serve food day after day and maintain such good quality. Thank you, and James too, for this food."

Chad raised his beer. "Here's to a man who showed us all how to live and to good friends and good food. May you find some peace in each new day." They raised their drinks and touched each other's glasses in the toast.

The sun was dropping quickly behind the mountains as the autumn chill brought goosebumps to their skin. There was very little talk as they ate. As they finished, Carla stood. "I'll clean up these plates and bring out some blackberry cobbler. That ought to make all of us sleepy, don't you think?"

Joshua looked at her and smiled. "Blackberry cobbler? That's my dad's. . ." he trailed off.

Chad smiled at Joshua in a show of support. "Don't know anyone who doesn't like blackberry cobbler. I have grandchildren, you know, so I suspect there's some vanilla ice cream in my freezer that might go right well with it. What do you say?"

Carla and Bella cleared the table. Bella leaned in conspiratorially. "Raise your hand if you want ice cream." All four of them raised their hands, and they all started laughing, even Joshua.

Joshua shook his head. "Anybody who doesn't like blackberry cobbler and ice cream. . . well, no way to explain it."

Bella and Carla set the bowls at each place, and Chad brought out the coffee cups and a mug of tea for Bella. They sat in silence and ate dessert. Chad was taking his last bite when Joshua spoke up.

"Don't know how to thank all of you. I've taken up your whole day, so I think I might need to head home."

The other three looked at each other and then at Joshua. He had returned his gaze to the mountains.

Carla took Joshua's hand. "Joshua, I'll be happy to drive you home. I can stay as long as you want. We can let Bella and Chad get on with their evening."

Bella was pleased that Carla had spoken up.

"Okay, well, let's go then." Joshua stood abruptly and headed for the front door

Bella recognized the robotic response. It made her sad to know he had many more days of moments like this. As they reached the front door, Bella hugged Carla and whispered, "Call me anytime." She stood up on her toes and kissed Joshua on the cheek. "Take care, Joshua. We'll talk tomorrow."

Chad walked them out to Carla's car. "Call anytime, day or night." He looked at Carla with a serious look that conveyed, "I mean it." She nodded.

As they drove off, Chad pulled his SUV into the garage. He started for the kitchen door and realized that, for the first time in many, many years, he did not have on his boots or his service weapon. *How did that happen? When was the last time I did not wear my weapon? Nora's wedding? Yes, Nora's wedding.*

Bella was putting dishes in the dishwasher and had already put the food in the fridge. He stood in the doorway for a few seconds admiring her. He loved watching her but didn't want her to do the work.

"Here, I can finish this up. You sit and drink your tea." He kissed her on the cheek. "What do you want to do with what's left of this evening?"

"Nothing, Chad." He turned from the dishwasher and looked at her. "Really, nothing. I was thinking I should have you take me home, but maybe you could get someone to do that tomorrow, if it's all right that I stay one more night. I know you have to go back to work, and I don't have enough clothes to stay down the mountain any longer."

Chad didn't hesitate. "Well, Miss Bella, you can stay forever, as far as I'm concerned. As for tonight, I like the idea of doing nothing. And, for tomorrow—we'll figure out tomorrow, tomorrow."

She looked over at him and smiled. "Good enough. Let's watch the last of the twilight, and if I may be so bold, I'll have a glass of wine."

"One wine coming up." He poured her a glass and prepared a cup of tea for himself; he had already had two beers today. He almost spilled the drinks when he walked onto the porch and saw her sitting there, imagining her there for the rest of their lives.

Chad watched Bella carefully. "Been a pretty hectic twenty-four hours, hasn't it?"

"Yes. Yes, it has. I'm sad about Joe, but I'm so glad we can be here for Joshua."

"Me too. I know I'm making a lot of promises these days, but I'm determined to be a better friend—to Joshua in particular."

"It seems the good thing that comes out of death is the reminder that life is about the living."

Chad took her hand. "Amen. And I plan to start living for more than my job."

She squeezed his hand, lifted her wine glass, and touched his raised glass of tea. "It's a pledge."

"Another glass?" Chad pointed to her wine glass.

"Thanks, no. I'm really tired and I think I need a full night's sleep. So, if you will excuse me, I think I'm going to call it a day."

Chad choked back the disappointment at not having more alone time with her tonight. He glanced at his watch and saw that it was only 8:30 p.m. This had been a challenging day for Bella on a short night of sleep. He understood, at least at some level, the impact on her of Joe's death. He leaned over and gave her a kiss. "Here's to a good night's sleep and a better tomorrow for all of us."

She kissed him back then stood to go. "Thanks for everything, Chad. Most of all, thanks for understanding my needs these last two days. Sweet dreams."

"Sweet dreams." He stood as she walked off. He sat back down and looked out towards the mountains and the night sky.

As soon as Bella settled into the bed after her shower, she realized she had not done her usual ritual of reviewing her day the previous night. She was determined she would do it tonight before the tiredness that was enveloping her took over. *My Not-So-Good List will be short tonight but deeply sad.* Joe's death, and in such a brutal way. Accompanying it, of course, was the impact on Joshua. She was about to move to her Good List when she remembered that she had been pretty disoriented in the morning. She hoped she would improve on how she dealt with trauma and bad news. *It isn't always easy when you're alone in the world.*

Then Bella focused on her Good List. *It doesn't seem quite right to have such a long Good List with all that's happening, but I do.* She had enjoyed spending more time with Carla, and she was happy

Carla could be supportive for Joshua. Bella smiled thinking about the quirks of fate that threw people together. *I hope Joshua can see Carla's affection for him.* She had helped Joshua today by calling the funeral home and making that connection for him, and she had talked with Pastor Fisk. *That was a good reminder for me that I want to be part of a church community.* She had visited Doc Jim to see the pup, and he was doing well. *I might have a dog before long.* She smiled to herself.

And then there was Chad. She had been having one-way conversations with her late husband for some time now. Before Matt passed away, he had told her he wanted her to have someone new in her life. The kindness, time, and obvious interest Chad had shown in her seemed like a pretty good sign to her. *Thanks, Matt. You'll always be my love, but I'm beginning to see that you were right. It's possible I could fall in love again. I miss you. Good night.*

Chapter 7

Look deeply into nature, and you'll understand everything better.
Albert Einstein, 1879-1955

Telling Harold

Chad and Bella had eaten a light breakfast on Monday morning and were headed to the County Offices to tell Harold Cooper about Joe. He could see Bella was lost in thought, and he figured she would speak once she had a chance to piece together her thoughts and emotions.

Bella's voice was soft when she eventually spoke. "Carla sounded quite confident this morning about opening the Valley Store. Joshua asked her to call Doug and Melody, and they all planned to be at the store by seven. She said Joshua decided to wait and tell them about Joe when they were all together."

Chad waited a moment before responding. "I think that was a good idea. Once they know, and Harold knows, it'll be easier for folks in the community to know. I'm surprised it's been quiet this long."

"Thanks for letting me stay with you a few more days; it'll make it easier for me to be available to help Joshua. Will it be a problem for you to get someone to take me home—to Drellag Caban? Unless, of course, Uber has found its way here."

"See, there you go, assuming there's no Uber." He laughed, clearly trying to lighten the mood. He knew he wasn't particularly good at it.

"Oh, Sheriff Chad Oliver, you have much to learn about me. I would have said I was assuming if I were. I didn't assume anything. I said, 'unless Uber has found its way here.'"

"Okay, okay, I surrender. Remind me not to try to play mind games with a professor of English."

"Oh, I wouldn't do that. We might actually find some mind games we enjoy together." She let the flirtation drop as they pulled into the parking lot of the county offices.

Chad looked at her. "Want to go in?"

"I haven't seen Harold in years, and he might find my presence a bit intrusive in this moment. You go ahead. I'll step out and get in a bit of a walk and some fresh air."

"Be back as soon as I can. And, by the way, the answer to your question is, 'No.'" He was out of the SUV and walking at a quick clip towards the door of the county offices. He looked over his shoulder and smiled at her.

The answer to my question is 'no'? What question? Bella shut the door to the SUV a little harder than needed. Then she realized she had asked him if it was a problem to get her a ride home. *You don't miss much, do you, Chad Oliver?* She stepped off at her own quick pace to sort out the emotions swirling through her. The loss of Joe and her attraction to Chad were pushing her brain six ways from Sunday.

While she felt it would take miles to walk out everything she was currently feeling, she didn't want to go too far since she wanted to see Chad when he returned and keep an eye on the unlocked SUV. *Hmmm, there was a time I wouldn't have considered the need to lock any vehicle here. Now it pops into my mind immediately.* She continued down the sidewalk, taking in the reds, golds, and oranges of the autumn leaves. An old song popped into her head and she began to hum "Autumn Leaves."

"Lovely! Why don't you sing it?" Bella turned at the woman's voice behind her.

Chad's daughter, Nora Oliver-Smith, stood a few feet behind her. She hadn't heard a car drive up.

"Where did you come from?" Bella looked around.

"I'd just dropped off some posters about the jamboree this Friday when dad came in. He told me you might appreciate some company while he talked with Harold, and I thought it was a great idea. May I walk with you?"

"Please, by all means." Her eyes almost begged Nora. "I assume your dad told you why he needed to talk to Harold?"

"No. No, he didn't. He just told me you were out here." Nora saw the stricken look in Bella's eyes. "What's wrong, Bella? Can I help?"

"You could do me a really big favor and sing that very melancholy song I was humming." Bella struggled because it wasn't her place to tell Nora, or anyone else, but as she had acknowledged at Chad's yesterday, sometimes a woman just needed to talk to a woman. The reality for Bella was she didn't have a woman friend here.

Nora gently took Bella's arm and stopped her from walking. She put herself in front of Bella so they were face to face. "Please, tell me what's troubling you. I learned to keep a friend's secrets long ago from the master of keeping things to himself."

Bella knew she meant Chad. She fought back tears. "Joe died Saturday evening."

Nora pulled her into an embrace. Nora would never have told anyone that her husband, Doc Fred, had already told her. Her voice was gentle. "Bella, I'm so sorry. Dad had told me that Joe used to hike with your father when they were boys. What a terrible loss." She stood quietly as she felt the silent sobs from the older woman; they held each other.

Bella settled herself then stepped back. "Thank you. Thank you for letting me have that moment of grief." She saw out of the corner of her eye that Chad was standing halfway between them and the door of the county offices, watching them. When she turned her head, he smiled at her and walked to his SUV, leaving the two women to themselves.

"Come on." Nora took Bella's hand and turned towards Chad. "Let's see how I can help." They both turned and walked in Chad's direction. Nora started softly singing, "Autumn Leaves." Bella held her hand tightly.

Chad watched the two women intently; his heart felt as full as when he first held his newborn grandchildren. *I can't mess this up! I might just find out what it is to have that love Nora keeps saying I deserve.* He was leaning against the SUV when they stopped in front of him. He had heard Nora singing. That warmed his heart too.

"Dad, Bella might need some female companionship. Think there's something I can do to help out?"

Chad smiled at his daughter. "Where are Mac and Lilly?" He was thinking he could go get his grandchildren.

"They're on a play date with friends. I can call Nancy. I'm sure she'll be happy to keep them for a while. I've got plenty of time. So, tell me what I can do."

Bella jumped in. "Oh, Nora, if you really mean it, you could take me to Drellag Caban… sorry, to my cabin, so I can get some clothes and my Jeep. That way I can stay down the mountain a few more days." Bella looked at Chad.

"Sounds like a fine plan. I'll swing by the station and check on a couple of things and Nora can let you in at my place. I should have given you a key."

Nora looked from her dad to Bella and back to her dad. She smiled from ear to ear. "Done and done! Stay right here, I'll pick you up." She pulled her phone out of her pocket as she headed towards the far end of the parking lot to her own SUV.

"Chad, thanks. I'm becoming very fond of Nora, and it'll be nice to have her company for a little while. Do you really think it's okay for her to ask her friend to keep the children?"

"Oh, I suspect she'll promise Mac there's a chance he can see you, and he would wait for the moon to rise and set a dozen times. I might just get jealous of that little boy's interest in you."

Bella warmed to the light banter. "Perhaps you should." She stepped over and kissed him on the cheek.

Chad pulled her in and kissed her on the lips, holding her tightly as his daughter pulled up beside them. "I'll see you when you get back. Just so you know, Harold is heading over to see Joshua at the store. I had a text from Carla."

He held up the text for her to read: "Best therapy. Doing okay. CL"

Bella smiled. "Oh, I'm glad. I hoped that being back into his routine would help him get through the day. It always helped me."

"Once I get home, we can figure out what else we need to do to help Joshua."

The warm smile in his gray eyes as he looked at her thrilled her. "Thanks, Chad. That helps. Thanks for everything." She kissed him lightly on the lips then patted her pocket to make sure she had her phone, wallet, and cabin keys. She stepped over to Nora's car.

Nora had her windows down. Bella could hear Nora singing one of her own Elvis favorites: "Can't Help Falling in Love." Chad opened the door for Bella and squeezed her hand. "See you soon. And you, Miss Nora, wait just a minute." He walked around her SUV, leaned in, and kissed her on the cheek. "Love you, my favorite child."

"Of course, I'm your favorite; you have no other choice!" She laughed and kissed her dad. "We gals have some things to do, but we should be back by lunch time. You might want to buy lunch for two ladies." She smiled at him. "Now, go save the planet, Daddy, or at least our mountains. Love you too."

He gave a quick wave as they drove off.

Actions With Unintended Consequences

Billy Williams was pacing around the desk in the holding area waiting on Deputy Susan Thomas. To be fair, he had only let her know he was at the station on his rapid walk down the sterile hall. He knew he had to get his agitation about the death of Joe Johnson out of his system before they interrogated Bobby Kirk. He could not mess this up. As Deputy Thomas approached, Billy nodded to the matron to get the suspect.

"Good morning. Sorry, it took me longer than I expected."

"Morning, it's okay. I needed time to walk off my personal feelings to make sure I don't cause us to mess this up." His voice was low and exacting.

"Understood. I'm still processing it myself. Never easy, is it?"

"Rarely, but objectivity and all the skill we have is paramount in this one. Did you review the tape on Jason Kirk?" Billy wasn't sure why he asked; he knew she would have seen it multiple times.

Susan nodded, affirming her review the tape. "What time did the deputies pick him up?"

"About midnight, but he had been drinking, so I told them to process him and we'd get to him first thing this morning. Didn't think I needed to wake you last night. Sorry it was so early this morning."

The deputy nodded as the matron brought out Bobby Kirk. He was short and stocky with unkempt dark hair that clearly needed to be washed. It matched the smudges on his face that looked like they may have been there for days. His hands were cuffed behind his back, and he was wearing ankle chains. Billy had told the matron to put Bobby's hands behind his back. He didn't want any chance this boy would grab something or one of them.

"Room 2 is open, Detective." The matron motioned with her head.

Deputy Thomas, who was only a few inches taller than Bobby, seemed to tower over him as he shuffled along. She pointed down the hall. "We're headed this way."

As they entered the room, the detective and deputy watched the young man as each tried to decide the best interrogation strategies to use with him. He did not appear hostile. Billy stared at him. *He's docile to the point of being creepy. What's going on with this boy?*

Bobby stopped when he entered the room and turned his head to look at Deputy Thomas. Billy noted that Bobby did not look his way at all.

"You can sit in that chair." Susan pointed to the one closest to the far wall of the room. She pulled her chair up to the table, her usual position when doing an interrogation with Billy. Billy stood against the wall closest to the door, adopting his favorite southern stance of arms crossed and one knee bent with his foot against the wall. The message was clear: I have nowhere to go and all day to get there.

As she sat down, Susan put the tape recorder on the table and glanced at Billy. He gave her an imperceptible nod to go ahead.

She started by giving the date and time. "This is Deputy Thomas with . . ."

"Detective Williams."

"Please state your name and date of birth." Her voice sounded almost motherly.

Bobby stared at her, finally glanced at Billy, and then turned back to Susan. His voice cracked. "My name is Bobby Kirk." He gave his date of birth, drawing it out like it was the longest day of his life. Maybe it was. They both already knew he was twenty and had dropped out of school the first day he could.

"Bobby, are you comfortable? Would you like some water?" Susan was as gracious as she would be to someone in her home.

Bobby shook his head.

"No, you're not comfortable? Or no, you don't want water?"

His eyes darted between the two law enforcement officers. "No water."

"Okay, then let's begin. I will tell you your rights under the Miranda law." She recited the required statement. "Do you understand your rights and responsibilities as I have just explained them to you?"

He nodded.

"I need you to answer, please, not just nod your head."

"Yeah. I do."

"Do you wish to have an attorney present?"

He let out a guffaw. "Ain't got no money for no lawyer."

"Do you understand that if you cannot afford a lawyer, one will be provided for you by the court?"

"Ain't nothing free. My pappy done told me, police done pick you up, just say what you know. Simple as that." He said police as poh-lease, dragging out the first syllable.

"Then you do not wish to have an attorney?" She had a slight smile and looked him in the eyes.

"Nope. Just ask me whatcha wants to know."

Billy looked at the young man, wondering how someone could be so calm and also be the person who pushed an old man so hard he hit his head, likely causing his death. *I wonder when he's going to switch gears?*

Susan began: "Where were you yesterday?"

"With cousin Jason. My pappy let me have his Alterra 300. We done took a ride in the hills."

"Which Jason is that?"

"Jason Kirk, only Jason I know." His voice took on an edge of agitation.

"Where else did you go?"

Billy was doing all he could not to throttle the kid. He couldn't understand how the boy was so calm.

"Jason wanted something to drink, so we done gone to the store."

"What store?"

Bobby's eyes showed confusion. "There ain't but one store here."

"The Valley Store?" She watched his face and decided she might have to use another approach. Her own voice took on more of an edge. "You mean the Valley Store, the one two blocks from this *jail*?"

"Yes, ma'am." Bobby recognized the demand in her tone.

"What did you do at the Valley Store?"

"Jason wanted a drink!"

"What kind of drink?"

"I dunno, juice of some kind. His pappy don't let him drink no cola."

"Who paid for it?"

"Me! Jason don't work."

"What did you buy for yourself?" She was now trying to find the balance between being a nice mother and one who wanted answers.

"Smokes."

"Did you pay for your cigarettes?" Her tone indicated she clearly expected an answer.

"Yeah." He dragged it out like he was trying to think about what else he could say.

"Was Mr. Joe there?"

"Yeah, ole fool. He done bent down to get my smokes and hit his head."

Billy came off the wall in such a quick movement that Bobby jerked back, a feral animal ready for flight or fight. Billy picked up the empty chair and slammed it down on the floor. The look in the boy's eyes was one of absolute fear. Both officers had seen it before. It was the look of someone accustomed to being threatened and beaten by an older male, usually his father.

Billy had the back of the chair facing Bobby and put his hands on the corners as though he were trying to control himself—he was.

"You listen *real* careful, Bobby." Billy glared at him. "You look at me when I talk to you." Billy knew there was a fine line between interrogating and abusing a suspect. He was walking it with the skill of a highwire walker at the moment. "I need the truth, the whole truth, and you better give it to me the first time." He let his words hang in the air. Bobby remained silent, and both he and Susan could see the boy was shaking now.

Billy dropped the volume of his voice, but not the intensity. "You do not want to lie to us. Do you hear me? We've seen the tapes from the camera in the Valley Store, so we know what happened. I know your pappy expects you to tell the truth." *I'll sure be telling Joshua he has to put cameras in that store. Now!*

All three sat in silence. Susan turned towards Billy. "Detective, would it be all right if I take off Bobby's handcuffs? I can see they must be making it hard for him to sit there and think straight."

Billy hated this part of a practiced routine. He would not be abusive or even domineering to a woman, but he knew Bobby had seen his father hit his mother. He understood too many kids grew up with that form of male dominance. Billy glared at her. "Deputy Thomas, let's be very clear here. If you undo those cuffs and he causes one bit of trouble, *you* will be responsible. Is *that* clear?" Billy hated himself for saying it.

"Yes, sir. I understand." She looked conspiratorially at Bobby, hoping he would think he could save her from the detective—likely, as he did his mother from his father. "You won't cause any problems, will you?"

"No, ma'am."

She asked him to stand and unlocked his wrist cuffs. She left the ankle chain locked.

Bobby sat down.

"Do you understand this deputy… this *woman* is doing you a solid? Do you?" Billy's voice was low, staccato, and just short of threatening.

"Yessir, I do."

"Speak up, boy, I can't hear you!"

"Yes, sir, I do," Bobby was loud but not shouting.

"Now, that's better. Talk like a man. You got that?"

Bobby nodded.

Susan's voice was almost a purr. "Bobby, let's go back to you buying cigarettes. What happened when Mr. Joe got the cigarettes out from under the counter?"

"I done told you. He slipped and hit his head."

Susan nodded, acting like that was perfectly understandable. "What happened when you went behind the counter?"

Bobby looked up at her.

Billy could swear he could see wheels spinning inside the boy's head. Did they see him

on tape? Didn't they?

"I tried to help him up." Bobby had a look of self-satisfaction.

Billy slapped the sides of the chair back and glared at Bobby.

Susan had already figured out the boy was probably not very high on the IQ scale and certainly not very sophisticated in the ways of the world. He had no juvenile record and no one in the station had ever encountered him before. She leaned slightly forward, as if coming between him and Billy.

"Bobby, that's not what happened, is it?"

Bobby's head snapped up. "No." Then he sounded like a runaway train. "I was trying to stop Jason. He done took money from that drawer the ole man opened. I don't know how much. But I was trying to run around and close that drawer."

Deputy Thomas shook her head. "Now, Bobby." She paused. "Detective Williams has already told you not to lie to us. It sure didn't look like you tried to close that drawer. Want to rethink what happened when Mr. Joe got you the cigarettes?"

The boy slumped in the chair, sliding his feet back and forth so the chains around his ankles scraped against the chair legs. Susan was glad the chairs were wood and not metal. She sat quietly but still leaned forward as if she was trying to protect him from Billy. Then she saw the tears on his face.

"I just wanted the cigarettes. That ole man's got a lotta money and all them cigarettes. Two cartons ain't nothing to him. That's all I took."

Billy leaned forward. His voice was very low and precise. "That's not all that happened, is it?" He continued to glare at the boy.

"No. I guess I bumped him when I tried to grab the smokes. He fell."

"Did you call 9-1-1?" Billy could barely contain his rage.

"What? You crazy?" Bobby sneered like he was talking to a buddy, then he caught himself. Billy was clearly the dominant figure. He corrected himself, "No, sir. We just hightailed it out of there. And fast."

Susan nodded. "We're pretty close to the truth now, Bobby, and that's good. But did Mr. Joe fall or did you push him? Remember, you need to tell the truth. It'll be worse if you don't."

Bobby started to whimper. "I want my mama. Can I talk to my mama?"

"Bobby, is your mother a lawyer?" Billy knew he needed this on the record.

"Nah." He was sniffling. "She cleans rooms. She ain't no lawyer."

"Do you want a lawyer at this time?" Billy wanted it on record.

"No, I said I don't want no lawyer."

"Then answer the deputy." Billy was firm but not pressuring in his tone.

"What question, ma'am?"

"Did Mr. Joe fall, or did you push him?"

Bobby lowered his head onto his hands. "I mighta pushed him, I just wanted the smokes. That's all. I can't help that he done gone and fell. Right?"

"And, just to be sure I understood you, Bobby, did you call 9-1-1?"

"No." He looked up at her.

Billy stood up. "Unless you have something else to say, that's all for now. Anything you want to say?" Tears continued to stream down Bobby's face, and Billy all but gagged watching the mucus drip from Bobby's nose to his mouth.

"No, sir."

"This is Detective Williams and . . ."

"Deputy Thomas, ending this session with... please say your name." She pointed to Bobby.

"Bobby Kirk." He could hardly say it.

She gave the time and walked over to put the wrist cuffs back on him. Billy quickly stepped out of the room. He was afraid he might lose his lunch watching the sad, pathetic boy wipe his face on his sleeve while knowing Bobby was about to go to jail for what may well be a significant portion of his life.

As soon as they returned Bobby to the matron, Deputy Thomas spoke to her. "Matron, Bobby wants to make his phone call."

"Sure thing, Deputy Thomas. I'll see that he gets it." Most folks in the mountains still had a landline, which made it possible to receive a collect call. All calls from inmates were collect. Most of the time they were not accepted. It did, however, alert whoever was on the receiving end that the person calling was in jail and wanted them. Might be the best this boy got today.

Not All Questions Get Answered

Billy looked at Susan as they walked away. "Good job in there. I've done good cop/bad cop with others, but you sure make it work."

"Not proud of that, Detective. Hardly seemed a fair fight, did it?"

"Did what we went in there to do. Doesn't mean we like it or want it. I want to be sure we know who did this to Mr. Joe." Billy shook his head slowly from side to side.

"Pretty clear that we know, isn't it?"

He could hear the sadness in her voice for a life ended abruptly and for one about to be cut short to a long time behind bars.

"I'll talk to the DA and let you know what she plans to do. Again, good work, Deputy. Good work." The double speak, common in these hills, was deeply ingrained. The phrases were often used as a way of reassuring the other person whatever was said was a fact, not important to the circumstance, or not offensive. The two parted as they reached the hallway to the small crime lab where Billy spent most of his time when he was in the station.

"Catch you later, Detective." She swiped herself out of the building with her ID card.

Billy swiped his card to enter the lab and took two steps inside to grab his mug from the shelf by the door. He felt like he needed a stiff drink after that interrogation, but coffee would have to do. He still needed to try and get Gertrude to talk and give up whoever was behind the prostitution ring. This one he had to do on his own.

Chapter 8

Sorting Things Out

Chad whistled as he walked into the station. *Nora is with Bella. Perfect.* He started his computer and several messages popped up. He glanced at the subject headings and decided he needed fresh coffee before delving into the details of the ongoing cases. He took his mug to the break room to wash it out and refill it, grateful no one was there to ask any questions about Joe. As he returned to his office, he caught sight of Sergeant Sylvia Whitehorse.

"Morning, Sheriff."

"Morning, Sergeant, I saw your message. If you can give me a bit of time to see what I need to get done today, I'd like to see you before you leave." He caught himself. "*If* you have time today." He knew she had rotated to the night shift, and he didn't want to keep her too late. However, there were several things he needed to discuss with her because he was eager to place an order for the new technology she was going to recommend. He knew they needed these tools to better serve the community.

"I'll be here when you're ready. I actually planned to be here until noon."

"Thanks. It shouldn't take long."

Chad closed his office door and settled in to read his messages. Detective Lewis, tracking ownership of the motels in Round City, had some new information and wanted to talk to him. Billy had information about the robbery and assault at the Valley Store, and he had reinterviewed Gertrude about the prostitution sting. There was a phone message taken by the desk deputy saying that Agent Quinn Isaacs of the Immigration Enforcement Agency wanted to talk to him today, but it wasn't urgent. Chad decided to start with Billy; he sent a message to meet at his office at eleven o'clock.

Billy's "10-4" popped on the screen immediately.

He dialed Quinn's number and hoped she would be available so he could check this one off his list.

"May I help you?" He knew it was Quinn.

"Por favor," Chad was proud he had looked up the word for "please" in Spanish.

"Oh, I see you need a lesson in Spanish pronunciation. I'm here to serve. The first word is pronounced 'pour' as in pour the tea. The second word starts 'fah.' 'Ah' like the doctor wants you to say when she puts a tongue depressor in your mouth, preceded by an 'f.' And the last part of the second word is like the word 'for' with a 'v' instead of an 'f.' So, it sounds like this, 'pour fah-vor.' Anything else you need today, sir?"

"Por favor!" Chad said it correctly this time. "I need to speak with a young woman who might need some lessons on showing respect to her elders. She available?"

"Checkmate. You win!" Quinn laughed. "Thanks for returning my call, Sheriff. Hope my humor didn't offend. Sam Nations did say you appreciate good humor."

"Might want to be careful what you believe from a Drug Enforcement agent." He was clearly amused. "And, as I think about it, I may need you to meet my lead detective. He could give you a run for your money."

"Is he single?"

That stopped Chad cold. "Well... as a matter of fact... he is." Chad had been single so long himself it never occurred to him to think about Billy as a single man who might like to meet a sharp woman.

"I'll tell you what. You show up some Friday for our bluegrass jamboree at The Corral and I'll introduce you. You're on your own after that."

"Might just take you up on that. However, the vacuum in my dating life is not why I wanted to talk to you."

Agent Isaacs filled him in on the immigrant family they had removed from the plateau on Friday. They were being interviewed, and they had family who were legally in the US. "Sometimes that helps, sometimes it doesn't. It's generally better than *not* having family here. Their request for asylum based on the trauma inflicted on them in Nicaragua will take time to verify. In the meantime, they will remain in detention here until a decision is made whether to deport them or not. Just wanted to update you. Any questions?"

Chad thought for a second. He was starting to understand the trust Sam had in this young woman. "No, Quinn, not on this family, but thanks for the update. It helps knowing they'll be treated fairly. I do, however, have another matter. Have time?"

"Give me the particulars and, if I need more, we can arrange a time to talk."

He explained they had busted a prostitution ring in the area. "Two were very young women, likely from south of the border, who appeared to be minors. Neither one of them would talk, even to Deputy Murphy in Spanish. I saw one of them at The Corral with one of our local commissioners."

"And?" Quinn waited.

"The commissioner was speaking very slowly to her. I never understood why folks think that helps when the person doesn't know the language. Anyway, I heard him tell her she would be fine and something like she would love it here."

Chad went on to explain to Agent Isaacs that he had followed Zimmerman to a house where the two had walked in together. "I immediately put surveillance on the place to gather information. A fight in front of the house on Friday night resulted in us entering."

Her response came quickly. "Chad, I can wrap up what I'm doing right now and head your way. May I try to interview the girls? I'm quite okay with Deputy Murphy being there too."

"Great! I was hoping you would be able to help. See you when you get here."

"10-4." Quinn hung up.

Chad leaned back in his chair and raised his arms above his head. An image of Bella flashed through his mind. *Oh boy, I may be way in over my head after lots of years with no distractions other than my work. Might be too old at fifty-eight to learn how to juggle a dating life, make time for friends, and still do my job.*

His mind shifted to his conversation with Carla in his kitchen yesterday. He remembered her insistence that she could handle the store for Joshua. He thought about the love and concern he had heard in her voice. He wondered how he had not realized the reason Carla was single all these years was how she felt about Joshua. *I never even wondered why she didn't have a boyfriend or husband. Guess I just assumed she wasn't interested. Boy, have my eyes been opened in the last two days. I'm a little slow on the uptake.* He shook his head, hoping to clear the personal thoughts that were crowding in. The knock on his door brought him back to the present.

The Valley Store

Joshua and Carla had been at the store since seven. When Doug and Melody arrived a few minutes later, Joshua started to tell them about Joe and couldn't.

"Joshua, why don't you go up and get those propane orders sorted out so we're ready for the folks that come to help with deliveries." He walked up the stairs without a word.

Carla pulled Doug and Melody to the side. Her voice was soft, caring. "Doug, Melody, this is going to be difficult to hear. Joe hit his head on the counter Saturday night and was seriously injured." She took a deep breath. "He didn't survive it." In looking from Melody to Doug, she didn't know whose face showed the most shock and sadness. "You can imagine this is a tough day. Joshua wanted to open the store, so he's really grateful you could come in and help." Neither of them said anything for several seconds.

Melody was the first to speak. "Miss Carla, I'm so sorry. Mr. Joe sent me home early on Saturday. I should have stayed."

Carla shook her head. "This is *not* your fault. Don't think that. Mr. Joshua wouldn't want you to feel that way." *Maybe we need to ask Pastor Fisk to talk to Melody.*

Melody nodded. "I'll help Mr. Joshua any way I can. Please make sure he knows that."

"He does, honey, he does. Thanks." Carla smiled at her.

Doug stood silently at the register, and Carla was afraid he was in shock. "Doug, can I get you something?"

"No, Carla, just going to need some time. Known Joe all my life, that I have." Doug choked back a sob.

Carla looked at them sympathetically. "I'm going to stay around and help out too. I think the best way we can help Joshua is by trying to act as normal as possible. Think we can do that?"

"I'll sure try." Melody tried to hold back the tears welling in her eyes.

"We'll get him through this." Doug turned to check the registers to avoid eye contact.

Carla went upstairs and saw that Joshua had printed out the propane delivery lists. He knew she had called the people on the list Chad had given her, and he was touched that all of them were more than willing to help out. As they reviewed the deliveries, Carla asked questions about general operations, and Joshua talked with her as if he explained these things every day. Carla felt like getting into his routine was helping Joshua to cope, and she was also glad that he and Bella had already spent some time at the store to get over the initial shock of being back.

"Wow! I love learning new things. This has been really interesting. I think we should get some coffee. What do you say?" Carla touched Joshua's arm.

"I could go for some." Joshua looked at his watch. "It's almost ten o'clock. Who did you say was coming in first?"

"Ken Bennett." She stood up.

They were headed down the stairs from his loft office when the front door opened, and Deputy Ken Bennett stepped aside to let a woman and little girl enter.

The woman thanked him, and then she saw Melody at the register. "Oh, hey, Melody. I thought you might be working today. Natalia is at The Corral."

"Hey, Miss Andrea. I know. She sent me a text. Hey, Karolina. How are you today?"

"I'm good," the little girl said in a quiet voice.

Joshua recognized the woman from her visits to the store, but he had never spoken with her. He was starting to see why his dad spent time talking to customers. You had to know the people who would keep your business going. He promised himself he would try to do better. He heard Melody's comment about Natalia. He stepped over to her.

"Welcome. I'm Joshua Johnson. We've not properly been introduced."

"Nice to meet you, Mr. Johnson, I'm Andrea. We like your store." She looked down at her daughter. "Don't we, Karolina?"

Karolina nodded.

"Please, call me Joshua." He realized Karolina had to crane her head all the way back to look up at his six-foot-four frame. He squatted down to be at eye level with her. "You can call me Joshua, too."

"Okay, Mr. Joshua. Nice to meet you. You can call me Karolina."

All the adults smiled. Carla giggled.

Karolina looked around from one to the other. She pulled on her mother's hand. Andrea bent over to hear what she had to say. She hugged her daughter. "Oh, honey, I think they just thought it was so sweet of you to tell Mr. Joshua your name."

Andrea stood up. "No, we've not met, but we always enjoy talking to Mr. Joe. Don't we, Karolina?" Karolina nodded. Andrea smiled. "Well, we'll let you get on with your day. We have shopping to do."

Joshua stood still for several seconds, trying to figure out how he was going to handle people talking about his dad, particularly once they knew what happened to him. He had avoided people talking about Jan; there would be no way to avoid them talking about Joe. He turned to where Carla was speaking to Ken Bennett.

"Thanks for coming, Ken. Joshua will take you out and show you the ropes. Here's the schedule. Just three runs this morning; do you have time to do them?"

Deputy Bennett looked at the list. "I know where they are, no problem getting it done." He reached over to shake hands with Joshua. "Why don't you show me the equipment and that big truck of yours? I think I'm trainable. Just so you know, I'm hazmat certified, so I'm good to go." The two men walked out to the propane storage area.

Carla turned to Melody. "Sounds like you and Natalia have a corner on the brains department over at the high school."

Melody laughed. "Well, Natalia does for sure. I just work hard."

"Girl, you listen to me." Carla moved closer and spoke softly. "I work hard. I lift trays of food and have even been known to wash dishes in the kitchen at The Corral. That's all physical work. It can be hard. I'd say what you do is *apply* yourself. You clearly have the brains to learn and then show that you have acquired all that knowledge. So, remember, applying yourself goes a long way in life."

"Yes, Miss Carla. I'll remember that. Thanks. I've tried to figure out what people mean when they say, 'if you work hard enough.' I like the idea of applying myself. That's a great way to think of it. Thanks again."

Carla patted her on the back of the hand and walked towards the rear of the store. She wanted to give Joshua space, but also wanted to know what was involved in the deliveries so she could help out if Joshua needed a break.

The two men were at the big propane tank when Carla walked up.

"Now, Ken," Joshua started, then turned and looked at Carla. "Do you want to know this stuff too?"

"Absolutely, go right ahead."

Fifteen minutes later, after Joshua explained things and answered questions, Carla took a piece of paper out of her pocket. She handed it to Joshua with a pen. "You just need to sign this, and Ken can take it with him."

Joshua looked perplexed. He looked down at the paper, read it, placed it on the door of the truck, and signed it. "Thanks, Carla. Good idea." The paper simply stated that Deputy Ken Bennett was authorized to drive the truck and make deliveries for the Valley Store and Propane Company.

Ken took the paper, shook their hands, and climbed in the truck. "Catch up with you when I get back." The truck started towards the front of the store.

Joshua reached out and pulled Carla into a hug; she returned his embrace with a pounding heart. He slowly released her, stepped back, and cleared his throat. "Thanks, Carla. Thanks for everything. I don't know if I could manage receiving our deliveries that are going to arrive shortly and gotten Ken ready for the propane deliveries without you." Neither said anything else as they walked up the steps to the loading dock.

Chapter 9

Picking Up the Pieces

"Nora, I can't tell you how much I appreciate your support right now. I was so surprised when you spoke to me at the county offices. I was so lost in my own thoughts I didn't even hear you walk up."

"The pleasure's all mine." Nora had a lilt in her voice. "I'll need directions from this point. I know you live off this county road, but I don't know where." Nora turned off Route 54 onto the county road up to Drellag Caban.

"Well, you can't miss me. I'm at the end of the road and the only one on the road, at least for now."

"Wow, that must be nice. I wish we could live farther out. Fred needs to be close to the hospital, so we'll live in the valley the rest of our lives. I'm not complaining, mind you. It would just be nice, once in a while, to spend some quiet time up on one of these mountains."

"My home is your home." Bella caught her breath as Nora over-corrected the steering wheel on one of the switchbacks.

"Sorry about that. I haven't driven switchbacks this sharp in a while."

"I'm the one who should apologize. I'm still a little disoriented over Joe's death. I did think I had rid myself of that sudden catch of breath when I'm startled, though. It used to drive Matt crazy."

"Matt?" Nora tried not to show too much curiosity.

"Oh, I forgot, you didn't know my late husband. Matt passed away almost five years ago. I can only imagine my behavior would drive your father nuts. I guess it's a good thing I had this little reminder."

"I wouldn't worry too much about what will drive my daddy crazy. I know him pretty well, and I'd say he's so smitten with you that anything short of being an ax murderer will go totally unseen!"

Bella hoped Nora couldn't see the heat she felt rising in her face. She was thankful they were approaching the grate across Bella's Creek and Nora's attention was fully on the road ahead.

"Oh, look! Arthur is working on my new fence. How could I have forgotten that he was installing it today?"

"Shall we stop and look?" Nora slowed her SUV.

"I don't want to keep you from the children too long. If you can spare the time, I could take just a couple of minutes to speak to him." Bella looked at Nora. "Oh, that's ridiculous, let me just tell him I'll stop on my way back down the mountain."

"Nonsense. I haven't seen Mr. Arthur in longer than a hound's ear. We'll stop." She drove towards the area where the men were working.

Bella could see the fence looked exactly like what he had shown her in his drawings. "I love that it fits right in with the woods, don't you? It makes me feel settled on this mountain."

"Yes, I think it looks like it was part of the land for decades. Nice job." She drove up to the grate and saw the water. "What a beautiful creek!"

"I love it too. My Grandmother Hazel named it Bella's Creek."

Nora chuckled. "Oh, wait until I tell my little Mac that you have a creek named for you. He will jump up and down for hours."

"You'll have to bring them up. I have eighty acres here. Lots of land to explore." Her voice became more animated as she began to share her plans. "Guess what, I'm going to put a guest cottage right up there." She pointed to the rise in the road. "It'll have a lovely view out over the valley and down here to the creek. You're welcome to come up anytime you want out of the valley."

"Wow, have you been planning that for a long time?"

"Only since the—" she stopped abruptly when Nora stepped on the brakes.

Nora looked at Bella. "Sorry about that. I was so distracted looking around that I forgot we were stopping. Mr. Arthur is going to think I'm crazy!"

Bella let her comment about planning the guest cottage drop and got out of the SUV. Arthur tipped his hat as she walked up.

"Morning, Arthur. Please excuse me for not calling you. I've been down in the valley, and it completely slipped my mind. Thank you for starting on the fence."

"Figured something had come up. Didn't think you'd mind... Oh, hey, Miss Nora." He tipped his cap to her as she walked around the SUV. "I was a bit concerned though when you didn't come to the door, what with your Wrangler here. Glad to see you're all right."

"Hey, Mr. Arthur. It's been way too long. How are you doing?"

"Fit as a fiddle, and twice as lively." He grinned at her.

Bella and Nora smiled.

"Good to hear. Good to hear." Nora headed towards the creek.

"Arthur, I'm truly sorry I didn't let you know I wasn't at home."

"No problem, Bella. We started pretty early and we're about to wrap it up soon."

"Unfortunately, I don't have time today to discuss the details, but I've decided to build the new cabin." She pointed. "Up there, right on the flat as you come onto the top, if we can make that work. I've also decided to ask you to try and repair the shed to as close to what it was as possible. I want the reminder of what my daddy built on this land. And, last but not least, would you look at what it'll take to close in the carport or build a garage attached to the cabin?"

"Whoa, Bella! You sure you want to do all that?"

"Arthur, I was pretty sure on Friday that was what I wanted to do. But after the events this weekend..." She looked at him knowing he had cleaned up the Valley Store.

He nodded and sadness showed in his eyes.

Bella continued, "I want it done as soon as you can make it happen. I want to make this property whole again and add a new element that will work in harmony with the land."

He nodded. "Did you decide on a prefab cabin, or are you going to design one?"

"I really liked the Overlook model. If I can arrange things in the next few days, do you think you would have time to do it before bad weather sets in?"

"I tell you what... I'll draw up the paperwork, and you can look at it and make sure you want to commit to all that. In terms of time, the best I can do is tell you we'll sure try to beat ole man winter."

She reached out and shook his hand. "Deal, Arthur. That's a deal. I don't know my plans over the next few days, so if you call me at the cabin and I don't answer, it's because I'm in the valley. My mobile phone works there, so just call me on that number. You have it, right?"

He opened his own mobile phone and recited her numbers.

"Correct. Thanks, Arthur. Thanks for everything. The fence is going to be perfect."

"My pleasure, Bella. My workers appreciate it too."

Bella walked over to Nora and looked out over the creek. Without a word, they turned at the same time and headed to Nora's SUV. Nora started to drive then stepped on the brakes quickly.

Nora laughed nervously. "*Please* don't tell my daddy I almost put you through the windshield twice. I just wasn't prepared for how lovely it is here." As she pulled her SUV up onto the flat of the land, she caught sight of the plywood covering the hole in the side of the shed. She parked the car and turned to look at Bella.

"Bella, this is a lovely setting: the broad mountain vistas, the gentle creek—all of it. It has to be a place you miss when you're not here." She stopped for a second and watched Bella's face carefully. "Is the damage to that building from the things that happened with those boys last month?"

"Yes, one of the ATVs plowed into it."

"I knew my daddy met you because of that case, but he doesn't tell me details and I don't ask. I should have asked if you were okay."

"Nora, I'm fine. I have to admit it was all a bit of a shock when it happened. Your dad, Joshua, and Joe were a big help in making me feel safe again and getting through it. As a writer, I often process my thoughts and feelings by writing a story; I was able to write one. So, please, don't bother your pretty head about it. Okay?" Bella could not believe she had just used a phrase her Grandmother Hazel had used so often when she was little. She looked at Nora, hoping she was not offended the old saying.

Nora nodded. "Good. I'm glad writing helps you. Maybe you'll share what you wrote with me one of these days."

The two women got out of the SUV.

"I will, Nora. Thanks for your interest. Come on now, let me show you Drellag Caban, and I'll get my things together."

Gathering Pieces

"Morning, Sheriff. How may I help you?" His dispatcher sounded cheerful.

"Good morning to you too, Cecelia. Would you please tell Sergeant Whitehorse I'm ready when she is?"

"Yes, sir, good as done. Anything else?"

"No, thanks. That'll do for now." He hung up, leaned back in his chair, and ran through everything he'd been trying to organize: what he might be able to delegate, what he had to handle, and how to make sure he had time to support Joshua. He hoped the news from his lead detective would help with the latter. A knock at the door signaled that Sergeant Whitehorse was available.

"Come in, Sylvia. Thanks for giving me a few minutes. I needed to get my head back in the game." They headed to the round table he used for meetings like this.

"Here to serve." Sylvia studied his eyes. "How are you doing? How's Joshua?"

"I'm fine, thanks." He sat for a few seconds. "Joshua? Well, it's going to take time, and the best we can do on our end is solve the crime that cost him his dad. Hoping Williams has some news on that front. I've asked him to join us."

His voice reflected the tiredness he felt from the weight of the events and his desire to solve the crimes that seemed to be stacking up like cordwood. He was relieved to talk to Sylvia since she knew about Joe; he hated feeling that he was keeping a secret from his staff, but he figured most people would learn about Joe's passing before the day was done.

"In the meantime, catch me up, please."

"Yes, sir. Agent Isaacs called and she was able to get here earlier than expected. She's in with the second of the two young girls picked up Friday night in the prostitution raid. Deputy Murphy was with her for the first one, but they agreed it was best for Agent Isaacs to take the second one by herself."

Chad had a puzzled look on his face. He looked down at his watch. *It's almost eleven o'clock? What have I been doing?*

Sylvia saw the look. She knew he rarely revealed what he was thinking. She continued, "The second girl is the one you saw with Commissioner Zimmerman. Agent Isaacs and Deputy Murphy agreed that the girl might be more willing to talk to someone she didn't connect with the folks in our office."

Chad nodded his head in understanding. "Any luck?"

"I think so. Agent Isaacs said she'd give you a full report when she was finished. No telling how long that will be since the first one lasted over an hour."

Chad looked at his watch again. *Where did the time go? It's only Monday. Lord help us.*

Sergeant Whitehorse was not accustomed to the sheriff being so distracted. She wondered if she should just sit and wait. When Chad stayed silent, she continued, "Not sure if Billy has updated you, but the DA seems pretty confident the grand jury will indict Steve Phillips on criminally negligent homicide in the overdose of Nick Brown. If so, she hopes the judge will set the trial date quickly. Hard to know how full the judge's calendar is. Given that Steve confessed to the trespassing and property damage at Dr. Anderson's property last month, he'll be headed out of here, even if she doesn't get an indictment for Brown's death."

Chad sat quietly and gave a quick nod of his head. "Sergeant, do you ever wonder how things went so wrong, so quickly for these young people? Seems just yesterday the worst we had was petty theft and Saturday night brawls."

"Well, I'll tell you, I'm either getting old or the world is changing faster than any of us can keep up with."

"You and me both. Okay, all that information is helpful, thanks. If you'll hang tight, I want to make a quick call to Lewis on the motel ownership in Round City, and then Billy should be here to update us."

She nodded.

Chad walked to his desk, moved the computer mouse to activate his screen, and picked up the phone to call the detective. The detective's line was busy, so Chad logged into his secure account and read the messages that popped up. He slapped his hand on his leg. "Good news, Sylvia. We can tie Zimmerman to the motels in Round City!"

Sylvia was surprised by his exclamation as she had not heard him on the phone. "What, sir?"

"I have a note here that our very own Detective Lewis worked his way through the maze of shell companies and found Zimmerman as the funder and sole owner at the end of the chain of those two motels in Round City. The pieces are starting to come together." He stood up to head back to the table, but swerved to answer the knock on his door. He pulled the door open so quickly that Billy's hand was in midair.

"Come in, Detective Williams. I believe you know Sergeant White-horse." He waved a hand towards the sergeant sitting at the table. Sylvia and Billy looked at him, trying to figure out who, or what, had invaded their normally placid sheriff.

"Fill us in, Detective." Chad was all business again.

"Yes, sir. Deputy Thomas and I interviewed Bobby Kirk. Just to recap, his cousin Jason Kirk told us the two boys went into the Valley Store on Saturday for juice and cigarettes. Jason also told us that Bobby pushed Mr. Joe, causing him to hit his head on the counter. Jason also confessed to taking the cash out of the drawer, claiming he gave it to his father."

"Got it, Billy, we need to know about *Bobby* Kirk."

Billy heard the impatience in Chad's voice. He outlined the interrogation, including the important part he felt Deputy Thomas played. "I don't have a decision from the DA yet, but based on Bobby Kirk's admission that he and Jason were in the store, the DA is likely to go for criminally negligent homicide, even though he claims he bumped or *might* have pushed Mr. Joe. She's reviewing the evidence and expects to have the autopsy report this afternoon. Honestly, I think she's a bit concerned none of these young men in the last month have asked for a lawyer. Even Phillips, whose family can clearly afford it, hasn't lawyered up."

"Good work, Billy. Sylvia, please tell Deputy Thomas I appreciate her part in all of this. Sounds like a good clean interrogation. Anything else?"

Billy looked from Chad to Sylvia, unsure whether he should share the information he had about Gertrude at this time. "Only if you want to know about my latest interrogation of Gertrude."

"Let's have it." Chad tried not to sound too impatient, but he found himself looking at his watch. He realized Bella and Nora would be back down the mountain soon. He knew Nora had a key and would stay with Bella until he got home—but he wanted to be there when Bella arrived.

"Well, I wouldn't say Gertrude is softening up, but I think she's getting a little edgy. She knows her priors are a problem in this, but she still seems pretty cocksure 'the commissioner' is going to take care of her. She doesn't act like taking money from men for sex with young girls is anything out of the ordinary."

"Has she asked for an attorney?" Sylvia waited for Billy's reply.

"Good question, Sergeant. Billy?" Chad nodded and glanced towards him.

"No. In fact, she's adamant about it. Given the number of folks I've interrogated recently without them requesting an attorney, it makes me wonder if there is some subliminal message floating through the air saying, 'no lawyer,' 'no lawyer.'"

Chad wondered if Billy could make a joke of everything. The buzz of his secure phone got his immediate attention and he pulled it from the clip on his belt. "Oliver here."

"Sheriff, sorry to disturb you, but Agent Isaacs needs you in the conference room as soon as you can make it."

"On my way."

He glanced at Sylvia and Billy as he jumped out of his chair. "Stay available, I'll call you. Got to go. May just have a new piece to this puzzle." He left the door open as he hurried out, indicating the other two were free to go.

Puzzle Pieces Prove Puzzling

The conference room's door was ajar as Chad rushed up to it. He knocked as he opened it, and Quinn Isaacs stood when he entered. "Sheriff, sorry to interrupt you, but I thought you would want to know where we are at the moment."

"Absolutely! I appreciate your time and the call. Sit, please."

They both sat and Chad saw she had a cup of coffee so he didn't have to offer. "What's up?"

"I've talked to both of the girls, and you were right; they're both very young. The first girl, who Deputy Murphy helped interview, is fourteen. Her family is from Guatemala, and she doesn't know where any of them are at the moment. She came across the border with her aunt, who she says is twenty, and they were separated by the men who brought them across." Quinn was as calm as two neighbors talking about the benefit of rain on the garden.

Chad absorbed the information. He knew this meant the girl would be leaving with Quinn Isaacs. He had no choice—Immigration had jurisdiction. He was hoping the second girl would be the link to Zimmerman.

Finally, he nodded his head. "My job is rarely easy, Quinn, but I do occasionally get to give people good news, and I get to celebrate that I live in a community where my family has been for over a hundred years. But I'm trying to imagine what happens in your work that you get to celebrate."

"Well, as surprising as it may seem, I do occasionally get to tell people they can legally be in this great land of opportunity—that makes all the rest of it doable. Besides, like you, I believe in the rule of law. When I enforce those laws and show compassion at the same time, it lets me sleep at night."

"Fair enough, young lady." Chad smiled. *It's good to know some-one of her caliber is working in immigration enforcement.*

She picked right up from where she had left off. "The second girl is sixteen and her story is a bit different. Neither of the girls knew each other before they were at the 'house on the hill.' That's how they referred to it. Let's just call the second girl Gabriela. That's not her real name, but I'm not sure the name she gave me is real either. She told me that she's from Mexico. She was trying to follow her boyfriend, who slipped across the border earlier in the year. He planned to go to California to find work so they could get married. The girl was nervous when she talked about the men who grabbed her on the border. She used the word 'secuestrada,' which means kidnapped. I was surprised at how emphatic she was that they were *not* police." She could see Chad's clenched fist on the arm of the chair.

"Gabriela told me she traveled in the back of a van with more than twenty girls, and they were dropped off at night at different places along the highway. By the time she was dropped off in 'las montañas,'" Quinn stopped and looked at him, "just trying to help your Spanish vocabulary." She smiled.

"Thanks. Even an old mountain boy like me can figure out you said mountains."

"Yeah... well, by the time she was dropped off, there were only four other girls. She told me almost all of the girls taken were under the age of seventeen."

"So, what else did you learn? About things locally?"

"She told me she was dropped off at a 'mo-tel.'" She grinned. "Hey, Sheriff, that's a freebie—same word in both languages!"

"Do you get lessons in torturing local law enforcement officers?" He cocked his head towards her and smiled.

"Nope, comes with practice. In fairness, you don't deserve it. Just trying to lighten the mood a bit." She paused. "The man you likely saw her with at the restaurant picked her up at the motel. She insisted the men kept calling him 'jefe,' which means..."

"Stop! I can figure that one out too. Chief! Dammit... Sorry, don't usually use profanity. I should have stepped over and spoken to him at The Corral." His face hardened.

"Sheriff... Chad, listen. This is tough stuff to deal with. I'm certainly determined to do my part to stop it, and I believe you are too. I have some ideas for how we might be able to get her help in learning specific details. We need to find out who she was calling 'el jefe.' We also need to figure out how the commissioner is involved—if he is."

"I'm all ears. I need to figure out as many pieces of this puzzle as I can. Then I hope we can decide the best way to put them together."

Chapter 10

Climb the mountains and get their good tidings. Nature's peace will flow into you as sunshine flows into trees. The winds will blow their own freshness into you, and the storms their energy, while cares will drop off like autumn leaves.

John Muir, 1838-1914

What Do I Need to Take?

Bella welcomed Nora to Drellag Caban and apologized for bringing her through the kitchen door. "I keep the screen door to the front porch locked to keep the animals out. But it means I can never bring anyone in through the official front door."

"I love entering a home through the kitchen. Seems to me it sends a message that the person coming in is part of the family."

"What a lovely way to think of it. I like that. Thanks. May I get you something to drink? Eat?" She walked to the kitchen sink and washed her hands. She opened the cabinet and took out two glasses.

"Looks like you're going to have something, so I'll join you. Water, tea, whatever you're having. I can help, you know."

"How about you let me do something for you? As clearly as you love those precious children of yours, I can imagine you get little time to yourself. Just make yourself at home and I'll take care of it. You might enjoy sitting out on the porch. Here, I'll show you."

"If it's all the same to you, I'm sure I can find my way out there. Thanks, Bella. It would be lovely to sit and take in the view."

Bella fixed them each a glass of tea, put a few crackers and cheese on a plate, and took it all out to the porch on a tray. "I see you found the best seat on the porch. Good for you." She set the tray down between them. "Help yourself. Oh, I forgot, I don't make sweet tea, do you need sugar?"

"I try to limit myself to the sugar I get hugging my children." Nora's smile was infectious.

"Well, I can testify to the joy of that. Lilly was sweet when they left the jamboree on Friday night. She stretched out of Fred's arms towards me and sweetly called, 'B'la, B'la' and I chose it to be Bella!"

"Oh, I'm quite sure that's exactly what she meant. She and Mac have their own language. I promise you Mac has not quit talking about you since last week."

She was moved by the comments and could feel the heat rising in her cheeks again as she sipped her tea. "I know you have lots to do every day. You might enjoy some quiet time here on the porch. I'll go get the things I need to stay down the mountain for a few days."

"Take your time, Bella." Nora allowed herself to relax into the rocker and enjoy the scenery; the ridgeline of the mountains was multiple shades of blue, capped by the hues of oranges, yellows, and reds on the changing leaves.

Bella checked to be sure all the windows were locked as she started to gather some clothes, her laptop, and the notes on the new cabin. She decided she would show the information to Chad and see what he thought of it. With her laptop, she could check emails while she was in the valley since she found answering messages on her computer much easier than on her iPhone. Satisfied she had what she needed and that the house was secure, she returned to the porch.

Nora's eyes were closed. Bella didn't want to disturb her and was about to duck back into the house when Nora turned to her. "I'm not asleep, although I'll tell you this might have been the most glorious few minutes of solitude I've had in a while."

"Being alone is overrated, trust me."

Nora heard the wistfulness in Bella's words.

Bella continued. "Sorry, I think Joe's death has stirred up difficult memories for me. I'm not usually so melancholy." She smiled, trying to reassure Nora—and herself.

Nora patted the chair next to her. "Sit, you could use some of this mountain air and scenery too. You'll be amazed at what five minutes can do for you."

Bella sat down and lightly squeezed Nora's hand. "Thanks for understanding."

The two women sat quietly rocking for several minutes, and then Nora started humming "The Lily of the Valley," a hymn from the 1800s. As she watched Bella close her eyes, she started quietly singing, "In sorrow He's my comfort, in trouble He's my stay; He tells me every care on Him to roll. He's the Lily of the Valley, the bright and morning star, He's the fairest of ten thousand to my soul." Nora returned to a quiet hum.

Bella rocked slowly to the rhythm of Nora's gentle humming. Without opening her eyes, Bella spoke. "That was one of my mother's favorite hymns. The Olivers in my family were Presbyterian," she opened her eyes and looked at Nora, "but, of course, you would know that. The Andersons in Knoxville were Baptists."

Nora stopped humming and sat up straight in her chair. "Might need you to back up on that. The Olivers in *your* family?"

Bella started laughing. "Sorry for the surprise. Yes, my great-grandfather Oliver built this cabin. I inherited it from my Grandmother Hazel—my daddy died when I was quite young." She saw Nora flinch. She assumed it was because she had mentioned her daddy's death. "My mother was an Anderson, and I married an Anderson. *No kin.*" She gave a slight wag of her finger. "And, yes, I have little doubt that you and your dad are my kinfolk somewhere back there among all the children of the Oliver brothers of Cades Cove." She watched Nora's face. "Problem?"

"No, none at all. It just caught me totally by surprise. Seeing you with my daddy today makes it seem highly likely we're going to get to know each other, I'm glad to say. Good to know we're already family." She winked at Bella. "That way, I can still spend time with you, even if my daddy does something stupid and lets you slip away."

This time the blush on Bella's face was unmistakable.

Nora looked at her and smiled.

"Thanks, Nora. It's nice to have a friend... and family." Bella's voice was soft.

The two women rocked in silence. Bella glanced at her watch and saw it was after eleven; she stood up suddenly. "Look at the time! I've taken you away from your children for far too long. Shall we head down the mountain?"

Nora stood up and walked over to check the latch on the porch screen door. "Good to go!"

Bella looked at Nora. "Nora, I don't know quite how to ask this. Your dad said there has to be an autopsy on Joe, so I'm assuming there won't be any kind of service 'til the end of the week."

Nora interrupted her. "I obviously haven't talked to Dad or Joshua. Joshua is pretty private. My guess is there will be a small funeral and burial with just Joshua's closest friends... which I'm sure would include you." Nora had seen the look on Bella's face. She gave her a gentle hug before continuing. "Then maybe there will be a community gathering to celebrate Joe's life, likely at the music grounds at The Corral. That would be my second guess. When any of it'll happen, I don't know."

Bella nodded. "Well, my dilemma is that I wasn't going to take the one outfit I brought with me from North Carolina that would be appropriate for a funeral. Do you think I should take it down with me?"

"I think you're fine either way. There's plenty of room at my dad's house, so you can take it down and leave it there if you want."

Bella noticed that Nora didn't seem at all uncomfortable about the fact that she was staying at Chad's. She decided she could always bring the suit back up with her if she came home before the funeral. It would be less awkward if she needed it on short notice. She returned to her bedroom and put her black pumps into her canvas bag and draped the hanging garment bag containing her black pantsuit over her arm.

"Okay, I'm ready. I'll let you go down the mountain first. I think I'll stop and close the gate, now that I have a fence."

"I think going ahead of you is a good idea on both counts."

"Both counts?" Bella raised an eyebrow.

"Yes, your place will be secure, and you won't have me running you off the road on the switchbacks."

Both women laughed as they walked out the door.

Bella locked the kitchen door and heard Nora say, "See you at my daddy's house."

Chapter 11

Delegating Responsibility

As sheriff, Chad knew he had the ultimate responsibility for everything that had an impact on his officers and the safety of the community. He also knew he was becoming distracted in a way he didn't recognize. He locked his hands behind his head, trying to process the distractions; he knew they were more personal than professional.

At least now I know that I'm interested in a long-term relationship with Bella. If I'm honest with myself, I knew Mary was never going to be a partner in this life of mine. . . or any other for that matter. She doesn't even come see her daughter or grandchildren. So, maybe having Bella in my life is new to me in more ways than just dating.

He had notified Sylvia and Billy to be in his office at eleven thirty to meet with him, Agent Isaacs, and Deputy Murphy. He looked at his watch and saw it was almost time for them to arrive. He couldn't decide whether to call Nora or not. He wanted to know if they were down the mountain, but it also felt like he was checking up on them. He closed his eyes and sat in the quiet.

Ten minutes later his personal mobile rang at the same time there was a knock on his door. He stood to open the door and pointed to the round table. The four walked in and sat down, leaving a space for Chad. He held up the ringing phone. "Excuse me for a moment." Chad stepped into the hall.

"Hey, Nora, what's up? Lose your key?"

"Ha, ha, Daddy. Very funny! Just came onto County Route 54. Thought I'd let you know we're headed to your place."

"Okay, honey, I'll be there as soon as I can. Everything okay?"

"If you're asking about your love interest, she's fine. Drives better than your daughter." Nora's longtime teasing was familiar to him—just not about a woman.

"Whoa, what's that supposed to mean?"

"The love interest? Or the driving?" Nora loved to banter with Chad.

"Should've known I was opening myself up for that one. Just tell me you're both driving safely."

"Always the sheriff, aren't you? Yes, Daddy, we're both driving safely. We'll be at your house in less than ten minutes, so get done what you need to do and get home. And that's an order."

"Yes, ma'am!" Chad smiled to himself. He could tell Nora liked Bella, and that made him happy—very happy, indeed. "Be there as soon as I can. Love you."

"Yeah, yeah, and apparently I'm not your only love anymore."

"You're getting a bit uppity, young lady. We'll have to talk about this later."

"Oh yes, Daddy. We *will* talk. Love you, Daddy."

Chad shook his head as the call disconnected, shifted his focus, and walked back into his office. It was obvious that introductions had been made. He sat down as Sylvia Whitehorse was explaining the round table to Agent Quinn Isaacs. "So, you see, even in modern times we can simulate the tribal talking circle just by facing each other at a round table. This eliminates the power a rectangular table gives to the person sitting at the head."

"Wow! It's enlightening that something in the business world today, that seems so modern as sitting at a round table, is deeply rooted in tribal custom. Thanks for sharing with me."

Chad waited until they finished. "Seems you've all met, so let's hear Agent Isaacs' plan. Then everyone can get on with their day."

"Please, call me Quinn." She did a quick summary of the interviews she had conducted with the two girls and thanked Deputy Murphy for her help. "By the way, Sheriff, Deputy Murphy's Spanish is excellent. I'm sure she can help out with your Spanish lessons."

Seeming to move as one, his deputy, his detective, and his sergeant turned to look at him.

"All right, all right, I did mention to Agent Isaacs—Quinn—that I want to learn Spanish. My first few attempts have been less than stellar."

Deputy Murphy jumped in. "Oh, sir, I'll be happy to help you in any way I can. You'll be surprised how quickly you can learn it."

"Sign me up, I'm teachable." Billy winked at Quinn.

Quinn looked at Billy. She realized he was the detective who liked to tease. He was handsome, in a school boyish way, and she decided to pay closer attention to him in this meeting.

Chad chuckled. "Okay, okay, we'll talk later about how we can make it happen, for all of us to learn some Spanish. Right now, though, we need to focus on what happened with these young girls, and what Quinn is proposing to help us solve some other issues in our community. Quinn, go on."

They all turned their attention to Quinn.

Quinn laid out a plan to gather more information with the help of Sam Nations from the DEA. Quinn would get him involved based on what Gabriela had shared about drugs in the house. "That about sums up my idea of how we might go about this."

Detective Billy Williams spoke first. "I think the plan is solid. It would also give me an angle to go at Gertrude, boss..." Billy stopped himself, remembering they had a visitor. "Sheriff. We still have the other young woman in holding. She's a local and legal age. She hasn't been willing to talk, but we might make progress with her using Quinn's plan. And didn't you say the deputies sent a girl home with her father before you arrived at the house? We could interview her too."

Deputy Murphy spoke next. "The only ones who speak Spanish are the two underage girls, and they're also illegal immigrants. Is it safe to assume that you will be taking them, Quinn?"

"Already have a team on the way to pick them up." The other three looked at Chad. Since this was news to them, they wondered if it was news to him. His face revealed nothing.

Chad looked around the table. "Anyone else?"

Billy started to raise his hand and caught himself. "One more thing. I can talk to the DA and see if she wants to make a deal with Gertrude. We could see if Gertrude's willing to return to the house as part of this plan. I think Gertrude being there would make it more likely to bait the trap."

Chad could see Sergeant Sylvia Whitehorse was biding her time. He expected nothing less of her. He sat silently, waiting to see how she would approach it.

"Sheriff," Quinn turned to look at Sylvia as she spoke up. "While I don't like the idea of Gertrude being able to make a deal, it's out of my hands. But who do we get to pose as Spanish-speaking immigrants to get picked up by 'el jefe' at the motel and brought to the house?"

Quinn did not hesitate. "No problem, Sergeant, no problem at all. We have IEA agents who look young enough to be your kid sister, and they do this stuff all the time. I'm guessing this kind of sting is not part of your normal day-to-day work here." She looked at each of them. "Lucky you."

Chad took charge. "Okay, let's run through this one more time, set a timeline to have things in play by the weekend, and move forward."

The five of them mapped out the plan and talked about potential flaws in it before agreeing Quinn would reach out to Agent Sam Nations of the Drug Enforcement Agency and Billy would talk with the DA.

"Sound work, folks." Chad was proud of this team. "Let's plan to meet on Wednesday afternoon to get an update and finalize the operation. Questions? Comments?"

They all shook their heads.

Chad stood, as did the others. "Thanks for your help, Quinn." Chad extended his hand.

She shook his hand. "Appreciate yours."

"Sergeant, can you give me a couple of minutes?"

Sylvia Whitehorse stood at the table as the others left. Billy closed the door on the way out.

"Sit, sit." He tried to figure out how to say what he wanted to say.

"First of all, I just want you to know that I knew Agent Isaacs was taking both of those girls."

She just nodded.

"Sergeant," he stopped. He took a breath and shifted his approach. "Sylvia, you're my senior sergeant, and I deeply respect you and your work. I hope you know that, even though I'm not the best at telling you. I am also at fault for not delegating more authority to you and the other sergeants. Life is starting to teach me some lessons."

She sat without saying a word. She looked at him, employee to boss, friend to friend.

"Right now, I need to be available to a friend who I have taken for granted for far too many years. I hate that it took him losing his father for me to realize it. Today is not the day to talk about how I can back off and give you sergeants more direct decision-making." He paused. "But I make you this promise; I'm going to have that conversation with all three of you. I'm asking you to think about it for a few days then talk with me. I respect your ideas and opinions, and it'll help me get it right." He looked at her. "One more thing. I'd like to see the technology equipment recommendations, but we'll put off going over it 'til next week."

Sylvia nodded. She knew the sting operation and Joe's death were the sheriff's focus right now.

"I haven't had much need of a personal life for a very long time, but I plan to change that too. As a starter, I'm aiming to reduce my eighty-hour weeks—soon. For now, however, are you available to take point for the next couple of days?"

"Happy to serve any way I can, Sheriff." She paused. "Chad."

He stood and so did she. "Thanks, Sylvia. Call me anytime you need me. I'll send a message to the other sergeants that you're on point. Now, you get out of here for today. I'm going to head out of here myself in just a couple of minutes."

"Let me know of anything you need me to do." She walked to the door. "And, when it's appropriate, please give my condolences to Joshua." She was about to shut his door when she added, "Please give my regards to Dr. Anderson."

He stared the closed door. *Oh, yeah, leave it to Sylvia to subtlety remind me how fast news spreads in these hills.*

Trying to Leave it Behind

Nora parked on the street below her dad's house and was out of her SUV before Bella pulled up behind her. She motioned for Bella to put her window down then gestured towards the top of the driveway. "Park up there on the pull-out pad. That way the always-on-call sheriff won't run you over if he flies out of here at the drop of a hat." Bella could hear the affection in Nora's voice as she joked at her dad's expense.

Nora looked around as she walked up the long driveway, thinking about the need to get someone to attend to her father's yard. *Funny,*

I haven't noticed how shabby all this looks. I'll have to speak to him about getting someone to clean up this mess. Bella was already taking her things out of her Wrangler when Nora reached her.

"Here, let me take some of that," Nora reached out to take something.

Bella handed her the hanging garment bag. "Thanks. I always try to make as few trips as I can to the car, and I generally end up carrying way too much!"

"Oh, I know the affliction. I've gotten even worse since I'm now also trying to herd two little ones at the same time. You'd think I could figure out a better system."

Nora unlocked the front door, pushed it back towards the wall to prop it open, and held the screen door for Bella. She watched Bella walk across the living room towards the bedrooms and wasn't surprised she went to Chad's guest room. Nora admitted to herself that she felt a little disappointed Bella didn't head into the master bedroom. *Probably better that I stay out of Daddy's love life.*

Nora followed and put Bella's hanging bag in the closet. "Let's decide what we want to do about lunch. I doubt my daddy has anything in the fridge."

Bella smiled. "Au contraire, your dad had food brought in yesterday. It's enough to feed the valley. We can make a spread for lunch. I can even check with Carla and see if she wants us to bring them something. Maybe Joshua needs a break from the store."

"Great idea! Let's do it." Nora headed to the kitchen.

Bella called Carla. "Hey, how are things over there?"

"Holding up pretty well, thanks. Been a few rough moments for Joshua, but I think you were right that it's good for him to be busy. What's up?"

"I just got back from Drellag Caban... oh, sorry, my cabin. There's a lot of food here at Chad's. Shall I bring you some, or do you guys want to take a break?"

"Let me check with Joshua. Can you hold on?" Carla walked over to Joshua and asked what he would like to do.

"Melody and Doug seem to have things under control. Today's deliveries are put away, and the propane for today is organized. Let's take a break and go eat."

Carla felt Joshua was so matter-of-fact because he had been in his routine. She didn't know how often he ever left the store during the workday but decided he seemed okay doing so.

"Bella, thanks for waiting. We'll be there in twenty or thirty minutes. See you then." Carla hung up.

Bella relayed the conversation to Nora. "That's good. Well, I'm not usually one to imbibe this early in the day, but I think we could have a mid-day glass of wine." She winked at Bella, "Half a glass? How about you?"

"I thought your dad only drank beer."

"He does. One a day, almost never more." She laughed. "You probably already know that."

Bella nodded. "Oh, yes, I had a glass of wine last night. What is wrong with my memory?"

Nora smiled. "He knows to keep Kim Crawford Sauvignon Blanc in the fridge for me." She opened the fridge to see it was packed with food. "None here. There's usually a spare in the fridge in the garage. Back in a second." She opened the kitchen door and went out. She could hear Bella laughing as she returned with the bottle of wine.

Bella was laughing so hard tears were running down her face. Nora turned and looked at her. "What's so funny?"

Bella caught her breath. "Was there any wine in the garage?"

"Voilà." Nora raised the bottle of wine.

Bella looked around.

Nora looked around the room to see what Bella could be worried about.

"I probably shouldn't tell you this. . . " Bella smiled.

"Come on, give!"

"Your dad came up for supper on Saturday, and he brought a bottle of Kim Crawford Sauvignon Blanc. I tried to figure out how he knew it was my favorite!"

Both women laughed heartily. Nora gave Bella a big hug. "Oh, I knew we were going to become good friends. I can't wait to figure out a way to play this one out on my daddy. This will be fun."

Bella returned the hug but was also unsure whether she had made a mistake in what she had said to Nora. *It will be great to have a female friend here, but maybe it will be awkward since she's Chad's daughter?* She decided to put the thought from her mind for the time being.

Nora poured them each half a glass of wine. She put some raw veggies on a plate and ranch dressing in a small bowl. "We can drink and munch while we fix lunch."

Nora's phone on the table buzzed and a text flashed on her screen. "Excuse me, it's Fred." She read the text. "He's home with the kids and will fix their lunch." She lifted her glass. "Here's to men who love their women and their children enough to do their part in raising them, even when they have twelve-hour days at work."

"He must have a hectic schedule!" Bella clinked Nora's glass.

"He does, but the great thing about a rural medicine practice is that he can make adjustments and be an active parent for the kids. That's really important to both of us."

"That's wonderful, Nora." Bella took the food that needed to be heated from the fridge and passed it to Nora.

They heard the garage door open. Nora leaned towards Bella. "I'll bet Dad beats his three-minute record in getting parked in the garage, his boots off facing out on the steps, and his service weapon in the gun safe." Nora saw the bewildered look on Bella's face. "That little ritual is how he says he can leave the job behind at the end of the day."

Nora looked into Bella's eyes. "I promise you I won't give away all his secrets. I'll let you figure out some things for yourself." She broke into an impish smile. "But, quick, before he gets here. Promise you'll call me anytime you have a question about my dad. Deal?"

"Deal." Bella was not quite sure what she had just agreed to.

Chad walked into the kitchen and put his gun in the safe before kissing Bella on the cheek. He then walked around the counter and kissed his daughter. "Greetings, ladies. Glad to see you found the wine and veggies. I need to do better about having food in the house."

"Points for you, Daddy. Grab a beer and join us."

"I'm good. Too early in the day for me. Any word on Joshua?" Chad sat and looked from Bella to Nora and back to Bella.

"He and Carla have been at the Valley Store all morning. They're on their way over to have lunch."

"Perfect. That's perfect. Let me help get this organized. Then we can sit on the porch and wait for them."

"Already got the food that needs to be warmed in the oven. So, let's head out." Nora walked towards the porch then looked back over her shoulder to make a comment. Her dad was kissing Bella; she turned and kept walking.

Bella and Chad walked onto the porch holding hands. Chad was carrying his glass of tea and Bella her wine. They both smiled at Nora.

"I'll finish up my wine and head home. Please let me know what I can do to help Joshua. Pastor Fisk called while I was on the way down the mountain from Drellag Caban and asked me if I was available to sing. Apparently, Joe had let the pastor know that he would like me to sing, 'Amazing Grace' and 'When the Roll is Called Up Yonder.' Of course, I will." She waited a beat. "Maybe you two would come over for dinner tonight?"

Chad smiled and nodded his head. "Thanks, Nora, on both counts. I'm sure Joshua will be pleased to have you sing. As for food, we may need to invite the whole valley to consume all the food that we have here. If Bella agrees, we'll ask for a raincheck on dinner."

Bella nodded and smiled. She was enjoying the ease of the exchange between father and daughter.

"Okay, I'm outta here. Don't often get to eat lunch with my husband and children on Monday, so I'm headed home." Nora picked up her glass. "Bella, thanks for a very special morning. I look forward to more of them. Daddy, be nice to her, you hear me? And don't run her off." She wagged her finger at him. She kissed Bella on the cheek and gave her dad a hug and a kiss as he stood to walk her out. "Don't worry, Sheriff, I've only had half a glass."

"And you, young lady, show some respect for your elders." Chad was equally playful in his admonishment.

Bella stayed seated and sipped her wine, absorbed in the warmth of this family. She loved how she felt embraced by them and the mountains, with the bouquet of fall colors in the leaves across the ridgeline.

She did not hear Chad as he walked up beside her. She almost spilled the last of her wine when he leaned in and kissed her. "Hm-mmm. . . wine and a sweet kiss. Nice combination."

"Chad Oliver, you're becoming quite devilish, I'd say."

"Oh, Dr. Anderson, I'm not *becoming* devilish. I always have been. You're only just beginning to see it." He sat down and put his hand on hers and squeezed it. "You doing okay?"

"I'll feel better when we see Joshua."

"I'll go check on the food. Need anything?" He stood.

She shook her head, smiled at him, and looked out to the mountains. He walked out quietly and left her to her thoughts.

Friends Provide Support

"Joshua, you've already had a long day. Maybe you want to eat and then go home and rest? What do you think?" Carla knew it was not uncommon for people who were going through trauma and loss to respond best when they were pointed towards things that were in their best interests.

Joshua looked at her. He was beginning to understand Carla in a way he had never seen her before. Although he considered her a friend, his interactions had been limited to meals at The Corral and Friday night jamborees. They had been dancing partners for years because Jan had never liked to dance, but Joshua had never given much thought to Carla otherwise.

"I don't know. Let's see how I feel after we have some lunch. Okay?"

"Of course."

They were silent for the remainder of the drive to Chad's house, but there was a lilt in Carla's voice as she called out "Hel-loooo!" and walked through the front door.

Bella went to Carla and gave her a hug. She pushed her gently back and looked her up and down. "Carla, what a lovely outfit. I love the flower print of your skirt."

Chad kissed Carla on the cheek. The last time he remembered doing that was when her parents were killed in a car wreck many years ago. *I have lost too much time in being a friend. Time to make that right.*

They all turned towards Joshua, who remained standing in the doorway. He looked at the three of them. "Hey, folks."

Bella stepped up and kissed him on the cheek. "What can I get y'all to drink?"

"I'll have ice tea, please." Carla walked out to the edge of the porch to get out of the way.

"I think I'll have an ice tea too." Joshua's sorrow was palpable. "Part of me wants to drink the rest of the beers that must be in that fridge and then send you to the store to bring more—but my dad deserved better from his son than one who would drink himself to oblivion."

Bella felt like a sledgehammer had hit her right in the chest. She could not imagine how Joshua was coping. His dad had been in his life almost every day for more than sixty years, and he lost him in such a tragic way. She could barely remember what it was like when she lost her father. She ached for Joshua and, in a small way, for herself since Joe was the last living link to her family's past. *I have always loved that my daddy and Joe grew up together in these hills.*

"Bella, are you okay?"

"Oh, Joshua, I'm sorry. You know my mind wanders off and I forget my manners. I'm okay. Let me get those drinks, and then we'll have some lunch."

"Fine with me." Joshua stepped back. "Fine with me."

Chapter 12

*Nevermore, however weary, should one faint by the way
who gains the blessings of one mountain day;
whatever his fate, long life, short life, stormy or calm, he is rich forever.*
John Muir, 1838-1914

Let's Make a Deal

Billy entered the small crime lab at the sheriff's office and saw Elizabeth Alexander bent over her lab table intently studying some piece of evidence. "Hey, Alexander."

"Afternoon, Detective, solving any crimes today?"

"Counting on you for that!"

"Well, sit yourself down in that chair over yonder, and I will regale you with my expertise."

"That sounds *real* promising. Will it keep until I get a cup of coffee?"

"No end of work to keep me busy in this fight of ours against crime. Go get your coffee."

Billy took his mug off the shelf by the door and headed for the break room. He idly tried to figure out which case Elizabeth wanted to share with him, but he knew it didn't matter in the long run. Whatever she had uncovered would make a difference in solving the case to which it was attached.

Elizabeth had been top of her class in forensic science at Middle Tennessee State University. The MTSU program was one of the best in the state, and they were lucky to have her: after her internship a few years ago, she returned to work in the valley when she graduated, but she could have gone anywhere. At one point she had said she wanted to go to graduate school and then the FBI. Although he would never want to keep her from her dreams, he hoped she would not leave any time soon. He knew it was her family's deep ties to the mountains that had kept her here—so far.

His coffee mug filled, he walked back into the lab and sat in his chair. "Okay, let's hear it from the best forensic tech in the valley."

"Ha, ha! I'm the *only* forensic tech in the valley. Lucky you!" Elizabeth grinned.

He usually let her humor slide. "Fair enough. Out with it."

"Since young Mr. *Bobby* Kirk is now resident in our fine facility, we have fingerprints on him."

Billy sat up straighter but stayed quiet. He was trying to learn from the sheriff.

"As you know, he was not in the system since he had no prior record. But ... ta da! I have a match from his prints at intake to two different prints from the shelf where the cigarette cartons are kept at the Valley Store."

"Good work, Alexander. Good work." He wanted to call the sheriff immediately, but he knew he needed to talk to the DA first to make sure all their ducks were in a row regarding the current case, the prostitution ring, and the sting operation.

Elizabeth bowed. "All in a day's work for a thorough forensic tech."

Billy laughed. "I have taught you some pretty bad habits, haven't I?"

"Well, I actually brought some of them with me. I'll give you credit for helping me refine them, though."

They both laughed.

"Thanks for getting that done. Now I have calls to make."

"Back to the grind." The words were at odds with Elizabeth's buoyant tone. She was a young woman who loved her work.

Billy sipped his coffee, made some notes on the proposed sting, and picked up his phone to call the DA.

"Afternoon, Madam District Attorney. Pleased to catch you on this fine day. Have a few minutes to spare?"

He told her they had matched Bobby Kirk's prints to those found on the shelf where the cigarettes were. He explained the shelf was not accessible without going behind the counter.

"Now if I can switch gears." Billy outlined the plan for the sting on the prostitution operation and asked if she was willing to consider making a deal with Gertrude and potentially the two local women who had been at the house. He reminded her that both women were over eighteen.

"I'm not crazy about making a deal with Gertrude." Peggy O'Haire waited a few seconds. "I need to do some research, and I'll get back to you. How soon do you need to know?"

"The sooner the better, but we won't present Gertrude with the idea until the team meets again on Wednesday. That work for you?"

"Perfect. I'll get back to you as soon as possible. Probably sooner on Kirk."

"Look to hear from you. And thanks." He hung up the phone and stared at the concrete block wall beside his desk. *I don't know that I ever thought my work in these hills would get so interesting or so complex. I think I like the challenge.*

Lunch and Conversation

Bella looked at the other three. "May I get anyone some blackberry cobbler?"

"None for me," Carla shook her head.

Bella looked at Joshua.

He was staring out at the mountains. "Blackberries are an interesting berry." His voice sounded separate from his body. "Strawberries and blueberries are relatively easy to harvest because they don't have thorns. But our mountain blackberries make you work for the reward. Many is the day I was scratched all over my hands and arms from picking those precious jewels."

Bella had her own experience with death and grieving, and she could relate to the random comments one made when in the midst of grief. "Joshua, remembering all the scratches from gathering blackberries makes me love them even more. I can eat them raw, as jam or preserves, and best of all as cobbler."

"I agree, Bella." Joshua smiled at her. "So, I *will* have some cobbler even though my lunch was more food than I usually eat in a day."

"Chad, any for you?" Bella stood.

"Thanks, no." Chad was headed for the kitchen with their stack of dirty plates. "I'll help, though."

They left Joshua and Carla on the porch. Chad put the dishes in the sink, rinsed off his hands, and turned around to look at Bella as she prepared two bowls of blackberry cobbler. He admired the ease with which she did things, and how comfortable she seemed at being in his kitchen. He hoped to have her there more often.

He walked towards the fridge. "Ice cream?"

"None for me, thanks. However, I do remember Joshua saying that there was nothing better than ice cream on blackberry cobbler. So, you can put some on his." She passed a bowl to Chad.

"Bella, if you'll take these out, I'll put the dishes in the dishwasher."

"Let me help with that. It won't take but a minute to take Joshua's dish out to him."

Chad's secure phone buzzed. Distracted by watching Bella, the phone startled him. "Sorry, this one I have to take."

Bella nodded and headed out to the porch. The dishes could wait, and she did not want to intrude on Chad's call.

"Oliver here."

"Hey, boss. Sorry to bother you, but Sergeant Whitehorse said I should call."

"Go ahead, Billy."

"The ME just called. He has ruled on the cause of death for Joe Johnson." Billy was more subdued than was normal for him.

"What's the CD, Detective?" Chad hoped the abbreviation he often used for "cause of death" would not be known if someone walked in off the porch. He was both anxious to know and annoyed that Billy was dragging it out.

"Blunt force trauma, which the ME attributes to Mr. Joe's head being slammed against the edge of the counter. He was very specific in using the word 'slammed.' He made it clear that falling would not have been enough force to cause the damage that was inflicted." Billy's professional demeanor started to crack; Joe had been friendly to everyone, and Chad could tell Billy's emotions were beginning to well up.

"Thanks for the call, Detective. I'll talk to you soon." Chad hung up and leaned against the counter. He knew the ruling meant charges against the Kirk cousins. He also knew it meant Joe's remains could be transferred to Round City. There was no good time, nor easy way, to tell Joshua. The tougher decision was whether to do it with or without Bella and Carla present. Joshua had the right to privacy, but Chad knew he had no one other than the three people he was with right now. He walked down the hall to his home office. This call he would make out of earshot.

Making Plans

"Here's your cobbler, Joshua." Bella set the bowl in front of him.

"Thanks, Bella, this looks great. Want some, Carla?"

"No, thanks. I've eaten enough to last for a month of Sundays. You enjoy it." She patted his hand, which was resting on the arm of the chair next to her. "I see you got some ice cream to boot."

"Nothing but the best." Joshua grinned like a little boy.

Bella looked out to the mountains. "I don't remember the last time I saw an autumn day with more variety and brilliance of color. It never ceases to amaze me how many shades of orange there are. I'm not an artist, but it makes me wonder why we think man can create the range of color that nature has."

Joshua looked at her. "Is it any different for an artist to try and create colors by mixing paints than it is for you as a writer to paint a picture with words?"

Bella stared back at him in surprise. The question would not have been out of place from his father, but Joshua had never been one to engage in particularly esoteric conversations.

Carla spoke up. "Joshua told me you're a writer, Bella. Don't you use different words to convey the nuance of an idea, or to refine the description of an object? Isn't that just a different canvas?"

Bella sat without saying a word. *Wow, I don't think I was ready for such thought-provoking conversation. I love it.* She smiled and turned towards them.

"I have to admit I find myself stumped by your questions. You made me realize how often I make an off-hand comment without really considering the merit of it. You have drawn me up short. I think my immediate response is that I do try to use words to more thoroughly convey an idea or describe an object. Thanks for making me consider my own use of language and the parallels to the visual arts."

Bella saw Chad out of the corner of her eye and realized he was trying to get her attention. "Excuse me, I'll be right back."

She walked towards Chad, who had moved back into the hallway and away from the dining room that led to the porch.

"Everything okay?"

"Need to run something by you. Given the circumstances, I'm not sure how to handle it." Chad was concerned about putting a decision on Bella that he had always made himself. At the same time, he was aware that he was starting to understand what it meant to have someone whose opinion you value to help you think through complex situations.

They stepped into the room he used as his home office. First, he pulled her into an embrace and kissed her. She hugged him and returned the lingering kiss.

"Why, Sheriff Oliver, it seems to me you know exactly how to handle things. You had the courtesy, given the circumstances, to kiss me out of sight of our friends." She stepped back and saw his expression was one of love and sadness.

"Chad, what's wrong? Please tell me how I can help."

Chad started slowly. "I need to tell Joshua we had to do an autopsy on his dad. We have two young men in custody who have confessed to being in the Valley Store, taking the money, and claim to have pushed Joe."

Bella squeezed his hand.

"The autopsy shows that Joe would have been slammed into the counter to cause the damage that occurred, and the medical examiner has ruled that as the cause of death. I just spoke with the district attorney, and she's deciding how to proceed. She had planned to take this case to the grand jury, but with such conclusive evidence and the fact that criminally negligent homicide is likely all she can get, she's inclined to have Billy Williams try to get the perp to plead guilty. The maximum sentence is six years." He let out a heavy sigh then looked intently at Bella. "It's been a long time since I was the one to directly deliver information to a family in a situation like this. And I have never had to tell a close friend."

Bella held his hand. "I can't imagine ever having to tell someone this news. But I've received some pretty bad news in my life, like when Matt was diagnosed with colon cancer." She stopped for a minute. He squeezed her hand. Her eyes moistened. "I think the most humane way is to provide enough information for the person to make any decision that has to be made, leaving the detail until the individual is ready to ask for it."

Chad nodded.

"Is part of your concern whether Carla and I should be there?"

"Yes, it is. He has the right to privacy, but I also know he has no one but us."

"You can give him a choice, you know?"

"How?"

Bella sat quietly for several seconds. "Perhaps you could tell him you have information on the case and ask if he would like to talk with you in your home office or on the porch?"

Chad nodded his head.

"If he indicates the porch, then you can ask if he wants us all to be there. If he says in your office, you can assume he wants to hear it privately."

Chad nodded. "I don't think it'll be easy for any of us, and least of all for Joshua. Let's get this done so we can help him make funeral arrangements. Joe's remains will be enroute to Round City shortly."

Chad leaned over and kissed her. "Thanks, Bella. It means more than I can tell you to be able to talk with you so I don't go blundering into this."

She kissed him lightly. "We'll get him through this. That's what friends do."

Bella stood and Chad followed her out to the porch.

"Everything okay?" Carla looked from one to the other. "Can I help with something?"

Chad pulled out a chair for Bella next to Joshua. They could see that Joshua was holding Carla's hand.

Chad walked around the table to face all three of them and sat down. Bella watched Joshua and Carla: Carla looked straight at Chad, but Joshua stared at the mountains.

"Joshua, I have some news related to your dad. Would you like to talk in my home office or here?"

Joshua looked like a startled animal. His eyes darted from Chad to Carla to Bella. Bella had previously thought she would step off the porch and let Chad talk with Joshua, but now she could see she needed to stay. *If Joshua wants me to stay.*

"They can stay, right, Chad?"

"Yes, that is entirely up to you... and them." Chad spoke slowly and carefully.

"Will you stay?" Joshua looked first to Carla and she nodded. He turned to Bella.

"Yes, Joshua, whatever you want."

"Then get it over with, Chad, please." Joshua's voice suggested he was resigned to whatever was coming.

Chad knew the best thing was to just say it. "Joshua, we arrested two young men who went to the Valley Store to buy juice and cigarettes. They committed what is known as a crime of opportunity. The evidence suggests that Joe died as a result of their crime."

Joshua sat without saying a word.

Bella looked at Chad and gave him a slight nod. She wanted to tell him he had been as humane as possible.

"They didn't go there to rob us?"

"No, Joshua, it doesn't look that way."

"What did they want?"

"Apparently they were at the counter and one of the young men decided he could just take a couple of cigarette cartons without paying for them."

"Did my dad try to stop him?"

"Yes, according to one of the young men."

"Did you have to do an autopsy on my dad?"

"Yes, by law we did. We had to know if the action of the crime contributed to his death. The medical examiner has ruled that it was the cause of death."

"I figured you had to do an autopsy because no one told me my dad's remains had been taken to the funeral home." His sad eyes looked around the table. "Thanks for not telling me."

The only sound was the call of an eastern towhee in the distance. "Drink-your-tea. Drink-your-tea."

"He should be at the funeral home in Round City by now, Joshua. I told Director Davis that I expected we would get you over there tomorrow."

"Tomorrow will be soon enough." Joshua did not wipe away the tears on his cheeks. He turned to Carla. "Could you take me home now? I want to go home. I need to talk to Pastor Fisk."

Carla stood, keeping hold of his hand.

He turned to Bella. "Would you call the pastor and ask him to come to my house?"

"Sure, Joshua. Do you want someone with you?" Bella asked. She hoped he would say Carla.

"Carla, can you stay for a little while? I know I've taken you away from work but if you could stay a little longer?"

"Whatever you need or want, Joshua."

Chad spoke up. "Joshua, any one of us, or all of us, will do whatever you need us to do. I have things covered at work so I can help however you need. If you'll allow me, I'd like to make a couple of suggestions."

Joshua looked at him and waited.

"I believe things are okay at your dad's house, but if you're okay with it, Bella and I can go by and just be sure."

Joshua nodded. "Thanks, Chad.

"Tomorrow morning, Bella and I could pick you and Carla up, if she can join us, and the four of us could ride to Round City. You can meet with the funeral director then we can have lunch. What do you think?"

Joshua nodded his head. "Might do us all good to get out of the valley."

The women nodded in agreement.

"Okay. I'll call Director Davis and set a time with him and let you know when we'll pick you up. The last thing for now is I suggest you close the store—at least tomorrow. Then you can decide what you want to do once you have made the final arrangements."

"Sure, sure. Doesn't matter now anyway. Dad's gone." Joshua struggled to hold back his tears, and the others knew he was talking through his grief.

Carla stood. "Come on, Joshua, I'll take you home." She hugged Bella and Chad and started for the front door. Joshua was right behind her. He watched her feet like he needed to follow in her footsteps—two people caught in a blizzard of emotions.

Bella waited until she heard Chad close the front door. She picked up her phone and called Pastor Fisk to explain the situation while Chad called the funeral home to set a time. He was putting the dishes in the dishwasher when she walked back into the kitchen.

"Pastor Fisk will go to Joshua's."

"Good. Things are set with Director Davis for ten tomorrow."

"Sounds good. Now, if you have some containers, let's freeze what we can of this food. I don't know about you, but I just can't eat any more of it for a while."

"Couldn't agree more. Bottom cabinet closest to the fridge has plenty of containers. Portion it out however you see fit." He paused, then turned to look at her. "Bella, thanks."

"Chad, seriously? For putting away food?"

He turned off the water from rinsing the dishes. "Bella."

She stopped putting the food in containers and turned to look at him.

"Thanks for being you. For being here with me and for your really good advice."

She walked over to the sink. She pulled him into an embrace. He did not resist.

She looked up at him. "Chad, I think the words you used were 'I could get used to this.'"

He nodded.

She smiled lovingly at him. "I could, too. But I'm also afraid."

"Afraid of what?" He leaned back from the hug and looked at her.

"Afraid that things are happening so fast, with so much emotion swirling around us that you might wake up one day soon and wonder why you thought you wanted to be with me."

"Then we're both on the same train. I'm totally aware of the heightened emotions at the moment, our own and dealing with the loss of Joe. I'm afraid you'll wake up one day and wonder why on earth you would be interested in me, especially with the job I have."

They were still holding each other.

She gave him a tight hug. "Maybe we could agree to give ourselves time to get through all that's happening right now?"

He nodded.

"I promise, I'll try not to scare you off." Her smile was infectious.

"It's a deal. And, just so you know, I've asked Sergeant White-horse to take lead for a few days so I can be here for Joshua, and for you."

"Good man. Let's finish this up and go check on Joe's house then close up the Valley Store and put a sign on it."

"Great, I can print something out from my computer if you'll tell me what to say. But we'll need to swing by Joshua's and get the key to lock up the store."

Bella reached into her pocket and pulled out a key. She showed it to him. "Carla slipped it into my hand before she left."

"Nothing gets by you gals, does it?"

"Not much, and don't you forget it."

Chapter 13

The End of a Difficult Day

Pastor Fisk arrived at Joshua's home soon after Joshua and Carla had returned. He knocked on the front door and let himself in. "Hey, Joshua, it's Albert." He was almost to the back porch as Joshua and Carla met him in the dining room.

"We're having some tea, Pastor, may I get you something to drink?"

"Tea would be great, Carla, thanks. Lovely evening, isn't it? Don't know when the fall colors have been so glorious." He accepted the glass of tea. "Thanks, Carla."

They walked out to the porch, and Joshua pointed to a rocking chair. "Have a seat." The two men stood until Carla was seated.

"Pastor...Albert, I need to know what information to give the director at the funeral home." Joshua let out a big sigh. "They sent my dad over to Round City today. I'm going to the funeral home tomorrow." He stopped for a second. "Guess you know, or figured out, they had to do an autopsy. Seems the boys who robbed us caused his death." Joshua's voice was so low it was hard to hear him clearly.

"Joshua, I don't know if this will help in any way, but you had a long time to prepare for Jan's passing. The loss of your dad was very sudden and in the most tragic way we can imagine, at the hands of another human being. So, I suspect it's hard to sort out your feelings about the loss of the two most significant people in your life." The pastor saw that Joshua was holding Carla's hand. He made no judgment.

"I don't know what to think or feel, Albert. Part of me wants to crawl in a hole and pull the dirt in over me. Part of me wants to jerk up those kids and shake them from here to kingdom come. Then I think, 'What's the point?' Nothing will bring my dad back."

Joshua rocked in silence for several minutes. Carla and Pastor Fisk followed his lead, letting him gather his thoughts.

"Chad told me that these boys didn't go to the store to rob us. They just took advantage of an old man there by himself. A 'crime of opportunity' he called it. If I'd come in earlier from my propane deliveries, it wouldn't have happened. I even called him before I did the last run, and Dad told me he was sending Melody home. Imagine, she could have been hurt or killed, too." His breathing was shallow and his words strained. "And maybe these boys are not such bad people and wouldn't have done anything if someone else had just been in the store."

Pastor Fisk waited a few seconds to see if Joshua was going to say anything else. "Joshua, that's one of the most charitable things a human being can say in these circumstances. You're willing to consider forgiving these young men. Far too many people focus on laying blame and carrying hate." He paused. "I'm confident your faith will lead you in the right path to come to grips with this terrible loss."

Carla had been listening to the conversation without speaking, and both men looked at her when she spoke up. "Pastor Fisk, I know it was before you came to our area, but my parents were killed by a flatlander driving too fast on one of our switchbacks out on the highway. I carried so much hate in my heart for way too many years.

I finally learned my hate was not going to bring back my parents or punish the driver any more than he was already being punished. When I was growing up and didn't understand why some people did mean things, my daddy used to say, 'His actions are to be judged by God and the law, not you and God.' I finally learned to believe that. I'm humbled by Joshua's ability to even consider forgiving them at this point. I know how hard it can be."

Joshua gripped Carla's hand tightly. "Carla, I never thought about how hard it was for you to lose your parents like that, and so young. Guess I just knew it had to be difficult. But I didn't think about what you were going through. It makes me think even more about how lucky I am to have you as a friend."

Pastor Fisk nodded.

"Have you made any decisions about who you want at the church service? Your dad had told me he would like Nora to sing. I've spoken with her, and she said she'd be honored."

"That's mighty fine of her. She has a lovely voice. Albert, do most people plan ahead like my dad?"

"No, Joshua, most of us know the end of our lives are inevitable, but most folks don't make decisions that would help out when it's their time."

Joshua nodded his head. He knew he had planned for Jan because her illness was over a long period of time, and it became evident the end was near. But he had no plans for himself. "I've been thinking about it, and I appreciate Dad thinking about me and knowing I wouldn't want a crowd. There are people who I think he would want there, if they want to be. As I said yesterday, Carla, James, Bella. Chad, Harold and Julie. Also, Melody meant the world to Dad. I'd also like Doug, Doc Fred, and our church pianist. Dad loved to hear her play." He took a breath. "Carla, do you think it would be all right if I ask Nora and the pastor to say a few words at the jamboree on Friday night to give others a chance to remember him?"

Carla did not hesitate. "Joshua, I think all of us would like to celebrate the life of a man who lived in these hills for, what, eighty-five years? He was always kind to everyone, and folks know that. I think that's a great plan."

"Then I think we're set, Pastor, unless you need something more from me."

Albert shook his head. "If you'll allow me, I'll say a prayer and leave you to your evening."

"A prayer is welcome, thanks."

The three of them bowed their heads, and Joshua rocked slowly as the pastor asked a blessing on all of them. In unison, they said, "Amen." Pastor Fisk rose and shook hands with Carla and Joshua. "I'll show myself out. Just give me a call after you talk to Director Davis, and then we'll finalize a time."

Joshua stood and walked him to the door. "Thanks, Albert. For everything."

Carla was standing in the dining room when he returned. "What can I do for you, Joshua?"

He walked up to her and took her in his arms. "Just hold me, Carla. Just hold me."

Carla held him close. *If you only knew, Joshua. If only you knew. I'd hold you forever.*

Wrapping Up the Day

Chad had a blank document open on his computer and turned to look at Bella. "What should I put on the sign for the door of the Valley Store?"

Bella thought for a moment. "Closed Tuesday: Family Emergency." She shook her head. "No, wait. It's not an emergency. Besides, I suspect the word about Joe's death will start to spread pretty quickly now. How about, 'Closed Tuesday: Sorry for the Inconvenience.' Then once we know more tomorrow, we can put up a more detailed sign if Joshua wants us to."

Chad nodded. He typed the document in letters large enough to be read from the bottom of the steps leading to the store's entrance, then printed it out and grabbed some tape from a drawer. "Okay, let's go do this."

Bella locked the front door while the sign was printing and walked in the kitchen as Chad was putting on his service weapon. She stopped and stepped back a few steps. She felt like she was intruding, like she had walked in on someone dressing.

Chad turned and saw her. "Are you okay?" He saw the look of confusion on her face.

She nodded and gave a slight smile.

Then it dawned on him. "Sorry, putting on my weapon is so much a part of leaving home that I didn't think about it. I don't have to wear it off-duty; I just do. Would you rather I didn't?"

"No. No, I'm fine, I just never thought about how easily, and I guess how routinely, you put on your weapon. I felt like I was intruding." Bella tried to make light of the moment.

He walked over to her. "I'll work on being more aware, okay? If you don't have a problem with it right now, I'd prefer to have it when we go to check Joe's house. I don't expect any issues, but it's hard to know how fast word has spread about Joe's passing." He stopped and looked at her. "Of course, I could send a deputy. Why don't I do that?"

"Chad, stop, please. You told Joshua we'd go check on Joe's house, and that's what we're going to do. Will you hand me my vest from the hook by the door, please?"

He handed it to her, opened the kitchen door, and stood waiting for her to walk out.

She stopped and kissed him. "I'll get used to it."

He hugged her and returned the kiss. "I look forward to getting used to that kiss. *You* are an amazing woman, Dr. Bella Anderson."

After she walked out, he reached around the doorframe to hit the button that opened the garage door. Once he slipped on his boots and jumped in the SUV, he saw she was standing on the driveway, waiting for him to drive out. When he got to where she was standing, he reached across the seat to open the door, but she beat him to it. She smiled and winked at him.

"Let's go to the Valley Store first. Doug and Melody have been there for a long time and there's no reason not to close up now. It's almost six o'clock."

"Good plan. It completely slipped my mind that they've been there since early morning and alone since Joshua and Carla left."

"I suspect they would stay 'til midnight for Joshua... and Joe." There was only one car in the parking lot when they arrived, and the person they assumed was the lone customer was exiting as they approached the front door.

"Evening, Sheriff. Ma'am."

"Evening, Walter. Give my regards to your missus." Chad hoped he hadn't been pestering Doug and Melody.

"Will do. Y'all have a nice evening too." Walter kept walking.

Once he heard the car door close, Chad turned to Bella. "Might be the fewest words Walter's said in years." Bella already knew Walter was viewed as the town gossip, and

they both laughed as they walked in.

"Evening, Sheriff, Dr. Anderson." Melody smiled at them. "Doug just stepped to the back."

"Been busy?" Chad looked around.

"Steady, but not too busy. Seems strange that no one is asking about Mr. Joe. Of course, I'm glad because I wouldn't know what to say."

Bella gave her a warm smile. "Melody, I have no doubt you would find the right words." She heard Chad click the lock on the front door. "We've come over to close up and let you know that the store won't be open tomorrow."

"Oh?" Doug had come from the back. "Joshua doin' okay?"

"Hey, Doug."

Chad extended his hand to shake with Doug. "We're taking Joshua to the funeral home in Round City tomorrow to finalize arrangements, so he asked us to close up and put a sign on the door. No words to express appreciation for the two of you holding the fort today. I know it means a lot to Joshua."

"Wouldn't have it any other way." The look in Doug's eyes showed a lifetime of friendship with the Johnsons.

"Me either." Melody tried to smile but her eyes brimmed with tears.

Bella saw the tears forming in Melody's eyes and walked over to her. She extended both of her hands to take Melody's. She wanted to hug her but didn't know how Melody would feel about that. Melody took Bella's hands.

"Dr. Anderson. . ."

"Call me Bella, please."

"Oh, okay, Miss Bella. I loved Mr. Joe. He was always so good to me and always, always encouraged me to do my best. I will miss him more than I can say."

"I know, Melody. And I have no doubt he loved you too. He bragged on you all the time. He was so proud of you for remaining at the top of your class. I know you'll continue to do well. I think he'll know that."

Chad stood mesmerized. *Does she always know the right thing to say?*

Doug stepped over to Chad. "What should we do with the cash drawers? We don't have the combination to the safe."

"Hmmm. . . guess we didn't think of that." Chad saw that Doug had the cash drawer out and the lid on it was closed. "Looks like they will stay secure." Melody ran out the tape on her cash register, folded it, and put in the cash drawer. Chad watched her. "Does that show the sales for today?"

"Yes, sir. The paper is just a back-up to the computer. We start with two-hundred dollars, and we put cash and any credit card receipts in the drawer. If we gave change right, the credit card receipts and cash should match the total sales, plus two-hundred dollars." She said it with the proficiency of a business owner.

Chad nodded. "Well, then I'm guessing you're both pretty good at making change. So, we'll take the drawers with us and drop them off to Joshua. Just to keep me honest, how about I sign a piece of paper and all three of you witness that I'm taking the cash drawers? That way, if there's anything off, I'm the one responsible." He grinned.

As he was talking, Bella had slipped up to the loft office to make sure everything was secure. She picked up a pad of paper and a pen and took them downstairs with her. Chad wrote a note that he was taking the cash drawers and signed it; all three signed as witnesses.

Doug laughed, "Now, ain't that a sight? Us witnessing the sheriff taking money from the Valley Store. If we can't trust the sheriff, ain't much sense in trusting anyone in these parts, is there?"

Chad reached out and shook Doug's hand. "Just trying to do the right thing in a tough situation, Doug." He stepped back. "Anything special I need to do to lock up?"

"Sheriff, I can show you the back doors, and we can make sure they're locked. I think Mr. Joshua locked them before he left this afternoon. Also, most of the lights turn off in the back, then we can do the one by the door when we go out."

Melody and Chad walked to the back, and Bella taped the sign to the inside of the door. After they returned to the registers, Chad picked up the cash drawers and all of them walked out, with Bella bringing up the rear to lock the door.

"Doug, Melody, can we give you a ride home?" Bella offered.

"By all means!" Chad said. He opened the back door of his SUV and gestured for them to take a seat.

Melody and Doug looked at each other. Each of them was used to walking home from the store.

Doug laughed. "That would be a hoot; me being taken home by the sheriff. Give me something to talk about at darts Saturday night."

He looked at Chad. "I promise, I won't make it too big of a story." He let out a big guffaw.

Melody shook her head. "Thanks all the same. I think I'll walk. The evening air feels pretty good, and I'd like to clear my head before I get home. I have some studying to do tonight. Thanks again. Night, Miss Bella, Mr. Doug, Sheriff." She walked off towards her home.

Doug only lived a few blocks from the store, so they dropped him off first, then Chad purposely turned on a street he knew would pass Melody's home on their way to check on Joe's house. The evening light was fading fast, and he wanted to make sure she was okay. She was walking to her front door as they passed. He honked. She turned and waved.

"Thanks for doing that." Bella put her hand on his arm.

"Thanks for thinking of it. I'm becoming all too aware of how engrossed I've gotten in my work. I've forgotten all the manners I ever had." They pulled up at Joe's.

"If you'll wait here, I'll just go around back and check on things. The front looks normal, but I'll double check." He got out and walked towards the back of Joe's house.

I don't think you've forgotten as many of your manners as you might think you have, Chad Oliver. Seems pretty thoughtful to me that you're checking on Joe's house, taking care to give Joshua the support he needs, and giving me lots of attention—something I've missed for years.

Chad gave her the okay sign as he walked towards the front door. She watched him open the screen, try to turn the front doorknob, then walk towards the front window to make sure it was closed. Chad opened the door to the SUV and got in.

"All secure. Let's drop these cash drawers off at Joshua's and head home. Work for you?"

"Sounds great."

Joshua didn't live far from his dad. "Oh, Carla's car isn't here. It does look like there's a light on in the house, though."

"I'll just take these up and check." Chad took the two cash drawers from the back seat and walked up to the front door. He knocked, and Joshua opened the door. Chad handed him the cash drawers and they spoke for a minute before he bounded back to the SUV.

"He seemed a bit upset that he forgot about the cash drawers, but I told him what we did and the note is in one of the drawers. That actually made him laugh. He sounded just like Doug, telling me that if he had to worry about the sheriff, there was no hope. Guess I'm glad to know folks feel that way."

Bella reached over and squeezed his arm. "And rightly so."

A few minutes later they were walking into the kitchen at Chad's house. He tied to distract her as he put away his service weapon. "Looks like the sun has gone down on this day. You must be starving."

"Not starving, but maybe we can figure out something. How do you feel about French toast?"

"I love French toast, but I don't think I have any syrup." He realized, once again, he would have to do better about having food in the house.

"Who needs syrup? You have blackberry preserves!" Bella's enthusiasm was contagious.

"That I do, and I have some ham steak too. I love breakfast food for supper. Let's do it."

The sky was cloudy and the moon barely visible behind it as they finished eating on the porch. They fixed the food together and ate it with small exchanges about the day and their mutual like of certain foods.

"I forgot to tell you I sent Joshua a text letting him know we'd need to leave his house at nine fifteen. Carla will meet us at Joshua's."

"Sounds like a plan. If I'm not appearing ungrateful, may I ask that we clean up these dishes? Then I'd like to take a shower and call it a day."

"I hope you can always tell me what you need, or want, and not feel you have to apologize for it. In spite of the reason for our time together today, I have thoroughly enjoyed having a whole day with you. I'll clean up the dishes. You go take care of Bella—for me." He leaned over and kissed her. "Now, go." There was a playfulness in his words.

Bella took a long shower and towel dried her hair. She couldn't believe it was only eight thirty, but she was tired. She plugged in her phone and set the alarm for seven o'clock so she didn't oversleep in the morning. She looked at her clothes in the closet and decided on a pair of gray corduroy slacks, a flowered cotton blouse, and her gray cardigan. She didn't bring any jewelry except the necklace Matt gave her for their twenty-fifth anniversary. She planned to wear that to the funeral, so she would not wear it tomorrow. *The earrings I've been wearing the last two days will just have to do.*

Satisfied she was ready for the morning, Bella climbed into bed. She was trying to think of what might be on her Not-So-Good List tonight. Sadness, she decided, covered most of the things that happened today. Sadness for Joshua and the loss of Joe's life, and the end of Joshua's family. Sadness that she knew that feeling of grief all too well. Sadness for the people in the community who knew and loved Joe. Sadness that two boys' lives were forever changed because they contributed to the death of another person. She lay in silence. She had nothing more for the list.

Bella's Good List was simple tonight. She didn't usually find one word to cover the things on her lists, but, somehow, friendship came to mind tonight. Friendship, and maybe more, if what she was feeling for Chad was any indication. She was grateful she was developing a friendship with Carla and pleased that Carla's friendship with Joshua might be blossoming too. She had thought about Matt today and felt like he had sent her a sign about having someone new in her life. She had been able to talk to Chad about different things and enjoyed the opportunity. She had missed those conversations since Matt died.

She closed her eyes tightly, opened them, and settled into the quiet. Sleep came quickly. It had been a long day.

Chad finished up the dishes and took a quick shower before heading to bed. He bent his arms, grasped his hands, and placed the back of his hands against his eyes. He often went to sleep like this, recapping his day. Tonight, he simply sighed and whispered to the room, "Thank you, Bella Anderson. Thank you for coming into my life. We will get Joshua through this. Sweet dreams."

Chapter 14

*Everybody needs beauty as well as bread, places to play in and pray in,
where Nature may heal and cheer and give strength to body
and soul alike.*

John Muir, 1838 – 1914

Early Morning Call

It was seven a.m. and Billy was already halfway through his first cup of coffee. He was in the middle of reviewing his case notes when his desk phone rang. "Williams here."

"Morning." He was pleased to hear from the DA. "Glad you're in. Grand jury is convening at eight. I'm taking the Steve Phillips case, and I'm asking for an indictment for criminally negligent homicide in the overdose death of Nick Brown. I think it's too soon after Mr. Johnson's death to take the case against the Kirk boys. Most people don't even know that Joe's gone yet. On the one hand, that's a prosecutor's dream: uncontaminated grand jury panel. But that man was too beloved in this community to expect fairness with them just finding out in the jury box."

"I hear you. So, what are you thinking?"

"I'd like you to take one more run at interrogating Bobby Kirk. Now that we know the ME's ruling, offer him another chance to lawyer up and see if we can get him to admit he pushed him hard enough to slam his head. Maybe he'll own up to it."

"He exercised his right to a phone call on Sunday. Called his mother collect, but she didn't accept the charges. No one has shown up at the station looking for him or Jason. Given they're cousins, I have to assume Jason's folks know about the attempted phone call."

"Maybe you should talk to Jason again too. Can you make that happen?"

"On it. Let me see if I can get Deputy Thomas. She's invaluable in our good cop/bad cop routine."

"I've listened to the tapes and seen the video multiple times. I'd say she's indispensable. Thanks, Billy. Talk to you soon."

"Pleasure to be of service, ma'am. Good luck with the grand jury."

He dialed Susan Thomas' mobile phone. She answered on the first ring and told him she was almost at the station; she would meet him in holding in fifteen minutes. Billy called the matron and asked her to get Jason Kirk ready, and then he would let her know how he wanted to handle Bobby. At the moment, he was thinking it might be helpful to have the two boys pass in the hall, but he wanted to talk to Susan first and get her thoughts on the strategy.

"Morning, Detective." Susan entered the holding area.

"Morning, Deputy." Billy motioned her over to the small room off the matron's desk.

"What's going on today?"

"The Kirk boys. ME officially ruled the CD on Joe Johnson. It was directly caused by having his head 'slammed' against the counter." Billy paused. "The ME was *very* specific on the use of the word 'slammed.'"

She nodded in understanding.

"So, let's see if we can get him to own it. We'll need to push him on wanting or denying a lawyer so it's as clean as we can make it."

"Got it." Her eyes were alert and her voice serious.

"I'm thinking we talk to Jason one more time, make sure he doesn't change his story. No evidence he was behind or on the counter. DA might cut him a deal if he corroborates." He waited to see if she would say anything. "One more thing. I wanted your take on having the matron bring Bobby down when we're finished with Jason and have you walk Jason back so they pass in the hall. What do you think?"

"Detective, I'm more than willing to do it." She paused. "I think the abuse these boys appear to have experienced, I assume from their fathers, might make it more useful if you walked Jason back. I could even stand outside the interrogation room with Bobby and say we have to wait for you to get back. You know, act like I'm afraid of you."

"Well, aren't you?" Billy scowled with a twinkle in his eyes.

"Sorry to disappoint you, Detective, but my husband has you by six inches in height and at least forty pounds, and I'm not even afraid of *him*." She had a big smile on her face. "Nothing personal, you understand?"

"No offense, *Deputy* Thomas!"

"None taken."

The tension broke away with the banter. Billy gave her a sad smile. *Joe. Joe is gone.* "Okay, I like your idea better. Let's do this thing." They stepped out to the matron's desk; she had Jason Kirk ready to go. They walked him to Room 2.

Billy and Susan followed Jason into the room, and Susan put the recorder on the table. Billy nodded to her to unlock Jason's hand-cuffs, then he stood against the wall with one foot propped on the wall—he was here for a fireside chat.

"This is Deputy Thomas and . . ."

"Detective Williams, with . . ." They both looked at Jason.

"Jason Kirk." He gave his date of birth.

"Morning, Jason, you're still under the Miranda warning we gave you on Sunday, but I'm going to repeat it so you're clear about your rights."

"No need. I know my rights. I don't want no lawyer. I done told you that." He looked at her with respect.

"And, Jason, just for the record, you know that if you cannot afford a lawyer, one will be provided for you. Do you understand that?"

"Yes, ma'am, still don't want no lawyer."

"Okay then. We just need to ask a few questions about Saturday night, and then I think we can wrap this up. So," she dragged out the word, "I want you to think about what happened when you went to the Valley Store. Can you do that for me?" She sounded like a teacher asking a favorite student to do her a favor.

"Yes, ma'am."

"Now, tell us one more time what happened when you got to the checkout counter to pay for the juice and get Bobby's cigarettes."

Jason started shaking, but his pupils were not dilated. Susan made a mental note to check whether the physician had seen him and approved his medication.

"Please!" Jason pleaded sorrowfully. "Bobby will kill me if he finds out I talked to you."

"Right now, you *need* to talk to me!"

The chain on his ankles began to rattle as he tapped his heels against the floor, but Jason started talking. He told exactly the same story he had told them before. His story was so perfectly identical that Billy wondered if the kid had seen the video recording. He nodded to Susan to continue.

"Thanks, Jason. Now Jason, do you know the difference in pushing someone out of the way and shoving them?"

Jason looked at her. "Yeah, pushing is like bumping into somebody in the hall at school. You don't mean to run into them, but you do and it pushes them against the wall. Shoving somebody means you push them real hard to get them out of your way."

Billy stood up, moved a chair to the center of the room, and sat in his customary position: back of chair forward and straddling the seat. He barely made a sound, but Jason glanced over at him.

Billy's voice was without emotion and no different than asking someone the time of day. "Very good, Jason. That's exactly right. So, now we need you to tell us... did Bobby push Mr. Joe, or did he shove him?"

"He shoved him. It was *real* hard. I've done been thinking about it, and I shoulda tried to stop him, but it happened too dang fast. Is Mr. Joe all right? He's a nice man."

Both the detective and deputy looked from the boy to each other. Billy could see that Susan was doing all she could not to offer sympathy to this boy. Billy was struggling himself. A stupid decision made by one boy messed up the other one for a lifetime—and cost a man his life.

"Jason," Deputy Thomas looked directly at him, and when she spoke her voice was calm, controlled. Billy had nodded to her, and she knew it meant she could tell the boy. "Mr. Joe Johnson did not survive. He died shortly after reaching the hospital."

Jason dropped his face onto his hands and wept. Billy looked at him. *For whatever learning problems this boy has, he's not stupid—nor is he a killer. He was in the wrong place at the wrong time—with the wrong person. This sucks.*

Deputy Thomas wondered if they should still have the boys pass in the hall. She knew that Bobby, for sure, would likely go away for six years. Even if he didn't confess to it as a shove, he had already admitted to pushing Mr. Joe. This recording would convince a jury that what Bobby called a push, and Jason called a shove, ended up the same way. But she knew how it played out was up to the DA, not her.

Billy stood up and walked to the door, "This is Detective Williams exiting room 2 at seven forty a.m." Susan watched him walk out. Jason continued to sob.

Billy took out his phone to call the matron; he told her to take Bobby to Room 1. He stepped back into Room 2 and logged onto the recording. "Jason, Deputy Thomas is going to take you back to the matron who will take you to your cell." Jason did not lift his head. Billy held up four fingers to Susan and mouthed, "Wait four minutes."

Susan nodded and breathed a sigh of relief. She was grateful that Billy was a decent guy. Nothing to be gained by putting this boy through any more than he was already putting himself through.

Billy knew it was a gamble either way to have Bobby see Jason, so he decided the better part of wisdom was to get Bobby to own up to it on his own. As the matron and Bobby walked towards him, Billy put on his sternest face and stared at Bobby. He hoped it sent a "don't mess with me" message.

The matron opened the door to Room 1 and Bobby walked in. Billy didn't need to have the deputy to interrogate this boy, but he wanted her to be part of it, so he watched Bobby sit down. Then he fiddled around taking his keys out of his pocket like he didn't know if he had a recorder on him. He knew the matron would wait and take Jason, so Susan would enter any minute. He heard a tap on the door just before the deputy walked in. He pulled the recorder out of his pocket and handed it to her when she came through the door.

"Use mine this time. I don't like the number of times your recorder messed up the last time we talked to this young man." Yet again he hated how he had to play the bad guy *to* Susan. He didn't mind being bad cop to a suspect, but not to her.

"Testing, testing." Susan played it back. "It seems to be working, Detective."

"Then let's get on with it."

"This is Deputy Thomas and..."

"Detective Williams, with... *with...* say your name and date of birth, *boy*." His emphasis on "with" and "boy" left no question who was in control, and Susan cast her eyes to the floor.

"Bobby Kirk." There was a slight tremble in his voice. He gave his date of birth.

Billy knew Bobby had not been in jail before, so he was hoping that he had found out it wasn't a great place to sleep, never mind a place to rest.

"Detective, would you like me to read Bobby his Miranda..."

Billy interrupted her. "Think I don't know it by heart, Detective?"

"Sorry, sir. Just trying to be helpful."

"Fine, then be useful. Read him his rights."

"Bobby Kirk, you have the right to..." When she finished, she looked at Bobby. "Do you understand these rights?"

"Yes, ma'am."

"Do you wish to have an attorney present?" Susan looked directly at him.

"I done told you I can't afford no attorney, and I don't want y'all giving me one. Just ask me what you gotta ask me."

"Since my recorder didn't work very well, I want you to tell us what you did all day on Saturday, three days ago."

Bobby recounted the same story about taking his dad's ATV and going for a ride with his cousin Jason. They then went to the Valley Store to get juice and cigarettes. He reiterated that Jason took money from the cash drawer.

"Now, just to be clear, Bobby ..." Susan's voice was soothing, motherly, "why was the cash drawer open?"

"'Cause Mr. Joe fell on the floor behind the counter."

"Did Jason go behind the counter?"

Billy stared at Bobby without saying a word while Susan asked the questions.

"Nah, I told you before, I did. I just wanted some extra cigarettes and that ole man had plenty. Besides, he has lots of money."

"And what happened when you went behind the counter?"

"He tried to stop me, and I pushed him outta the way." Bobby had no inflection in his voice.

"Do you know the difference in pushing someone and shoving them? Between shoving someone, and shoving them *against* something?" Susan knew she was on thin ice, but she deliberately didn't use the word "slammed" from the ME's report.

"Yeah. Why?"

Billy slapped the back of the chair. He had pulled it up and sat down during the time Susan was talking to the boy, but Bobby had not even looked at him. The noise caused Bobby to jerk his head up.

"Did you hear her?" Billy dragged out every word—his face as hard as granite.

Bobby nodded his head quickly. "Yes, sir, I heard her. I know the difference."

"Then you tell her the difference, now!"

"Ma'am, if you push someone it's like an accident 'cause you didn't see them or something. Shoving is harder cause you want them out of your way." He didn't look at Billy.

"Thank you, Bobby, that's right. Now, did you push Mr. Joe, or did you shove him?"

Bobby took a couple of halting breaths. "I shoved him. I wanted him outta my way."

"Boy, speak up." Billy was as stern as he dared without sounding like he was being abusive.

Bobby's voice was now trembling. "I said I shoved him. I didn't mean for him to hit his head so hard. But he did."

Susan didn't miss a beat. "Did you call 9-1-1, Bobby?"

"No. I done told you before, we just hightailed it outta there." His earlier bravado had disappeared.

Billy stood up, knowing the camera was recording along with the audio recorder. "Bobby Kirk, you're under arrest for the murder of Mr. Joe Johnson. You have been read your Miranda rights; do you wish to hear them again?"

"No, sir," Bobby sputtered. "Did he die?"

"Yes, Mr. Joe Johnson died shortly after you shoved him into the counter. Do you wish to speak to an attorney?"

"No, sir." He deflated as quickly as a balloon pricked by a pin, and his voice was barely audible. "What's gonna happen to me?" Then he looked at Billy. "What's gonna happen to Jason? He didn't shove Mr. Joe, I done it. You can't say he done it. He didn't."

"The district attorney will speak with the judge, and a decision will be made on the next steps. You will be informed what will happen when the district attorney makes a decision. Do you understand that?"

"Yessir."

"This is Detective Williams and..."

"Deputy Thomas returning..." she looked at Bobby.

"Bobby Kirk."

She saw the tears in his eye. "To his cell at eight fifteen a.m."

The three exited the room.

Trip to Round City

It was eight thirty and Bella knew Chad was up. She had seen the light under the door to his home office and his bedroom door was open. The smell of coffee wafted towards her as she walked quietly down the hall. She had checked her email when she first woke up and there was nothing that needed her immediate attention. She made a cup of tea and sat down at the counter with her Louise Penny book, *The Kingdom of the Blind.* One look at the cover and she decided now might not be the best time to read about drugs and murder. She did not hear Chad walk in but sensed his presence.

"Good morning, lovely lady, reading a good book?" Chad looked at the cover.

"Good morning to you." Her smile reached her eyes when she looked up at him. "I decided *not* reading this particular book was the better part of wisdom this morning."

"May I?" He reached for the book. She handed it to him, and he read the inside cover. "Interesting, I didn't know you had a penchant for detective stories."

"Hmmm… not sure how you would know. Do I dare tell you I'm trying to write a mystery?" She had a sheepish grin on her face. "I've been working on it for several years."

"Glad you told me. Let me know if I can help." He winked at her. "I'm sure we'll talk more about this as time goes on. For now, what would you like to eat? We need to leave in about thirty minutes."

She stood up and walked to the fridge. "How about I fix you breakfast?"

"I'm a milk and cereal person, but I can fix you something else."

"Milk and cereal it is. You get the cereal; I'll get the milk." She opened the fridge.

They finished their breakfast and he looked at her. "I texted Joshua we'd be there closer to nine, hope that's okay. I realized this morning we really need to allow time for the leaf-lookers on the roads this time of year."

"Absolutely. Let's clean up these dishes, and I'll go brush my teeth. I just need to grab my phone and wallet. Did I tell you I hate carrying a purse?"

"You did not; so do I!" They both laughed. He pulled her into a hug. "How about a better way to start the day?" He leaned down and gave her a lingering kiss.

"Well, I'd say that was a great way to start the day. Thanks. Now, if you'll excuse me, I'll be back in a flash."

He could see the heat rising in her face. He smiled; he didn't want to be the only one affected by their kiss.

Joshua and Carla were sitting on his front porch when Chad and Bella arrived. Joshua had on gray slacks, an open neck white shirt, and a blue blazer. He was carrying a suit bag. Carla had on a deep purple dress with pale lavender flecks and black pumps. Bella thought they made a nice-looking couple. *I would love to see both of them happy.* She looked at Chad. The gray of his eyes was heightened against the dark blue pullover sweater and pale blue shirt he wore with dark blue corduroy slacks. She loved how easy it was to be with him and how much she was enjoying his company.

"Bella, it's not easy to know what to say. I would love it if the four of us were getting together to go on a double date. I think I see that in Joshua and Carla's future. But that is not what this day is about."

"Chad, just be yourself. You're a smart man and you read people really well. Let's just show Joshua our friendship, and the rest will take care of itself."

Joshua opened the back door and Carla climbed in.

Chad released the lock on the back of the SUV and got out to hang up the suit bag. He reached towards Joshua to take it.

"Carla and I went to Dad's house this morning to get his suit." Without anything further, Joshua handed the hanging bag to Chad.

The two men shook hands and Joshua continued around to get in the SUV.

"Glad you thought about the leaf-lookers, Chad. No reason we shouldn't be among them today; it's such a lovely morning. Won't be long before the leaves start to fall in large numbers."

Bella had her window down. "Is that too much breeze in the back?"

Carla tapped her on the shoulder. "Not for me. Thanks for asking."

"Good for me." Joshua could barely be heard.

Bella turned around and looked at Carla. "Listen. Do you hear the 'drink-you-tea' of the eastern towhee?"

They were all quiet and listening. Carla spoke first. "I don't think I ever realized that their call was 'drink-your-tea.' I love it." They drove on in silence, but Carla had her window down now too.

Chad looked in the rearview mirror when Carla gasped. "Look! There are two ospreys on that tree." She laughed. "Oops, I didn't think about the fact we were past it before you could see them."

"I'm just enjoying all the colors of the leaves. One of the nice things about delivering propane this time of year; you get to see the leaves up close and personal." Joshua's words sounded distant, almost detached. "Thanks for coming with me."

They rode for the next fifteen minutes in silence; each was lost in thought, watching the leaves pass by. As they pulled out onto the highway to go to Round City, Bella raised her window and Carla followed suit. Chad pulled into the parking lot of the funeral home at ten minutes before ten.

Chad turned and looked at Joshua. "Want any of us to go in with you? We can wait here or on the porch if you prefer."

Joshua looked surprised. "I just expected y'all would go in too. It'd be a help to have y'all with me; I just did all this by myself for Jan."

As they walked to the entrance, Joshua reached for Carla's hand as she walked up beside him. Chad and Bella walked behind them side by side but not holding hands. Chad and Bella looked at each other and exchanged smiles.

"Mr. Johnson, Ms. Long, Sheriff Oliver, and you must be Dr. Anderson." Director Davis greeted them as they walked in, shaking hands with each one. A hand seemed to appear from nowhere and take the suit bag Chad had retrieved from the back of the SUV.

"Right this way." The director pointed towards a room where the double French doors were opened to reveal a small conference table and a cluster of armchairs upholstered in a soft shade of blue. The room itself was painted a pale, calming yellow. He introduced the woman in the room as Sue Martin, one of his co-directors.

"Anyone care for something to drink?" They all declined. "Have a seat, please, wherever you're comfortable." Joshua headed for an armchair. The others followed.

"I'm truly sorry for your loss, Joshua. Just no easy way to say it." The director sounded sincere in his comments, even for someone who had to say it many times in his job.

"Thanks, Dan. Nope, no easy way. If it's okay with you, I'd like to discuss arrangements for my dad and his burial. You know he already has a plot next to my mother."

"Yes, Joshua, he does. I don't know if you recall, but he also made complete arrangements for himself at the time your mother passed."

Joshua sat stone faced. "I didn't remember, but I'm not surprised."

"Everything is taken care of as he prepaid his expenses. If you want to make any changes, you can just let me know."

"No! I would never change what my dad wanted." His volume lessened as he finished the sentence. "Sorry, I didn't mean to sound harsh. It's just a lot to process right now."

"Sure, Joshua, I understand. All I need is your signature accepting his plan, and then to get details on the day and time of the service and burial. Your dad provided information for the obituary, and I have a draft here to share with you. You may add or delete anything you wish. We'll also need to know which papers you want it in. With your permission, we'll also publish it on our website. It seems today more people look at the website than read the papers."

Joshua extended his hand for the folder the director was holding. He started to read the draft obituary and a tear rolled down his face. He handed it across to Bella. "Would you read it, please? You were the English professor. Dad loved that you were a professor and so good with words."

Bella took the paper and wondered if she could manage to read it without crying herself.

"Joshua, I think this is lovely. It has the simplicity that I think your dad cherished about being a mountain man, and the depth of love he had for you, your mother, Jan, and the community in our hills." She paused for a moment.

"Thanks, Bella. Anything I need to add?"

"I believe you might want to put something like, 'There will be a private funeral and burial.'"

"Yes, please. Dan, I want that in there."

Bella looked at him. "Do you want to add that there will be a celebration of his life during the jamboree on Friday night at The Corral?"

Joshua was nodding his head. "Yes, that too, please."

"Absolutely, whatever you wish. Do you have a time for the service and burial?"

"No, could you just arrange it with Pastor Fisk and let me know?"

"Certainly, we can try to reach him now." He nodded to Ms. Martin, who left the room.

They sat in silence for several minutes. Bella looked around at each person. *Isn't it strange how the usual rituals—small talk and chats about the weather—disappear when dealing with death? It was the same when Matt died; no one seemed to know what to say.*

Ms. Martin returned, interrupting Bella's thoughts by handing her a piece of paper. She also gave a note to Dan; he glanced over it then turned his attention back to the group.

"Joshua, Pastor Fisk has spoken with Ms. Oliver-Smith and the pianist, and both can be available at four o'clock tomorrow or nine on Thursday morning. We can do either of those times. Which would you prefer?"

Joshua did not hesitate. "Tomorrow at four. Dad wouldn't want Melody to miss school."

"Dr. Anderson has the revised obituary; does it reflect what you wanted?"

"Joshua, would you like to read it, or have me read it aloud?"

"Read it aloud, please, Bella. Let's see what Carla and Chad think."

When she finished, Joshua looked at Carla. "What do you think?"

Carla had a comforting smile on her face. "It's a nice remembrance."

Chad nodded. "I agree."

"Please be sure it's placed in *The Tuesday Tattler*. If you'll tell me where to sign, Director Davis, we'll be on our way."

Bella winced, remembering that she hadn't known Joshua's wife had passed away because she quit reading the obituaries in *The Tuesday Tattler* after Matt died. *I wonder what else I might have missed by trying to avoid my own loss.*

After completing the paperwork, Joshua headed straight for the door. The others expressed their thanks and shook hands with Director Davis before following Joshua out. He was waiting at the bottom step of the porch.

"I'm buying lunch, you decide where." Joshua headed for Chad's SUV.

Chad looked at Carla and Bella.

Bella shrugged. "Don't ask me."

Carla laughed. "Okay, let's go to down to Main Street. I know a good place."

Chapter 15

Help May Not Be Enough

Susan Thomas was the senior deputy in the sheriff's department, so she was on call when additional support was needed. She had just returned from a short lunch in the break room when her mobile rang. She did not recognize the number.

"Please, come help Lottie, now. *Please.*" The woman's voice was a low whisper. The line went dead.

"Lottie? Lottie? Who is. . ." Deputy Thomas remembered that Lottie was Jason Kirk's mother. She called dispatch. "I'm on my way to the Kirk residence on Dickson Road. Send backup and alert an ambulance to be ready if I need them." She heard the dispatcher say, "10-4."

Within two minutes of receiving the call, Susan was out the back door and in her SUV. She flicked on her flashing lights and siren as she headed to the Kirk home, trying to figure out who called. She knew it wasn't Lottie herself, and she finally realized it had to be Mrs. Brown across the street. Susan let out a big sigh; she was relieved to know giving Lottie her card had paid off. Lottie gave it to Mrs. Brown: two abused women helping each other.

As she turned onto Dickson Road, she saw two deputies were already there. One deputy had his weapon drawn, and the other was positioned behind their vehicle with his weapon drawn. She turned off her siren but left her lights flashing.

Mr. Kirk was sitting in a chair under the tree with his wife on her knees in front of him. He had a handful of her hair and was pulling on it with his left hand. He had a baseball bat in his right hand.

"Sir," the deputy in the yard spoke calmly. "Put the bat down. Nobody needs to get hurt here."

"Ain't putting the damn bat down 'til this woman tells me where my boy is, or I beat it outta her." Mr. Kirk's voice was a bellow.

Deputy Thomas knew she should not intervene with a man who was abusive to his wife unless it was life and death. The presence of a female police officer would likely just irritate him. She said a silent prayer of gratitude for her short hair and the tinted windows on the SUV. The deputies knew she'd let them handle it, and more importantly they knew she'd back them up.

The deputy behind his SUV spoke up. "Hey, buddy, ain't no woman worth going to jail for, no matter how annoying they are. Right?"

"Might be worth it. 'bout time I taught her a lesson or two."

"This ain't the day, buddy. We'd have to do some police work that we really don't want to do. You get my meaning?"

Lottie Kirk was shrinking as close to the ground as she could and not have her husband pull the hair out of her head.

Deputy Thomas was trying to figure out if Lottie wanted to give the deputy room to aim his weapon and take out her husband. What Lottie couldn't know was that this particular deputy regularly won marksman competitions among law enforcement officers in the state. He was calculating which way the bat would fly if he hit the man in the hand.

"C'mon, buddy. Kirk, is it?" the second deputy continued. "Just throw that bat away from your woman there, and let's sort this out. Maybe we can help find your boy."

The bat was swaying slightly in Mr. Kirk's hand. Susan was afraid he would drop it given the angle at which his arm was canted, and then a bad situation could become exponentially worse.

"Y'all don't care 'bout my boy," Kirk yelled, his slurred speech indicating he already had too much beer in him.

"Kirk, listen up. I'll come over there and get your wife. If she did something wrong with your boy, I'll personally take her to jail and see that she gets locked up for a long time."

"Ha, she ain't done nothing *with* him. I ain't stupid. She just ain't tellin' me where he is. That's a damn sight worse. Lying to *me!* I ain't takin' that from her or no other woman. You got that?"

"I got it." The deputy tried to sound like he was just as hateful to women, but it was all he could do not to choke. "Need to know you want to end this, so let me see you put that bat down." The deputy walked out from behind the car and towards Mr. Kirk. Susan put her window down. Her weapon was ready, and she had her other hand on the door handle to jump out if needed.

In a flash, Kirk threw the bat over his head into the high grass behind him. He let Lottie's hair go and sneered at her. "Go get me a damn beer, woman!"

Lottie ran to the porch like a frightened kitten. The two deputies descended on Kirk and had him on his feet and his hands in cuffs within seconds. Susan jumped out of her SUV and ran to Lottie. She called dispatch. "Send a bus." Lottie was going to the hospital. Susan knew the staff there would check her for injuries and try to convince her to get help. Mr. Kirk was about to find out about his son. The deputies had him in their SUV by the time Susan reached Lottie.

"Lottie, look at me." Deputy Thomas was calm but firm. "You were really brave there, and smart. I saw how you tucked your body to protect yourself. Now, I'm going to get you some help, and you're going to have a few days to rest up."

Lottie's body went limp. "Won't matter none. Today, tomorrow, one of these days he won't take time, he'll just hit, and that'll be the end of me. I done know it." Her was voice a whimper.

Susan knew that now was not the time to convince Lottie that she had choices. She just rested her hand on Lottie's foot and tapped it gently; victims of abuse were both scared of being touched and in desperate need of a caring hand. Susan saw the ambulance turning the corner and heading their way. The deputies turned the corner going the other way, taking Mr. Kirk to jail.

"Sheriff, ma'am, don't send me in that am-bue-lance." It was a victim's plea to spare her another reason for her husband to beat her.

"We have to make sure you're okay, Lottie. It'll be all right." Susan would see if the women's shelter had funds to take care of the ambulance costs. They usually did. As the ambulance pulled into the driveway, Susan could see Mrs. Brown across the street looking out her front window. Susan gave a thumbs-up. Even if Mr. Brown were to see her, she knew he would have no reason to think anything other than she was signaling to the ambulance driver.

After she convinced Lottie to let her go into the house to get her purse, Deputy Thomas had a quick look around as she checked to make sure the doors and windows were locked; the house would be empty for at least a few days. The house was sparsely furnished with tattered furniture, but it was immaculate. Susan was pretty sure Lottie scrubbed the floors three times a day.

She locked the front door on her way out then handed the purse to Lottie. After waving off the ambulance, she got in her SUV and put her head against the headrest for a moment, taking a deep breath to clear her head before driving off.

Five minutes later, she pulled into the Emergency Room at the hospital and went in to give Lottie the news that her son was in jail. Lottie needed to hear it while there were folks to help her through it.

Lunch, Friends, and Legal Matters

The Blossom Bistro in downtown Round City turned out to be the perfect place for lunch. The attempts at a Parisian atmosphere almost looked authentic, but fortunately did not include tiny bistro chairs. The eight tables with their red checked tablecloths were far enough apart to provide some privacy while still giving an intimate feel. The front cabinet full of croissants, pain au chocolate, and Napoleon pastries made it feel complete, albeit out of place in this rural mountain town.

Bella looked at Carla. "Good choice. The food was excellent; a perfect lunch menu."

"How about dessert? Those pastries look good, and I see on the chalkboard they have 'moose made out of chocolate.'" Joshua laughed, dragging out the Os in moose. "That's what my dad always called it."

Carla smiled at him. "I'll split one with you, Joshua, in honor of Joe."

"Deal. Bella? Chad?"

Chad shook his head. "I'll enjoy watching you enjoy yours."

"Me too. I'm full."

Joshua's phone buzzed, and he glanced around the room before realizing it was his. He looked at the caller ID. "Sorry, I'll step out and take this." He stood, and they heard him say, "Joshua here."

When Joshua returned, the chocolate mousse was at his place. He put it in front of Carla. "I'll just taste it, then you enjoy it, Carla." Joshua ate one spoonful of the mousse then put his spoon down. Carla looked concerned but began to eat the mousse herself, hoping that a bit of normality would encourage Joshua to say what was on his mind.

Finally, he spoke. "That was the attorney my dad and I use. I just didn't feel like talking this morning, so I sent him a text that I needed to talk to him later today. He's going to come to my house this afternoon. I told him I was with y'all, and he said you needed to be there for part of it, if you can." He looked at them expectantly.

All three nodded their heads.

The server approached and Joshua took the bill. Chad offered to leave the tip, but Joshua would not hear of it. "My treat, all around."

The drive back to the valley was filled with quiet talk about the warm days and cool nights of autumn, and the perfect weather that was forecast for Friday night's blue grass jamboree and sing-along.

Once they were on County Route 54, Bella put her window down. "Isn't it amazing that even with the movement of the car, the sounds and calls of the birds travel right through?"

"Okay, I know Dr. Anderson here is the professor, but here's a quiz question. What does 'last singing of the whippoorwill' mean?" Chad waited to see if anyone would answer. "Well, bless my soul! I'm not the only descendent of a European settler who says something without knowing what it means."

Bella grinned. "Well, Sheriff Oliver, do elucidate."

"Whippoorwill males sing through the night to protect and attract their mate. They stop singing at first light and then camouflage themselves in the trees and bushes." Chad glanced at Bella and beamed. "That lesson is courtesy of Sergeant Whitehorse and her husband, Chief Smallwood."

Joshua focused on the last part of what Chad said. "I haven't seen Mike Smallwood in a while. Sylvia's usually the one who comes in the store. When did you see him?"

"He helped us out with a case recently. In fact, he helped solve the mystery of the light we were seeing from time-to-time northwest of Bella's property."

"Oh, really?" Bella seemed surprised.

"Oops, my bad. Isn't that what the young folks say now?" Chad laughed. "Carla, you may be more in the dark about the mysterious light than anyone."

Carla gave a gentle push on Chad's seat. "Very funny, Chad. *Enlighten* me, then."

Bella smiled at the light banter which she knew was a valuable distraction for Joshua. She told Carla that she had seen a light in the middle of the night several weeks ago before the meth lab blew up. "I just assumed the light was associated with the lab."

Chad spoke up. "I wasn't convinced, so we continued to investigate and turns out there was an area being used to shelter illegal immigrants. The light was from a flashlight they used to get to the area for their makeshift outhouse."

"Wow! You managed to find them? That's impressive." Carla patted Chad's shoulder.

"Just diligent police work. It also introduced us to a very fine agent from Immigration Enforcement who I think will help us make sure we welcome our legal immigrants while managing the illegal ones; most of these folks are just looking for a better life."

"I'm relieved to know you found the source of the light. And, well, I hope the immigrants get treated fairly." Bella's voice expressed her relief and her concern.

"More convinced than ever that they will be." Chad reached over and touched her hand on the arm rest. "Hope you all get to meet Agent Quinn Isaacs one of these days."

Chad pulled into the driveway at Joshua's home. Joshua's attorney, Gray Olson, was sitting on the porch.

"I didn't know he'd be here this fast. Can y'all stay?"

"Sure." Carla nodded her head and patted Joshua's hand.

Bella and Chad agreed.

They all walked to the porch and Gray Olson spoke first. "Miss Carla, nice to see you." He kissed her on the cheek. "Chad, Joshua." He shook hands with each of them in turn. "And I don't believe I've met this lovely lady."

"Hey, I'm Bella Anderson." She extended her hand to shake his.

Joshua didn't let her say anymore. "She's part of the Oliver clan." Then he looked at Chad. "Are you two related?" His eyes darted from Bella to Chad.

Carla giggled. "Kissin' cousins, most likely."

Bella laughed.

So did Chad.

"Oh, back there somewhere, best we can figure out without doing a genealogical study. But, more to the point, Gray, Bella's land up the mountain has been in her family since the late 1800s; she's got deep roots here."

"Well, good to know. Nice to meet you, Miss Bella."

Chad looked at Bella. "Gray was my dad's junior partner for a number of years, but he now heads the firm. He's a fine lawyer."

"For a lawyer." Carla's banter was out of her mouth before she thought about the situation.

Gray laughed the loudest. "Joshua, if I could speak to you for a few minutes alone, then I need to talk to the four of you together."

"Sure." Joshua unlocked the front door. "We'll meet you guys on the porch. Help yourselves to whatever you want to drink. Gray, we'll go in my office."

Carla offered to get drinks while Bella and Chad opened up the doors to the porch and pulled up the rockers so the five of them could see each other and the mountains. Carla came out with a tray of glasses filled with ice, a pitcher of ice tea, and napkins. "You might think I'd done this once or twice in my life."

"And you do it best of anyone." Chad bowed his head in respect. He picked up the pitcher to fill the glasses and then handed them to the two women.

They sat for several minutes, rocking as mountain folks do, and took in the view of the ridgeline across the mountains and the trees half colored with leaves and half bare. They heard footsteps. Chad poured tea for the two men as they sat.

"Joshua has asked that I explain this part of Joe's last will and testament to the three of you, and then he and I can finish up later."

Joshua looked at each of them. "You're welcome to stay as long as you want, but I'm guessing you have plenty of your own things to be getting on with. I'll just say I'd like you to seriously consider what Gray is going to tell you. And, well," he hesitated, "I hope you'll say yes."

Gray explained that more than forty years ago, when Joshua graduated from college and came back home to help in the business, Joe and his wife started a fund that would generate scholarships for students in the valley.

"A while back, Joe added a caveat to the fund that it should first go to the highest achieving female student who had financial need, and she would receive the equivalent of a full ride at the University of Tennessee, not to exceed the cost of her chosen university. The student may, of course, choose to attend any university. If there were more funds generated in a year than needed to fully fund a single student, the money should be divided and allocated as determined by the committee overseeing the scholarship. But, again, it should go to a girl, or girls."

Bella looked at Joshua, who saw the inquiry in her eyes. He nodded his head slightly; she knew the first recipient would be Melody.

Gray continued. "Once the scholarship committee is established, I will share a letter Joe left that will explain his reasons."

Joshua looked at each of his friends. "Dad specified that if you were available to serve, I should ask the three of you. Carla, he knew that you know everyone in these hills, and he felt you'd make sure we didn't overlook someone the money could help. Chad, he wanted you because he respected your skills of observation, your objectivity, and fairness. Bella, I don't think I need to say why he chose you. But I will. He told everybody you were the brightest human being, man or woman, he ever met and had the most common sense of anyone he knew. He loved your daddy, his best friend growing up, and he loved you. He felt you would be the best to make sure the committee considers that the student has a pretty good chance of being successful in college, especially for any money not going to the top student. He included that the fund should pay your expenses to come for meetings if you were in North Carolina." Joshua stopped, let out a breath, and his shoulders drooped.

Gray spoke up. "Mr. Joe asked that you make your decision within forty-eight hours of being notified so that Joshua had time to find someone else if you were not able to serve. Once the committee is formed, should one of you be unable to serve in the future, it's the responsibility of the other three to choose a replacement. The last thing is to let you know that Mr. Joe and I met with Dr. Amanda Bennett, and she assured us that there is a system in place for students to apply for scholarships. Once the Johnson Foundation has this committee, you would have access to consider those students. Do you have any questions?"

They all sat quietly. Bella rocked as she looked out to the mountains. She smiled as a tear ran down her face. *I know one young lady who will be ecstatic. Joe Johnson, you're a saint.* Bella knew she would serve, but she was not going to say it now. She didn't want to unduly influence the other two.

"Joshua, Mr. Olson, I'm humbled by this request. May I let you know tomorrow? I want to make sure I can do justice to this honor."

Gray saw that Chad and Carla were nodding their heads in agreement with Bella.

"Under the provisions of the will, I need to know by Thursday afternoon at this time. The committee will meet to go over the particulars related to the funding of the scholarship, management of the trust, and establishment of processes. I assure you, Mr. Joe thought this out to the last detail."

Joshua looked at each of them. "Thanks for considering this. It's really important to me."

Gray stood. "Joshua, we'll talk in the next few days. I'll leave you to your evening. It was nice to see you Miss Carla, Chad, and to finally meet the legendary Miss Bella."

Bella blushed, stood, and extended her hand. "Gray, it's been a privilege to meet you, and I look forward to getting to know you better. I'll be in touch."

Carla stood and hugged Gray. "Proud of all you've done, Gray. Keep up the good work."

Joshua walked Gray to the door. Carla sat back down in the rocker and started humming: "Come, ye thankful people, come."

Chapter 16

Earth has no sorrow that earth cannot heal.

John Muir, 1838 – 1914

Ending This Day

Bella and Chad made their goodbyes to Joshua and Carla.

"Something you need or would like to do?" Chad opened her door.

Bella looked at him. "Are you always so thoughtful?"

"Would like to be; sometimes I miss the mark."

She chuckled. "Don't we all? I look forward to learning when you might miss the mark." She took a breath. "There are a couple of things I'd like to do, how about you?"

"Let's see if we can make them all work. You first."

"I'd like to swing by Doc Jim's home, if you think it's okay, and check on the pup. Then I would like to talk with you about my plans for repairing my shed and building a cabin. Party-pooper that I am these days, I need an early night. Tomorrow is going to be an emotional day for me. For all of us."

Chad turned onto Doc Jim's street. He pulled up in front of his house, and Doc Jim waved from the porch.

Bella started to get out.

"Can we take a minute first?"

She looked at him and pulled her hand off the door handle. She turned to him.

"I'm good with all that and look forward to hearing about your plans. I need to check in with Sergeant Whitehorse, and I'm going to have to try and reschedule a meeting set for tomorrow afternoon to the morning. Sorry, can't avoid it."

"Before you continue, if not apologizing for what you need or want applies to me, it has to apply to you, too."

"Fair enough." Chad nodded. "Fair enough. Let's go see this pup."

"Evening, Bella and Chad." Doc Jim gave them a wave.

The pup came to the top of the steps, his tail wagging. He sat on his haunches and waited.

"Good boy!" Doc Jim reached over and petted the pup. "Got his name yet, Bella?"

She smiled as she walked up to the pup and put the back of her hand towards him. "Evening, Doc Jim. Evening, boy, you're looking more fit every day." She looked up at Doc Jim. "No name yet. It sure brings a smile to my heart to see how he's flourishing under your care."

"He's a fine animal. He'll make a good pet for you up on your mountain. Pull up a chair, if you have time."

"Wish we could but ..." Bella looked at Chad. He nodded. "Well, not sure if you've heard but Joe passed away on Saturday. We're trying to support Joshua right now. I'm sure you understand."

"That is sad news indeed. Hadn't heard. This community without Joe will be hard to imagine. That man could have gone to any city and made his fortune, but he chose to stay home and provide for our community. May he rest in peace."

"Amen. You'll understand that we need to run, but I'm glad to see you and the pup doing well. We'll be back to check on him... and you. You're pretty important to this community too."

"Thank you, Chad. Does the spirit good to spend some time with friendly folks. I'll look forward to it. Love the animals but I spend a good bit of time by myself these days, what with my kids in Knoxville.

No complaints, mind you. They call every day. Just good to see a local face now and again."

"It's a promise." Bella touched his arm. "You can count on it. I'll stop by on Thursday or Friday and see if you think this boy is going to be coming home with me."

"Looks like it. No rush. We'll be right here."

They said their goodbyes, and five minutes later they were walking into Chad's kitchen. "Not sure how you feel about frozen pizza, but I can put one in the oven, and I think there's some salad left."

"Perfect. If you get the pizza started, I'll excuse myself for a few minutes, and then fix the salad. Maybe we can talk over the shed and cabin while we eat?" Bella smiled at him.

"Sounds like a plan. I'll take care of my phone call, and we'll be ready to settle in for the evening."

Bella gave him a kiss and danced off to her room. She felt like a teenager excited about her first boyfriend.

Chad turned on the oven and propped the phone between his ear and shoulder as he took the pizza out of the freezer. "Sergeant Whitehorse, good evening. Do you have a couple of minutes?"

"Ninety percent of the time," She chuckled.

"More than fair. I need to change the meeting for tomorrow afternoon to the morning if we can get Agent Isaacs earlier. Joshua is doing a private service and burial at four tomorrow, so I want to be available for him. The earlier in the day, the better it is for me." He slid the pizza onto a baking tray and placed it in the oven.

"Sure, Sheriff. Just to be clear, the meeting will include you, me, Deputy Thomas, Detective Williams, and Agent Quinn Isaacs, right? I'll see that Deputy Murphy is briefed when she returns from leave."

"That's it. I'm hoping our folks can make it work around Quinn's schedule."

"We will. Now, how's Joshua? Anything we can do?"

"Let me think on it. Oh, thanks! You reminded me I need to go put a sign on the door of the Valley Store that it'll be closed tomorrow."

"I can take care of that, Chad." This was now her friend, not her boss, who needed her assistance. "What should it say?"

"Just a minute." She could hear he was talking to someone and guessed it was Dr. Anderson. No, she *hoped* it was Dr. Anderson.

"Thanks for taking care of it, Sylvia. Just put 'Family requests your understanding during our closure.' That way Joshua can open when he's ready. Thanks for everything, Sylvia. See you in the morning."

"See you in the morning. Happy to help." She hesitated. "Oh, and tell Dr. Anderson 'Hey' when you see her." She hung up.

Is she psychic? Oh, she must have heard me ask Bella what to put on the sign. Guess she thinks I need a reminder that folks are watching. Well, let them look!

Bella took the salads out to the porch. Chad followed with the pizza and their drinks.

Chad lifted his Fat Tire ale to Bella's glass of Kim Crawford Sauvignon Blanc. "To Joe, who made this community a better place for being among us. To Joshua, may his heart find peace in the loving memories of a great family. And to us." He stopped.

"*Salud!*" Bella winked.

Chad clinked his bottle to her glass and sighed. "Spanish?"

She nodded and smiled. "It means both cheers and health. Now you know almost all the Spanish I know."

Chad looked at the pamphlet about the prefab cabins Bella had placed in the center of the table. Bella looked out to the mountains as the sun started to fade behind the ridgeline. It would be dark quickly; the sunset came early this time of year.

"Are you considering this specific cabin, or just one done by this company?"

"That one. The size is right. I like the layout and the fact that it has two porches."

Chad nodded. "Looks like it may have really high ceilings. Is there a second floor?"

"No, I can have a loft put in and dormers, which I might do even if I don't put a loft right now; they will bring in more light. Arthur is drawing up papers for me on the cost of installing it, fixing the shed, and either closing in my carport or building a garage onto the cabin."

"You've decided to repair the shed?"

"Yes, I'd pretty much decided that last week, but... well, the events of the weekend made me realize I *want* to preserve the shed. My daddy built it. He had always planned to have a painting done on the side that has no windows or doors. He didn't live long enough to make it happen. I have lots of ideas of what to put, but I need to think about that part a bit more."

"Does Arthur know The Log Cabin Company?"

"He recommended them." Suddenly she looked concerned. "*Why*? Is there a problem with the company?"

He laughed. "No, not that I know of. You're hearing the voice of the ever-cautious sheriff speaking. If Arthur has worked with them, I would trust them. You might just want to do a quick check and make sure there are no filings against them. Gray could do that for you, if you want."

"Good idea. I should have an attorney here. The one I have in North Carolina would expect me to have someone who practices in Tennessee. I have some other things I've been thinking about with the land too. I've just haven't gotten around to talking to an attorney. I'll ask Gray if he can take me as a client when I call him about the scholarship committee."

"Speaking of that ..."

"Yes?"

"I would be honored to accept Joe's request. I have to check with the county attorney and make sure there's no conflict."

"Sure, that makes sense. I'm surprised the county is large enough to employ an attorney."

"We're not. State statute allows smaller counties to contract those services. Ours used to be my dad. Now it's Gray." Before she could ask, he jumped in. "He'll tell me if it's a conflict for him to advise me as county attorney since he represents Joe."

"Well, fine sir, just as that sun is about to fade behind the mountain. . ." she watched the blue-black sky dropping with it, "I'm fading too. Thank you for thinking about my potential construction projects. I'll appreciate your thoughts, if you have time."

"I will make time." He leaned over and kissed her, and they held hands as they watched the sun disappear. A shooting star flew across the sky; they both saw it, squeezing each other's hand tightly at the same time.

Bella leaned on Chad's shoulder, and he rested his head on hers. Bella sighed. "I'm choosing to take that shooting star as the universe giving me, and us, a sign."

They cleared the table and cleaned up the kitchen. Chad turned out the kitchen light as they walked down the hall. At her bedroom, Chad embraced her and gave her a lingering kiss. "I could get used to this. And, if I'm not being too forward, I have great hopes that one of these days we'll walk to the end of the hall together."

She returned his kiss. "Play your cards right, sir, and you could end up with the winning hand. Good night, kind sir." She walked into the guest bedroom.

Chad turned and went into his home office across the hall.

After getting ready for bed, Bella lay there for a few minutes, taking deep breaths and slowly exhaling. She thought about her Not-So-Good List. She decided that, yet again, one word came to mind: grief. Grief for Joe, grief for Joshua, and grief for a community that had just lost, she believed, it's oldest living resident. *I'll have to ask Chad about that.* She was relieved there was no more to unburden to the Not-So-Good List. Grief was enough.

Another deep inhale and slow exhale as she thought about her Good List. She had thought about her daddy today and her desire to fix the shed he built. She had visited the pup and Doc Jim. *I will make a point of visiting Doc Jim regularly.* Figuring out a name for the pup could be fun, she decided, and definitely a good thing. She was making friends in the valley and saw there was a possibility that Joshua might find a new companion in Carla. As for Chad, well, she definitely had him on her Good List. *It's happening so fast; I didn't plan for this.* She pulled the sheet and quilt up around her neck. *Maybe the best things don't need to be planned.* She was sound asleep in minutes.

Preparing for Tomorrow

Chad knew there was no way he could read any of the reports on technology equipment from Sylvia, even though he probably wouldn't be able to fall asleep for hours. He reviewed the station blotter for the day's reports and was dismayed to see the call to the Kirk's house. Based on the notes, Deputy Thomas and the other two deputies handled it well. If possible, he would try to get an update from her tomorrow morning before their planning meeting.

He saw the report from Detective Williams that the grand jury had rendered an indictment of criminally negligent homicide on Steve Phillips in the overdose death of Nick Brown. He wondered if the boy would now ask for any attorney. Sitting back in his chair, he remembered that Nick Brown lived across the street from the Kirks. He shook his head. *Only two families on that road, and neither one able to help the other live a better life. We have work to do in building community support.*

A new calendar appointment revealed that Agent Quinn Isaacs was available to meet at eight, and Sylvia had confirmed it with their staff. She noted that DEA Agent Sam Nations would attend as well. *That's good. Glad Quinn reached Sam. We'll all be fresh and should be able to make a plan and finalize it in a couple of hours at the outside.*

He went back and reviewed the Detective Lewis's notes about the chain of shell companies owning the motels in Round City and the final piece that put Commissioner Zimmerman at the head. *Doesn't mean he knows what's going on in his motels... but it doesn't mean he doesn't. If we can prove his ownership, then his financial disclosures when he ran for office were fraudulent. One more thing...* He made a note to talk with the police chief in Round City as he had promised. He would wait until they had a plan for solving the possible link of the commissioner with the prostitution in the valley. One more quick scan of his emails, then he shut down his computer to prepare for bed.

As he got out of the shower, he looked at himself in the mirror. He couldn't remember if he had studied himself in the mirror since his divorce. He recalled several times before the divorce when he had to literally look himself in the eye and remember that he was staying in the marriage for Nora. Now, he admitted that maybe he should have made a different decision, but it was too late for that type of second guessing. This intense look at himself was very different. *You, my friend, are falling in love with Bella Anderson. Maybe I'm already in love with her. It's taking all the patience I may ever have to leave her at the guest room door. But maybe being a patient man will all be worthwhile.* He flipped off the light switch then crawled into bed, raised his arms, and put the back of his folded hands over his eyes. "Good night, lovely Bella. Sweet dreams."

Everything Ready for Tomorrow

Joshua sat in his recliner, drinking a pale ale. Harold and Julie had stopped by and brought supper, which they shared with him and Carla. They didn't stay long after cleaning up the dishes. Carla had left about an hour ago, and he just wanted to sit in the dark. He could have watched *NCIS* in real time tonight, not something he usually did, but this was not a night for watching crime. He was living it. *Pastor Fisk, I hope you're right that I can find my way to forgive these boys. I have never been a violent man, but this could push even the calmest person over the edge.* He tried to put it out of his mind and be the gracious man his dad had always been. *Dad apparently fought back. Shouldn't I?* He wasn't even sure how you would fight the outcome. He would talk to Chad about what would happen to these boys. He prayed their punishment by the law would let him find peace.

He stared into the darkness of the room and felt the loneliness of an empty house. He had enjoyed the company of Carla, Bella, and Chad. Admittedly, he didn't like what brought them here, but it made him realize he didn't have to be alone. He and Jan used to have people over three or four times a month. *I want things to be active and fun again. If I've learned no other lesson, it's that none of us knows when our time is up.*

Lying in bed later, he stared at the ceiling. *I miss you, Dad. I hope you're reunited with Mom and Jan. That alone can sustain me through this. I hope the service and then the jamboree will do you justice.*

He found his thoughts drifting to Carla. She had been with him most of the time since he arrived at the hospital on Saturday. He had always considered her a friend, but he was starting to realize that their businesses kept both families pretty busy, so they hadn't seen each other much socially except at jamborees. And, of course, he had the love of his life, Jan. *I miss you more than ever, Jan. I'm not sure I'm cut out to be alone. I know you told me you hoped I'd find someone else to love. I just didn't think I needed someone, and I sure never thought someone could take your place. I've never seen Carla the way I have these last few days. I don't know why, but I think she...* his eyes closed, and he was sound asleep.

Chapter 17

And into the woods I go, to lose my mind and find my soul.

John Muir, 1838 – 1914

Putting Things into Place

Chad left home as quietly as he could, leaving a note for Bella. "6:30 a.m. Help yourself to whatever you need. See you by noon or will call." Once at his desk, he made a list of the things he needed to get done this morning and did a quick scan of new reports from various law enforcement agencies. *This may be a good time to think about how I can give the sergeants more authority and distribute the control that I have held so tightly.* He sent a text to Deputy Thomas to see him before or after the meeting, whichever worked for her. It was seven forty-five when there was a knock on his door.

"Morning, Deputy Thomas, come in and have a seat." Chad shut the door and walked to the table. "Hope things are going well in your life."

"Better than a pig in a poke. And you, sir?"

"Doing well, thanks. Some rough days right now, as you know. Looks like you had to deal with a side effect of Jason Kirk's arrest."

"Partly about Jason's arrest. Mostly it's a man who drinks too much and beats his wife. I suspect he will find any reason he can to continue to do both."

"Do we know anything about his relationship with his son?"

"If Jason is to be believed. . ." she looked at the sheriff. "And I do believe him, he's the object of his dad's abuse too. He told us he took the money from the cash drawer for his dad. If we can find evidence of that, we'll get his dad, too."

Chad nodded. "And yesterday's call?"

"I left my card with Mrs. Kirk when we went to talk to her after Jason was arrested. Her neighbor across the road, Mrs. Brown, called me. . ." She stopped as it was apparent the sheriff wanted to say something.

"Did Mrs. Brown have your card?"

"No, so that gives me some hope the two women might be willing to find help for their situations." Susan had a wan smile. "As you know, with the HIPPA laws it's hard to get anything specific about a medical patient. But I checked at the hospital this morning and Mrs. Kirk is still there. She was not physically hurt in front of us, but I don't know what may have happened before we got there. Mr. Kirk is in holding. Not sure if Detective Williams has talked with him yet."

"Okay, thanks for the update. Thanks most of all for giving Mrs. Kirk your card. Were you able to check with the women's shelter to see if they could help out?"

"Yes, they'll take care of the ambulance cost. The hospital counselor will let Mrs. Kirk know she can go to the shelter from the hospital. I hope she will. Time will tell."

The knock on the door signaled the rest of the team had arrived. Chad opened the door to find the hallway full as IEA Agent Quinn Isaacs, Sergeant Whitehorse, Detective Williams, and DEA Agent Sam Nations made small talk.

Chad ushed them into his office. It was a tight fit, but they all found a seat at the round table as he welcomed them. "Thanks for coming, all of you. I'm well aware it made an early morning for some of you, but circumstances required it. Sylvia told me she has advised you of the passing of Joe Johnson. Quinn, you're the only one of us who didn't know him. Joe was a pillar of our community; it's a great loss." Heads nodded around the table. "To the matter at hand, Deputy Murphy is on leave, but she'll be back tomorrow, and Sergeant Whitehorse will bring her up to speed. Now, Billy will bring us to date on the position of the DA on Gertrude and the two local women who were at the 'house on the hill.'"

"The best the DA is willing to offer on Gertrude is to let her do her time at Bledsoe instead of shipping her to Nashville. Neither of the two young women have any priors, so she will negotiate for time served and a hundred dollar fine, if we need them. Otherwise, she's inclined to let them sit in jail for a while but give them a minimum fine. The maximum fine of five hundred dollars might just put them back to their old tricks." He watched Chad to see if he was in trouble for his joke.

Agent Quinn Isaacs spoke up. "Agent Nations and I have spoken, and we would rather not use the two women you're holding. Between our two agencies, we can put four women in the house with Gertrude: two who look like the two you have in custody, and two we can use as bait for Zimmerman starting in Round City. Those two are both bilingual, and, as I said the other day, they could pass for sixteen."

Chad nodded. "Sam, where are we on the drug angle in this? Is there any evidence to support the information Quinn got from one of the Spanish-speaking young women she took into custody?"

"First, let me just say that as a member of this community, I'm deeply saddened at the loss of Joe. Sad for the loss of his life and sad for our community. On the matter we're discussing, we've had no leads on what appears to be fentanyl reaching this community or I would have told you. However, what Quinn shared fits the pattern of distribution we're finding in other small communities. In the larger, more populated areas, we get a range of distribution points including street sales, malpractice among physicians, and everything in between. Smaller communities tend to be more socially tight-knit, so the chain of distribution tends to follow other illegal activity." Everyone at the table nodded their heads.

"Makes sense." Chad looked around the table. "Any evidence of drug use in the women we have in holding?"

Sylvia Whitehorse shook her head. "None. None with Gertrude either."

"Sounds like the illegal immigrants were being used to ferry the drugs to patrons, leaving the local women out of it. Less chance of talk in the community. Gertrude involved?"

Sam shrugged, "It stands to reason that she was the conduit for the distribution. Quinn, did you learn anything about that?"

"The most I could get was 'el jefe said twenty dollars for one pill.'"

"But how did they get the pills?" Chad tried not to sound frustrated. He was champing at the bit to get Commissioner Zimmerman if he was involved, but this operation had to be done correctly.

Quinn didn't hesitate. "The girl was explicit that there would be five little plastic bags with one pill each, and she had to leave either the pills or the money in the drawer of a table in the room at the end of the night; it would be gone in the morning when she woke up. Apparently, the girls had to go out back of the house every day at midday, and when they came back the pills were in the drawer. So, we don't know who might have come in the front door."

Deputy Thomas added, "When Quinn and Murphy interviewed the youngest girl, she said their clients didn't start coming around until the evening. So, it seems there would be plenty of time during the day for the pills to be put in the rooms without the girls seeing who put it there. The girls watched television in the living room during the day after they scrubbed the bathroom, did the laundry, and completed whatever else Gertrude gave them to do."

Quinn was deliberate when she spoke. "You have to understand these girls are young. They were being sexually used *and* abused. They don't speak the language, and we certainly can't expect that they were looking for things in order to answer our questions. For my two cents, Gertrude should have to give up the source of the drugs to get her deal."

Chad waited a beat. "Anyone else with background to share? We need to lay out our timeline and plan for repopulating the 'house on the hill,' and make sure we have the resources in place and the strategy down solid."

The group spent the next hour examining the plan shared by Agent Isaacs. The two agents from the federal agencies had experience and understood the local issues and concerns, while the local part of the team had training but little experience in this kind of a sting. However, the local officers provided their deep knowledge of the community and information from the two men who had been arrested Friday night. They also had custody of Gertrude, who could make the house seem no different than it was when it was closed down.

"Then we're set?" Chad looked around the table. "Everyone know what they're to do?" He was satisfied the competency of these law enforcement officers would make things work, and he was confident they would put an end to the crime in the "house on the hill." However, he also wanted to be confident that he could get to the head of the operation, whether it was Zimmerman or otherwise. On that matter, he wasn't sure whether their trap would be enough to catch 'el jefe.'

Making Her Own Plans

Bella smiled at the note Chad had left and took it out to the porch with her while she drank a cup of tea and ate a bowl of cereal. She had not seen his handwriting before; it was bold. *This puts a check in the plus column for thoughtfulness, Chad Oliver.*

With her computer on the table, along with the brochure on the cabin, she moved aside the cereal bowl and opened the file of her notes on the pros and cons of managing the repairs on the shed. She realized she had not told her insurance company about it. *Should I? How does that work when a crime is involved?*

She decided to call her insurance agent in North Carolina. He had worked with an agent in Tennessee to put a rider on her home-owner's insurance in North Carolina that covered Drellag Caban and her property. *Maybe I should separate the two?* Her agent answered the phone, and Bella got caught up in a haze of questions and explanations, facts and figures.

By the time Bella had a chance to look up and check her watch, it was almost eleven thirty. She had the answers about her insurance, a claim was filed, and the insurance company would work with the court on recovery. Regardless, the repairs were covered, and she was ready to proceed with the next part of her day. She picked up the phone and dialed Gray Olson.

"Gray, thank you for taking my call."

"And thank you for calling. I'm hoping you're calling to tell me you'll serve on the scholarship committee."

"I am. I know I'll need to learn more about processes and goals, but I would be honored to serve at Joe's request. While I have you on the phone, I'm planning to spend more time at Drellag Caban than in the past, and I would like to know if you're taking new clients."

"First, may I ask what Drellag Caban is?"

"Oh, sorry, it's the cabin my great-grandfather built. I inherited the property, which is about eighty acres. I will need legal advice about it at some point."

"Is there a reason for the name?"

"Yes. Drellag is Scottish for 'dragonfly,' and Caban is the Welsh word for 'cabin.' I'm a big fan of dragonflies."

"Well, that makes sense then, doesn't it?" He paused a second. "I'd be happy to meet with you to discuss how I might be of service. Is there any pressing matter suggesting we should meet sooner rather than later?"

"I will need a contract reviewed fairly quickly." She told him about the damage to her shed, the building of the new cabin, and the garage.

"Sounds like a pretty ambitious project. I've reviewed a number of contracts with Arthur Gillett, and they're pretty straightforward. If you can get me a copy of his contract and the contract for the sale of the cabin, I'll review them, and then we can meet at your earliest convenience. I'm pleased to hear you have spoken with your insurance agent. It's hard enough to deal with having your property violated; you don't need to deal with the courts for restitution. That said, we can talk about punitive and other compensatory damages related to what happened on your property as well."

"Oh my, that never entered my mind. I will need to think about how I feel on the matter of punitive damages. We can talk when we meet. Do you have any time this week? I think I should have the two contracts, and the time to think about it all, by Friday."

"How's ten on Friday for you?"

"Perfect, I'll see you then."

"Bella, thank you for agreeing to serve on the scholarship committee. You'll be a valuable member. I'll see you on Friday."

The call ended, and she sat looking at her phone. She had never even considered punitive or compensatory damages. She knew from years of reading detective and spy novels that emotional distress was often a charge in crimes like the ones on her property, yet she never considered it and knew she was not likely to pursue it. She would listen to what Gray had to say, though. She heard the kitchen door open and could hear the garage door closing. *How long have I been out here?* She picked up her cereal bowl and empty mug and walked into the kitchen at the same time Chad did.

He looked at his watch. "Good morning." He walked over and kissed her. His embrace was more one of greeting, but she held on. "Hey, what's up? Not that I'm dismayed by the hug, but I'm guessing that's more than a hello hug." He leaned back but did not let go of her. Their eyes locked.

"Figured me out already, have you?"

"Oh, I don't know if that will ever happen, but I'm a pretty good observer and all my senses are telling me you have more than 'good morning' on your mind."

"I just got off the phone with Gray, but we can talk about that in a minute. How was your morning? It must have been something pretty serious to take you in so early." She stopped. "That was stupid. I have no idea what time you normally go to work."

They both laughed.

"At the moment I'm trying to work out what a new normal might be, but as you know I had a meeting that had to be held today. My old normal was anywhere from six to eight a.m., depending on what was happening in our fair hills." He paused. "That looks like an empty mug; shall I get us each some tea so we can sit on the porch and catch up?"

"That would be perfect. I'll switch to ice tea, please. I'll just put these dishes in the dishwasher, then we can sit and enjoy some of the beauty of this day. I'm glad you were able to get away from work."

"Wish it could have been sooner. Now, you go on out. I'll be there in a minute."

Shortly, Chad set the glasses of tea on the table and kissed Bella on top of the head as he did so. She loved the gesture and the gentle caring it showed. He sat and looked at her. "Tell me about your morning."

"I'm prone to way too many details; I can ruin a movie if you ask me what it was about." She laughed. "After almost five years of talking mostly to myself at home, a listening ear is likely to be abused." Her raised eyebrows and upturned eyes sent a pleading "Will you forgive me?" look. "I'll try to give you the highlights, and you ask for detail if you need or want it, okay?"

Bella told Chad that she had a text from Arthur who had a contract drawn up on the shed, garage, and installing the prefab cabin. She had called the cabin salesman, Macklin Evans, and he was going to email her a contract. "Gray can see me at ten on Friday. I generally trust myself to make decisions and to think through the pros and cons. I can show you my list if you're interested."

She then told him about the insurance claim and Gray's comments on punitive and compensatory damages related to the damage to her land. "If I can talk this through with you after I meet with Gray on Friday, or maybe sometime over the weekend, then I'll be ready to finalize things the first of the week."

"I think you have this well in hand and, once you talk to Gray, you'll have the legal perspective. I assume the contracts are pretty straightforward, and I'm confident Gray will make sure your interests are protected. What he can't help you weigh, relative to filing for punitive and compensatory damages against those responsible, is how much you want to go through if the DA can't settle it out of court. I'm not saying that to discourage you, I just want you to think about it."

She leaned over and kissed him slowly, then looked him directly in the eyes. "That, dear Chad, is exactly what I needed to hear. I'm not one to generally give up without a fight, but the older I get, the more I'm prone to decide the cost-benefit ratio to my mental and physical well-being. Enough about me. Anything you want to share about your morning?"

"Accomplished what I went there to do, and some other things as well. Made some promised phone calls and had a few minutes to catch up with Sam Nations. I asked him your question about Joe being the oldest native resident in these hills."

"Oh, great. What did he say?" Bella was genuinely interested.

"There's a tribal member living in a pretty remote area north of Sam's folks who's ninety-eight. That makes him the oldest 'tribal native,' as Sam put it. He did think Joe was the oldest European descendent who was native to this area."

"Thanks for asking him."

"Oh, and one more thing. Nora is getting the signs ready to go up tomorrow for the jamboree and sing-along and the celebration of Joe's life. Some of the tribal folks come most of the time, like Sylvia Whitehorse and Mike Smallwood, but not many others. Sylvia told me that she expected most of the tribe would come Friday night to honor Joe. Sam told me everyone knows Joe saved this community by giving them a place to buy groceries at a fair price, and never overcharged native people, which was a problem in other parts of the mountains."

"I hope this celebration of Joe's life might bring other forms of healing for our community."

"That would be nice, wouldn't it?" Chad smiled at her.

"Speaking of Nora, I'm glad she's going to sing this afternoon. I talked to Joshua, and although the funeral home would send a car for him, he didn't want that. He asked if we could pick him up. I told him we would. I hope that's okay."

"Bella, there's a part of me that, for a long time, I allowed to convince myself that the failure of my marriage was not my fault. Maybe it's age talking, but no relationship is one-sided. I have a good idea that what you and I seem to be feeling could lead to something long-term, and that feels pretty good to me. I'm not rushing you, in any way, but we're both old enough to know that we have to be honest with each other and navigate the rough parts, even for a friendship. I'll try to tell you when something is a concern or bothers me. I need you to do the same. We both made a commitment to Joshua to support him through this. I would expect nothing less than you agreeing to us picking him up. We good?"

"Works for me. He needs us to pick him up at three fifteen. He'll meet with Pastor Fisk before the service. Let's figure out something for a quick lunch, then we'll need to get ready. At least, I'll need some time to get ready. I walked around your yard for a while this morning. It was nice to lose myself in the woods. However, I'll feel better if I shower before I dress for the funeral."

"Done and done, as my Nora is fond of saying." He rose and headed to the kitchen. She put her computer in her bedroom and joined him to make lunch.

Chapter 18

*One can make a day of any size and regulate the rising and setting
of his own sun and the brightness of its shining.*

John Muir, 1838-1914

Choices to be Made

Billy had arranged for the DA to meet with Steve Phillips at one thirty
on Friday. The DA would offer Steve a plea deal on the trespassing
and property damage at Dr. Anderson's property, and a criminally
negligent homicide charge in the drug overdose of Nick Brown. Billy
wanted to make sure Steve understood he had the right to have
an attorney present, although Phillips had already indicated multiple times he did not want a lawyer. He was eighteen, legally an
adult in these charges, but he still lived at home with his parents—
Commissioner and Mrs. Zimmerman. He had not asked to call them,
and they hadn't tried to reach him; they knew where he was. But
judgement day was coming and Billy had to check whether Steve
was going to negotiate for himself or not.

Billy waited for Deputy Thomas to join him ahead of their chat
with Steve. He would also follow up with Gertrude, and the DA
would talk with her tomorrow. They wanted her back in the "house
on the hill" before Friday.

"Hey, Billy, sorry I'm running a bit late. The follow-up with Quinn
took a little longer than I expected. Needed to make sure we had

good information for the two DEA agents who are impersonating our local women in the 'house on the hill.'"

"No problem. Let's get Steve Phillips wrapped up and ready to deliver to the DA." He walked towards the holding area and saw that the matron had Steve ready to go.

"You again?" Steve's old smirk returned.

"Good afternoon, Mr. Phillips."

"Yeah, good afternoon to you, Williams. Madam deputy... you *are* just a deputy, right?"

Susan Thomas ignored him and unlocked the door to Room 2. She stepped aside and let Steve shuffle by her to the chair against the far wall of the room.

After the recording was started and all three of them had stated their names and Steve his date of birth, Steve opened his hands and stretched as far as he could with the chains attached to his waist. "Please, ma'am, unshackle me, I bring danger to no man." The overwrought theatrics of his delivery would have been out of place even in a middle school play.

Billy turned his chair around, scraped it across the floor, and sat. "Seriously, boy, you shouldn't have skipped your English classes. That's not Shakespeare, and it's a third-rate performance. Let's skip the drama and let this fine deputy read you your rights."

"I'm tired of telling you I know my rights. I don't want a lawyer, so get on with it!" Steve all but spit out each word.

"To clarify, you're waiving your right to representation and are prepared to talk to us on your own?" Susan's voice was cool and calm.

"Yep, you got it. Finally!" His sneer returned. "Now, that only took how many times for you to understand? Handcuffs, please?" He winked at her.

"Aww." Billy looked at Susan Thomas. "What do you say we give this young man a break? Take off the wrist cuffs?"

"Detective, if that's what you want." Susan pretended to be annoyed.

Billy nodded at her, and she uncuffed Steve.

"Not really sure we're going to be here long enough to warrant taking them off, but hey, you're lucky, I'm feeling generous today." Billy gave Steve a smirk of his own.

"I told you, I want out of here, now! I'll pay for the damn shed—"

"Manners, Mr. Phillips, there's a lady present." Billy's voice was quiet but stern.

"I'll pay for the shed. How much can it be?"

"That's a conversation you can have with the district attorney on Friday at one thirty p.m. In the meantime, we're here to give you the opportunity to tell us you want a lawyer to represent you in that meeting." He quickly added, "Good guys that we are and all that." He didn't care that it was recorded.

"Let's see... I'm in the south. If I speak as slow as molasses, like y'all talk, y'all might understand." The sarcasm dripped out of him. "I... do... not... want... a... lawyer!"

"Fine then. On Friday, our district attorney will meet with you and inform of your right to a trial, or if you're having a really good day, she might offer you a deal. You will be charged with criminal trespass, destruction of personal property in the commission of that trespass, and criminally negligent homicide in the death of Nick Brown." He looked at Susan Thomas. "That about cover it, Deputy?"

"Almost. There could be punitive and other compensatory damages, I believe."

"What the hell... heck does that mean?" Steve stared at her.

"Why, Steve, I thought they taught you high-level vocabulary at that fine Mountain Villages Academy. Aren't *you* surprised, Detective?" Susan was not playing the good cop this time.

"I am, but let's cut him some slack. He's had more than a few days in our fine facility with some not-so-well-educated folks." He looked at Steve and played sympathetic. "Basically, it means you could be liable for damages to the emotional well-being of the landowner. I believe you wrecked the gate, tore up the ground, and destroyed heaven only knows what was inside that shed."

"I wasn't driving!" Steve shouted.

"Sorry to have to tell you, but it was your ATV, and you gave Nick Brown permission to drive it. So, it's your responsibility. And we'll add that Nick isn't with us any longer to tell his side of it. Now, I'm no attorney, but I've seen enough of these cases to know that juries are pretty sympathetic in these parts to destruction of property and the emotional toll that has on the property owner. But, hey, you might find a different situation."

"Detective, I'm concerned that Mr. Phillips here doesn't seem to be hearing the part about homicide. Last time I checked that carries a term up to six years in prison. Is that right?"

"Last I knew. Of course, there may be new sentencing guidelines. But, Steve, did you know... well, of course you don't, you're not a lawyer. The vandalism laws in Tennessee have stiffer penalties than the homicide charges. Those sentencing guidelines are based on value of the damage. I'd guess you're looking at ten thousand dollars or more in damage, so that's three to fifteen years in prison and a fine up to ten thousand dollars." Billy had been prepped by the DA on the penalties.

Steve sat staring at him. "You're just trying to scare me. I'm not going to jail or paying that kind of fine. And I don't need an attorney to make it happen. I'll just call my dear ole stepdad. So, I'll take my phone call now."

Well, well, we've finally found what you think is your bargaining chip. It's not going to be your stepfather. The question will be whether he insists on you lawyering up.

"Very well, Deputy, please put on his cuffs. The matron will assist you with making your call when she can work it into her schedule. This is Detective Williams, and..."

"Deputy Thomas, escorting..."

"How many times do I have to say my name? Steve Phillips!"

"From Room 2 to the matron at holding." She turned off the recorder and put it in her pocket.

Billy let her walk him down the hall. Next up, Gertrude.

The Gathering of Friends

Bella was taking a shower when she heard the buzz of a text message. She quickly finished her shower, grabbed her towel, and looked at the phone. It was from Carla: "Meet you @ JJs." Bella was not surprised that Carla would ride with them from Joshua's. It dawned on her that they'd made no plans with Joshua for after the service and burial. It would be supper time. She decided to text Carla back. "Should we plan supper after the service?" She started toweling her hair dry.

Carla's response came back almost immediately: "James has the back room set up at The Corral and a fish dinner ready to serve."

After thanking Carla, Bella turned her attention to getting ready. She dressed in her black pantsuit, white silk shell top, and put on the necklace Matt had given her along with the earrings she always wore with it. She ran the brush through her hair one more time and opened the door to walk out. Chad was just stepping out of his room. He had on a black wool suit, with a starched white shirt and red tie, and black dress shoes. They stopped and looked at each other.

"Sorry for the occasion, Dr. Anderson, but I must say you look stunning."

"And you look pretty spiffy yourself, Sheriff Oliver." Bella leaned in and kissed him.

"Doing okay?" Chad waited a second. "I don't have a lot of experience at knowing whether I should ask when I think something is difficult, or just let you know if you need to talk, I'll listen." He looked at her, his eyes pleading for direction.

"Please ask anytime. I want to tell you how I'm doing. I also don't want you to think I expect you to navigate the memories and loss for me. I'm doing okay. Thanks for asking."

He kissed her gently and took her hand.

"Then we'll just bumble our way through this together. Here's my bumble for the moment. You can wait out here, or you can come with me to the kitchen, but I'm going to wear my sidearm."

"I'll wait for you in the car so we can get going once you're ready. I don't want to keep Joshua waiting." Chad opened the door leading to the garage so she could go out, then he took his weapon out of the gun safe. Bella made no comment about it when Chad got in the car, and they drove to Joshua's house in comfortable silence.

Joshua and Carla held hands as they walked down the steps. Chad got out and opened the door for Carla, and Joshua walked around the SUV. Chad kissed Carla on the cheek. "Afternoon, Carla. You look lovely. Sorry for the occasion that brings us together."

"Thanks, Chad. Helps to have a fine gentleman, who's looking pretty handsome himself, give me a compliment. Don't have much chance to dress up in my line of work."

"I hear you." Chad smiled at her while he shut the door.

Joshua patted Bella on the shoulder when he got in. "Thanks, Bella. I'm much more comfortable for us to be together than riding in a funeral home car. Hope you don't mind that I asked Harold first. He and Julie are coming to the service directly from work, so it's going to be tight for them."

"We're happy to do it, Joshua."

The ride to the church was quiet, and they were there in five minutes; nothing was very far when you lived in the valley. Chad drove around to the pastor's office at the back so Joshua could meet with him before the service. Chad looked in the rearview mirror just as Joshua leaned over and kissed Carla on the cheek. "See you inside."

"Oh my, Carla, is someone picking up Melody?" Bella turned to look at Carla. "I didn't think about her having to walk."

"Me either. I can call her and see."

"We can easily go get her; we have plenty of time before four."

Carla called and found out Melody had planned to walk. Chad and Bella left to get Melody and Carla stayed so Joshua wouldn't be concerned if he came out and they were all three gone.

"Thanks, Sheriff. Miss Bella. I didn't mind walking, but I didn't want to sit alone."

Bella put her hand out, and Melody took it. "We'll sit together."

Chad followed them to the church and waved as Harold and Julie, as well as Doug and his wife, drove up. Chad had seen Nora's car around the back of the church and assumed she and the pianist were warming up. The pianist was playing softly as they entered the small, white clapboard church. Carla was sitting in the front pew with Joshua. Harold, Joshua's oldest friend, and his wife, Julie, joined Joshua and Carla, who looked to see if James had been able to come after all. He was not there. Bella, Chad, and Melody sat in the pew behind them. When Doug and his wife came in, they sat next to Melody.

Mourning Loss and Celebrating a Life

At four o'clock, Pastor Fisk entered the sanctuary. The casket was already at the foot of the communion table as Joe had not wanted pallbearers. The small group stood, and Bella noticed that Joshua swayed a bit. She was glad that Chad was standing behind him.

After the call to worship and a prayer of invocation, Pastor Fisk read passages from the Old and New Testaments, and his final passage was from John 14:1-3. Bella heard the beginning words, "Do not let your hearts be troubled." She had memories of hearing these very words for the funerals of Matt, her mother, and Grandmother Hazel. She imagined the same reading was given for her own daddy; she just didn't remember.

"... go and prepare a place for you, I will come back and take you to be with me that you also may be where I am," Pastor Fisk read.

Lost in her own thoughts, Bella caught the ending of the scripture. *I pray all of you, my family, are looking out for Joe.* The pastor then shared a short homily of thanksgiving for Joe's life and the promise of God's love. He gave his pastoral prayer and sat down.

There was a soft beginning of the hymn "Amazing Grace," and Nora started singing. Bella felt a hand on her shoulder. She and Chad turned at the same time to see it was Doc Fred, Nora's husband and Chad's son-in-law. Bella imagined he might have had trouble getting away from the hospital. She reached up and squeezed his hand.

Pastor Fisk asked everyone to stand and open their hymnals and join in the singing of "Eternal Father, Strong to Save." They started singing, and Joshua suddenly sat down. Carla sat next to him and held his hand. Bella reached forward and put her hand on his shoulder. She didn't know if it was just too much overall, or if there was something about this particular hymn.

After the hymn, the pastor led them in the Lord's Prayer and gave a benediction. The pianist started playing "My Faith Looks Up to Thee," and Nora started singing, joined by Pastor Fisk. When they sang, "Wipe sorrow's tears away..." Joshua stood up. Pastor Fisk walked over to him so they could exit together.

Joshua's friends trailed behind him, and the small group walked up the hill to the cemetery while the funeral attendants rolled the casket out to the grave. Joshua sat in the middle of three chairs with Carla and Bella beside him. The others stood in a semi-circle around the casket.

Pastor Fisk gave a prayer and then asked if anyone wanted to speak. No one did. Instead, Nora started singing, "Abide with Me." Bella didn't realize she had been humming it on the way to the grave, and Joshua whispered, "Sing with her, please." Bella sang quietly and others who knew the hymn joined in as Joe's casket was lowered into the earth. At the final line, "In life, in death, O Lord, abide with me," Bella felt the words drift off to the mountains on the chilled evening breeze.

Before they walked back to the church, Carla spoke to the pastor. "Pastor Fisk, if you and Mrs. Fisk could join us, my brother and I have a fish dinner for all of us in the private dining room at The Corral. I think James called your wife." She looked around the small group. "We hope you'll all join us." Joshua took her hand and headed for the parking lot.

Bella spoke to Melody, "Do you need to call home?"

"Do you think the sheriff could stop by my house, and I'll run in and ask my mama?"

"Absolutely." Bella realized Melody had taken her hand and she felt her tremble. Bella stopped walking and turned to face her. "Oh, sweet girl, Mr. Joe loved you, and he was so proud of you. It's okay to cry. We all miss him too." The two stood facing each other and Bella took both of Melody's hands.

"Thanks, Miss Bella, I'm going to miss him so much."

"I know." Bella gently squeezed Melody's hands. "I know."

Supper With Friends

James had the room set and flowers on the table. Bella thought the room looked lovely and was a fitting and appropriate tribute to Joe. She noticed how people seated themselves at the long trestle table. Melody sat between her and Chad—directly across from Joshua, Carla, the pastor, and his wife. Nora and Fred were next to Bella. Harold and Julie sat next to Joshua. Doug and his wife were at the end. The pianist was unable to join them. There was quiet conversation among the friends at the table.

Bella turned to Nora. "Do you know anything about Joe's choice of the hymn, 'Eternal Father, Strong to Save?'"

"Sorry to chime in." The two women looked at Joshua. "I don't think my dad focused so much on the words, but he liked what he called 'the strength of the music.' He also knew that I want to go to the ocean someday. He would tease me about watching *NCIS*. I just like that it's about the military service that protects those oceans for us."

Nora smiled at Joshua. "It's a lovely hymn. When it's sung in four parts, it's one of the most melodic hymns I know. I'm glad to know why Joe asked for it."

Once they were finished with the food and the plates had been cleared from the table, Joshua stood up. The soft talking stopped.

"Everyone here knows that I'm not one for big speeches. But I've had a lot of time to think over these last few days, and I," he stopped, his voice cracking. He took a moment to recover and continued, "I just want to say, thank you. Thank you for being my friends, for being friends to my dad. He was the finest man I've ever known."

"Absolutely."

"Amen."

"For sure."

"Truer words never were."

"My dad is gone. I believe, I hope, he's reunited with his God and my mom. Now though, in this moment, Dad would want us to live. He would want us to celebrate the blessings of life. He believed he had many. One of the things my dad and mom did many years ago was to establish a college scholarship fund that will cover all expenses for one student from our high school each year."

Joshua stopped and looked at Melody. "I hope the first recipient of that scholarship will choose the University of Tennessee. But it'll be her choice. She should go where she wants to go. On behalf of my parents, I'm pleased to share with you tonight that the first scholarship will go to Melody Emmerson." His six-foot-four-inch height allowed him to reach easily across the table. He extended his hand to her. "You have earned it."

Tears streamed down Melody's face. Everyone stood and clapped. Joshua lifted his tea glass. "Congratulations, Melody, we're so proud of you."

Others followed suit.

Then Chad lifted his glass. "Here's to Joe and Joshua Johnson, may there be more people like you in the world." Everyone touched glasses.

Bella turned and hugged Melody. "Congratulations, I'm so excited for you." Everyone began to congratulate Melody, and there were calls of "Speech, speech!"

Melody walked around the table and hugged Joshua. "Thank you isn't enough, Mr. Joshua. I wish I could thank Mr. Joe. I'll make you proud. I promise."

Joshua had tears in his eyes. "Melody, I'm glad we could help your dreams come true."

"Mr. Joshua, thank you again for supper and the scholarship. I'm sorry to say this, but I have an exam in the morning, and I need to go study." Gentle laughter burst from the group, and Melody's words served as a signal for everyone to begin to gather their belongings and head for the door.

Joshua called out behind them. "Doug and I will reopen the Valley Store tomorrow morning. Hope y'all will stop in."

"You bet."

"Absolutely."

"See you there."

Good Night, Bella

"I suppose we had a pretty good idea that was going to happen for Melody. I think it was a perfect way to pay tribute to Joe at the end of this day." Bella and Chad were sitting on his porch in the last of twilight.

"Couldn't have been better."

"Chad," Bella turned to look at him. She had finished her glass of wine and Chad his beer. "I have loved this time together. I'm sorry for the event that made it happen, but this has been very special for me. You've made it easier for me to navigate my emotions around the loss of Joe and the loss of the last tie to my daddy." She stopped and looked at him. He just waited.

"But..."

"I feared there would be a 'but.'" He tried to smile.

"You have a sheriff's department to run, and I need to head up the mountain."

"Do you want to go tonight?" He hoped she would not.

"I have my Jeep here, so I can get myself home. If it works for you, I'll go in the morning."

He leaned over and kissed her. "Promise me I get Friday night with you at the jamboree, please."

"Who could refuse those puppy dog eyes?" She laughed. "No one I'd rather be with. We can sort out details between now and then. Fair enough?"

"Fair enough. Speaking of puppy dogs, we'll need to sort out getting your new pup up the mountain. Hope you have a name ready." He took her hand in his and they watched the sun drop behind the ridgeline, flashing golds and reds off the leaves remaining on the trees. The blue-black sky appeared as quickly as the shutter on a camera; darkness arrived.

They parted at his guest room door. He was still hoping there would be a day she walked to the end of the hall with him.

Bella snuggled into bed. Her Not-So-Good List wasn't needed on this night. Her Good List started with reflections on the life of Joe Johnson, and the connection he had given her to her daddy for almost fifty years. She was so proud of Joshua for making this a day of celebration. And, as she thought about it further, she realized how much there was to celebrate: Joshua's parents cared enough about education and young lives to build a scholarship fund to send a deserving student to university. Melody, who worked side-by-side with Mr. Joe throughout high school, was going to get the first scholarship. Although it wouldn't bring Joe back, Bella thought it might help console Melody that she had been in his thoughts.

She turned her attention inward. *I'm happy that Carla is stepping up to help Joshua, and I hope he can see what I see: that she has loved him for a very long time. And last, but far from least, Matt was with me today. Maybe he settled a bit knowing that I'm getting to know Chad and may not end up spending the rest of my life alone. Makes it a good day on the wings of Joe. Thanks, Mr. Joe, for being my friend.* She curled up, rolled on her side, and went to sleep.

At the end of the hall, Chad's hands were in their usual position for his end of the day reflection, with his elbows bent, fingers interlaced, and the backs of his hands resting on his forehead. *Joshua, I know how tough it is to lose your dad; I still miss mine. I vow, though, you and I are going to be the leaders our dads expected of us. I also promise I'll be more attentive as a friend.* He smiled as he thought of Bella. *I'm not sure how two people in their late fifties will navigate this dance of courtship, but I'm so looking forward to the adventure. Sweet dreams, Bella.*

Chapter 19

Drellag Caban: Home

Bella felt her heart race as she took each switchback on the county road up to Drellag Caban; the anticipation of returning home always thrilled her. The higher she climbed, the fewer leaves there were on the trees; she was determined to sit out by the shed to experience the view across the valley at some point today. She wanted to enjoy what Chad had once referred to as the "painter's palette of color" below.

As she stopped at the gate to her land, she basked in the warm feeling of being home. She had replayed Chad's parting words in her mind all the way up the mountain: *Each day is a new beginning. I like starting mine with you.* He had kissed her and assured her he would call later in the day. She turned off the engine so she could walk the fence that now separated her land along Bella's Creek, much as the original did in the pen-and-ink drawing she loved so much. *I wish I could remember when the old fence rotted through and collapsed. Oh well, now I know that no ATVs can get onto my property from the road.* The early morning light was creeping across the mountains. The swoop of an osprey caught her eye as she examined the fence closest to the creek. *Drellag Caban, I'm home.*

The crest at the top of the road, where she always caught her breath at the beauty across the mountains, was going to be the perfect place for her new cabin. This morning, though, she drove up to her carport, excited to get a jump on a busy day.

She started by opening the windows and the French doors to the porch to allow the cool morning breeze to bring fresh air into the cabin. After putting in a load of laundry, she set her laptop on her writing table to organize her thoughts and finalize all the construction that was about to take place.

The tea kettle whistled before she could even open her laptop, and she went to make a cup of Earl Grey tea. She would normally use a mug, but this morning seemed to call for her special teacup, the one with the delicately hand painted dragonfly. As she puttered around the kitchen, it reminded her that she wanted to do something. *What was it? I know I made a mental note of. . . something.* She looked around the room but couldn't imagine what she was trying to recall. She shrugged her shoulders, picked up her cup of tea, and went back to her writing desk.

An hour later, she had read through the contracts from Macklin Evans on the prefab log cabin, and the one from Arthur Gillett to install it, repair the shed, and build a garage. It made sense to her that a garage was better than trying to close in the carport; it wasn't that well built to begin with. An email from her insurance agent indicated an adjuster would be out later in the day, and their settlement offer on her claim would follow shortly. She made a note to talk to Gray about the insurance settlement tomorrow.

She finally remembered why she was looking around the kitchen and jotted a reminder on a scrap of paper to ask Arthur to change out the overhead light and build a shelf for a microwave. *Maybe I'll just go ahead and order one online. I don't care how long it takes to get here.* She knew there was one more thing she wanted done but couldn't remember what. *Oh well, it'll come to me eventually.*

She put her jeans in the dryer and hung the rest of her laundry to dry on a rack in the small second bedroom. Bella fixed her favorite comfort food for lunch: a peanut butter sandwich. She pulled on her boots, picked up her sandwich and Yeti mug, and headed out to sit by the shed. It was a little after noon and the day was perfect. She nestled in the taller grasses, enjoying the feel of the breeze in her hair. Carl Patrick was scheduled to do one last check on the road and one more cut before winter, so she would take advantage of it before he did.

Chad had been right. The color was breathtaking: now the shades were mostly burnt orange, brownish reds, and mottled yellows. She leaned back against the shed and let her mind wander as she absently ate her sandwich. The first images of what she would have painted on the wall of the shed, once it was repaired, played in her mind. She wanted it to be a tribute to her daddy and at the same time draw the viewer's eye out to the mountains and valley. A picture was taking shape.

The Valley Store Reopens

Joshua was surprised but happy Carla had offered to meet him at the store at seven on Thursday morning, and the hours since then had flown by in a blur of bookkeeping and checking the stock. He couldn't believe it was already two o'clock; he hadn't eaten yet, and he was grateful Carla had stepped in to get lunch ready in the back of the store.

"You good, Doug?"

"Better than a hog wallowing in mud."

"Then I'm going to go back and have a bite of lunch."

"Miss Carla made chili, and it's really good. She had James send some fresh corn bread over and that made the meal. Enjoy it."

Joshua walked into the storeroom. Carla had the table set and was about to place a mug of coffee on it. She kissed him on the cheek. "You look tired. Let's eat." She smiled at him.

Their conversation while they ate was easy and comfortable.

"Thanks, Carla, this is really tasty. Appreciate all your help this morning. It's been good to be busy. The bookwork takes a lot of attention, but I've made a point to step down and speak to customers."

"James has told me the bookwork at The Corral takes concentration. Not sure how you do it in an open office."

"You sure you don't need to be at The Corral? Seems like more leaf-lookers than normal this year."

"It's good for James to spend some time on the floor. Makes him appreciate me more." Carla winked at Joshua.

"Do you like serving?"

"I don't mind it. Have to say, though, the older I get, the less interesting it is. Used to be that I was the one who came up with new menus. I also handled the inside remodel... that was about the time you did up the Valley Store, I think. Lately I haven't been able to flex my creative muscles. Although we add new things to the menu and have daily specials, folks tend to want the same ole things—not complaining, mind you."

"Didn't sound like complaining. Guess I haven't thought about the demands of different businesses since I graduated from university. Sorta settled in here, made changes in the slow way we do in these hills, and we've tried to meet the needs of the newcomers. That's busy enough for me."

"I'm with you on that." Slowly, Carla continued, "You know, we're always getting applicants for servers and busboys." She hesitated again. "If you need me to help out on the register until you decide what you want to do, I can make that happen. No need to rush into getting a new cashier."

"Really? You would do that?"

"Happy to do it. You know our head server, Cheri. She handles all the scheduling now. I wasn't joking when I told you I'm at the restaurant as a server just to have something to do. So, what do you say?"

"Well, it would really help out. I know Doug will help as much as he can, but it's hard on him to come every day. He's not as old as my dad, but I think he's in his late seventies. Do you want to think about it?"

"Nope. I'll let James know, and I'll look forward to learning something new."

Joshua reached across the table and placed her empty bowl in his. He stood to walk to the sink, leaning over to kiss Carla on the cheek along the way. "You're the best, Carla."

Never a Dull Day at the Sheriff's Office

Chad answered the phone. "Thanks, Cecilia, I'll speak with Agent Isaacs."

"Good morning, Quinn."

"Are you in California?"

"No, why?"

"Well, here in Tennessee, it's afternoon, at least on this side of the mountains."

Chad looked at his watch and saw it was already one thirty. "So it is; what's up?"

"Just wanted to let you know we're preparing to set our part of the operation in motion late this evening in Round City. We've been onto a guy for a while that we think is the link to 'el jefe' and, with any luck, he'll fall for our team when they try to give these 'girls' to him."

Chad sat taking in the information. He had talked with the police chief in Round City earlier in the morning and told him that his detective had traced ownership of the two motels to Commissioner Zimmerman, but he had not told him about the sting. He wouldn't at this point. It may not involve the motels, and that part of the operation belonged to Immigration Enforcement, even though the actual sting was happening in Chad's jurisdiction.

"Quinn, how involved is Chief Nelson on your side of the operation?"

"Not really at liberty to discuss anything with him until after the fact. Before you say anything, I know agency cooperation is ideal, but I have bosses too."

"Got it." He wasn't sure her position was any different than his own. He also knew that Chief Nelson's brother was the regional assistant director for the State Bureau of Investigation, and Chief Nelson might know if the SBI and IEA folks talked to each other. *Wouldn't it be wonderful if we all trusted each other?*

"Any word on Gertrude?" Quinn's question brought his attention back to the conversation.

"The DA and Detective Williams spoke with Gertrude this morning, and she took the deal. Our DA is pretty tough. DA O'Haire made it clear to Gertrude that the deal will be nullified if she tries to pass on the fact that the two women going in with her are law enforcement. Gertrude knows that if there's any deviation from the plan, she won't go to Bledsoe *and* she'll go away for the maximum time. Being the madam of a house of prostitution isn't the toughest job Gertrude ever had. She'll do her part and keep her mouth shut—I hope." Chad knew Gertrude wanted to be near her daughter and grandkids; it helped to have a bargaining chip.

"The DEA agents that will walk out the door of your facility with Gertrude are pretty tough themselves, and they'll keep her away from a phone. I promise you they won't miss a thing she says to anyone who shows up at 'the house on the hill,' or even a text."

"Sounds like you know them." Chad was focused on the overall sting, which would happen Saturday night if all the cards fell into place, but his thoughts were being crowded by Bella and the fact that he had already let it become early afternoon without calling her.

"Sheriff Oliver, are you still there?"

"Sorry, let myself get distracted. Sounds like things are organized and going according to plan. I had a deputy take down the crime scene tape yesterday, so I'm sure the word will spread once Gertrude is back this afternoon."

"These operations rarely run like clockwork, just so you know. I work hard to anticipate the unintended outcomes, but you just never know. I have a question for you, if you have a minute."

"Sure, how can I help?"

"I want to be on your side of the mountains the next couple of days and wondered if there was someone who rented rooms, like a bed and breakfast, where I wouldn't stand out too much having odd hours."

"The only official B&Bs we have are likely booked solid right now with leaf-lookers." Inspiration struck. "Listen, I have an idea, but don't know if it's feasible. I'll text you a message when I figure something out. That okay? I'm assuming this is for Friday and Saturday night?"

"Yes, that would be great. Thanks. Look to hear from you soon."

"Good. Talk to you later, Agent Isaacs." Chad decided he would talk to Bella about his idea for accommodation and see what she thought. He dialed her number.

Creative Thinking Saves the Day

"Drellag Caban, may I help you?" Bella answered the phone on the second ring.

"Good afternoon, Bella." Chad's voice was low and warm.

"Good afternoon to you! How's your day going?"

"Didn't expect so much time to pass since I saw you 'til this phone call."

"See, that's what expectations can do for you, cause you to feel you must explain." She waited a beat. "I'm happy for any time you call. While I don't know the intricacies of your work, I can appreciate that it must take a great deal of concentrated thought and lots of instantaneous decisions. So, let's add, 'no apologies needed,' to that list of what we accept in each other. Deal?"

Chad sat for several seconds, unable to speak. *Where on earth did this woman come from? I can't be this fortunate in life! I just can't.*

"Chad, did I lose you?"

"Just trying to figure out what planet you're from. Don't know if I've met anyone with so much patience."

"Oh, don't get too excited. I have my limits, but they generally come when others are thoughtless or cruel. Anyway, I don't think you told me if we have a deal." There was a smile in the lilt of her voice.

"Signed, sealed, and delivered. And, Bella, remember I told you I have a lot to learn from you? I had no idea how true that was going to be. Thanks. Now, how is your day going?"

"It's going well, thanks. Laundry is done and the floors are swept." She started laughing. "Sounds like a 'housewife' chore list, doesn't it? Did I tell you I don't do 'housewife' very well?"

"Don't need a housewife. Plenty of people happy to do that work and get paid for it. I'm getting a pretty good picture that you're the person I thought I would never find."

"And what would that be, fine sir?" She liked the flirtation.

"A partner in life." He was struck by the simplicity of it as the words came out.

"Sounds like an interesting journey to explore." She continued. "I'll tell you what I've done today. It will give you much more to consider about whether you want a potential partnership." She told him she had reviewed the contracts on all the construction and new cabin, and then spent time sitting out by the shed enjoying the mountains and the trees. "The painting for the wall is taking shape in my head, so if you know someone who can execute the ideas when I'm finished, let me know. When you called, I was working on a poem.

I'm trying to write an ode to Joe." She took a breath. "Now you know some of the many places my crazy brain can take me."

"I love hearing all of it. Thanks for sharing." He paused, not sure how to ask her what she thought about his idea to help Quinn out. "Wondering if I can run an idea by you that would help me solve a problem for a situation I'm dealing with right now?"

"Sure, I'm always happy to listen, and you'll find I almost always have an opinion. That said, you can take or leave that opinion as you choose. Fair enough?"

"Couldn't ask for anything more. You know, broadly, that I'm dealing with a case involving the trafficking of minors." He waited to see if she was going to say anything. She didn't. "I'm working with other law enforcement agencies to try and bring an end to it, at least in our hills. One of the lead agents in another agency is a single female, and she needs a place to stay Friday and Saturday night."

Bella jumped in. "Oh, Chad, she's welcome to stay here. Would that help out?"

He shook his head. He had not even considered that as a possibility. "That's very kind of you to offer, but, in this case, I think given the likely nighttime aspects of this, it might be too much for her to get up your mountain. Also, she might be concerned about getting back down if she's needed during the night."

"That makes sense. What are you thinking?"

"She could stay at my place, but I was hoping you would stay down the mountain tomorrow night after the jamboree. I had planned to talk to you about that part of my thinking later. Anyway, I wanted your thoughts about me approaching Joshua to see if she could stay at Joe's house. Do you think it's too soon? The location would be ideal for her; it's close to the station and the operation."

"Give me a minute." It was clear in her tone that she was already thinking about the possibility. "The easy part is me staying down the mountain tomorrow night. I have to come down in the morning to see Gray on the legal stuff. I was planning to go to the library after my meeting and stay for the jamboree, and it's easier if I don't have to drive back after. So, I accept your kind offer. Now, regarding Joe's place ..." her voice trailed off as she weighed her thoughts against Joshua's current mindset.

"Joshua and Carla picked up his dad's suit, so it might actually make it easier for him to go back again with a purpose. It would also be a way of putting 'life,' so to speak, back in Joe's home. From my experience, one of the things about these early days of grief is you want to be busy, and having something to do to help someone else can start the healing. I think that would hold true for Joshua. He's a kind and gentle person. So, I'd say to ask him. But do you have a back-up plan if he's not comfortable?"

"I think so. She could stay at Nora's. They have a guest cottage, but I'd rather not do that since the agent's here officially, and there are my young grandchildren to consider at Nora's."

"Do you think it would be dangerous for them if she stays there?"

"No, I just like to plan for as many contingencies as I can."

"Well, I'd say to start with Joshua. If that doesn't work out, call me back. In the meantime, I'll play around with scenarios. I love a good puzzle."

"Thanks, Bella. I like being able to problem-solve with you. What does the rest of your day hold?"

"I'm waiting on the insurance adjuster to look at the shed. In fact, I think I hear a vehicle coming up the road. Then I'm going back to the poem, and the rest of the day I hope to finish the book I've been reading. That's my day. I won't ask you to enumerate yours as I know your work is confidential, but I'll ask you to tell me one thing: what are you going to do that's good for Chad Oliver today?"

"I just did it. I've talked to you." His warmth and sincerity were evident.

"That's very nice of you to say. You brought joy to my day. Thanks. Now go take care of our hills, Sheriff Oliver. Talk to you soon."

"Bye, Bella. Thanks." He hung up and leaned back in his chair, wondering when he had ever felt so happy to spend personal time with a woman other than his daughter.

The Sun Sets and the Moon Rises

The insurance adjuster was there for about forty-five minutes and told Bella she would get their settlement offer within twenty-four hours, maybe even later in the evening. The woman had been very efficient. She asked questions verifying the age of the structure, the conditions under which the damage occurred, and she indicated she had a copy of the report from the sheriff's office. Bella reviewed the sketch the adjuster had drawn and took pictures with her mobile phone of the paperwork so she could reference them if needed.

The sun was low in the sky. Bella took some vegetable soup from the freezer and heated it on the stovetop. *Yep, a microwave would make it a lot easier on a day like today.* She put on her vest and took a wool throw out to put around her legs if she got too chilly. This week had been a rollercoaster of emotions, with a lot of time spent away from her beloved Drellag Caban. The comfort of eating on her porch would be one more step to feeling like she was home, and she figured the soup would make it doable: she would be warm inside and out.

As she ate, she watched the stars as they began to appear in the blue-black sky, looking like diamonds scattered across a piece of jeweler's velvet. She recalled a quote she had once read from the naturalist John Muir: "We all travel the Milky Way together, trees and men." *Ahhh, Mr. Muir, and even women.*

Once it was fully dark, Bella retreated from the porch and locked the door, then washed out her bowl and left it in the dish drainer. It felt like weeks since she had been home. *It is home. I have a pretty good feeling it's going to become my only home.* It was almost eight o'clock. She picked up the phone and dialed Chad's personal number.

Chad answered. "Hello there."

"Have a minute?"

"For you, almost any time, and I'm working on *any* time." She could hear the smile in his voice.

"Just called to finalize tomorrow, see if you were able to work things out for the female LEO, and . . ."

"Did you just say LEO?" Chad sounded surprised. "Where did you learn that?"

"Why, Sheriff Oliver! Number one, I read many, many books." She paused a beat. "Actually, your deputy, Amy Murphy, told me when she was up here last month. Something about LEOs will eat you out of house and home, but forensic techs are bottomless pits."

Chad roared with laughter. "Well, that's the truth, and I even know some LEOs who will give the techs a run for their money when it comes to eating."

"Glad I could make you laugh."

"I needed it, thanks. Yes, I talked to Joshua, and he was happy to help out. He told me he thought it would make him feel useful. Seems someone advised me that might be the case. What do you need from me about plans?"

"My meeting with Gray is at ten, and I can go to the library after that. Just need to know what time to plan to meet you?"

"I'm in good shape for the morning, so how about we meet at The Corral, and I'll buy you breakfast? Then I can give you a key to my house, and you can go whenever you want. You might want to rest before the jamboree. I should be able to get away by mid-afternoon, if all goes well. I told Joshua that we'd meet him and Carla at The Corral for supper about five thirty. We can then walk out to the music grounds with him. He's a little nervous about the Celebration of Life for Joe." He had thought about asking Bella to stay Saturday night but decided he wouldn't have to worry about her if she was up on the mountain, especially if anything went wrong with the sting on Saturday night.

"Then I think that answers my questions. I hope you have a good rest of the night. Are you home?"

"Yes, got here about an hour ago. The rest of my night is going to be in slumber, I hope."

"Mine too. Dream of me."

"No doubt about that, Bella. No doubt at all. Sweet dreams."

"Good night, Chad, see you for breakfast. Does eight thirty work?"

"Perfect. Looking forward to it."

"Me too." She hung up the phone then sat for a minute to let the good feeling sink in.

The house was closed up, so she needed only to make sure the kitchen door was locked and the porch light on. Done and done. She crawled into bed and turned to look at the silver frame holding the picture of her and Matt on their twenty-fifth anniversary. *Well, love of my life, I'm struggling with my love and loyalty to you, and what I think I'm feeling for Chad. I trust your words of encouragement to share my life with another man; I just don't know if I trust myself to find the balance in being true to both of you.* She was grateful for nothing on her Not-So-Good List tonight.

Her Good List was topped with many thoughts about Chad; he was kind, thoughtful, playful, intelligent, and had been very patient with her need for time, especially with the loss of Joe. She added thinking of—and talking to—Matt to her Good List. She felt she had a good grasp on the construction projects, and she would take care of the last things that needed to be done in the cabin. She had finished reading Louise Penny's book *Kingdom of the Blind* today, and she drafted a poem to Joe. *Drellag Caban, I'm home. I'm making progress on those wonderful new memories I promised.* She touched the anniversary picture and pulled the quilt up to her neck.

"Good night, Chad. I'm glad you've come into my life."

Chapter 20

Climb the mountains and get their good tidings.
Nature's peace will flow into you as sunshine flows into trees.

John Muir, 1838 – 1914

Let the Day Begin

Bella was headed down the mountain by eight, delighted to have the windows of her Wrangler down to enjoy the cool breeze. She loved the delicate color of the pale sky above the hills before the brightness that came when the sun crested the mountain tops. The "drink-your-tea" call of the eastern towhee was bound to float across the air at this hour. She loved that this was a bird that did not migrate in the winter. It was a settled bird, just as she wanted to be.

She glanced at her overnight bag on the passenger seat. Since she was only staying one night, it had not taken her long to pack her things, grab her computer, and be on the road. She had planned her wardrobe carefully to keep the bag light: being inside most of the day meant she only needed to wear jeans and her flannel shirt and vest. The jamboree would require another layer, so the first thing she had packed was her silk thermal underwear to keep her warm. *Maybe I should see about getting a second pair and leaving some clothes at Chad's house to avoid carrying them back and forth?* She smiled to herself and shook her head. *Whoa, Bella, let's try to take this one day at a time.*

She wasn't sure if she pulled into the side parking lot of The Corral at the same time as Chad, or if he was standing there waiting for her. It didn't matter; he was at her driver's door before she could open it. He opened the door, stepped into the open space, leaned in, and kissed her. She eagerly returned the kiss, surprised at her own need for the connection.

"Good morning, lovely lady. Allow me." Chad stepped back, swooping his hand back to usher her out of the Jeep.

"Well, that's quite a nice start to the morning." She laughed at the gesture, but to make a point she stepped ahead of him and opened the door to the restaurant.

"Oh, it's going to be *that* kind of morning?" Chad chuckled and shook his head.

"Better get used to it." She laughed and playfully pushed him through the door. "Will this ruin the reputation of the rough and tough local sheriff?"

"Not a chance." He saw Sam Nations stand up at a corner table in the back.

"Giving us your table?" Chad gestured to Sam.

"Wasn't planning on company, but I'd be honored if you and Dr. Anderson would join me." Then the playfulness he had observed as they walked in made him think twice. "Unless this is a private party?" He winked at Chad.

Chad looked at Bella. "Up to you. Think you can enjoy your breakfast eating with this mouthy young whippersnapper?"

"Ouch!" Sam pulled out a chair for Bella. "Please sit, whether the old man does or not. Might actually be preferable if he didn't."

"Okay, gentlemen, as much as a lady might enjoy the jousting of two fine men, this one would be honored to sit with both of you."

Cheri put water on the table for Bella and Chad. "Coffee?"

"The lady will have..." Chad stopped himself. He extended his hand to her with a questioning look.

"Hot tea, please. Cheri, isn't it? You've served me and... several times at the front of the restaurant. I'm Bella Anderson. How's Carla?" She had stopped herself before she mentioned Matt. *Why did I stop? He* is *my late husband. I could have said his name.*

"Nice to see you again. Miss Carla is doing real fine. She's going to be over at the Valley Store for a while helping out Mr. Joshua. So, in the meantime, I'll take the locals. Tea it is. Coffee, Sheriff?"

"Yes, please, Cheri."

Bella spoke before she left. "Cheri, just a minute, please. Have you ordered Sam?" He nodded. "I think we can save you a trip and order now, if that works better for you?" She raised her eyebrows to Chad, with a questioning look.

"What will you have, Bella?" Chad deferred to her.

Bella ordered a scrambled egg, ham, and a biscuit.

"I'll have my usual." Chad nodded at Cheri.

Bella turned to Sam as Cheri stepped away. "What brings you home?"

"Oh, just a little work to be done on this side of the mountain. Gives me a chance to have some time with my folks. Not had a lot of time for visiting them lately. How're you doing?"

"I'm well, thank you. As you must know, it's been a sad week in the valley. I hope you can come tonight to the jamboree to help celebrate Joe's life."

"Wouldn't miss it for the world. My folks are coming too. Mr. Joe was a kind and fair man. He always treated the people of our tribe with respect and appreciation for our traditions. One time he told me that as much as he loved this land, he regretted how so many Europeans acquired it. Seems he traced the land he bought for the store and his home before he bought it. It was bought legally by Europeans through the US government agreement with tribes in the 1700s, so he was okay buying it." He paused. "But that's a conversation for another day."

Bella looked intently at Sam. "Since I've been up here full time, I've realized how ignorant I am of our community and its history. I hope to learn more so I can be a contributing member of our shared place, and I hope you will continue to educate me."

"My pleasure. Now, what brings the two of you out to breakfast today?"

"I'll let Chad answer that one." Bella stood up. "If y'all will excuse me." Both men stood and Bella headed for the ladies' room.

As soon as she was out of earshot, Sam slapped Chad on the back. "Way to go, Chad. That was a pretty familiar interchange I observed as you walked in the door. Proud of you."

"For your information, *young* man, I met Bella in the parking lot. True enough, though, I invited her to breakfast."

Sam interrupted him. "I'll take that. You should have listened to me and taken her to dinner in Round City, but I'll take inviting her to breakfast. Good move." He slapped Chad on the back. "With fear of beating a dead horse, it seems pretty good to me that two fine people like yourselves get to know each other. Just remember, I'm the one who told you to ask her out."

"Well, you'll have to share those honors with Nora, but just so neither of you get the idea it was an original thought with you, I was intrigued by her the first time I met her in the Valley Store." He stopped as Bella walked towards the table. "It's all good, Sam." He smiled as Bella approached. "All good."

Cheri arrived with their food just as Bella sat down. "Anything I can get you?" Cheri looked at them. "Y'all need jelly or preserves?" She refilled Sam and Chad's coffee.

Bella said, "Blackberry preserves would be great. Thanks, Cheri."

"You've got it. Anything else?"

Sam looked around the table. "No, I think we're good. Thanks."

He looked at Bella. "How are things up on your land these days?"

"Everything's going well, thanks. My new fence was installed this week and repairs to the shed will soon be done. You'll have to come up and visit sometime."

"I'll take you up on that."

"I saw a sign about the upcoming powwow. I'd love to learn about the history of it."

"While we have always had tribal dancing and singing, the pow-wows started as a way to sell curatives to the European settlers. Sure you want the history?" She nodded, so he continued. "Powwow is an Algonquin word that has been adopted pretty universally across tribes. These days our goal is to celebrate our traditions and hope to educate folks who aren't familiar with them. Hope y'all can come."

"Would love to. I saw the schedule was published in *The Tuesday Tattler*, so I'll look at it closely. Thanks. In my profession... well, my former profession, we have a saying that I think applies to this conversation: 'Never a day wasted when you learn something.'" She smiled at Sam.

"Goes for me too," Chad nodded.

"Happy to help." Sam looked at his watch. "Time for me to skedaddle. Hope you have a good day, and see you at the jamboree tonight."

"Have a good day, Sam." Bella smiled at him.

Chad stood and shook hands.

"Do you need to head out too?" Bella looked up at Chad.

"Shortly, but I would like to hear what you have planned for the day." He sat back down and handed her a keychain with a bear cub and a key.

"Thanks, cute bear cub." A smile crept across her face. "Any bears endangered in getting this cutie?"

Chad shook his head. "Should have seen that one coming. No. No bears endangered. My ear drums, maybe." Bella looked puzzled. "It's a gift from Mac. He gave me two of them a while back. I called and asked him if I could give one to Miss Bella. Not sure my hearing has recovered yet. He was so excited, he was yelling, 'Yes, Grandpa, please, please, please!' I'm telling you; I may have to tell that little boy to back off."

Bella laughed so hard she almost spilled her mug of tea. "Oh, Chad, I hope they're coming tonight so I can thank him properly."

"They'll be there. He made sure I knew that *he* wanted to see Miss Bella tonight."

"Good deal." Bella winked at him. "Now, how about your day?"

"I asked first."

"Library after I meet with Gray. I have some research to do and emails to write. Since I have a bit of time before my meeting, I'm going to stop by and see Joshua and Carla. I need a few things from the store, but, more importantly, I want to see if I can help in any way."

"Sounds like a busy day. I have some work to do fighting crime in our little corner of the world. That said, I think I can be home around four. Would you confirm with Joshua and Carla that we're meeting here for supper at five thirty?"

"Will do."

Bella saw that Sam had paid his bill on the way out. She was curious why he left by the front door.

Chad got Cheri's attention and asked for the check. "Oh, Sheriff, Sam took care of the check. Thought you knew. He did ask me to give you this." She handed him a piece of paper.

Bella stood and had walked a few steps from the table when Chad caught up with her after leaving a tip.

She looked at him puzzled. "Problem?"

"You might as well read this note. If you don't know how talk flies in a small community, you'll find out sooner or later." He handed her the paper.

Proud of you, Grandpa. Don't mess this up. She's a good catch.

Bella looked at the note and then at Chad. "Is there a back story I should know?"

"In the interest of full disclosure, Sam and my lovely daughter have let me know in no uncertain terms, and on more than one occasion, that I better 'get to know that smart and lovely lady.' And Nora's latest words were 'don't mess this up!'" He feigned shock.

They were standing by her Jeep. She leaned in and kissed him. "Well, okay then, Sheriff, don't mess this up!" She winked at him and got in her vehicle. "See you later. Enjoy your day."

He stood watching her pull out of the parking space. *One of these days I have to find out why she backs into parking spaces.*

The Valley Store

The propane truck was driving towards the back of the Valley Store as Bella pulled into the parking lot. She wondered if the folks from the sheriff's department were still helping out or if Joshua was driving. The signs for the jamboree tonight and the powwow were both stapled to a new bulletin board to the side of the front door. *Is this your doing, Carla? Good idea! Can't miss it walking in.*

"Morning." The silver bell above the door jingled as she walked in.

"Morning, Bella." Carla glanced at the door as she spoke then turned her attention back to the customer in front of her. "Thanks, Mr. Wallace. Tell your wife I said 'hey'."

Bella stepped to the side to hold the door open as Mr. Wallace walked out. "Thanks for shopping at the Valley Store."

He stopped on the porch and turned around. "Ladies, I don't know what Joshua's paying you, but you're worth every penny. Thank you for starting my day with a smile." He nodded to Bella and continued down the stairs to the parking lot.

Carla laughed as she came out from behind the cash register. "We're not a bad tag team. Let me know if you're looking to come out of retirement. What brings you down to the valley so early this morning?"

"I have some shopping to do. I'll catch up with you in a few minutes. Joshua around?"

"He should be back anytime. He had a propane delivery."

"Oh, I'm glad he felt like doing it. Anyone helping him with that?"

"Couple of the folks from the sheriff's department offered to take the longer runs so Joshua wouldn't be away from the store for so long. Couple of those will be done this afternoon."

"Aren't we lucky to live in a community that's so supportive?"

"That's sounding a bit permanent, Bella. Have we convinced you to stay?"

"Leaning that way, Carla."

"Well, anything I can do to convince you, let me know. I'm all about a shopping trip to Knoxville from time to time if you miss the city."

Bella laughed. "Now, that's an inducement. Thanks."

The bell jingled, and Carla turned. "Morning, folks. New to these parts?"

Bella went about getting a few things she needed at the cabin and pulled out her get-when-you-go-down-the-mountain list. *Eggs and milk. Well, they'll have to wait 'til I go home tomorrow. Guess I'll come back and shop on my way home.*

She walked towards the front and heard Joshua call out, "Hey, Bella."

She turned. "Hey, Joshua. Well, I must say, you're looking as spry as a spring chicken."

He leaned down and kissed her on the cheek. "Looking pretty spiffy yourself. Jeans and a plaid shirt suit you."

"Aw, get on with you." She kissed his cheek in return. They both laughed. "Looks like Carla has things under control up front. Have a minute to chat?"

"Sure. Cup of tea?" Joshua stood at the counter in the storeroom.

"I'm good. I'd just like a few minutes with my friend, that's all." They sat at the small table. "Anything I can do for you, Joshua?"

"Not that I can think of. Carla is a blessing, for sure. She's a take-charge kind of gal, and I can see I needed some shaking up, or shaking loose, or... heck, maybe both."

"Most of us do at one time or another. Not afraid to take charge back when you want it, are you?" She was serious but tried to make it sound lighthearted.

"May not want to, Bella." He went quiet for a moment. "I've always been thankful to have my dad around almost every day of my life. The longest time away was when I was at UT Knoxville. And, God as my witness, I loved my mother and my wife to the ends of the earth." He paused. "I've been thinking about all those kinds of things."

She reached over and touched his hand. "Joshua, that's a good thing. If the most horrible losses in our lives don't shake up our thinking, well, I don't know what will."

"Thanks, Bella. I hope you can hear this in the way I mean it."

She waited.

"If there was a way to make it official, I'd ask you to be my sister. I love being with you and God knows there's nobody I've known longer who I trust, even with all the years you were away from here. But, if you can't be my sister, I need you as my friend."

She squeezed his hand. "Well, it so happens I'm meeting with Gray Olson in a little while, and I can ask him if there's a way to make it official. I'd be honored to be your sister, and I always wanted a brother." The look on his face caused her to regroup. "Relax, there doesn't have to be any legal paperwork involved. As a little girl I used to do 'pinky swears' with my friends." She held up her pinky finger and curved it. "So, let's pinky swear that we're brother and sister forever."

Joshua extended his finger. "I like this a whole lot better than what the boys used to do. Harold and I became 'blood brothers' by cutting ourselves and touching our bloody fingers together." He laughed loudly.

"Well, either way, it's official. Now, what does my big brother need today?"

"I need you to tell me. . ." He hesitated, and then looked her right in the eye. "Tell me it's okay that I'm seeing Carla in ways that never occurred to me—in more romantic ways."

"Joshua, I'm full of opinions and more than willing to share them. But you have to promise me that you know what I'm going to say is just that: my opinion."

"Fair enough. Fair enough."

"In my experience, loss of our loved ones takes our hearts and minds places we never thought we'd go. We have loss, sadness, love, hate, fear, and relief for our loved ones being out of pain. In my opinion, no one can tell you what your heart feels. It's yours. If you're worried about what people will say if you have a personal interest in Carla, don't. It doesn't matter. The people who care about you want you to be happy. If someone doesn't like your decision, they don't matter anyway."

"Funny, Harold told me something like that a few weeks ago." Joshua averted his eyes. *I don't think I'll be mentioning it was about you. Now I can see that, at the time, I was just grateful for your attention and friendship.* "Did I tell you he's like a brother to me? So, can you handle two brothers?"

She started laughing. "You might want to consult with him on that! I'm a strong believer that the more people who love you in life, the better off you are." She watched him for several seconds. She saw the contemplative Joshua returning. "Penny for your thoughts!"

"I'm not totally sure how I should feel less than a week after my dad's passing and six weeks after my wife's. But I know this: I want to live every day I have left."

"Me too, brother! Let's start tonight. Chad already told me we're meeting at The Corral at five thirty, so I'll see you there. Any problem closing the store?"

"None. Carla already has a sign ready to go on that new bulletin board to invite people to celebrate dad's life at the jamboree."

"Perfect!" They stood and walked to the front together.

"I decided to buy groceries on my way home tomorrow."

Carla nodded. "Oh, do you need a place to stay tonight?"

Bella looked from Joshua to Carla. *What the heck.* "I'm good, thanks. Chad has given me total access to his guest room anytime I need it." She winked at Carla. "See you at five thirty. Have a nice afternoon."

"Bye, Bella," Carla and Joshua said in unison. She looked back over her shoulder as she walked out the front door and saw them standing with their arms around each other. Bella smiled at several customers as they walked towards the door. "Happy shopping."

A Sheriff's Work Is Never Done

Chad arrived at the station, expecting to get caught up on several things, but the messages on his computer screen indicated otherwise.

Need to see you re: Steve Phillips deal. BW.

Technology list in your inbox. SW.

Murphy here, up to speed. AM.

He typed a response to Billy Williams: "C U in 15." He had just touched the send button when his phone rang.

"Oliver here."

"Sheriff, Agent Isaacs is on the phone. Second call from her this morning." His dispatcher was courteous but made the point it was a return call.

"Put her through, please."

"Hey, Quinn. Sorry I missed your other call. Any time it's urgent, just tell dispatch or call my phone."

"Not urgent. And good morning to you. Just wanted you to know that the guy we've suspected is the intermediary for 'el jefe', whoever *he* turns out to be, picked up one of our 'girls' last night."

Chad felt his heart rate pick up. The hunt was on.

"We're tailing at a distance, and I'll let you know if she's headed your way. Are Murphy and Thomas set to hang out at The Corral over lunch hour?"

"Yes, they are. So, why didn't the guy take both of the agents—"

She interrupted him and laughed. "Whoa. We haven't put her in play yet. Wanted to see if he'd take this bait. I have to tell you the most worrisome part, heck, the scariest, is knowing these women go in with no weapons and no means of contact. Don't get me wrong, they're well trained and competent women, but these are some bad actors, and you just never know what they will do, especially if they get spooked. Anyway, the team will make her available tonight. Let's just hope the current one makes it to the valley and not somewhere else."

"Yeah." Chad spoke very slowly. *I don't know if there is enough training in the world to convince me that I'd want my daughter taking the risk these women are willing to take. But, thank God, they are.*

"So, let's see what the day brings. Thanks for arranging for me to stay at Mr. Johnson's home. Joshua sounded really nice on the phone. I'm going to be over there around three to check in with him, then I'll check in with you."

"Great, Quinn. Call my mobile. And, hey, thanks. Thanks for being the bright and obviously capable professional you are *and* for helping me keep crime down in these hills."

"Gotcha, Chad. See you later today. Looking forward to the jamboree."

"Later, Quinn." He hung up and stared straight ahead. *Who knows, maybe we can show others that DEA, IEA, and local law enforcement can work together and trust each other. Might help to curb some of the crime in this country.*

Legalese

Bella drove up to the small, unassuming concrete building. It had charm from the subtle green, beige, and white striped canvas awnings over the windows and hedges planted beneath them. The door was painted a dark green and accented with a brass knocker, door handle, and plaque reading, "Oliver, Olson, and Olson, Attorneys-at-Law." The plaque caused her to stop for a moment. She knew Chad's father was deceased, so why was he first on the plaque? She was about to knock on the door when it opened.

"Dr. Anderson!" Gray Olson smiled. "Come in. Saw you drive up. We don't rest much on ceremony around here. Just come in anytime. Not usually all that busy to need to have someone answer the door." He directed her to a front room.

"I'm so accustomed to visiting the office of an attorney in a fairly big city that I appreciate less formality. Do you have a receptionist?"

"My wife helps out when I can't be disturbed, but she's pretty adamant about not working Fridays!" He laughed. "Can't blame her. I wouldn't either, but I get paid. She doesn't."

"Then I'd say that makes you a pretty lucky man."

"Without a doubt."

Gray handed her several documents and an information sheet. "These cover our services, and the information sheet will ensure I have all the particulars on your properties, your current attorney of record, that sort of thing. If you decide you want us to represent you, you can fill that out and get it back to me."

"Who is the 'us?'"

"Oh, sorry, my sister is the other Olson. She splits her time between here and Knoxville. She likes some of the big city client work and, most of all, she likes living in the big city."

"Got it. If I'm not being too forward, I see that Mr. Oliver's name is still on the plaque on the door. May I ask why?"

Gray started laughing. "Well, which do you want first, the serious or the funny?"

"I'm guessing the funny is too good to pass up. Let's start there."

"As things have grown more in these parts, we don't know everyone anymore. If someone calls or comes through the door that's acting a little too highfalutin', we tell them that we have to consult with Mr. Oliver. Then someone calls them back and says Mr. Oliver is unable to take on any new clients."

Bella laughed and shook her head. "Oh my, that's a great story. Have you ever used it?"

"No, but it gets a laugh out of folks when I tell it." He had a big grin. "The real reason the name is still there is that Chad's grandfather and father practiced law here for over seventy-five years between them. Most folks aren't interested in rural practice; poor folks can't pay much. But, like the Olivers, I believe everyone is entitled to fair representation. I love living where I grew up, and so does my wife. I'm grateful to the Olivers for taking me on as a wet-behind-the-ears new attorney years ago."

"It seems to me it's always good to remember the folks who helped you along the way. I've had several mentors in my lifetime and was always grateful for their wise counsel."

"I hear you. Now, to your contracts. I've reviewed both, and I think the structure and clarity of obligations on their part, and yours, is clear. Do you have any experience with Arthur Gillett?"

"Yes, about ten years ago he did some major renovations on Drellag Caban for me to make it a four-season cabin. I have to say this is the latest I've been up here in years, and I'm pleased with the insulation. Why do you ask?"

"I can't advise you on the fairness of the costs in these contracts. Given that you've dealt with him before, I'm assuming you've made the decision that you were satisfied with the value for the price."

"I've spent most of my life in a city, so I'd say I got great value for the money. That part isn't a concern for me. On the last work, I had Arthur provide me with his liability insurance and bond, and I verified his license with Harold at the county offices. Is there something else I should do?"

"Good for you. The only advice I would give otherwise is to make sure that no liens have been placed against your property for nonpayment by any suppliers or subcontractors before you pay the final bill. We can do that for you if you want."

"Ah, that's one I didn't know about. Thanks. We can talk before I get to that point. So, I'm good to sign these contracts?"

"Legally, yes. Have you given this enough thought that you won't have buyer's remorse?"

"Thanks for asking. I'm careful about doing pros and cons and sleeping on things. I have talked to Chad about it for another perspective. I trust Arthur. I have no choice but to fix the shed, and the cabin and garage are something I want to do. I also wanted to let you know I heard from my insurance agent, and I'm satisfied with what they will pay out on the shed. They will deal with the district attorney as I understand it. I have no interest in suing for punitive or any other damages. Can you give me a reason I should?"

They chatted about the advantages and disadvantages of pursuing anything other than what the insurance company would pay, and Gray answered all her questions about what would be involved if she wanted to take things further. The discussion convinced her that her first instinct was the way forward.

"I want to move on. I'm trying very hard to restore the spirit of Drellag Caban and my land. I don't want the negativity or stress with the options you've outlined. I'll be fine."

"Then I think we're all set."

"What do I owe you?"

"First visit and review of your contracts is gratis. I hope you'll decide you want me to represent you in Tennessee, and most of all I hope you stay in these hills permanently. You'll be a great full-time addition to our community."

"Thanks, Gray. If it's okay with you, I'll sign these contracts and ask you to fax the one to The Log Cabin Company on Monday. I'll take the one for Arthur, and I'll get this form back to you next week."

"Sure. Go ahead and sign, and I'll witness your signature. Just to keep it on the up and up, I'll even let you show me your driver's license." He grinned. "Then just give me a call and we'll send it right along."

"Thanks. I'll do that. Meantime, thanks for your time and advice. I appreciate it greatly. See you at the jamboree?"

"Wouldn't miss it. Mr. Joe was pretty special to all of us. I'll make a point of introducing you to my wife. She was very taken with your trio on stage last week."

Bella felt the heat rising in her face. She was pleased her unexpected performance with Nora and Sylvia had gone well, but she wasn't sure if she was prepared for an encore. "I look forward to meeting her. See you soon."

"Have a good day, Bella."

Chapter 21

Waiting

Deputy Amy Murphy walked into The Corral and joined Deputy Susan Thomas at the front table that gave them a view of the whole dining room.

"Hey, Susan, rough duty today, eh?"

"Could be worse, right? How are you, Amy?"

The two women, both in uniform, settled in and chatted about work in general, families, and life in the hills. They avoided the topic that brought them here. After being there for almost two hours, they both wanted—and didn't want—to see a county commissioner bring a young Mexican girl through the door.

"Sheriff?" Their young server asked tentatively. Both women kept themselves from rolling their eyes—a tempting reaction to the assumption that anyone in uniform was a sheriff. Amy looked at the nametag of the server and wondered who her family was. She didn't recognize her.

"Patty, I'm Deputy Murphy. How can I help you?"

"Well, I was just wondering. Is it hard to get in the sheriff's department?"

Susan pulled out her card. As head deputy, she was always ready to talk to anyone interested in joining law enforcement. "Hey, Patty, I'm Deputy Thomas. Give me a call, and we can talk about what you would need to do to join the force; I'll be happy to answer any questions."

Patty put the card in her pocket. "Thanks a lot. Can I get you anything right now?"

"We're good. Look to hear from you." Susan smiled at the young woman.

"Good luck." Amy watched Patty as she walked away.

The front door opened and Commissioner Zimmerman walked in. A petite female was with him. She had smooth copper skin, dark brown hair, and her eyes were downcast. They were seated on the opposite side of the dining room from the deputies.

Susan turned her phone towards Amy. "Sure glad Quinn showed me her picture."

"Oh, good. Let me see. I hate that I was out the first of the week."

"No doubt, she's the one. You comfortable with how we're going to play this?"

"Can't wait!" Amy watched as the two settled in at a table. The deputies finished up their coffee, paid for their meals, and prepared to move.

Murphy headed for the restroom and left Thomas looking at her phone. She had no idea how they were going to get the girl to speak in front of the commissioner and not give this away, but she was confident if anyone could do it, Murphy would. Susan stood and walked towards the commissioner, pretending she had just spotted him.

"Good afternoon, Commissioner, nice to see you today." She smiled at them both.

"Good afternoon, Deputy..." He looked up at her nametag. "Thomas." It was obvious he did not want to prolong the exchange, but he *was* a politician.

"So glad to run into you. I have a question about that new road proposal you've been talking about at the county meetings." She turned to the young woman. "So sorry, excuse me. I don't think we've met. I'm Deputy Thomas." The Immigration Enforcement agent looked down at the table.

"Oh, she's my niece, visiting from up north on fall break, and she's quite shy. She's studying Spanish in school, and she's only supposed to speak in Spanish when we go out in public. You know, for practice." He grinned from ear to ear.

Wonder how long it took him to think that one up? "Well, real sorry I don't speak Spanish."

Susan turned to look at Deputy Murphy as she walked up. "Commissioner," she nodded. "Did I hear you say you needed something translated into Spanish?"

"Translated? No, no. The commissioner was telling me his niece here is studying Spanish and can only speak Spanish while out in public on her visit to our lovely mountains."

"No hay problema. Como estás?" Amy Murphy asked the agent if she was okay.

"Bien," the young woman answered, keeping her head down.

"Necessitas ayuda ahora?"

The young woman shook her head, indicating she did not need help at the moment.

Deputy Susan Thomas smiled as she looked at the commissioner. "All Greek to me. How about you?"

"Can't understand a word they're saying." He snickered. "I even told ... uh, my niece this would be a pretty one-sided outing. Me talking, her listening."

"Well, lucky for you." Susan smiled, trying not to gag. "At least *she* can understand *you*. We had some Spanish speaking girls here recently, and they didn't understand a word of English." Susan saw the commissioner's face shift from jovial to alert. *I seem to have struck a nerve.*

"Verificaré que hicimos contacto." Murphy looked directly at the IEA agent. The young woman kept her head down and nodded, acknowledging that the two law enforcement officers had made contact.

"What did you just say to her?" Zimmerman sounded anxious.

"I told her I was glad we'd met. You know, 'contacto.' Well, we've kept you from your meal long enough."

"Yes, Commissioner, sorry to interrupt your visit with your niece. I'll catch up with you later to understand that proposal you made. Maybe there's some way we can work with the community on it." Deputy Thomas thought he looked slightly less spooked after Amy's explanation, and she hoped they had pulled off the contact meeting without him getting suspicious.

He nodded. "Sure. That'd be great. Thanks, ladies."

The two deputies turned and walked out the front door. Once they were safely in their patrol car, Murphy spoke first, "Well, that seemed to work out. Good thing Quinn told me to use the 'we made contact' message."

"Ha! You did it like a pro. Even though I knew you already had something specific to say worked out with Agent Isaacs, it still it sounded like a fine howdy-do conversation. Good job!"

Library Visit

Bella walked into the library, satisfied she would be comfortable with Gray Olson as her attorney in Tennessee. She texted Arthur to ask when he wanted to pick up the signed contract and let him know she was in the valley today. In her call to Macklin about the new cabin, he told her he was available tomorrow to show her the Overlook model and finalize things. *I'm glad I told him I'd call if I decide to come over; it saves me a trip if I'm not feeling up to it. Either way, he knows Gray will fax the contract on Monday.*

"Bella, hey, nice to see you." The librarian had been on the phone and not seen Bella until she was standing in front of her.

"Hey, Dona. Just returning the books I got recently, and I'll take a couple more of the ones you recommended. I've been wanting to read the new Robert Galbraith novel, *Lethal White*. Have you read it?"

"Yes, I think you'll like it. Working on your own book?"

"Well, let's just say that kernels of ideas are starting to form. It hasn't been the week to write."

"I was sorry to hear about Mr. Joe. Going to the jamboree tonight?"

"Wouldn't miss it for the world. If you'll let me know another book or two off your list of recommendations, I'll go do my email and then find them on the shelves."

"No need, I'll get them for you. Internet's been spotty today. Hope it works."

Bella spent the next two hours reading and answering messages. She also worked on the poem she wanted to write for Joe. A friend had emailed her an article about writing a story or poem in the one hundred forty characters of a "tweet," and she played with that format. She read it again. "You graced us. Then left us. Hearts once full, bereft. Service to others, our tribute to you." *I doubt if it'll be the only thing I ever write about Joe, but it was fun to try something different. Need to do some more work on it.*

An email popped up on her screen, startling her. She had been away from living with the internet, and she was no longer accustomed to new messages appearing instantaneously. It was from Bonnie, her editor at *Stories to be Told*. As with most writers, she viewed the email with anticipation and dread. *Was my story, "High on a Mountain: Altitude and Drugs," accepted?* She decided to go get a bottle of water before she read the email. On her way back, she heard Dona call her name.

"Bella, here are your books."

Bella pulled her wallet out of her jeans and handed Dona her library card. "Thanks, Dona." The books safely stowed in her bag, she sat down and opened her water and the protein bar she had been glad to find in the vending machine. *It's now or never. Let's see what Bonnie has to say.*

"Bella, great news. . ." she read. The long sigh of relief she exhaled never seemed any shorter, no matter how many publications she had. Bonnie went on to tell her that the official letter from the editorial board should catch up with her soon. She leaned back in the chair and relished the moment. Then it dawned on her: for the first time in a long time, she had someone with whom to share this good news—Chad. Matt had always been happy for her when her work was accepted for publication, as she had been for him.

It was two fifteen. Bella decided she would start one of her new books and leave around three fifty to get to Chad's house around the same time he did. She settled into the chair and looked at the titles. She decided on something light for a change and was grateful Dona knew she liked Patrick Taylor's books. This one was titled *An Irish Country Cottage: An Irish Country Novel*. She flipped it open to the first page and began to read.

Two Cases Down

Detective Williams was not surprised when DA Peggy O'Haire told him no one had called to say they would attend her plea offer to Steve Phillips. *Maybe your stepdad has more reasons to keep away from the law than you. Too bad, Stevie.* He knocked on the sheriff's door. It opened.

"Detective, come in."

"Morning, Sheriff, or I guess almost afternoon."

"Indeed, it is."

"Time flies when you're fighting crime." Billy was surprised Chad rolled his eyes.

Chad was seated at his round table. "What's on your agenda?"

"Steve Phillips. Wanted to let you know that Peggy O'Haire has had no one call or show up saying they would represent Steve at the plea offer. I listened to the recording of the phone call he requested to make. He didn't get to talk to dear ole stepdad, but his mother took his call. Boss, I don't know how a woman can be so coldhearted to her own child. He told her he was going to prison for years if he didn't get help."

"And?"

"And, with absolutely no concern for her son, she told him: 'Stevie, you know your dad controls the money. I can't help you, son. I told you not to hang out with that white trash.' Boss, I almost slammed my fist against the wall."

"Billy, you know we don't get to choose who comes through our doors. As for his mother's reaction, well, there's a reason my daddy used say, 'a hit dog always hollers.'"

"Yeah, what's that?"

"From where I sit, she knows she has made the choice of her comfortable life over her son. He hit her right between the eyes asking for help. So, she screams that it's all his fault."

"Yeah, I guess so." Billy paused as he thought about what Chad said. "Not sure what the DA will offer him in the end, but it looks like he'll be headed out of here today."

"Let me know." Chad watched Billy nod his head and remembered that he was about Billy's age when he felt like he finally understood another of his dad's sayings. *It takes all kinds to make this world.*"

Billy continued. "Gertrude and the two DEA agents are in place. Sergeant Whitehorse told me there was an uptick in drive-by activity last night at the 'house on the hill,' but no customers. Like you said in our briefing, the men would be watching to see if they were at risk of being arrested."

"The truck out front didn't entice anyone in?"

"Apparently not. Any word from Thomas and Murphy?" Billy was interested to know what had happened with the two deputies.

"Yes. Not sure if he *is* 'el jefe,' but Zimmerman showed up with one of the IEA agents at The Corral. We'll see how the night plays out. Just remember, we have no plans to move until tomorrow night."

"I know, boss. I know. Well, thanks for lending me an ear. I'm headed to meet with DA O'Haire and Mr. Steve Phillips."

"It's out of your hands now. You did your part, and you and Susan did it well. Protect the DA and let her do her job."

"Got it, Sheriff. Thanks."

Billy walked straight from Chad's office to the conference room to meet up with the DA.

"You again?" Steve glared at Billy as two deputies escorted him into the room. The sneer on his face was worse than before.

Billy ignored him. The deputies led Steve to a chair and took their places behind him. They did not uncuff him. This was the DA's meeting, and she would be unlikely to allow them to take off the cuffs. Billy was in charge of the recording, and he already knew the cameras in the ceiling were on.

"This is. . ."

"District Attorney O'Haire."

"Detective Williams and. . ."

The two deputies gave their names and Billy looked at Steve.

"And. . ."

"I hope this is the last time I have to tell you. I'm Steve Phillips." He gave his date of birth and tried to slam his wrists on the table but the chain around his waist prevented that. He growled.

Billy read him his Miranda rights. "Do you understand. . ."

"And, again, for the last time, I know my rights. I don't want an attorney. Just get on with it!"

"Mr. Phillips." DA O'Haire read the list of charges against him. "You have confessed to criminal trespassing and property damage in the commission of a crime. Is that correct?"

He nodded his head. "Okay, okay, I know I have to say it. Yes, that *is* correct."

"The grand jury of this county has indicted you on the charge of criminally negligent homicide in the death of Mr. Nick Brown who died in your presence by overdose of an illegal substance. You're entitled to a hearing before the judge, or a trial by jury on this charge. I will explain the maximum penalty for each of these charges and will then ask you for your decision in handling the matter." She enumerated the maximum prison time for each charge, the maximum fine, and the cost of restitution for the shed on the landowner's property. She further explained that if he were unable to pay any fines or restitution, any financial interests he held or assets in his name could be attached.

"In other words, they will be seized and sold, with the proceeds going to the state of Tennessee and the landowner." She paused, staring directly at him. "Do you have any questions?"

"$20,000.00 for that old shed?" Steve's anger was rising. "Who appraised that?"

"Mr. Phillips, the landowner's insurance adjuster made an appraisal based on the extent of damages to—I believe I'm correct in saying this—a historical building. But you are, of course, entitled to an independent appraisal if you defend yourself, or have an attorney for a hearing or trial." Peggy O'Haire was accustomed to dealing with aggressive comments and questions, and Billy had never seen her vary from this matter-of-fact approach. He wondered how long Steve was going to drag this out.

"Well, I might just do that!" Steve was getting more belligerent.

"Mr. Phillips, are you telling me you want a hearing or a trial?" Peggy asked, feigning interest in his comment.

Steve deflated. "No use. No one cares anyway. The good news for the landowner is my good ole stepdad let me put the ATVs in my name. So, attach away. Serves the old man right."

"Mr. Phillips. . ." Peggy started, her voice stern and serious.

"Hold on a minute!" His voice rose. Billy could sense Steve was caught between his tendency to argue and the potential for self-preservation. He dropped the attitude. "I think Williams said you could make me a deal. What are you offering?"

"Well, Mr. Phillips, the cumulative penalty for these charges is twenty-one years in prison and a fine of $13,000, plus restitution and court costs. If we go to trial, you might be allowed to serve the terms for the two major charges concurrently, so that would drop the maximum to fifteen years. The minimum for criminally negligent homicide, a Class E felony, is three years." She stopped and let that hang in the air.

"So, what's the deal?" Steve started tapping his heels on the floor.

"Well, you see, Mr. Phillips, I'd just as soon go to trial because I'm pretty confident I can get the maximum sentence, not concurrent. I have a confession from you and a grand jury indictment on the homicide charge. So, I'm not inclined to be too lenient."

Billy had admired Peggy O'Haire for many years, and this was a particularly strong performance. The two deputies stood like sentries behind Steve.

"I want a deal. I don't want to go to trial, or let the judge decide. What's the deal?" Steve's anxiety was clearly rising. One of the deputies put his hand on Steve's shoulder in response to his bouncing in the chair.

"Mr. Phillips, I'm prepared to offer you six years in prison, with the possibility of parole, a total fine of $5,000.00, and restitution to the landowner for $20,000.00."

Steve slid down in his chair. "What if my ATVs don't pay all of it?"

"There are ways to work out your payment. That does not have to be handled at this time. Do you want time to consider the plea offer?"

"I'll take it. What do I have to do?"

"We have to go before the judge. He will want to make sure you freely made the decision to accept the plea deal and were in no way coerced or offered other incentives to make a plea. Do you wish to go forward?"

"Yes." Steve Phillips lowered his head.

"The judge may have an opening on his docket this afternoon. You will be notified. Do you have any questions?"

He shook his head. "No."

All present stated their names and exited the conference room. Billy and Peggy stood outside the door as Steve was escorted to holding.

"The judge already told me he will give him a hearing at three. Can we get him to Round City by then?"

"He's all yours. We'll transport him. Thanks, Peggy. Before you go, I appreciate the way you've helped us this week. It's been more than we're used to dealing with on this side of the mountain; Gertrude done, Steve done, and I'm guessing you're working on a deal for the Kirk boys?"

"Yes, I think it was right not to take it to the grand jury on Tuesday. We'll let the Kirk boys cool their heels with you for a week or so. Then I'll convene the grand jury and get that one moving. Need anything else?"

"No. Just hoping the things that have piled up here recently don't become our new normal."

"Me too." The DA reached out and shook Billy's hand before leaving the station.

Billy walked down the hall to tell Sheriff Oliver. He'd take his chances with getting lectured for not calling first.

Chapter 22

One touch of nature makes the whole world kin.

John Muir, 1838 – 1914

Preparations

"It seems like everyone in the valley has been in today." Joshua looked at Carla. "As much as I avoided people when Jan passed away, I've realized it's some comfort to hear people talk about what my dad meant to them. Wonder why we don't tell people those things when they're alive?"

"Good question, Joshua. I have a lifetime of not doing that. Maybe we could start a new trend. What do you think?"

"I think that's a good plan." He stopped. "Hmmm... you know Dad and I spoke about this just a few weeks ago." Both looked up as the silver bell above the door jingled.

"Afternoon, folks, welcome," Carla beamed as she greeted customers. She looked at Joshua. "We'll finish this conversation another time."

"Yes, ma'am, we shall. Let's plan to lock up at four so we can get cleaned up before supper." He smiled and headed up the stairs to his loft office.

Getting Everyone Ready

Nora Oliver-Smith sat at her piano singing to Lilly, who sat on her lap; it was her favorite way to warm up her voice. Mac came running in the room.

"Mommy, how long 'til I see Miss Bella? Huh, how long?"

"Come here, sweetie." She pulled him up beside her on the wooden piano bench. She loved having enough space for her children to sit with her.

"Mac, I'm so happy you're excited to see Miss Bella. She wants to see you too. I need you to remember to walk in the house, not run." She kissed the top of his head. "Mommy is going to warm up her voice for a few more minutes, then we're going to eat supper, change our clothes, and it'll be time to go. I'd like you to take a rest. Daddy and I might let you stay at the jamboree a little longer tonight. Would you like that?"

"Yes, Mommy. That means I can be with Miss Bella longer. I'll go rest."

"Where are you going to do that?"

"I think I'll lay on the sofa and listen to you warm your voice." He yawned. "I love you, Mommy."

"I love you more."

"I love you more than you love me." Mac's voice faded.

"It cannot be." Nora knew he would be asleep in no time. She could already feel Lilly's slowed breathing against her chest. She put her in the Pack-and-Play she kept near the piano.

"Mommy, sing, please." Mac's voice was heavy with sleep.

Nora decided against "When the Roll is Called Up Yonder," which she would sing tonight at Joe's request; it was a little too lively to ensure sleep. She had finished her arpeggios and musical scales before Mac came in the room, so she began crooning "Mountain Lullaby" to get him settled. Thirty minutes later, with her two little ones napping and her voice warmed up, Nora reviewed her family's plans for the evening. She and Fred had already talked with Mac to explain that Mr. Joe had passed away. They wanted him to experience the Celebration of Life that would be part of the jamboree, but Fred would monitor Mac's interactions so he would not hear people talk about how Joe had died. Supper was ready, and she would feed the children before they left. If Fred was late at the hospital, he would meet them at the music grounds. She knew her dad would watch the kids until Fred arrived, allowing her to help the Greg Brothers set up. Everything seemed to be in order; she decided to sit down in the great room and put her feet up on the ottoman to soak up the gentleness of her children napping.

Checking Items Off the List

Chad took advantage of the few minutes of quiet to look over the incident reports for the last week and make sure he had a handle on what was going on in the community. He was pleased with the work Sergeant Whitehorse had taken on and the overall commitment of his department to chip in and help; they recognized the impact losing Joe would have on Joshua and the community. The knock on his door drew his attention away from his reading. He stood and stretched, then opened the door to find Billy Williams standing there.

"Hey, Billy, come on in. I need to get some water. Want some?"

"Beer an option?"

"Afraid not, at least not at the moment." He looked at his lead detective and was concerned. "Back in two minutes. Have a seat." He realized his own distractions with Joe's death, Joshua's needs, and Bella's presence had made him less attentive to the needs of his staff. *I need to get with it. Time for Billy to take some time off.*

He walked back in with two bottles of water, put one in front of Billy, and sat down.

"Thanks."

"No problem. The hangdog look on your face, though, tells me you might have a problem. What's up?"

Billy sat without animation, taking his time unscrewing the cap on the water bottle. Chad knew Billy had a tendency to turn the cap so fast he often ended up spilling water on himself; now, he lacked his usual energy. Chad waited.

"I was miserable when I walked out of the conference room, knowing that an eighteen-year-old boy is going away for six years, and his mother was too worried about her own comfort to try and help her son. His life will never be the same. Did he have any idea that being with Nick Brown when he overdosed would put him here? Do we teach kids that? Do they even care to learn it?"

Chad let him talk.

"Not sure I had a perfect childhood, what with the bullying I took for my name being William Williams. Even calling me 'Billy' didn't help much. One thing I always had was parents who showed me love and taught me right from wrong. They spent lots of time with me to make sure I knew it." He took a deep breath. "Now I do my job every day and take it seriously, but in the last month we've had three dead boys, and two others whose lives are pretty messed up. Does it really matter that they were eighteen or twenty years old? Adults in the eyes of the law? I just don't know."

After several seconds, when it was clear Billy had wound down and wasn't going to say anymore, Chad spoke. "You do know, Billy. That's why you're lead detective. You think about and analyze things from every angle. Sure, you get a bit flippant sometimes, and I have to rein you in, but I also know it's how you cope. You aren't being a smart-aleck just to be a smart-aleck. If we take off our hats that require us to uphold the law, we can see that these are people's lives. They're young people who we, as a community, have failed."

Billy nodded his head. "I know, boss, and that's what's eatin' at me. How could I have stopped this?" He took a swig of water, "Hell, even Gertrude never had a chance. Her daddy abused her from the time she was three. We just didn't know it until her teenage brother caught and killed the old man, and then *he* went to jail. Sorry, boss, it's been a rough few weeks."

"That it has, Billy. Tonight, we're going to come together as a community . . ." Chad suddenly had an idea. "I'd like to ask a favor."

"Anytime. What do you need?"

"Tonight, we're going to celebrate the life of the oldest European descendent in these hills. Agent Quinn Isaacs is going to join us, and she has not been to one of our jamborees. I'm tied up with Joshua, so could you make her feel welcome here?"

"Sure, boss, whatever you need."

Chad was surprised at the flat reaction from Billy. He appeared to be numb.

"That's what I need. Thanks. Then when we get through tomorrow night, I want to see a leave form that you're taking at least a week off in the next week or so."

Billy jerked his head towards Chad. "What? I don't have time..."

"You don't have a choice. You take leave... or I'll put you on leave. Got it?"

"Yessir."

"Now, it sounds like Steve Phillips took the plea deal. What did she offer him?"

"Six years, with the possibility of parole in three, I think. On top of that, there's a $5,000 fine, court costs, and $20,000 restitution to Dr. Anderson."

"Okay, sounds fair to me. When you get back off leave, I plan to have a meeting with our leadership team. Let's see if we can get ourselves more prevention oriented with these kids. Good with that?"

"Sure, sounds fine. Oh, and boss, Peggy O'Haire has a heavy load in Round City right now and will wait a week or two before convening the grand jury on the Kirk boys. She also feels the community needs some time to heal from Joe's death. She wants the grand jury to have time to deal with the loss."

"I know it'll be harder on Joshua to have it drag out, but it makes sense. Besides, we're not in charge and don't need to be. Those boys aren't going anywhere, nor is the elder Mr. Kirk. Let him cool his heels, too. From what Susan Thomas tells me, his wife could use a break. Now, you go home and put your feet up for a little while, and I'll see you at the jamboree."

Billy looked at Chad. "Are you getting out of here, too?"

"Absolutely. Plan to be out the door in the next twenty minutes. See you soon."

Meeting at Chad's

Bella could not get focused on the new book. She decided to take a chance and run by Doc Jim's to see the pup. It had been a week since she and Chad had found him; if no one had claimed him, maybe she would take him home with her tomorrow. Before packing up, she browsed online for a few minutes to research Doc Jim's hunch that the dog was a sheprador, a mix between a German shepherd and a Labrador retriever. The photos she came across certainly looked like the pup, and she smiled considering the names a friend's goddaughters had suggested. *I'll have to think about the names the girls gave me, especially for a sheprador that lives on top of a mountain.* She closed her laptop, made sure she had not dropped any crumbs from her protein bar, and stopped to say goodbye to Dona.

"Hope to hear you sing tonight, Bella." Dona smiled as Bella approached the check-out.

"Well, I hope to hear everyone singing, you included." Bella winked at Dona.

As she drove up the road to Doc Jim's, she began to wonder whether she should drop in unannounced, but Doc Jim was sitting in his usual place on his porch as she pulled up, the pup at his feet. She was two steps onto the walk when the pup jumped up and went to the top of the stairs, his tail wagging.

"Hello, boy." She reached out her hand and he licked it. She leaned in and petted him.

"No need for an approach anymore. I didn't even have to tell him it was you. He must know your footsteps already. That's a good thing."

"Get on with you, Doc Jim. I'm glad to see you too."

"Got time to sit for a spell?"

"If you can spare a few minutes, Doc Jim, so can I." She shook his outstretched hand.

"Just call me Jim. Saves me calling you Doc Bella. Doesn't seem fitting to your academic accomplishments, and I'd trip over Dr. Anderson."

"Deal, Jim."

"Heading to the jamboree?"

"Yes, Chad and I are meeting Carla and Joshua for supper at The Corral first, so I won't have long, but I wanted to check and see what you thought about me taking this little guy home tomorrow."

"I think that's a good plan. I've given him his shots since I doubt he's had them. I'd say you're good to go. I'm up with the songbirds, so come anytime that works for you." Jim spoke in the slow mountain talk that comes with rocking on a porch.

"Thanks, Jim. I'll settle up on his care when I get here."

"No need, I'll stick Chad with the bill." He roared with laughter. "Just kidding. Glad to get him ready for a good home. He's been a right good companion for me. My cats give me attention when it suits *them*, but that's something I've always loved about dogs: they're suckers for attention whenever *you* want to give it."

Bella stayed for a few minutes and spoke with Jim about the community and his life as a veterinarian. "It's nice to chat, Jim. I'll stop by from time to time, if that works."

"I'd be honored, Bella, anytime. Look forward to learning about your ties to these hills, and your academic career. Joe always did brag on you."

Bella wondered how many more things were going to make her blush. "Oh, Joe just felt an allegiance to my daddy, I think. Thanks for believing him, though. See you two tomorrow." She petted the pup and turned to wave as she reached her Jeep.

Jim called after her. "Don't be a stranger."

It was almost four when she reached Chad's house, and the garage door was closing as she drove up the hill. She parked on the parking pad to the right of the garage and grabbed her canvas bag with her clothes and toiletries along with the bag containing her computer and library books. She decided to pull out the books and leave them in the car. *No point in forgetting them at Chad's house and being without reading material.* She had a bag in each hand and was almost to the steps when the front door opened.

"Hey!" Chad called out as he headed for the steps. He stopped. "Help!"

Bella put the bags down and looked around to see if something was wrong. "Was that a question? Do you want help? Or are you saying, 'Help! *I'm* in trouble?'" She stood with her head craned back, looking up at him on the porch.

"Help, as in I don't know what I should or shouldn't do."

"What do you want to do?"

"I want to run down these steps, sweep you into my arms, and then carry your things inside."

"Then what's stopping you? Your sock feet?"

He bounded down the steps, picked her up in an embrace, and kissed her. She responded enthusiastically. "Welcome!" He looked into her eyes and let her feet return to the ground. He picked up her two bags, took her hand, and they walked into the house.

"Glass of wine?"

"Are you going to have a beer?"

"No, I generally don't when I'm going to be out in public. Old habits die hard for a lawman."

"Do lawwomen have the same concerns?" She cocked her head at him, smiled, and then leaned in to give him a kiss. "Sometimes I can't help myself. Don't take me too seriously." She dragged out the last two words. "Glass of tea will be fine. Thanks."

They sat out on the back porch and shared the events of their day. Chad didn't talk about any specifics, but he did share his concern about Billy Williams.

"Sounds like you handled it well. Will he take leave?"

"I'm sure he will. I might have to admit to some manipulation that could help him to get his head on straight."

"Oh, and what would that be?"

"I asked him to make sure the immigration agent has someone to talk to at the jamboree."

"And why would that give him a reason to get his head on straight, as you say?"

"Well, she's about his age, single, smart as a whip, attractive, and will definitely give him a run for his money in the jokester department."

"Why, listen to you, Mr. Matchmaker!"

"Whoa, not trying to be a matchmaker. I just figured if he spent some time with her, he might start thinking about having a life outside of work. Quinn may or may not be part of that time."

"Quinn? Does she have a first name?"

"Yep. Quinn."

"Okay then. Here's to Quinn giving Billy a run for his money." They clinked their ice tea glasses.

"About time I get ready if we're going to be there by five thirty. We'll meet my brother at The Corral: who I'm pretty sure *is* going to be with his love interest." Bella had a smirk on her face.

"Your brother? I thought you were an only child." Chad looked confused.

Bella told him about the conversation with Joshua.

Chad smiled to himself. *Well, good for you, ole buddy. And thanks for removing the competition for this woman sitting beside me.* He turned to Bella, leaned over, and kissed her more passionately than he had earlier.

"Well then, Miss Bella, let's get to supper and the jamboree. I'm pretty sure there's another admirer of yours champing at the bit to see you, four-years-old though he is."

"I am flattered by his enthusiasm. He's a sweet little boy." She kissed him on the forehead as she stood up and headed to the guest room.

Four Friends Share Supper

Joshua smiled. "This was a great idea. I like having a picnic at the jamboree, but I think it might have been too much for tonight."

"I think it's nice to just sit and relax and know we can leave the cleanup to James." Carla grinned from ear to ear.

Bella had her fork halfway to her mouth. "The food, as always, is great. Do you have a different theme on Fridays?"

Carla shrugged. "Depends. I know that Joshua likes lasagna and we don't make it very often, so I asked James to have it tonight. The dancing we're likely to do calls for a heavy dose of carbs. Hope you don't mind."

Chad held up the glass dispenser with dressing in it. "It's delicious. The salad is good too. Is this a new salad dressing? Don't think I've had it before."

"A friend of mine recommended it, and I found it on the internet. One of the best Italian salad dressings I've had. Glad you like it."

They were chatting among themselves when the door to the room opened and all four turned as Mac came into the room, tugging hard on Nora's hand. "Mommy, it's Miss Bella and Grandpa. May I go?"

She shrugged and laughed. "Yes, but do *not* jump up on Miss Bella."

Mac walked as fast as he thought he could without getting into trouble for running. Bella turned and opened her arms. He leaned in and she pulled him up on her lap. "Hello, my special friend. How are you?"

Nora looked from one to the other. "Sorry to intrude. Fred is running behind, and I need to get out to the Greg Brothers. May I impose?"

"Come here, Miss Lilly." Carla reached her arms out. Lilly stretched from Nora's arms to Carla's.

Chad chuckled. "Guess I'm chopped liver."

"Competition is tough, Daddy. But you're still number one with me." She walked behind him, put her arms around his neck, and leaned down to kiss him on the head. "Love you, Daddy."

Chad leaned his head back and kissed her on the chin. "Love you more."

"Already been on that round today." She laughed

Joshua looked confused. "Round? What round?"

"Oh, sorry. When I was little, I would tell Daddy that I loved him. He would say, 'I love you more.' Then I would say, 'I love you more than you love me.' And he would end it by saying, 'It cannot be.'" She smiled. "Mac and I had that 'round' this afternoon."

"That's really special." Carla had a big smile. "Don't you think so, Joshua?"

"Looks like these kids will take care of you older kids, so I'm going to run." Nora kissed her children, gave a hug to each of the adults, and headed out.

"Looks like we're the ones who got lucky tonight." Carla grinned.

"Amen," Joshua said. Lilly reached out to Joshua and climbed from Carla's lap into his.

Once their supper was finished, Chad took his grandchildren to the bathroom.

Bella looked at Joshua. "It's going to be a special night."

"I hope so. For my dad's sake."

They stood as Chad returned, and the six of them headed out to get the chairs out of their SUVs and find a place to sit for the jamboree.

Chapter 23

Jamboree

The sun was dropping quickly behind the mountain ridge, revealing the waxing gibbous moon that would illuminate the sharp craggy edges of the hills. Bella couldn't imagine a more beautiful backdrop to the music and dancing that would fill the air and float off to the far reaches, bouncing back from the rock surfaces that were now visible through the barren trees. Mac held Bella's hand on the way out to the jamboree, and Chad carried Lilly. Joshua and Carla had gone ahead of them to get chairs when they ran into James at the edge of the parking lot.

"Hey, Sis, Joshua. I've put chairs for all of you right over there." He pointed to an area where Joshua could see a big banner strung between two big trees. The banner read: "RIP Joe, you were the best of us!" Joshua feared his knees would collapse under him. Carla felt his hand tighten against hers and she squeezed back.

She stretched up on her tiptoes and whispered in his ear, "You've got this, Joshua." He held her hand tightly and kept walking. They made it to the seats under the banner. It was then that Joshua took in the crowd and realized most of the community must be here. The Greg Brothers were warming up, and Nora was singing softly.

"Miss Bella, did Grandpa give you the bear?" Mac's eyes showed concern.

It took Bella a second to remember the bear on the keychain. She lifted him up on her lap. "Mac, he did give it to me. It was so sweet of you both to share it with me. I like the cute little bear cub."

"Good. He will protect your keys. Bears are strong." He had an air of confidence that only a four-year-old can muster.

"That he will, Mac. Thanks so much."

Nora had left a blanket on the ground by the chairs, and Chad put Lilly down to play. Mac looked up at Bella. "I have to go play with my sister now. You'll be okay, I'm right here." Bella smiled and gave him a quick hug as he slid off her lap. He began a game of peekaboo with Lilly, both of them laughing uncontrollably each time Mac revealed his face. Bella couldn't help but laugh along with their sheer joy.

She looked up after a few minutes and saw Fred picking his way through the crowd. She waved to him to make sure he saw them, and Mac glanced up when he arrived.

"Daddy, look Miss Bella is here." He did not get up to greet his father.

"Glad to see I'm not the only one being ignored like I was chopped liver." Chad stood and slapped his son-in-law on the back. "Don't be countin' on any attention from Mac tonight. He's under Miss Bella's spell."

"Well, isn't that a fine howdy do?" Fred laughed as he bent to pick up his daughter and give her a hug.

Lilly squealed. "Da, da."

Not to be outdone, Mac pulled on Fred's pant leg and Fred squatted down. "I'm glad to see Miss Bella too. Give me a hug, or I'll be madder than a wet hen." Mac laughed and hugged his daddy.

"Evening, Bella. Thanks for being a trooper with these two rug rats." Fred smiled as he sat down on the blanket with his children.

"Pleasure's all mine, I assure you." Her words were drowned out as the band started up with the always popular "Rocky Top," and everyone was suddenly on their feet singing and clapping. Mac grabbed both of Lilly's hands and started hopping around to the beat of the music.

At the end of the song there were shouts:

"One more time!"

"Again!"

"Let's hear it!"

The Greg Brothers played one more refrain. People dropped back into their seats on the last call of "Rocky Top, Tennessee."

Nora welcomed the band and the crowd then called on Joshua and Carla to begin the dancing. The band started up with "Bonaparte's Retreat" as Carla and Joshua moved to the platform for the dancers. Everyone was on their feet clapping for them. As soon as they stepped up on the dance floor, the Greg Brothers started with "Pig in a Pen," and over an hour of dancing and singing followed.

Bella and Chad were talking with Fred when Sam Nations walked over.

"Found these two wandering around like lost puppies." Sam pointed to Quinn and Billy. "Pretty sure the detective here can explain the jamboree part of the evening to this big city gal, but I don't know if he knows the dance our folks are going to do."

"Thanks, Sam." Billy glared at him. "I think Quinn knows about jamborees and clogging. What do *you* plan to tell us?"

"I thought Miss Bella, the most educated one of this bunch... Oh, sorry, Doc Smith, didn't see you sitting down there. The two fine doctors here..."

"Okay, okay!" Chad put up his hands in mock surrender. "Pull up a chair, folks, and let Sam enlighten us with whatever is stuck in his craw."

Sam positioned himself in front of the group. "Seriously, I thought you might like to know about the dance some of our tribe members are doing in honor of Mr. Joe. It's our healing dance. We believe this dance realigns our spirits and provides healing and comfort to bring us peace."

Bella smiled at Sam. "Thanks, Sam. How lovely. Although I'm sure I would enjoy the artistry of the dance, I like knowing the beliefs." She looked at the others sitting with them, and decided she would ask her question, hoping it didn't offend Sam. "I have a question, not related to the dance."

"Sure, what's that?"

"Is there a reason you don't use the side door at The Corral like other locals?"

Chad watched Sam. "I learned about that recently myself. Mind if I give it a shot, Sam?"

"Look forward to it."

"Chief Whitehorse recently told me he uses the front door in honor of all of his ancestors who were never allowed to enter the front door of any business owned by European settlers. There may be another reason Sam wants to share."

"You nailed it. Mind you, this is not about The Corral or the family that owns it. They always welcomed us, from the time Carla and James' folks started it. But we know the sting of the humiliation of our forefathers in many places, so we honor them in this small way. We don't do it to make a point. We do it to honor those who came before us."

Bella sat without saying a word and, like the other adults, nodded her head in understanding.

Sam clapped his hands together. "Hey, this is a night to celebrate the life of a man who showed all of us what it means to be kind and gentle and funny. So, let's leave this heavy talk for another day. What do you say?"

Billy clapped Sam on the back. "Come on then, Sam. Let's take Miss Quinn up to that dance floor and teach her a few clogging steps."

"Whoa, not me. Two left feet and all that. You two have fun," Sam said. He shook Billy's hand and gave him a gentle push towards the dance floor.

Billy grabbed Quinn's hand. "Let's do this!"

Chad smiled to himself, relieved that the night might let Billy leave some of the angst of the past several weeks behind.

As more people gathered on the dance floor, Carla steered Joshua out of the crowd of dancers. When they approached Bella and Chad, Joshua was taken aback by the lineup of people under the banner waiting to speak to him. His normally reflective self struggled with the thought of speaking to everyone, but he knew they wanted to express their condolences and respect for his dad. That gave him the strength to face the crowd. *Having Carla with me will make it easier. She'll talk to all of them. I can do this.* They greeted and spoke to each person, and Carla kept the line moving.

Soon the music stopped, and everyone turned towards the stage as Pastor Fisk walked up the steps. Nora requested a moment of silence, and the pastor asked a blessing on the people gathered to celebrate the life of Joe Johnson and a special prayer of comfort for Joshua. Although his prayer was as gentle as the life Joe lived, everyone present gave a loud "Amen" when he finished.

The Greg Brothers immediately started playing, "Go Tell it on the Mountain," and Nora invited the crowd to sing. They joined in enthusiastically, and Joshua sat down, letting the music wash over him. Mac walked over, and Joshua picked him up.

"Hey, Mac. Thanks for coming to sit with me."

"Sure, Mr. Joshua. We made a prayer to Mr. Joe and told him we'd take care of you."

Tears welled in Joshua's eyes. He bounced Mac on his knee in time to the music.

Bella looked down and smiled at the scene. She knew all too well the need for unassuming connections in the time of grief, something children did easily. *I wonder at what age we lose the ability to just 'be' with another person? No words, just human connection.*

Nora stepped to the microphone. "Anyone who would like to share something about Mr. Joe, please come forward." She walked down the steps and handed the microphone to the first person.

Twenty or so folks came forward and talked about Joe.

"He was kind."

"He was always fair."

"He helped out when folks were hungry."

"Never a selfish bone in his body."

And so the tributes went. Pastor Fisk stepped back to the microphone. "Heavenly Father," he began as a quiet came over the crowd. This community of hill and valley folks, native tribe and European descendants, knew a link to their heritage was gone. It was a time of coming together and acknowledging their common humanity. At the sound of the pastor's "Amen," there was an echoing and resounding "Amen!" throughout the crowd.

"If you'll turn your attention to the dance floor, we have a special honor tonight in tribute to Mr. Joe. Chief Whitehorse, please." All eyes turned to the dance floor. Nora handed the microphone to the chief.

"Tonight, we honor a great man, Joe Johnson. We will perform our healing dance to pray that this night we come together in harmony and healing." He handed the microphone back to Nora. The intricacies and individual movement of the dancers from the local tribe was watched by all. One of the deputies on duty moved closer to a man who was known to shout profanities at natives, but even he was respectful tonight. Everyone clapped at the end of the dance as the dancers moved off the floor.

"Mr. Joe," Nora began as she was drowned out by chants of "Joe! Joe! Joe!" until she lifted her hands, palms out signaling for quiet.

"Mr. Joe had a special request for the following hymn. I hope you'll join in. Then I'm asking Miss Bella, Miss Sylvia, and Miss Nancy to join me up here to lead us in our last number."

She turned and looked at the Greg Brothers, and they started to play, "When the Roll is Called Up Yonder." Nora began to sing: "When the roll is called up yonder, I'll be there. When the roll is called up yonder, I'll be there." The people in the crowd started to sing with her, joined arms, and swayed.

Chad leaned over to Bella and pointed to Lilly, who was sound asleep in Fred's lap. "Time for you to head to the stage." Mac began to pull on Bella's hand. "And I think there's a little boy who might like to go with you." Bella smiled and let Mac pull her to her feet. They headed to the stage together, running into Sylvia Whitehorse on their way there. Bella extended her hand and Sylvia took it. Nancy Olson was already at the bottom of the steps. As the last chorus was sung, Nora nodded to them to come up on the stage.

Nora began. "Tonight has been a special gathering at our jamboree. When we're feeling a little cross or tired, I hope we'll remember the example Mr. Joe set for us every day, every time we were around him. He was kind, gentle, always had a smile, and we all counted on his sense of humor. He was truly an amazing man." The band started to play "Amazing Grace."

"Amazing Grace, how sweet the sound," Nora sang softly. She extended her hands to the other three women to join her then reached down to pick up her son. "That saved a wretch like me," they all sang. After the first verse, the crowd joined in, and, as the last verse started, Bella, Nancy, and Sylvia stepped away to leave Nora and Mac on stage.

Bella was overwhelmed with the quiet energy in the crowd as everyone stood singing with Nora, swaying slightly and holding hands. *This* is *my community. I promise you, Joe, that just as I want to restore the magic to Drellag Caban, I will work to help bring this community together for the good of everyone. Thanks for gracing us with your life, and for loving my daddy and me.* Chad walked up to meet her and could see the mixture of love and sadness on her face. He pulled her into his arms, and they too swayed with the last of the music as the Greg Brothers played the ending and folks quietly sang, "When we've been there ten thousand years, bright shining as the sun, we've no less days to sing God's praise, than when we'd first begun."

Take Me Home

Joshua wasn't sure how much longer he could stay on his feet. "Ready?" He turned to Carla. She nodded, grateful her brother knew they would want to try and get away without having to worry about gathering up chairs. Fred had Lilly on his shoulder, and Chad picked up the blanket, folded it, and tucked it under his arm. He took Bella's hand. Nora, who usually stayed and helped the band put away their equipment, had been sent on her way by the oldest Greg brother. She carried Mac and joined the small group as they headed towards their cars. They said their goodnights, exchanged hugs and handshakes, and all smiled. Mac looked at Bella. "Miss Bella, you sing almost as good as my mommy. Keep trying."

Bella kissed him on the cheek as his head rested on Nora's. "Good night, sweet Mac. I hope to see you again soon."

"Okay," Mac was fighting to keep his eyes open.

"Thanks, Bella." Nora kissed her on the cheek. "Thanks for coming into our lives." She stepped around Bella. "Excuse us." Chad and Bella stopped. "Night, Daddy. Treat Bella right, you hear me?" She kissed her daddy, and he kissed her back. Chad kissed his grandson's head.

"Doing the best I can."

"If you need him to do better, let me know." Nora smiled at Bella and walked off.

Chad and Bella called "Goodnight" in unison as Nora waved her hand high above her head.

Gray Olson walked up beside Bella with his wife, Nancy. "Bella, I want to introduce my wife."

Bella and Chad stopped and turned towards the couple. Chad and Gray slapped each other on the back. Bella extended her hand to Nancy. "I thought that might be you on stage. You're Nora's friend too, aren't you?"

"One and the same: wife and friend." Nancy shook hands with Bella then turned and kissed Chad on the cheek. "Hey, Chad. Good to see you keeping company with a fine lady like Miss Bella."

"You have a lovely voice. Now that I've made the connection, please let me thank you for taking Mac and Lilly the other day so Nora could help me out."

"Always fun to have them with our kids. We left them home with my mom tonight, but we would love for you to meet them."

"I'd love that. Let me know where and when." Bella's voice was kind and sincere.

"We'll do that. It's a promise." Nancy gave a slight wave as she and Gray walked on.

Chad opened the passenger door of his SUV for Bella. She climbed in and rested her head against the headrest; she didn't move when Chad got in.

"Tired?"

"In a really good way. How about you?"

"I'd agree with that. If it's not too chilly for you, I think a drink on the porch under this beautiful moon will be the perfect ending to this day."

"Deal." Bella leaned over and kissed him.

Calling it a Night

Chad looked at her. "I reckon this is an evening we'll remember for some time to come."

"Do you ever wonder where so many of our sayings originated?" She was sipping her wine, and Chad was drinking his beer.

"Sometimes. Have to admit, I don't have a lot of experience examining the intricacies of language like you do, madam professor." The good humor in his tone was apparent.

"Hearing you say 'reckon' made the phrase 'heavens to Betsy' pop into my head. Then I thought, 'why Betsy?'" She started laughing. "I *have* told you I have these weird, random thoughts, right?"

"Only one of your many endearing charms, Miss Bella. I do have to say that sitting with you on the porch in the moonlight, without competition from my grandson I might add, is a great way to end the day."

Bella lifted her glass to his bottle and smiled. "I'll give you most of that. Your grandson *is* charming, but I don't know if I have the stamina to keep up with him."

Chad started laughing as he clinked his bottle to her glass. His secure phone buzzed. *Just one night... can't I have one evening not interrupted by this phone?* He looked at Bella and shrugged.

"Oliver here."

Their drinks finished, Bella took the empty bottle from Chad and walked into the kitchen so he could take his call. *Never imagined the life of a sheriff. Wonder if he ever feels his time is his own?* She rinsed out the glass and put it in the dishwasher and his beer bottle in the recycle bin. She turned out the kitchen light and headed for the guest room. Chad met her halfway. He pulled her into a hug. They stood silently in a close embrace.

"Sorry. I warned you ... "

She interrupted him by putting her finger on his lips. "Shhh... I don't need an apology. It's okay. Actually, it makes me feel more secure knowing our sheriff is on duty."

"Yeah, like a dull toothache."

"I'm going to bid you goodnight and let you deal with whatever is calling you to crime prevention. Thanks for a lovely evening and for being my support as I deal with the loss of Joe. Sweet dreams." She kissed him and stepped into his guest room.

"Good night, Bella. Dream of me."

She turned and looked at him. "Back atcha."

Chad turned and went into his office. He couldn't believe his good fortune to have met this woman. He turned on his computer and sat down to read the report that the desk sergeant had called about.

Bella took a shower, towel dried her hair, and climbed into bed. She lay thinking of her day. She was relieved to have nothing on her Not-So-Good List tonight, nothing at all. *Well, maybe the abrupt ending to it with the phone call. Guess I'll have to get used to it if this man is going to be in my life.*

Then she thought of her Good List. Definitely number one tonight was the life of Joe Johnson. He had always been kind to her, shared memories of her daddy, and now she knew how much he meant to the community. She added time with Carla, Joshua, and the Oliver-Smith family at the jamboree. She was grateful for Sam Nations, who seemed comfortable helping her learn about native life in these mountains. Although she felt awkward being called up on the stage, she enjoyed singing with Nora, Sylvia, and Nancy; she added it to her Good List, along with the invitation to meet Nancy and Gray's family. It suddenly dawned on her that she had forgotten to tell Chad about her story being published. She added it to her Good List that she thought about Matt, and she knew he would be pleased for her publication. She felt sleep coming on quickly, and her last thoughts were of Chad. *You're making my Good List every night, Chad Oliver. I wish you sweet dreams.*

Chad shut the door to his home office so the light didn't seep through the bottom of the guest room door and disturb Bella. The report he had read indicated the plainclothes deputy had followed the commissioner back to Round City with the IEA agent posing as a young Mexican girl. Zimmerman left her sitting in the lobby of one of the motels he owned. Zimmerman then came back around seven and picked her up and took her to the 'house on the hill'. *Guess the encounter with Thomas and Murphy spooked him.* The team had expected Zimmerman to take the young woman directly to the 'house on the hill' from The Corral. *Wonder if he knew we were tailing him?*

The two DEA agents posing as the local women who went to the house with Gertrude both had mobile phones. Quinn Isaacs had reported receiving a text saying that Zimmerman had taken the IEA agent into the house around seven and Gertrude put her in a room. They could hear a heated argument between Gertrude and Zimmerman. Gertrude had apparently not given anything away, and Zimmerman left yelling, "You better get this business back up and running now!"

Chad leaned back and sighed. While he wasn't convinced that this information was urgent enough to interrupt his evening with Bella, he realized that his sergeant was accustomed to sending him messages and calling at any hour. *Guess that means that the grapevine isn't growing so fast that they all know there's a woman in my life now. Oh well, time to see if I can sleep.*

He logged off his computer, took a shower, and went to bed. Tonight, he laced his fingers together across his chest as he stared at the ceiling. He knew he needed his head in the game for the unfolding operation. There was no telling what the next few days would bring. *I just want to catch Zimmerman and whoever else is part of his shenanigans.* He stopped himself. He knew the commissioner was up to more than shenanigans. He couldn't let himself be naïve; the next several days would bring some serious police work.

His thoughts turned to Joshua and Joe, and the knowledge that he would need to manage his role as sheriff and friend in the coming days as decisions were made about the Kirk boys. Lastly, his thoughts turned to Bella. *Please don't get discouraged by the demands of my job. I promise you, Bella, I'm going to back out of many of the things I took on because I had nothing else to do.* He smiled as he fell asleep thinking of Bella.

Chapter 24

Headed to Drellag Caban

As dawn broke on Saturday morning, Bella sat drinking her cup of tea on Chad's porch while enjoying the last song of the whippoorwills as the early morning light started its ascent over the mountaintops. She was looking forward to returning to Drellag Caban. She heard Chad's footfalls down the hall and called out to him, "Good morning."

"Good morning to you." He stepped onto the porch and leaned over to give her a kiss. "I'm not sure if it was the anticipation of your presence when I awoke or the smell of the coffee, but in both cases, thanks."

"I think that's 'in either case.'"

"Only if you mean 'either.' I mean 'both.'" He winked at her.

"Well, well. The teacher learns a lesson. Fair enough." She bowed her head in respect.

"Would you like more tea while I'm in the kitchen?"

"I'm good at the moment, thanks though."

Chad returned with his coffee. As he sat down next to her, he asked quietly, "Hear that?"

"The whippoorwills? Yes, I was sitting here thinking about what you told me about the last call of the whippoorwills. Maybe this is the last call before migration; they seem very active this morning."

"Speaking of activity this morning, what's on your agenda?"

"Spending time with you. Whatever you can spare. Then I need to buy some groceries and dog food, after which I'll swing by Doc Jim's and pick up the pup. I was going to go to Round City to the prefab cabin displays, but I decided I don't need to do that. I know what I want. I signed the contract with Gray yesterday, and he'll fax it to them on Monday. I can pay the deposit by credit card, so I'm good to go." She looked at him and grinned. "Worn out yet?"

"Not quite yet."

"It'll take some time to help the pup get settled into a routine."

"Have a name for him?"

"Promise you won't laugh?"

"I'll try. Best I can promise." He grinned.

"One of my dear friends has two sweet, young goddaughters who were visiting her yesterday. She and I were exchanging emails, and she asked them what I should name my new dog. After some apparently serious deliberation, they came up with a shortlist of their favorites: Dex, Syrup, Wizard, and Peanut."

"Sounds like you have some good choices there. What did you decide?"

"Drum roll, please." Chad lightly tapped his hands on the table. "Dex the Wizard." She raised her eyebrows and looked up at him. "What do you think?"

"I think that's a mouthful when you call a dog home." He laughed

"I know. I think I'll call him Wizard and, if he doesn't respond to that, I'll try Dex. I'm telling Doc Jim to list him as Dex the Wizard, though."

"Then Wizard it is! Does Jim know you're coming by?"

"Yes." She nodded. "In all of the activity yesterday I forgot to tell you two things. One is that I stopped by and had a short visit with Jim and the pup soon to be called Wizard. The second is that the story I submitted to my editor at *Stories to be Told* was accepted for publication by their editorial board."

He leaned over and kissed her. "Congratulations on both the pup and the publication. Do I get to read your story one of these days, or do I have to wait on it to come out in print?"

"Happy to email it to you, or you can wait. Up to you."

"At least tell me the title."

"'High on a Mountain: Altitude and Drugs.'" She looked from the mountains towards Chad.

He sat very still; his face was like granite.

"Chad, are you in there?" A chill ran up her spine. *Is he angry?*

"You wrote about what happened on your land?" His voice was as cold as his face was hard.

"Excuse me." She had a long history of avoiding conflict, and her voice trembled as she stood and left the porch.

Chad did not move.

Saturday at the Valley Store

Joshua couldn't believe how busy they were so early on Saturday morning, then he remembered they closed early yesterday. He had urged Carla to sleep in this morning, but she had been waiting for him when he got to the store at six thirty.

"Whew, that rush was almost like breakfast at The Corral."

"Guess I never thought about what it was like for you trying to get orders, deliver them, and keep people's coffee mugs filled. Speaking of which, want some coffee?"

"Sure, that'd be great. No one's in the parking lot, I'll walk back with you."

Joshua poured them each a mug of coffee then positioned himself where he could see the front door. "Thanks, Carla. Thanks for everything."

"Get on with you on a Saturday morning, Joshua Johnson. I'm happy to help out, and frankly it's a nice change of pace from running around in the restaurant. Might have to up my exercise though; not as much activity here as I get there."

"Guess I never thought about it. Dad was always the one up front. I get plenty of exercise stocking shelves and moving inventory around back here. Guess I wasn't very attentive to what it must have been like for him."

"Oh, I'm pretty sure after so many of years of helping with the stock and inventory, he was probably grateful to be standing in the front. I'm not complaining, mind you. Just don't want to lose my girlish figure."

Joshua set his coffee mug on the counter and stepped towards her. "Don't think you're likely to have to worry about that. You look …" he reached out to embrace her just as the silver bell above the front door began to jingle. "Mighty fine to me," he finished, dropped his arms, and walked out into the store.

Carla's heart was racing from the anticipation of Joshua's spontaneous attention. She felt the sudden thud of disappointment as he walked away.

Going Home

Bella sat on the edge of the bed, torn between taking her things to her Jeep to clear her head in the morning air and just taking time to try to understand Chad's reaction. She had never seen him so stern, so unyielding. As she stood to get her toiletry bag from the bathroom, there was a knock on the door. She took a deep breath and walked over to open it.

"May I come in?"

She had to tamp down the temptation to say, "It's your home." She waved her hand in an arc, ushering him in. "Sure."

Chad walked over to one of the armchairs in his guest room and sat down. "Will you sit with me for a few minutes?" His voice was contrite, and she could hear the plea in it.

She sat without saying a word. Her laptop computer sat on the table between them. She had a fierce urge to open her computer and show him the story, but she waited to see what he had to say.

"I didn't know your late husband. . . maybe you had your ups and downs. I suppose most folks do. What *is* apparent to me is that you loved him deeply and clearly shared many more things in common than you and I have." He stopped and stared at the wall in front of him. He saw the sheets neatly folded on the end of the bed. A soft smile appeared on his lips as he recalled her comments about the things her mother had taught her. He took a deep breath. "I'm not making excuses for my reaction, but I would like to share a story with you."

"Chad, I—"

"Please, Bella, I need to tell you this."

She stayed silent and settled back into the chair.

"Over the last fourteen years, I've had a lot of time to think about the failure of my marriage. I'm not stupid; I know I own a lot of it. I love my work and what I do for our community. I used to tell Mary what happened at work, but I never considered what it meant for her to carry that burden and try to live in the community. We stopped talking—except for the few things we had to say to get through the day—when I found out she was telling the women in her bridge club about cases I shared with her."

He let out a big sigh. "Who knows? It's highly unlikely we would have made the marriage work even without that. I stayed married for Nora; now, I sometimes wonder if that was a mistake. What I know wasn't a mistake was ending the marriage. I'm not sure what Mary's life is like in Knoxville and, sadly, I don't care. I hate it for Nora that, for the most part, her mother ignores her and the children. She addresses what I'm sure she sees as the obligatory days: birthdays, Christmas." He stopped.

Bella sat looking at him. She wanted to reach out and touch him, to give him comfort, but she sensed he needed to say what was on his mind.

"This isn't about Mary, and it's only a little bit about Mary and me. My reaction to hearing the title of your story was purely, and wrongly, about my history with Mary. I should have asked you to tell me about the story. If I had a concern after hearing about it, then I should have said something. I'm deeply sorry." He looked at her when he apologized. "I *am* sorry, Bella. You didn't deserve my reaction."

"I accept your apology." Her smile came from her core as she reached over and touched his hand. "I don't know what it is to spend so many years of your life with someone you don't want to be with. I loved Matt with all my heart—all my being—and he loved me. We had very few disagreements in our twenty-five years, but even those we worked out. I have no doubt you have sensed some of my conflict in entering into ..." she shrugged and raised her eyebrows, "whatever this is I think we're both feeling. It's challenging not to feel disloyal to Matt's memory." Her voice trailed off with the tinge of sadness that accompanied these thoughts.

"Hey!" Chad smiled at her. He felt even worse for bringing her these sad memories. He stood up and took her hand. "Let's go out to the porch and start this day over. What do you say?"

She smiled and took his hand, picking up her laptop with the other and walking with him. As soon as they reached the porch, Chad picked up their mugs and went to the kitchen. He returned and set her tea in front of her, then sat down.

"English professors encourage writers to read their writing aloud. I read this aloud to myself, but I could have asked you to listen to it before I submitted it. I don't know why that didn't occur to me. I can read it to you now... or you can read it. Which do you want?"

"I'd be honored if you would read it to me."

Bella read the story of her personal reaction to the invasion and destruction of her property. "'Even in the most idyllic settings in the high mountains, one has to work diligently to restore the spirit of tranquility when invaded by the reality of drugs in our modern world.' The end." She looked at him.

"That's a powerful and beautiful story, Bella. Thank you for reading it to me. You mentioned once that you write to process things. This story helps me understand that."

"Thank you for listening. I'll be more attentive to sharing my work, but you have to be willing to say, 'enough.' Okay?" She smiled at him.

I was such a jerk. This woman sits here thirty minutes later accepting me as the jerk that I can be. "I'm the one who gets the best end of that deal." The sincerity she had come to expect returned to his voice.

She leaned over and kissed him, putting her hand behind his neck and pulling him into the kiss. He did not object.

"Now, let's get some breakfast so you can tell me what you're doing today, and then I'm headed out to pick up a cute..." She winked at him. "... pup."

They both laughed.

Chad made ham and scrambled eggs while Bella made toast. She took the blackberry preserves out of the fridge. "Remember the conversation about our mothers and their expectation of proper behavior?"

"Yes, what about it?"

"Did you always have to put the preserves or jam in a bowl on the table?"

"Oh, yes, and the ketchup, mayo, and mustard."

Bella began laughing so hard she started to choke. She stood by the counter for a moment. "Several weeks ago, I finally gave myself permission to put the condiments on my food in the kitchen, and not into a dish on the table before I could use it."

Chad chuckled as he put the food on plates. "Do you think our mothers are shocked at us making fun of all their efforts to teach us good manners?"

"I'm pretty sure mine figured out long ago that I would learn but not always follow."

Bella put the toast on a small plate and covered it with a napkin, then spooned the preserves into a bowl. She carried both out to the porch.

Halfway through their breakfast, Chad spoke. "You wanted to know about my day. I have to go to work today and will likely work well into the night. We're working with DEA and Immigration, and I need make sure things are going according to plan."

"Then you need to give it your full attention. I'll just issue an open invitation that if, and I do mean *if*, you're free tomorrow and want to get away, come up anytime and stay for supper. If you can't, I understand."

Chad stared at her. "Did God throw away the mold after he made you?"

"More than likely. Heaven forbid there should be two of me on the planet."

"Well, we'll have that debate another day."

"For now, let's enjoy one of His best creations: these mountains." Bella pointed towards the ridgeline. The grayish white light of the sky began turning to yellow just before the sun peeped over the mountaintop.

Thirty minutes later, the kitchen was cleaned up and her things were in her Jeep. They stood at the driver's door as Chad kissed her. "Bella, I *am* sorry."

"We can talk more about this later if you want, but in my life it's done. You apologized; I accepted your apology. I try not to dwell on the negative. For me, it's enough that we both learned from the experience. I'll try to do better about sharing so you don't have to guess what I'm thinking and doing. Fair enough?"

"More than fair. Now, drive safely. Tell Wizard he's one lucky dog, and I'll call you later in the day."

"See you soon." She blew him a kiss as she drove away.

Wizard Has a Home

When she arrived at the Valley Store, Bella was pleased to see so many cars in the parking lot. She knew all too well how important it was for Joshua to be busy while he dealt with the grief of losing his dad.

"Morning, Carla. You look pretty bright-eyed and bushy-tailed for someone who danced the night away."

"Shoot, that was just a walk in the park. Serious dancing is when you do it all day *and* half the night." Carla laughed so loudly that Joshua looked down from his office loft.

"Might've known it would be you two gals." Joshua stood and started down the stairs. "Morning, Bella. How are you?"

"Good, Joshua, and you?" She gave him a kiss on the cheek.

"Just fine, thanks. What can we do for you today?"

"Need a few groceries and some dog food."

"Dog food?" Joshua looked puzzled.

"There's been so much going on that I didn't tell you a dog wandered onto my land. He's been with Doc Jim getting fixed up. No one has claimed him, so Jim says I can have him."

"What a lucky pup," Carla smiled and nodded her head. "Be good for you to have some company up on your mountain."

"It will. I'm going to name him Dex the Wizard."

Joshua grinned. "Well, who doesn't want their very own Wizard?"

"I'll let you get on with your customers. Let's get together soon," Bella headed further into the store and gathered the things she needed. Returning to the front, she spoke softly to Carla. "Is Joshua doing okay?"

"Seems to be. I'm keeping an eye on him."

"I'm sure you'll take good care of him" Bella smiled and reached over to squeeze Carla's hand. "See you soon." She called up to Joshua, "Take care, Joshua."

"Have fun with Wizard."

As she drove to Doc Jim's, Bella thought back to the puppy training courses she and Matt had done over a decade ago with their last dog. *My memory is a little hazy, but I think I'm ready for the challenge. Who says you can't teach an old dog owner new tricks?*

After they exchanged pleasantries, Doc Jim got down to business: he outlined the training he had started with Wizard then put a metal dog crate in the back seat. He handed Wizard's leash to Bella and lifted the dog into the back of her Jeep. "Any other questions about finishing up his training using the crate, or how to train him to stay close to your cabin?"

"I think I understand. It's evident you've done a lot of work with him in just a week. I'll call if I have any questions."

"Anytime, Bella, anytime. Now you two have fun together. He's going to make you a fine companion."

After bidding Jim farewell, Bella began the drive home, glancing in the rearview mirror every few minutes to make sure Wizard was okay. Throughout the journey, his nose was pressed against the window. *It looks like he's enjoying the autumn scenery as well.* As she approached her gate, Bella found herself talking out loud. "We're home, Wizard. I just need to open the gate, and then you'll be able to settle in."

Once they were parked at the cabin, Bella spoke as if the cabin and the dog would acknowledge her introduction. "Drellag Caban, meet Wizard. Wizard, this is your home, Drellag Caban." She put on his leash and lifted him down from the back. She didn't want him to do any damage to his paw pad, although she had seen it was healing nicely. As she walked Wizard through the house, she took an old blanket from the shelf in the second bedroom and put it against the short wall of the kitchen. It was a location where he could see her in any of the main areas of the cabin. He sat down on the blanket; she petted and praised him.

"We're going to get along just fine, Wizard. Yes, we are."

She left him on the blanket and was amazed he responded to the command to stay. Doc Jim had trained him quickly: smart dog. Bella got her groceries, canvas bag, and computer bag and put things away. She had bought dog dishes at the store and put them in the sink to wash them out before giving Wizard water and food.

We have a new companion, Drellag Caban, Wizard is going to bring magic into our lives.

A House Is Not Always a Home

Chad had reviewed their plans for the next few days with Sergeant Whitehorse and then sent her home. She had put in extra duty this week covering for his absence during the time Joshua needed him. *Time to get down to brass tacks. We can't blow this operation.*

"Oliver here."

"Agent Isaacs, sir. Shall I put her through?"

"Yes, thanks, Cecelia. Hope you're doing well."

"Just fine, sir. Here she is."

"Hey, Quinn, did you survive our little jamboree?"

"I did some clogging at university, but I have to admit it takes a toll on unused muscles. Sleeping until eleven was a real luxury this morning. Thanks for including me last night and letting me learn more about this community. Billy was a big help in orienting me to the local folks."

"Glad to hear it. Billy's a good guy. Now, what's the word on the 'house on the hill?'"

"Moved a couple of trucks so it looked like customers, and two of our male agents entered and exited the house on the schedule your team suggested. Still no local takers yet. It's Saturday, so I'm expecting we'll get some action tonight. Seems there were drugs in the four bedrooms when our female agents arrived. Someone must have gone in after the yellow tape was removed."

"What? How did someone go in and us not see them? I've had someone there around the clock."

"Don't know the answer to that, Chad. Maybe there's someone further up the road that's involved. I didn't think to ask you to check out the residents at other houses on the street. My bad."

Chad sat silently for several seconds. "No, it's on me. I'll get someone on that as soon as I hang up. Could be a name will pop up that's familiar to us, or we'll find a rental with a new occupant. Anything else I need to know?"

"We're following Zimmerman, but I have to tell you, Chad, I think this one's going to get stretched out. So, whatever happens over the weekend isn't likely to be the final trap for him. Is that a problem for you?"

"Yes and no. I want to stop whatever he's doing, but I'm also smart enough to know he's a much bigger fish than the 'house on the hill' activity. If we can catch whoever is behind the drugs going into that house and shut down the place, we send a strong message to the men who are frequenting it, I can be patient as we gather information on Zimmerman. Are we bringing in the FBI?"

"My bosses want to meet after we get through this weekend, and they'd like you to be part of that meeting. Are you good with that?"

"Oh, yeah, I want my detective to get the credit he deserves for tracking down the ownership of those motels in Round City."

"Okay, I'll see what I can do to get that organized for the first of the week. In the meantime, my phone seems to be working here and when I'm at the 'house on the hill,' so call if something comes up.

Thanks again for arranging for me to stay at Joe's house. Joshua and Carla have been delightful hosts."

"Glad it worked out for all concerned. You have my numbers. See you when I see you. Thanks, Quinn."

"Later."

Chad sat back, looked at his watch, and saw that it was already three in the afternoon. *Where did the day go?* He walked to the break room to get the sandwich he made before he left home. No one was in there and he was able to make a quick exit back to his desk. He called the detectives' room; Billy answered.

"Hey, boss, what's up?"

"Surprised to hear your charming voice."

"Here to serve."

"Good. If you have a few minutes, come down and help me brainstorm some information we need to track down quickly."

"Be there in five."

Chad decided he would take his time eating his sandwich, and Billy would just have to excuse his poor manners. Just as he took a bite of his sandwich there was a knock on the door. *Seriously, Billy, five minutes?!* He stood and opened the door.

Billy saw Chad's sandwich on his desk. "Sorry, do you need time to eat? Want me to come back?"

"No, I'll just ask you to excuse me while I eat. It's been a long time since breakfast. Pull up a chair."

Billy grabbed a chair from the round table and moved it closer to Chad's desk. Even though he now understood the round table was intended to encourage problem solving, he liked the informality of sitting down like this with the sheriff.

"What's up, boss?"

"Anyone in the detective shop besides you?"

"Just Alexander. She's running some forensics on dead wildlife showing up near the Mountain Villages. There are concerns that someone is poisoning them, maybe to keep the animals away from their fancy homes."

Chad nodded as he ate his sandwich. He took a drink of water. "Here's what we need to get done. Maybe you and I can divide and conquer. We need to look at houses on the road above and below the 'house on the hill,' see if we know the folks, and figure out who they are if we don't."

"Easy enough to run a list of property owners on that road. Simpson's on the desk today, and he normally rides that sector. He'll know the regular folks and if there's been any change lately."

"Guess that's why I pay you the big bucks! You run that list, and I'll go talk to Simpson."

"Boss, finish your sandwich first. Besides, I need to talk to you about something else."

Chad leaned back in his chair and picked up the last of his sandwich. "I'm all ears."

"Well, I wanted to ask you... Nah, I wanted to tell you thanks for asking me to accompany Quinn last night. It was fun to introduce her to some locals and do some clogging. I haven't danced like that in years. It was great being totally distracted from all that's been bugging me." He paused. "Well, anyway, thanks."

Chad nodded and popped the last piece of the sandwich in his mouth. He didn't want to say anything until Billy finished.

"And..." Billy hesitated. "I guess I do want to ask a question. Is there some kind of conflict of interest if I ask Quinn out to dinner sometime?"

Chad took his time chewing his sandwich. He knew Billy would not interrupt him. *Well now, Billy, I just wanted to distract you. I guess whoever thought love was in the air in the spring never spent a fall in these mountains. Looks to me like we have three men in this valley acting like lovesick moon calves.* He snapped himself back to the moment.

"Not my job to monitor your personal life, Detective. Don't let it interfere with the work." Then he smiled and gave Billy a thumbs-up.

"Got it, boss. Now I'll get on that list of residents. Thanks." Billy stood, extended his hand to Chad, and left.

Chad walked to the front and explained what he was after to Simpson.

"Boss," Simpson kept his voice low, although no one was in the front area, "there's only one house that's had any changes recently. It had a for sale sign on it for years, and it finally sold maybe six or eight months ago. It's on the same side of the road as the house where we took out those folks last week, maybe a quarter mile or so on up the hill. It's a dump."

Chad patted him on the back. "Thanks, Simpson, you've just made this day much easier. Do me a favor, please, and ask Cecelia to see if she can reach Agent Nations for me. I need to stop down the hall on my way to my office, but tell her I'll be right there. Thanks, thanks again."

Simpson smiled. "Just doing my job, Sheriff." He picked up the phone to call dispatch.

Chad was whistling as he walked down the hall. Two deputies passed him. "Good afternoon, Sheriff. Sounds like a good day."

"Mine just got a whole lot better. Hope y'all are having a good one too." He kept walking.

As he walked out of the men's room across from his office, he could hear his phone ringing behind the closed door. He stepped quickly to get it. "Oliver here."

Chapter 25

The End of This Day

Bella went about her day, changing the sheets on her bed, doing laundry, and cleaning the cabin she felt had been neglected for too long. Wizard did not seem to be at all disturbed by her movements; even running the vacuum over her braided rugs was met with equanimity. She made it a point to stop and pet him from time to time.

"You, my Wizard, have so much to learn about life on this mountaintop. We're about make some pretty big changes. I hope you like them." His tail thumped against the blanket, punctuating each word.

Once the cleaning was finished and the laundry hung to dry or folded and put away, she walked into the kitchen to look at what she might fix for supper. *Hmmm... need to think about supper for tomorrow night in case Chad can get away.* She had plenty of fresh vegetables from her shopping in the morning, and she had chicken in the freezer. She could make fried chicken, potato salad, and a green salad tomorrow. For tonight she decided to have a salad with the last of the ham steak she had in the fridge; that would be plenty.

She looked at the clock and was surprised to see it was almost five o'clock. "Come, Wizard. Let's take a quick walk outside and then we'll sit on the porch." She decided to let him out without his leash. She opened the screen door and he headed for one of the big trees. After he finished relieving himself, he turned his head to look at her. "Good boy, Wizard. Come." She clapped her hands once and he ran towards her. She praised him and was about to sit down with a glass of tea and her book when the kitchen phone rang.

"Drellag Caban, may I help you?"

"Evening, Ms. Anderson, this is Macklin Evans. Hope I'm not too late returning your call."

"Not at all. I hope you received the message that I decided I don't need to come over. I signed the contract on the Overlook cabin model and my attorney, Mr. Olson, will fax it to you on Monday. Once you sign it, you can fax it back to him. Does that work for you?"

"Yes, ma'am, that'll be fine. Thanks for your confidence in us."

"Gray will let me know when he has the contract back, and I'll call and give you my credit card for the down payment. Any problem with that?"

"That will be just fine. I've talked with Arthur Gillett, and he expects he can have permits by the end of next week, and I've already reserved the logs for your cabin. As soon as he pulls the permits, we'll get this delivered."

"Wow, that's great. I was expecting to have to wait. I know Arthur has to do foundation work, but maybe we can beat winter. Thank you so much."

"No, ma'am, thank you. We aim to make you a satisfied customer. If there's nothing else, I'll wait to hear from you next week."

"Oh, one more thing. If I decide I want the dormers, when would you need to know that?"

"Would you do the loft as well?"

"Not at this time."

"Then Arthur can do the dormers, he takes care of the roof mate-rials. Just talk to him."

"Perfect. That's all I needed to know. Have a nice rest of the weekend."

"Good evening, ma'am."

Bella hung up the phone, excited that she was really going to get her guest cottage. She pulled her hand away from the handset and was startled when it rang again.

"Drellag Caban, may I help you?"

"Wondering what I have to do to get a reservation for supper tomorrow?" She felt the warmth in Chad's voice through the phone.

"Just tell me the time that works for you, and you're set."

She really doesn't hold a grudge even though I deserve it. "Just called to say hey and hope you've had a good day. How's Wizard?"

"I've had a good day, thanks. And before long I'll teach Wizard to say hello for himself."

"*That* I look forward to hearing."

"I finished my lick and a promise housekeeping, and we were just going to sit on the porch. Oh, and The Log Cabin Company called. We're all set for the new cabin. You might not believe this, but they have a set of logs in stock. He'll deliver them as soon as Arthur pulls the permits."

"Too bad our county offices are so busy that it might take months for that to happen." His voice was deadpan.

"Nice try, Sheriff. I happen to know the county manager and last night at the jamboree he told me there should be no problem."

"Foiled again." Chad laughed.

"How about you? Busy day? Busy night ahead?"

"Yes, and yes. The good news is we caught a break this afternoon, and this may go better than I had hoped."

"Then I'll hope it goes well, crime is averted or stopped, and you're safe doing it."

"Safety, yours and ours, is always foremost in our thoughts. That does bring me to a question."

"Ask away."

"Any limitations you want to put on the hour of the day, or night, I can call?"

"Chad Oliver, even for a man raised by a proper southern lady speaking to a woman raised by a similar one, you should know you don't have to ask, or apologize for the time of day or night you call. I think I remember a night last month when your call came close to midnight."

"Indeed, it did, but that was from the sheriff. I'm asking as Chad."

"Anytime. You just might need to let it ring longer in the middle of the night. I'm a deep sleeper. Wait! I may have an assistant in Wizard who can make sure I wake up when the phone rings. We'll have to try it sometime." The lightness of her tone made him smile.

"Thanks, Bella. I don't plan to make a habit of it, but there is something reassuring about knowing I can call you at any hour. I promise I won't abuse it."

"For me too, Chad. And I won't call you too often in the middle of the night." She smiled even though she knew he couldn't see her.

"Hate to run, but duty calls. Just wanted to wish you a lovely evening and tell you I plan to take you up on your offer for tomorrow. I'll call you when I know what time I can get up there."

"I'll look forward to your call. Be safe and go stomp out crime. Good night, Chad."

"Good night, Bella. I..." he stopped himself from saying "I love you," even though he wanted to. "I hope you sleep well."

"Good night, Chad." There was a click on the line as he ended the call, but she stood for a moment, holding the phone to her ear. The awful beeping that comes when a landline isn't hung up snapped her out of her reverie. She put the handset back in its cradle, then noticed Wizard was sitting at her feet, his eyes telegraphing that he was ready to be fed.

"Hold your horses, Wizard. I'm going to make my salad, and then we'll take my dinner and yours out to the porch and enjoy the end of this day."

She ended up not opening her book. She sat and ate her salad with her dog at her feet. She loved the quiet of the mountains, save the call of the birds and the whistling of the wind. Now she could add Wizard's soft breathing to the mix of sounds. She was content.

Wizard finished eating his dinner. "Let's take a walk, Wizard. It'll be dark soon and I don't want it to be too late when we go out. Doc Jim assured me you'd sleep the night away in your crate. Won't be too long that you won't need that crate to make it through the night. Come on, let's go."

She set her dishes in the sink, put on her vest and boots, and clipped Wizard's leash to his collar. They set out on a walk down to the gate and back. As they walked back up the road, the sun dropped behind the mountain like a basketball going into a hoop on a three-point shot. The blue-black of the sky lit up with thousands of twinkling stars, interrupted only by the ambient light from her porch.

"Let's run this one home, Wizard." She was reasonably confident as she unhooked his leash, but she also hoped she wouldn't regret it. Wizard took off and ran to the cabin. He was sitting on the bottom step panting when she reached him. She squatted and pulled him into a hug. They stayed that way for several seconds, Wizard's head resting on her shoulder. They were both panting.

Bella closed up the house and headed for the shower. Once she was ready for bed, she put Wizard in his crate just outside her bedroom door. "Good night, sweet Wizard. Tomorrow we can take a hike and you can learn the lay of the land."

She curled up in bed and looked at the picture of her and Matt. She reached out and touched his face. *Well, love of my life, there's a new male in Drellag Caban. I think you would approve of this sheprador. And, in the interest of full disclosure, there's another man in my life, Chad. I think you would like him. Just promise you won't let go of me. No matter how this plays out, you'll always be in my heart.*

Bella considered her Not-So-Good List. Chad's reaction to her telling him the title to her story. She knew now she could have handled it differently, and she would in the future. She couldn't help but wonder what other deeply buried scars lurked in Chad, and maybe even in herself.

On the bright side, her Good List was full tonight. She and Chad had handled the mishap by listening and talking it through. She felt that held promise for the future. Joshua and Carla seemed to be working well together at the Valley Store, and she wished good things for their future. Wizard was her new four-legged companion. He was a smart dog and seemed to learn quickly, and she looked forward to many years together. She thought of Matt and her mother today. *Grandmother Hazel, you're always with me here. I hope you know that. Daddy, the shed will be fixed soon, and I'm going to get the side painted. I think you'd like my ideas.*

She stretched. She had left the window in her bedroom slightly open and felt the cold October air chill the room. She rolled onto her side and whispered out the window, "Take care of Chad and all those who serve with him."

All the Planning in the World

Chad's secure phone rang, and he smiled when he saw the name flash up on the caller ID. "Hey, Sam!"

"What's up, Sheriff?"

"Been trying to reach you. Are you close by?"

"Just got back from Round City. I'm headed to The Corral to pick up something to eat then I'll head your way. Can I bring you something?"

"Some vegetable soup and cornbread would be greatly appreciated. See you when you get here."

Twenty minutes later there was a knock on his door. "Have a seat at the table. I'll wash my hands and join you." Chad had lost track of the time while focusing on the information about the sale and possible tenant in the house up the road from their target. It was almost dark, and he knew things would start to pick up at the "house on the hill" if there were going to be customers tonight.

"Thanks, Sam." Chad pulled up a chair and pulled out his wallet. He put a ten-dollar bill on the table. "That should cover it and your services."

"Oh, you can't afford my services. So, just put your money away. I've got this one. Next one's on you. Then we'll go back to buying our own. How's that?"

Chad left the money on the table. "Did you get the word that there were drugs in the rooms at the 'house on the hill' when your agents arrived?"

"Yep. But we can't figure out how all the eyes on the place missed it."

"That one had me stumped too." There was a knock on the door. Chad stood up to answer it, unable to imagine who it could be. Quinn Isaacs was standing in the hallway.

"Private party, or can anyone join?"

"Glad you got the message." Sam pushed the bag of food towards a chair. "Sorry, Chad, forgot to tell you I called Quinn to join us."

"The more the merrier." Chad wondered if he would get used to the more free-flowing ways the young agents operated. "As I was saying—" Chad began.

"Before I so rudely interrupted the boys club?" Quinn smiled demurely.

"Before I knew you were joining us." Chad's retort was just as quick. "We've found some evidence that might help us sort out how the drugs were already in the house when the women arrived."

"Do tell," Quinn and Sam said almost in unison.

Chad gave them the details about the house about a half mile up the road from the "house on the hill." They then kicked around some ideas about how to approach it and not run off whoever was living there. "Deputy Simpson indicated it's a dump, but in these hills that doesn't mean no one lives there. When one of my folks say it,

I usually know it means, 'none of your friends or family would live there.'"

Quinn looked at Chad. "I say the three of us check out the house up the road. With DEA and IEA agents inside the 'house on the hill,' and your folks on the outside, Chad, it's well covered no matter what happens. You're arresting anyone who enters the door and seeks services through Gertrude, right?"

"Absolutely. We'll arrest every one of them, and once we have the lead on the drugs, we'll do it with fanfare. I want that operation ended and out of my community." His voice took on a hard edge.

"Whoa, Chad, we're on your side, remember?" Sam put his hands up in the air.

That's twice today that cold anger has made an appearance. What's going on in my head? "You're right, Sam. Sorry. To both of you."

Quinn looked directly at him. "No problem, Sheriff. That passion gives me all the more reason to be on this team, temporary though it is."

Chad looked at his watch. "It's after eight and we missed any advantage of daylight, but we should still have a pretty good moon, and there is no other real light up on that hill. I'd like to stop and speak to my deputies on the way up. One vehicle or more?"

"I'll take mine. Quinn, if you go with me, we can look like a lost couple and, heck, we can even argue like an old married couple if we need to. We'll go ahead and see what we can see."

"Fair enough. I'll be up to meet you in less than thirty minutes. It'll take fifteen to get up there from here."

"Thanks for dinner and the company, gentlemen." Quinn did a mock curtsy as she stood. "I'll stop down the hall and meet you in front, Sam. Later, Chad."

"Later." Chad walked to his desk. *People get killed who don't have their head in the game. You don't get that right with someone else's life, and you sure aren't going to take that chance with your own. Not now. Not with Bella in the mix.* He called dispatch and told them where he was headed, then he rang Billy on his mobile to see if he had tracked down ownership of the property likely being used to get the drugs to the "house on the hill." Billy assured him he would call as soon as he had the intel. Chad was satisfied he had done everything possible on his end; he headed out, stopping near the deputies positioned in a dilapidated truck in front of the "house on the hill."

"Evening, boys," Chad spoke in a friendly voice as he approached the truck from across the street. "Got some business here?" He was beginning to wonder if there might be listening devices planted in the nearby trees. "How about you show me some ID?" Although his SUV was unmarked, Chad knew it was well known in the region, and *he* was certainly known to most folks. He moved closer to the window.

The deputy behind the steering wheel looked at the sheriff. "What's with the tough cop routine, sir? And was that Sam who just drove up the road with some lady? Sure hope so, he was weaving like he was on a two-week drunk."

"I need to know what you boys are doing here." Chad's voice was rather loud and he leaned in to speak to them, acting like he was trying to hear the person in the passenger seat. "Need to say this fast, guys. We're heading up to a house a half a mile up the road; it might be a drug distribution point. So, stay alert and call for backup if you hear any gunshots. Dispatch knows we're up here, but I didn't order backup." He stepped back from the vehicle.

"Now, you boys make sure you listen carefully. You have the right to sit along the road and visit anywhere you want, but take my advice and don't be too long. Makes you look mighty suspicious." He walked across the street to his SUV, got in, and headed up the road.

Two trucks pulled in behind the deputies and two men got out and headed up the steps to the "house on the hill."

"When it rains it pours." The deputy on the passenger side opened his door. "If we're the ones to arrest these men once they go inside, I'm thinking we better alert dispatch now."

"I'm with you. Better safe than sorry." He picked up his radio and called it in. "Listen, we've got a bunch of federal agents inside that house who can help out, so it'll only take one of us to officially arrest them. I'll stay out here in case the sheriff needs help."

"Good plan. I've got an incoming text, so that must mean they've approached Gertrude and one of the DEA agents is alerting us. I'm headed in."

He got out and headed up the walk, taking the steps two at a time.

The deputy behind the driver's seat put the key back in the ignition so he could start up and get up the hill on a second's notice.

Things Can Still Go Awry

Sam and Quinn parked beyond the house they had identified and were walking down the road on opposite sides. They had worked on a routine and hoped it didn't backfire.

Quinn yelled at Sam. "I told you to get gas before we started out. I wouldn't be trying to walk back to this hick community if you'd listen once in a while."

"Give me a break! A buddy of mine told me there was something interesting to see up this way. How'd I know we didn't have enough gas to make it from Round City?"

"You could've known it would get dark in a place with no streetlights!"

They saw headlights coming up the hill and assumed it was Chad. The grass around the property was about a foot high, and the house itself looked long neglected. The only light in the old place seemed to be coming from a huge television screen.

Chad stopped and spoke loudly. "You folks need some help?"

"Not if he had listened to me." Her voice was so vicious Chad was glad he knew she wasn't really mad at either one of them. Suddenly they both realized Sam was almost up to the front window of the house.

Chad turned off his SUV and got out. "Do you have a vest on, Quinn?"

"Never leave home without it."

"What does Sam think he's doing?"

"He told me if it seemed okay when you arrived, he was going to head up because we'd seen the light from the TV."

"Glad you know what he's thinking. This is not the way to scout a possible distribution point. I'm headed around back. You cover Sam." Chad took off up the drive and around the end of the house.

Sam banged on the door and shouted. "Open up, DEA."

Quinn hoped he had a warrant and just hadn't told her. The night was so still the only thing she could hear was a lone mockingbird. Then the light went out on the television and she heard a door slam. Sam was still at the front door. The next thing she heard was multiple gunshots. "Sam!"

She had her weapon aimed above the hood of Chad's SUV and turned her head as she saw flashing blue lights coming up the road. Chad's radio in the SUV chirped and she couldn't decide whether to answer it or stay on point, ready to shoot if needed. Two SUVs pulled up, and Deputy Thomas jumped out. "Who are you?" she called out.

Quinn recognized her voice, "It's Quinn, that you, Susan?"

"10-4. What's going on?"

Susan Thomas moved in next to Quinn to hear what she had to say and waved the other deputies towards Sam. Just as they advanced, there was another shot and Sam toppled on the steps. Susan pulled out her radio and called for an ambulance and more back-up.

Quinn did not like the way this was playing out. Sam didn't tell her everything he knew. She could feel it in her bones. She heard another shot. This one came from inside the house. The three deputies dropped back, and the group huddled to make a plan. Quinn was the only one who knew that Chad had gone to the back of the house.

Chapter 26

Keep close to Nature's heart... and break clear away, once in a while,
and climb a mountain or spend a week in the woods.
Wash your spirit clean.
John Muir, 1838 – 1914

Early Morning Hours

In the brisk cold that is familiar in the mountains at two in the morning, Forensic technician Elizabeth Alexander and Detective Billy Williams were huddled with the team sent from the DEA. The two dead bodies, one in the house and one in the backyard, were first on the agenda to get cleared so they could be transported to the morgue. Sam had been at the hospital for several hours, and the report was that he had a through-and-through shot that just missed the femoral artery in his right leg and grazed the patella of his left knee; he was going to make it.

Agent Quinn Isaacs and Deputy Susan Thomas were at the back of the house. Sergeant Whitehorse had come to take charge of the overall coordination with the DEA. Multiple arrests had been made at the "house on the hill," and Gertrude had been taken back to jail. She would leave for Bledsoe after being debriefed tomorrow. The DEA and IEA agents posing as workers in the "house on the hill" had joined the team at the site of the shooting.

Sergeant Whitehorse got everyone's attention. "This is DEA Special Agent Maureen O'Connor, and for those of you I have not met,

I'm Sergeant Sylvia Whitehorse. We have a joint forensic team working the scene inside the house and the backyard. We have received word that Special Agent Sam Nations is out of danger and is expected to make a full recovery. Those members of our department not otherwise assigned are dismissed. We will provide a detailed briefing at your next shift. DEA and IEA agents can report to your lead agent present. Questions?"

The people assembled looked at her expectantly. Finally, one of the deputies from the sheriff's department spoke up. "Sarge, where's our boss? We would like to know before we go home."

Sylvia was about to speak when all eyes turned from her to Chad as he walked down the driveway. A loud, raucous cheer went up from the crowd. Chad raised his hands, palms out, to quiet the group.

"You'll wake the sleeping, and maybe the dead, with that echoing across these mountains. Appreciate the support, just needed to get my report to Agent Quinn and Deputy Thomas so there's no forgetting any details. Now, those of you who have been dismissed, do what the sergeant told you. Get some rest. Tomorrow's a new day... well, today's a new day. Thanks, everyone."

The folks from Chad's department each came and shook hands with him and spoke to him before leaving. Then came a chorus of "Night, Sheriff," "Night, Sarge."

Chad spoke to the IEA and DEA agents and thanked them for coming. He walked over to Sylvia Whitehorse. "Thanks, Sergeant. We're going to get to the bottom of what happened here tonight, but for now we just need to work the scene. Unless you need me, I'm headed to the hospital and then my office. You can reach me there."

"Take care, sir. We need you, but not here. I know you'll get to the bottom of it."

"No, Sylvia, *we'll* get to the bottom of it. Thanks for managing this scene." He clapped her on the shoulder then hopped into his SUV. *Another weekend visit to the hospital; I really hope this doesn't become a habit.*

He was met by a nurse when he arrived at the emergency room. "Dr. Smith would like to see you. Come with me." He followed the nurse through the key-controlled double doors to the back of the ER.

Fred waved him over; they entered a small room and closed the door. "Hey, Dad, are *you* okay?" Fred looked his father-in-law up and down. "Apparently there was some police radio chatter involving our sheriff's well-being. Let me check you out."

"Fred... Son, thanks for the concern. I'm fine. It's never a good day when you take a life, but it's what I'm trained to do when someone shoots at me or someone I'm sworn to protect."

"Then why all the chatter?"

"I was at the back of a very dark, dilapidated drug distribution house with limited human resources."

Fred looked at him in surprise. "You had limited resources at a shootout?"

"Not my doing. It comes as close as I ever need to get to experience the Wild West. You got the only customer for your hospital, and he's a good guy. The other two will be headed to the morgue."

"Okay then. Our patient is heavily sedated, and there are two DEA agents outside his room. So, nothing for you here tonight. My prescription for you is to go home and get some sleep."

"Sleep will wait. I just need to see Sam for myself, and then I'll be at the office. I promise some shuteye in a few hours, but only for a few hours. I have a busy day."

"Dad, enough. Whatever it is that happened here tonight didn't just start on this day or yesterday. You'll get to the bottom of it, but not if you're exhausted. Don't make me send your daughter to put you in line."

Chad started laughing and then caught himself. "I surrender. Here's what you can tell my daughter... The matter I dealt with tonight *will* get resolved, and we *will* keep on the trail until we get the folks at the head of the snake. But that is *not* why my sleep will be abbreviated today."

"Why then?"

"Because I'm going up on a mountain to take a hike with a very pretty lady and her new dog. Then I'm going to enjoy supper on her porch. And the night will bring what the night will bring."

Fred pulled his father-in-law into a bear hug. "Way to go, Dad. I've been worried that Nora might try to make good on her threat to have me tell you how to date a woman in today's world. I have no idea! Sounds like you don't need lessons."

Chad slapped his son-in-law on the back. "Now, off to file my paperwork and then home to sleep."

New Beginnings

Bella hurried in from the porch to answer the phone. She saw on the kitchen wall clock that it was noon. "Drellag Caban, may I help you?"

"Let me count the ways."

"Hey," Bella dragged out the southern 'a' in hey. "Was hoping I'd hear from you today."

"Me too. But that's a story for another day. The question for today is this: are you up for a hike with a very tired sheriff and a pup named Wizard?"

"Just appear at my door and your wish is my command."

"You might want to put a condition or two on that line." He had a smile in his voice.

"Maybe, maybe not. A hike with two fine males and fried chicken after. You're on. Will I see you soon?"

"Look out your door. I'll be there right after I lose my phone signa..."

Bella pulled the long cord on the wall phone and moved to the kitchen door. A wide smile crossed her face as she heard the famil-iar sound of the heavy engine in his SUV. *I feel more settled on this mountain every day. Welcome to my home, Chad.*

About the Author

Jacque Jacobs resides in Vero Beach, Florida, where she is active in the *Tuesday Writers* of the Laura (Riding) Jackson Foundation (LRJF). She serves as a member of the Board of Directors and Vice-President for Operations of the Foundation. She is also a Board member for the United Way of Indian River County and a member of the Board of the Vero Friends of the Atlantic Classical Orchestra. She strongly believes that your own life is greatly enriched when you work to improve the quality of life for each person in your community.

Author's Note

Over the last five years I have spent a great deal of time in my volunteer work for the Laura (Riding) Jackson Foundation of Vero Beach. Laura (Riding) Jackson (1901-1991) was as devoted to words as perhaps any writer ever has been. In the move of her historic house in 2019, I was the Board member who worked most closely with the project manager and mover. This 1910 Florida Vernacular house in which Laura lived from 1943 – 1991 will move you in ways you can't imagine, if you take time to sit quietly and experience it. Writing this novel series and spearheading preservation of this house collided for me in 2020 when I thought about the solitary life this woman of words spent in a house with few creature comforts. I woke early on December 21, 2020, and wrote—Passion for your creative spirit is more satisfying than chasing creature comforts. I am grateful for a lifetime of following my passions.